Hominid

A novel by Nicholas Jonathan Green

No part of this publication may be reproduced, distributed, or transmitted in any form or by any means, including photocopying, recording, or other electronic or mechanical methods, without the prior written permission of the author, except in the case of brief quotations embodied in authorised critical reviews and certain other non-commercial uses permitted by copyright law. Any references to historical events, real people, or real places are used fictitiously, and with only fictional intent.

First printing edition 2023

© All Rights Reserved

'To the gods within us: well met.'

jo

The land was the sky.

It began to rain. The rain began to fill the potholes in the decrepit lane. Her car complained as she drove over them. The jolt of it made her want to curse, but she didn't. She rarely swore. She thought swearing to be infra dig. This is not to say she had a high opinion of herself. Indeed, she was often humbler than pie (with gravy). It was that she had been taught not to be uncouth by parents whom she had thought couth. She had been slightly wrong.

She was hurrying home from work. Her head was full to the edge of folly with all that mattered least. This annoyed her. She preferred to think of things that she thought mattered. She thought life had taken this away from her. She still loved being wrong.

She glanced up. She saw crows trundle graphite skies.

'Whodunnit,' she said for no learnable reason.

As if in response, several crows cawed. The murder then split, shredding the grey with indolence. Crows veered in different directions along the same instincts.

'Raw,' she cawed this crow-day aloud to them.

Then she roared. When she was alone like this she liked to roar. Perhaps this was a reaction to a conservative upbringing, and the routines and banalities of a conventional early life. These days, convention made her want to explode like a big dead sun.

She thought she liked the word 'roar'. She liked words almost as much as she loved laughter. She didn't know how any word meant anything, and she didn't know what meaning was. She invented new words. She turned old words backwards. She turned them inside out. She everted them. She inverted them. She never, ever perverted them. If she could have eaten words she would have done so. The thought of this made her laugh again.

Then she saw the baby. She suddenly forgot about crows and words.

She came upon it on a slow bend in the crippled lane. What she saw at first was no more than a pallor. She knew without knowing that it was not memory, or litter, or animal. She knew that this was swaddling cotton, but this swaddle was abandoned.

Who would do this? Who could? Why? When? How? She wished to roar again, but this time with anger. She couldn't quite see the baby yet; nor could she quite hear it: her car windows were shut because it was winter. Today there was no horizon. A day without a point of view usually made her happy. Not this day. Under this day someone had abandoned a baby.

Instinct told her the baby was crying. She slowed the car down. The crime of the cotton in the long grass beckoned. Now she saw that yes, the cotton was dirty with time. Yes, it was soiled. It was weathered. Seeing this patina made a fist inside her. How long had the baby been here? Outrage turned to rage. The horror of a crying baby alone in long grass stabbed her.

Suddenly now, the only thing of importance to Dashiell Ann Salter who could roar was the baby in the abandonment. She therefore stopped the car and got out.

The sky was the land.

*

Bringing the baby home had been simple. Its arrival had been harder.

It was a Tuesday like many Tuesdays. Tuesdays brought Dashiell home from work with work to do. She would do this work, and then welcome her daughter Tally home from day care. Her husband Jericho would then return from work. Today, he was soaked by nearly the coldest rain. Wet with curses, Jericho kissed Dashiell hello.

Their kissing had evolved in the crucible of marriage from romance into something else. This other thing was not better or worse than romance. It was different. Their hello kiss was a habit. It contained no memory of sex. It was a dry kiss, from which romance and desire had evaporated like dew on a remembered hill. It was a kiss that wore a mask of contentment that had, in time, become a real face – as masks do. This kiss was their usual and always greeting, and Tuesday could do little about it. January could care about them not at all.

Jericho saw the baby in her arms in the nearly white, the soiled white: the dirty. 'And this?' Jericho was long of body but short of speech. Also: 'What the hell?'

At teatime, the carer brought Tally home. The routine was: greet Tally with a smile. Tally sometimes unwilling to smile and at other times seemingly cheerful. Dashiell to greet the carer with another smile, quite different. Why was Jericho home from work so early? Nothing doing in houses then. No, things doing in houses. Just home early to be at home. 'The only upside of being the boss.' Then Jericho kissed Tally and again Dashiell. Still, however: 'What the hell?' This time with anger.

'What else was I supposed to do?' Dashiell washed the baby as she spoke when they were in the bathroom later. 'Sometimes it's essential to do the wrong thing. You know that. What else?'

'Have you called someone?'

'Who?'

'The council? The police? Ghostbusters?'

Then she merely washed the crying from the baby. The baby seemed to enjoy the cool of her water and her attention: Dashiell only had eyes for this baby boy – this gift, as she saw him. Of course she did. Jericho didn't mind her sudden preoccupation. It was natural. They had talked about having another baby. Jericho had been less than keen.

'He can't stay,' he said gently over an hour later. The statement seemed to slow the marble air. They were in the bedroom now. She had laid the newly swaddled baby on their bed. She lay beside the baby. She nurtured him with play and smiles. It made Jericho smile. Jericho knew Dashiell would soon 'see sense', however. She would soon yield the baby up for adoption because, he was 'sure', Dashiell valued their marriage and another child was, in Jericho's mind, the last thing they needed as a couple. Tally was their full-time commitment, and it was for Tally's sake above all else that Jericho wanted Dashiell to yield the baby.

Some instinct now told Jericho that the baby's inclusion in their little family, should he stay, would turn out badly for Tally and thus for them all. He never shared his foreboding with Dashiell or anyone else, however, even when his prescience was horrifically confirmed.

Now, Dashiell said nothing to him in reply; so Jericho pressed the point gently: 'Tell me why I'm wrong,' he said.

He sensed her demeanour change in response to his insistence. The change was not in his favour. Not at all.

He waited.

Yes, she agreed eventually, the baby's parents must be found. Yes, their hands were already full with Tally. Their hands were tied by love. How could the baby stay the night, even one night, anyway? mused Jericho. What would they feed him? He must have a home to go to.

Dashiell was half-hearted in her responses.

'People don't just leave babies by the road,' said Jericho evenly, filling another silence with what he saw as reason and a husband smile. Even as he spoke, he knew his reasoning was pointless. He knew she would hold this baby close to her until time took him away.

Dread seduced Jericho's marching heart.

'Well now they do,' she said.

Jericho looked at his hands. They were full of questions.

'How could he stay the night?' Dashiell said. 'Well he could stay the night by not being anywhere else, at night: tonight,' she said in that way she said things sometimes – the way she had once said them when they were at passion's knee. Her logic delighted him, even now. He still deified her smile. Still he could not defy it. He wished to do neither.

Tally entered the room in her wheelchair. Jericho and Dashiell smiled at her by long habit. Dashiell gave Tally the baby to hold. Tally's smile in response jewelled Dashiell's eyes with emotion. Holding a baby in a wheelchair can be difficult. Minimal use of arms can make this harder. Jericho thought he had not seen Dashiell cry for far too long. 'Vulcan!' he often called her. It was their little joke. Now, she laughed and cried at the same time. Same thing, laughter and tears, she often said. 'Go high enough and things that seem different low down are the same.' Dashiell had said that to him soon after they had met. Jericho had been, to quote Baloo as he liked to do, solid gone from then on.

Now, Jericho nearly wished he could remember how to cry.

The sky was an ocean.

*

'We don't know who it belongs to.' Over morning coffee the next day, Jericho again tried to reason with her, this most reasonable of people.

'It?'

Later, Jericho made some calls. During weeks, people with training came. Yes, the Salters were within their rights to care for the baby, but only if the baby's biological parents or legal guardians could not be found. Finding the baby's parents and returning him to them at first seemed possible – even likely. There would be a reunion of emotion. People would be double thanked. Tears would kneel to gravity. There would be greetings and hope. People would inhale.

This was clearly abandonment, however; so perhaps the baby's real parents didn't want to be found.

At first, Jericho went to great lengths to try to find the baby's biological parents or legal guardians. He made no headway in this. At last, it seemed he never would. Dashiell knew in her silences – where she kept things – they would never be found. Dashiell did not know how she knew this, or what knowledge is.

In the y of a Tuesday, Jericho stated the obvious to Dashiell: Tally was almost certainly pretending to have accepted the baby into their home. In her heart, Tally must surely resent it. 'You said it yourself: we're all actors,' he reminded her. 'Tally doesn't just need all our care,' he continued, 'she wants it, and want and need are, quote, east and west.'

'Stop quoting me,' Dashiell replied. 'I'm not worth quoting. Anyway. What Tally wants beyond anything is not to need anyone. I hate it when you make me state the obvious.'

'Sometimes the obvious needs stating,' was all Jericho would say.

Jericho always worried when he knew Dashiell was denying her better judgement. Good judgement was something Dashiell usually had in abundance. Not quite the best, it was better than most. Now, the urge to protect and nurture had overridden this judgement.

Jericho knew that Dashiell was determined to give the baby all the love and attention he could ever need. Dashiell's mother had been crow-cold and distant. All things are caused.

They both knew that their daughter Tally needed every ounce of their love and care, however. Paraplegia had damned Tally's atoms, so she needed her parents much more than a healthy child might. Tally loathed being a burden. Tally loathed herself.

Time seemed to pass.

The baby's parents still hadn't been found. Who had been looking? Social services, yes; but how hard had they looked, really? Who cared who the baby was, really? The state did, or pretended to. People must be accounted for. Their existence and origins must be mapped and noted. That the state needed to know such things was no longer questioned, as neither would be the appending of this basic information with data about their stated politics, retail choices, sexual orientation, and then even location, so that they could be tracked as they exercised the free will they lacked.

Free of will, Jericho grew more worried as winter surrendered to the first rumours of spring. By April, strange things began to happen.

A blood test was required to ascertain the child's true parentage ('how did you come about the baby again, Mrs Salter? You found him?') by DNA matching. Already guarding the baby's uniqueness instinctively, Dashiell found herself unwilling to take the baby to the doctor's surgery, where the blood test would normally have taken place. Expecting push-back on this, instead she was offered a home visit by an NHS admin staffer, who could not have been more polite or helpful.

Three weeks later, the blood test was attempted.

A young NHS staffer arrived. Over-polite and overworked, he prepared to draw a modicum of the baby's blood for testing; but he couldn't get the needle into the baby's arm. The needle bent when the young man tried to push it in gently. Appearing unfazed, the man tried again with a fresh needle. The fresh needle failed as the first one had. Maintaining his professional calm but smiling his puzzlement, the man stated the obvious: This was strange. Dashiell agreed. What might cause such a phenomenon? The young man was embarrassed, so his weary smile coughed out laughter that was like an old tractor failing to start on a cold morning. He pondered while Dashiell lavished him with smiling platitudes designed to distract and defuse, to which he underreacted. As she thus sought to reduce the situation to some bizarre fluke, a familiar fist grew in Dashiell's midst. She heard a chemical roar within. A murder of crows took sudden flight in her heart.

The young man prepared to leave politely. He made a throwaway comment about the throwaway needles. He requested that Dashiell make an appointment to repeat the blood test attempt 'when all the little gremlins have gone to sleep!'. Wishing her 'and baby' well, he then left.

Dashiell was overwhelmed by relief at his departure. Blunt foreboding swamped her. They must not create a special case for him, her thoughts pleaded. He was just a normal child, couldn't they see!? His blood was fine anyway. What need to test? This was just a faulty batch of needles, surely. Not to worry. All was well. She prayed the one-handed prayer of the devout unbeliever.

This was the first of many strange things.

*

Dashiell loved the baby more than she dared to.

By June, the baby's presence was causing a bright havoc. Jericho questioned her frequently about 'the issue'. He would say things like, 'He can't stay,' and she would say nothing with skill.

Already Dashiell couldn't imagine his absence. Jericho knew this, and it troubled him. Part of the trouble was logistical. They both worked full time. They required fulltime care for Tally. Now, the baby had to be cared for by a new nanny called Amelia. Amelia cost money. Property development and estate management were not making Jericho rich. Dashiell's work as a teacher was modestly paid. Dust motes collided.

They both knew the emotional turmoil that the baby was causing would influence their relationship. They had been tumbling along fine, as lucky marriages can. The baby had changed everything. It was not that Jericho required much of Dashiell. At times, she wished he required more, and that she needed him more, too. No. It was many obvious things. One of them was what they both knew was growing in Tally's subconscious like bindweed: the sense that really, mummy wanted a child that worked properly, didn't she? A child that wasn't broken. A child that would one day run and laugh and kiss the air.

Didn't she.

By what metric might love be measured? By grain, by scruple, by dram, by ounce, by pound? In the other heavy language of the metre? By what Imperial System? By what Trojan betrayal? Horses could not be made of wood anyway. It was silly. Silly Hector.

If love can't be measured, how can it exist? How can water heal if it can't be cut? What is the triple point of love? This was silly! said Dashiell's mind as she tried to find sleep in the bed of their marriage; but love was losing its way: The bed always needed making. In youth, her thought prattled, love is a quick fluid that in time, freezes; yet only as a fluid would it yield to gravity's command. Love would find a level and a shape. Yes. It would settle. Colder, its murmur would slow to a whisper, and then to silence. Only in old age could that silence be understood. Would she understand?

Again, Dashiell wished these thoughts would stop. She wished that now the baby was asleep in his cot by their once erotic bed, sleep would claim her as it also refused to claim Jericho beside her. His breathing told her all. Dashiell wished sleep would claim and hush them both now at the night's feet as fervently as she wished the baby's real parents would never claim him.

Love had kissed them with its cruelty.

*

Languages are countries.

Strange things now fled in abundance from him. He didn't cry. He barely ate. He made them feel serene in a way that unsettled them. The umbilical of their marriage creaked under the strain of his presence, yet they were too amazed by him to notice. He wasn't possible. What was possible? What was truth? What was sanity, now?

Reality played games with them.

One thought was never far from their minds: the child wasn't theirs. This truth lay in the back of Jericho's throat like a constriction of mould. He resolved to tell the foundling the truth as soon as the baby could understand him. Jericho didn't know that the baby could already understand them all – talking or silent. Jericho would soon find out.

Dashiell made Jericho promise that he never would tell the child the truth of his parentage, however. They argued. It killed her yearning for his sex like a sick dog.

They had moved the baby into the adjoining room. Dashiell hated this, but Jericho couldn't sleep with him in their bedroom. In that adjoining room, the baby lay in the memory of moonlight and listened to their hearts beating next door. He loved this sound. He was exposed to a permanent cacophony of sound. He had already learnt to filter out much that he didn't want to hear while listening to that which interested him. It was a matter of self-preservation. His parent's heartbeats interested him. He considered one of these two drumbeats to belong to his parent but not the other. He had no idea why he felt this.

Dashiell became afraid.

He could run faster than an adult at an age when normal babies can barely crawl. This made Dashiell madly happy and physically sick with incredulity. She tried to hide the baby's ability to run from Jericho and Tally to protect them from the impossible. Soon, of course, they found out anyway. Jericho said and did nothing when it happened; yet his shocked mind was ablaze. When Tally saw the baby run too, she laughed loudly with a kind of joy that made them hurt. She shrieked with wonder. She knew he was the new Buddha. Of course he was.

'Go-go-go, Thumping Jack Flash! We must tell the world!' Tally said. Her face was the saddest mask of wildest joy. Dashiell looked at her sharply in a way that said: no, we must tell no one, ever; so Dashiell and Tally argued. 'He's exactly what the world needs!' said Tally. 'Like First Contact! He's First Contact. Everything's up to its neck in, I don't know mum – utter crap, and here's this thing, this infant who is, I don't know – reality's dream! You must understand. When the world finds out about him everything will change!'

'No darling,' answered Dashiell. 'The world will suspect him of being a charlatan or worse, too different to cope with, and so it will ignore him until it's destroyed him.'

'How can you be so negative, mum? Bloody hell!'

Arguments feel worse on Sundays. This Sunday was no exception. Tally harangued Dashiell, who took her usual refuge in silence. Jericho stayed out of it as he usually did. He pretended to read newspapers that enervated him and saddened him. He then followed his incredulity outside, where it escaped his expletive throat with ease.

The baby found their reactions to him fascinating. Why were they now so shocked that he could walk and run when a month earlier he had spoken! Not one word, but a sentence! What was walking at six months, when he could speak at four months!? Then, he had said to Dashiell: 'No one will ever hurt you except me, mummy.' The baby held her eyes as he said this. To hold his eyes was to fall without hope or wish of landing. Dashiell had been beyond any reaction. Shock can do this. The book of the mind can be utterly empty and numb, but the writer is in a state of gaudy frenzy. It took Dashiell a week to turn a page.

She had not told Jericho or Tally of the baby's talking. Dashiell had asked the baby not to speak in front of them. He had agreed. 'I understand, mummy,' he said with a certain sort of smile.

That afternoon he spoke in front of Jericho anyway. Dashiell wondered if this was out of spite, mischief, or in rebellion. She chose mischief. Perhaps he was an imagined Loki in a smile of myth. 'The property market's due a boom,' the baby said to Jericho as Jericho entered the house after work one Thursday that was well suited to rain. Jericho's mouth opened, then shut, then opened again. He then looked at Dashiell, who was marking some of her pupils' work at the kitchen table. Dashiell didn't look up. 'Can I get you a bowl to swim around in pointlessly, oh fish of gold?' she said.

Later that day, the baby ascended the stairs three steps at a time. He then looked at them all from the top of the stairs and smiled. This made them want to laugh and cry too. 'Same thing', cried Tally, relishing her newfound insanity.

'Go high enough, mum – fly – and things that seem different down here turn out to be the same thing up here. You were right! Look at him up there!' In her wheelchair, Tally gazed up at him at the top of the stairs. She laughed with the vertigo of the possible.

Dashiell tried not to worry and to laugh and hiccup and panic and exist and work at the same time. Multitasking was certainly her thing. All this made the baby laugh.

He was exceptional at laughing too.

*

The incident with the needle had been reported, of course. As arranged, an NHS field nurse came to try the blood test again. Dashiell offered him sweet Darjeeling tea, flapjack, and impressive conversation in the silly hope that he could be distracted. Obviously, he couldn't. Attempts went ahead. More needles were blunted. The attempt stopped only when the baby broke one of the nurse's arms when he lashed out in what the nurse assumed must be pain. The nurse was wrong. It seemed to Dashiell that the baby could feel no pain – or anything else – physically. When Dashiell embraced him or washed him, he seemed to feel nothing. It seemed his skin would be silent forever.

Nursing his broken arm and in agony, the nurse had no idea what to do. He had never experienced this. Wasn't this what happened last time? Dashiell apologised. A baby breaking a man's arm was simply an impossible thing. Dashiell apologised again. Perhaps some Paracetamol?

The baby cried because he had caused the nurse pain. It took Dashiell several minutes to hush him; and then he whimpered on, lost in a little horror.

'Have you noticed anything unusual about him otherwise?' the nurse said with brave humour.

Dashiell pretended to think. She swore the baby caught her eye as she did so. She felt an extreme compunction to laugh loudly.

'How's he eating?' grimaced the nurse.

'Fine.'

In fact the baby ate nothing but warm bread and drank nothing but cold water and sunlight.

Later, when the broken nurse had gone and Jericho returned from work, Jericho studied the baby's skin as if to explain the impossible. Experimenting, Jericho pushed a toothpick against the baby's skin gently. The skin and flesh remained flat where concavity should have occurred. He pushed the toothpick a little harder. Again, the baby's skin did not yield. The toothpick snapped. They laughed, but that was because they were unsettled to the point of breakdown. The baby knew this.

'What's going on, Jerry?' she said. Her eyes were suddenly tearful and desperate.

The baby knew that what she meant was: 'Make my love go away. Make this stop. I need to find a way back to a world I can deal with. I can't deal with this. *We* can't deal with this.'

Lost, and lost for words, Jericho could only embrace her in a state of empathy. It was the last time they would ever embrace in exactly this way again. The baby knew this, too. It made him cry, and that made Dashiell comfort him.

'See?' she said of her tyrant instincts.

Jericho saw.

'Gottle O'Geer,' Dashiell said, lost in the lethal safety of her mind.

'Make mine a double,' Jericho laughed; and so they let humour save them again for a while.

*

As promised, the baby disguised his abnormalities when he was out with her in the village or shopping in the town nearby; but Dashiell was concerned that his nanny Amelia would speak outwardly of his walking or talking or impervious skin. Dashiell therefore relieved Amelia of her duties. This meant that Dashiell would have to look after the baby full-time. That meant she had to give up her teaching job. When she had told Jericho of her concerns and plans, he struggled with his anger. He struggled because he was tired, they were poor, and he was human.

'For God sake, Dash!' He had called her Dash when they first met. He now called her this because he unconsciously wanted to take them back to that time. He couldn't.

She knew this. She had so much to say that she said nothing in response. She felt sorry, but not the need to apologise. He knew this.

'I know you love him, but if we should be looking after anyone, it should be Tally,' he said when the silence finally became unwieldy. Of course their main commitment was to Tally. Of course they would never let her down; and now, here was Dashiell letting her down - or so Jericho saw it. Jericho knew that Tally would one day see it that way, too; and that day wasn't far away.

'I can't support us all,' Jericho continued quietly. He hated saying it. He wished he could support them all. He wished he had been a professional surfer, too.

'What else was I supposed to do!?' she snapped, waking the baby from an early evening doze.

The baby looked at them. Jericho found his gaze worse than troubling, and somehow better than brandysnaps. The baby understood. As people do at the strangest of times, Jericho burst out laughing. Humour had been their bridge. It had always been their way of coping.

'Our own foundling. He's got your eyes.' Jericho heard himself saying. Jealousy's child lodged in his throat and made it heavy and perverse.

They could hear Tally sing as she washed upstairs.

'I've told you all I can tell you,' said Dashiell.

Jericho stopped laughing suddenly when the baby said, 'Just give me patience, please, and some water. I already love your love.' The baby looked out of the window now as he shocked them with these words. In the west, the day finally bled to death. Night was born in superb gore.

I already love your love.

*

In his tiny bedroom, he found his life's keel and his sail in the oceans of his thought.

In that simple room, he read the book of his contemplations and scattered them on the ceiling. There, they vexed and soared and dazzled like things. There, they focussed to a point at night and waited like good linen. In the morning, they woke (though he rarely slept) when the sun awoke and followed it across the sky's imagination. When the sky was tall in summer, his heart went on tiptoes. When the sky wept, his crux wept. He loved the sullen rage of winter clouds, which migrated from past to future without intent. What lay above them? One day, he would find out, he vowed. Now, when his mind took wing, he felt no need for freedom. In this, he was truly free.

Three years after Dashiell found him, he saw a programme about the sun on television. He watched it with obsessive interest. Later, he found a book on the sun in the living room. He spent hours looking at diagrams of the sun in silent wonder; so Dashiell bought him a DVD documentary about the sun. He watched it several times. When actual footage of the sun was shown, he went closer to the television, so he could watch the surface roil and clutch and flare. Suddenly aware of Dashiell watching him, he met her gaze as he met the sun's gaze. It was a gaze of recognition.

A paediatrician who liked to whistle visited almost a year after the first blood test failed. He seemed intent on finding out why it had failed. He couldn't. After he left ('Most strange – more bad needles? How odd!'), they feared the worst; but in time, the matter seemed to go away of its own accord. The baby was registered as 'orphan', and that seemed to be that.

The nurse's arm had long since healed of course. He had attributed the episode in a telephone conversation with Dashiell to 'some sort of misunderstanding'. He had seemed embarrassed. He had sounded drunk. No, babies clearly don't break grown men's arms. No, something else must have happened; what it was didn't matter now anyway, did it?

It mattered to Jericho. It mattered more every day.

Jericho became amazed at how long he, Jericho, held on to his rationality. This child – this foundling – could not be real; yet what else could be? It was all rather like dreaming.

Jericho thought he was dreaming when the child fashioned intricate, briefly symmetrical patterns in vortices in his bathwater, or sight-read Bach, or solved quantum field equations with absurd ease. Then, actually, Jericho felt more awake than he had ever felt. He felt mercilessly alive.

As the child grew, amazement became their norm. Normality became impossible. Impossibility became normal. Clearly, they had all fallen asleep one day nearly four years ago and were now all dreaming the same dream; because if they were awake or sane …

On occasion, Jericho's feelings – incredulity, confusion, panic – vented without warning.

'We have to tell someone!'

'Why? They'll only take him away from us.'

It was more obvious than breakfast cereal that this was what Jericho wanted.

'He'll be persecuted,' Dashiell continued.

'You don't know that. He could be looked after.'

'You mean prodded and poked and put behind glass he'll shatter with a whisper.'

'He's impossible, Dash.'

'I know. What do you want me to do about it?'

They then spoke for a while without words or movement as they once had. Without the distractions and inadequacies of words, they understood each other naturally.

Dashiell and Jericho struggled with their own different battles with the impossible; but they were united in their concerns for Tally. The change in their daughter since Dashiell had found the child and brought him home was worrying. Dashiell and Jericho worried that Tally felt that the boy's abilities seemed to amplify her disabilities. They feared that she had begun to shrivel in the light of his growing splendour, as Tally saw it, and that there was nothing they could do about it.

Naturally, Dashiell sought to reassure Tally. 'Darling. You're amazing!' said Dashiell to her brightly in the d of a Sunday, after Tally read aloud one of her famous monologues.

'Yes, but who's ever going to sex me?' was Tally's naked reply.

The question broke Dashiell's heart.

Later, alone, Tally's words echoed in Dashiell's essence. She now forced herself to acknowledge what she had long denied: that a sickness had been born in her on the day she had found him. It was a sickness called joy. Joy had a brother whose name was fear. The sickness and its sibling never stopped growing. A cloying rose grew deep within her. Its thorns were black claws. She worried that it had scratched her youth from her. Jericho reassured her in a way that seemed dutiful.

'You're hot. Live with it.'

She knew he didn't mean it. He had found her sexy once and she, him; but life is life.

So she studied herself in the naked mirror and was protected by a terror she could understand. Then she laughed like a divine savage.

*

The baby became a boy. Boys go to school. To have tutored him at home would have been to draw more attention to him. Was he addled? What was the reason he might not attend primary school? There was none. He was like any other boy. Precisely. He therefore went to school.

The school at which Dashiell had worked was the nearest to them, and the best of the local bunch. Dashiell felt growing dread as his first day at the school approached. She was scared that his 'abnormalities' would be discovered. She was also, she realised, jealous.

She had found the baby. She had nurtured him. She had given up her job and so part of her identity to devote herself to him. Now, she was about to hand him over into the care of others. Were they worthy? Why was she any worthier? What if they found out?

That must never happen.

Dashiell dropped him off at primary school stuffed full of promises. Tally insisted on coming, despite the palaver of getting her wheelchair into the car.

'You have to promise you won't speak like an adult, or do algebra with ease, or lift the teacher's car up, or punch – above all don't punch anyone! Or pinch them!' Dashiell said to him as they all got out of the car.

'Oh, ducky! Promise me you'll pinch somebody,' Tally implored, her eyes living.

'Tally!' Dashiell admonished gently. The gentleness was a code for her guilt.

The foundling pulled a face at Tally, then said to Dashiell, 'I promise.' He held her gaze with his universal eyes. Everything about everything was present in his eyes. Dashiell adored and dreaded what she saw in them. Might this gaze give him away? No. No one would ever see him as she did. Please, please, please don't let him become an outsider like me. Please? Protect my boy from his perfection. Thank you. Now off you go and be a good boy and remember what I told you.

I promise.

Dashiell and Tally watched him wonder off into the playground and towards the schoolhouse. Dashiell's trepidation was slightly eased when the headmistress Mrs

Delaney greeted her warmly and asked if she might have any interest in part-time work?

'You are missed around here you know, dear.'

So it turned out that good things came to keep an eye on all the strange things that had happened. Dashiell accepted the offer of work. It would enable her to bolster the household's finances. Perhaps working at the school he attended would also allow Dashiell to protect him, too – he who, it seemed, already needed no one's protection.

His invincibility was only physical, however. Saying goodbye that day to his mother and his sister hurt him. He was as exceptional at feeling pain as he was at dealing with it, however. Pain and strength therefore collided in him as Dashiell and Tally walked away. Neither would yield.

His eyes darkened as Dashiell and Tally walked away in a way that made Mrs Delaney glance and glance again. Poor boy. There was something peculiar about his eyes, though. Why did they seem so familiar, yet so strange? Mrs Delaney couldn't quite think, she was sure; so she made him feel as welcome as all the other new pupils, and went about her ways.

He hid his tears ineptly.

'It'll be alright.' The voice belonged to a boy about the same age as him. His name was Kenton Young. Kenton extended a comically formal hand. The foundling shook it formally. In her office, Mrs Delaney saw them do it. It made her smile.

'I like to be called Kenton if possible'.

Kenton soon became his best friend. They played together at break time and lunchtime. The foundling helped Kenton with classwork that Kenton found difficult. Kenton wasn't surprised his new friend didn't find anything difficult because children just accept things while questioning everything. Mrs Salter's dark-haired son was just one of those children who could do everything. The end.

One day soon, Kenton asked him around to tea and to play after school. He therefore got to meet Kenton's parents Thomas and Bella Young. They seemed strange; but that was because, he thought, adults are just strange things who can't-be-understood. He was therefore unaware of what some might call abnormalities in Thomas and Bella's relationship, and in Bella's behaviour.

It was while having tea at the Youngs' that the foundling first met Kenton's sister: Shanti. Shanti came home from the girls' school and joined them at the tea table. When she did so, he stared at her for an amount of time that Bella Young became inwardly uncomfortable with, but which Thomas Young ignored.

'Children are what they are, dear. What do you mean he stared? Shanti's beautiful. Of course he stared. I would,' Thomas said to Bella that evening as they got into their separate beds. Bella didn't respond. I would. Yes, you would, she thought; but then so might I have, once.

The foundling soon asked if he could come round for tea almost every day. Kenton always said yes, so Bella had to start making excuses. She did so with a smile full of teeth unnaturally straight and white. This was how Bella was glad to see herself: unnaturally straight and white. Slightly above nature, actually. Slightly chosen by a higher cause.

When he went to the Young's house for tea or to play, it was now in the hope of seeing Shanti. In hope, he would play and watch TV with Kenton. They were best, best friends. They were 'blood brothers, blood', as Kenton used to say, rap hugging him like a gangsta rap gangsta.

'You're flipping lucky to have a sister like Shanti,' he said to Kenton one day when Shanti failed to come home while he was there.

'She smells of pickled onions,' said Kenton with his eyes glued to the TV.

'I like pickled onions.' Indeed, the foundling asked Dashiell if they had any pickled onions that night. Having none, Dashiell bought some the next day. The next day, he ate the whole jar. Nothing happened for about half an hour. He then burped which such pungent force that it shattered one of the kitchen windows.

'Bloody blimey! Nuclear pickle waste from war smell! Call the smelly navy!' roared Tally. She fell about laughing.

'As worse as pickles are' he said, wiping the laughter from her eyes gently.

Tally and the foundling then had yet another burping competition. Dashiell tried to disapprove. She had studied acting.

Pickled onion or not, he fell vertically in love with Shanti Young over tea at the Young's at 27, Slate Avenue quite close to the village hall. 'Fortunate' to get close to her one day on the stairs, he found out that she didn't smell of pickled onions at all. He thought she smelt of heather on summer hills. He imagined therefore that she might just taste of summer itself. Kenton found his best friend's interest in his sister made him feel slightly strange, but children just accept things the way they are while questioning everything.

Kenton's feelings made Bella Young think, which made Thomas Young go to the golf club.

*

At school, Glenn Holm told him that when you are seven years old your heart turns brown, so you can make yourself burp at will. He had no idea who Will was. There was also a girl called Jane May. Everybody knew Jane May was mad because she had big curly hair and she could shake her head violently without getting dizzy.

He looked forward to being seven. He knew Jane wasn't mad.

*

Beneath a Saturday in early May, he was changed forever by the rapture of birdsong.

There was woodland nearby, where Tally wished to go. When Dashiell and Jericho were doing chores in town, he therefore pushed Tally away from the kitchen table in her wheelchair and out of the back door without so much as a by-your-leave.

'Rhetorical question,' she said when they were halfway down the road.

'You'll see.'

'You already know what rhetorical means? Holy shit!' laughed Tally.

At the age of five, he was barely taller than her wheelchair. He could push her with no apparent effort, however. That made Tally laugh her blocked drain laugh and swear like ten troupers.

Their neighbour Mr Bourncleave saw them go. Mr Bourncleave found it grotesquely irresponsible that the Salters would allow a small child to push a disadvantaged child to heaven knows where. He watched them until they were out of sight. He then withdrew behind the scoff of the kitchen curtains and disapproved of disapproval.

He pushed Tally to the woodland. Tally talked a bit and sang a bit as they went. Then they reached the woods. He pushed her some way into the trees, then stopped.

'Have you brought me here to put me out of my misery?'

'Of course.'

He sat down on the ground beside her. Seeming scarce at first, birdsong seemed to grow to become a paean to the thing of existence. To him, it became colours and flavours. He thought that its beauty was so far beyond description that it was hopeless, and what was life without hope's burden? He found that thought rather delicious.

The trick was to see the birds that were singing this song or that. It was almost impossible. Unless they moved, the birds were invisible even to him, who could see for clear-day miles. He gave up trying, and let moment of the woods stretch out to the furthest of all far things within him.

They sat together. There they were. Then they held hands. The spectrum of sounds washed them. The birdsong overlapped and separated and became silver and nougat and shimmering and bronze and nothing to do with sound and everything to do with experience. Vortices of song swirled and disappeared into fathoms where otters flashed, and light darted amongst fish steadfast in their scales, and where dreams gobbled the chainmail bubbles worn by the dive of a kingfisher.

The beauty of it drained them of intent and flooded them with significance. They sat together as they were. Seconds and aeons fled to them and from them. Sunlight painted tree branches until an hour passed, and then another. Hereabouts on branch, on high, or in Doomsday fields and wetlands once perhaps the Barn Owl, the Icterine Warbler, the Meadow Pipit, the Parasitic Jaeger, the Siskin, the Blue-headed Wagtail, the Common Linnet, the Twite, the Chaffinch, the Velvet Scoter, the Yellowhammer, Temminck's Stint, the Black-tailed Godwit, the Chiffchaff, the Dunlin, the Ruff, the Blue Tit, the Common Buzzard, the Eurasian Thick-knee, the Bullfinch, the Red-necked phalarope, and even the Stone Curlew may have woven air into sounds that people may have found sublime, distracting, or calls to vital slaughter.

In truth, what he and Tally now heard were the territorial claims and mating calls of no more than five sparrows, a few starlings, and a solitary blackbird. In truth, so little was left of what once was. For the moment, however, it seemed to them both that they had been welcomed into the hall of eternity by a humble hand that shook with the effort of trying to grasp a beauty that cannot be grasped any more than now can.

Suddenly it was time to go home. He carried her in her wheelchair back to the real fable they shared with Dashiell and Jericho that was called a home. As they went, he told her jokes that turned her weeping from one sort to another, and then they were the same, and forever changed.

*

When he became seven years old (and Tally was thirteen), he discovered that he couldn't make himself burp at will, though he now knew who Will was.

It was about this time that Dashiell allowed him and Tally to take in a stray cat that appeared in the garden. A week later (the summer solstice), he let the cat outside because it seemed to him that was where it belonged. It sniffed around the garden for a while, then got through a hole in the garden fence and disappeared. He thought about following it and bringing it back, but he felt that if the cat sought freedom, that was what he would give it. When Tally found out the cat had gone, she cried for a day and didn't speak to him for a week.

*

He thought that human time might be the first moment of a flower in colour. He thought it might be the memory of winter. He thought it might be footsteps in unknown rooms. He thought it might be the creep of mould on walls built by long-dead hands, or branches moving in the last of afternoon; or raindrops forsaken by rain on insolent railings; or the mark left by absent jewellery on old flesh; or the courage of windows; and shadows gathered under accustomed furniture; and the wear of a carpet where egress and ingress meet; and experience that cannot be described; and unchanging change; and an average road on an average day, and the road rising to a hill at dawn.

In the S of a Sunday, he discovered what horses meant to him.

Dashiell led them out into early August fields. The throat of the gale was on the gorse. The rain eased off as they walked. Soon, only drizzle withered the puddles on the footpath. He saw a fallen tree branch. To him it looked like discarded lightning.

He stopped and looked down at a puddle at his feet. Dashiell stopped and looked with him. Beneath them, their quivering rain-selves looked up and pondered them. She could feel his million questions. He heard the dim patter of the drizzle. The sky shivered. Silence took flight. Then a happy boy was suddenly dancing in puddles. Their puddle-reflections therefore shattered happily.

Then he stopped making the puddles laugh. He seemed to sense something. It seemed to him that the air was haunted by a time before he existed – if such a thing existed. He looked up at Dashiell too quickly for her to look away to disguise her emotions; and so he saw the rain die in her eyes.

A raven roared in a tree nearby. The bird seemed affronted by their presence. Jagged and reluctant, it hurled away into the gangster landscape. History lived in the land.

'Look, darling. There.' She pointed.

Then he saw them: horses. The things he had sensed. There were two of them locked out of time near a fence. He breathed in sharply. He knew he would never breathe out.

'What are they waiting for?'

'They're not waiting for anything. Well some dry hay, maybe, or some oats. I see what you mean though. They do look like they're in a queue of themselves.'

He looked at her quizzically in response. His expression made Dashiell laugh. She was grateful. There he was, already as handsome as the white wind beside him.

He had seen horses before of course, but never like this. Never this close. Dashiell led him closer still. As they approached the horses, one looked at them. He was spellbound. This was an epiphany for him, she could see. She felt his little hand safe in hers. It made her happy.

'I can't say anything about them,' he said of the horses eventually. One jerked its head at some crucial whimsy. The other whinnied. The woman with rain in her eyes and the child by her side promised neither of them the chance of food. They were therefore irrelevant; so the horses turned into sudden running muscle and mane and instinct. The wet earth thumped their weight.

Mummy was OK, surely? Was mummy OK? Mummy?

He would never be able to define the word 'horse'.

*

In the moon of a Monday, he discovered a thing he could call home.

That thing was fire.

Fire cleansed him. Fire personified him. Fire reiterated him.

It was November 5th. Dashiell and Jericho had built a bonfire in the back garden. The back garden was a bit small for such things, so they built a small bonfire. Tally and the foundling were allowed to hold sparklers. Tally used them to write ephemera on their retinas. She challenged them to guess what she was writing. She wrote fast to try to thwart them.

'Balderdash!' guessed Dashiell.

'Mum. You saying I'm writing balderdash or that I wrote bloody balderdash?'

'Both,' smiled Dashiell.

'Mum! Shit!' said Tally. Her smile vanished into the dark in that way it did when her mood swung like this. Tally's moods swung like church bells at the hours and their fractions. They were all used to them. The foundling thought them fascinating, but deadly sad. He thought they were just the-way-things-are. Jericho just carried on tending the fire and swigging a beer that wasn't as cold as it used to be. Dashiell drained the wine from her glass in one yes please gulp.

'You're writing bollocks,' said the foundling to Tally.

'Yay! Top of the class, clever clogs. Bloody hell! Your go then!' said Tally. Her anger was a black spark.

'Come on now!' Dashiell's attempt to upbraid the foundling for his language was half-hearted. If she was annoyed with him, why was she laughing (though he now knew that people laughed because they are serious)?

'But Tally taught me to say it!' was his earnest defence.

'He's bloody showing off again aren't you, shit-wit? Wit shit. Pant shit. Look at him.' Tally laughed at him. For the first time, the foundling felt anger. He didn't know it yet, but his anger would grope its way to life's nipple. There, it would feed and grow, and gain identity. The identity would evolve, and seek outlets for havoc. He would fight it. The conflict would be as worlds colliding; but not yet. Not for a long time. Now, he just wished Tally wouldn't laugh at him.

'I'm not showing off. But I can let off if you want,' he answered. His diversion worked: Tally stopped laughing at him. Instead, she guffawed and farted to pre-empt him. 'Beat that, pipsqueak. He's a big show-off.' Tally's jet eyes ravished the fire as she spoke.

'Tally. Come on darling. Don't,' said Dashiell.

'Well if I don't, he won't know how much we love the little bleeder, will he? Will you, bro?' She turned to the foundling and offered him her sparkler as parlay. His sparkler had gone out. He was now more interested in the bonfire, however. The paper, cardboard, and tinder had caught, igniting the small wood above. The logs above that, though at first loathe, were soon smouldering too. Flames leapt around them and up into the cold night like similes.

Jericho put his empty beer bottle down to find the next firework to light. 'So – Roman Candle or Catherine wheel, sports fans?'

Dashiell's scream cut Tally to the quick.

The foundling had walked into the bonfire, where he now stood in wonder. Dashiell's instincts sent her into the fire to grab him, but Jericho stayed her to save her.

The foundling's weight, though yet slight, made the burning wood collapse around him; yet enough of it remained to immolate him. Soon, he was drenched by fire. He thought that the flames were like wild blown hair. He thought the fire was where nights began in the throats of stories.

Jericho made to leap into the fire to pull him to safety, but Dashiell found herself stopping him as he had stopped her. She stopped him because something told her the boy would come to no harm. She also didn't want Jericho to suffer. Her instinctive care for Jericho made the foundling just as happy as his new friend fire did. He laughed as the flames welcomed him. He had found his home.

Dashiell's restraining grip on him still, Jericho stared. His face was a mask of terrible wonder.

Beside her parents, Tally looked at the foundling amid the flames with a distant, marvelling grief. Her eyes danced with tears, which turned them into mirrors. In these mirrors was reflected her little brother standing smiling in the fire. His clothes had burnt away, leaving him naked and happy. He pulled silly am-dram faces as if to say, 'Ah! That's better! That's nice!'

Dashiell released Jericho from the grip of her care.

Then they just watched the foundling and did not know what they knew and did not know what they didn't know not quite here and not quite now in the garden of fire with its sudden palms and its animal pages and its devotion to beauty and its evocations and its ancient alchemy that showed one thing to be another, and another to be something else, and this fable of itself a rumour of sanctuary among the north for ancestors besieged by the monsters of cold and the stripping of land by settlers for crop and the deracination of people because they were people and the devolution of appearance into reality and the deconstruction of that reality into the humility that arises from insight like a boy from fire on a cold November evening invented by a 17th Century anarchist when in fact a neighbour called Jeremy Shwondler was watching and not understanding how a boy can stand naked and smiling in a bonfire when surely the world should be swoosh! and boohoo! and baked potatoes cooked in cooking foil in the magma at the bottom of memory under the branches of flame near the top of the bonfire so that Jeremy Shwondler might grow a stomach and a pit of cold with fear of the impossible seeding and budding in his safe world so that its predictable walls might Jericho like trumpets as brassy as fire's caprice and rush inside to tell his wife that 'Stone the crows, Julie. Come and look at this! and so another rumour spawned in a village already heavy with anecdotes like the belly of a gravid beast seeking a place to birth and the jelly and waters of the birth spilling out over the rocky shoulder of the red earth saying without a word it's just a blue ball of time like iron in the absolute that is space that is as cold as perfection and impossible and the infinity of indifference and the infinity of joy that is life especially when it's made of the living smile of a wee child who has found a new toy to play with and that wee toy is fire.

*

A month later, the Circus Minimis pitched its tent midway between the village and the town nearby.

Dashiell saw a poster advertising the circus visit outside the local post office.

'So who wants to go?' she said after lunch. It was Saturday.

Tally and the foundling rammed their right arms into the air, classroom style, and shouted 'me, me, me, me,' louder and louder to try to drown each other out.

'All right!' Jericho finally exclaimed to silence them. He was smiling, but as smiles often are, it was a mask. The property market was due a boom. Marriage is marriage.

'Well dad clearly needs to go,' said Dashiell with an angle. She didn't meet Jericho's eyes.

That evening's performance began at 7 pm. To the foundling, that afternoon seemed to take forever. 'A watched kettle never boils,' smiled Dashiell to him at about 3.30 pm.

'Is it teatime then?' he replied with a kettle whistle sound and flickering innocence.

'It will always be teatime, noodle.'

Dashiell was compelled to kiss him on the forehead.

By chance, Tally saw Dashiell kiss him thus as she wheeled herself past the kitchen window outside on her way back from taking the rubbish out – a chore she insisted on doing. By chance, her reflection on the window became superimposed on the image of her real mother kissing her not-real-brother in the kitchen. Tally fancied the superimposition scarred her retinas in some way. She remembered how she and her found-brother stared at a lamp at night, then when 'ready!' looked away and at each other. Giggling, they had watched the memory of the lamp in their eyes orange-fizz and firework-fade. Now, Tally heard herself giggle bitterly as she wheeled herself up her special ramp and back inside the house. The house felt slightly less welcoming than it had a minute earlier.

Eventually it was 7 pm and they were in the Circus Minimis big top, which was the smallest circus tent any of them had ever been in. It was barely ten metres in diameter including the audience seats, of which there were only four rows. All the other seats were taken by locals, some of whom the foundling recognised. Did some of them avoid looking at the Salter family? Did Tally deliberately seek out their gazes and hold them with the blazing coals of her eyes until they looked away? He also thought that he lip-read someone in the audience say of the Salter family, 'at least they're where they belong'. Perhaps he was wrong; yet he felt the seeds of anger being planted in his core. He knew instinctively that these seeds must not take root, nor the crop flourish. He therefore had another marshmallow, pulled a face at Tally, and focussed on their surroundings.

Everything about the Circus Minimis was small. Even the horses were Shetland ponies. As a crazy ukulele tune was played by a trio of buffoons, one such horse entered the tiny performance ring now. It pulled a tiny cart driven by a tattooed juggler wearing a stovepipe hat.

'That's why it's called Circus Minimis. Minimum means the least of something. It's the opposite of maximum – though you knew that didn't you?' Dashiell said to him as she offered him another marshmallow. Was she annoyed? The foundling hadn't yet eaten the marshmallow she gave him five minutes earlier: it lodged un-chewed in his sugar melting mouth. Realising this, she gave him a look that said, 'eat-up', and 'why can't you eat it?', which meant, 'why can't you be more normal, so I don't have to endure casual ostracism and the ruin of my marriage to this man I still love?' She said none of this, of course. She didn't need to. Her found-son knew what her look meant, too.

'Are you a mini-mum or a maxi-mum,' he replied, and she smiled her smile. Tally saw it.

The performance comprised the usual clowning and acts. The foundling particularly liked the strong man act. A short interval followed. They remained seated while most people got up and used the facilities or crushed the bar. He wasn't sure why they remained seated instead of mingling with others like this. He wasn't sure why Jericho looked at nothing in a particular way while he sucked a boiled sweet, either; or if mummy was aware that daddy seemed unhappy in this happy place. It didn't seem to matter. They were at the circus. Tally was laughing and cramming her mouth with sweets until she couldn't speak, and crying with laughter as she did so. She often cried like this.

Interval over, it was time for the high-wire performance. A wire had been stretched between two towers at either side of the performance ring. While the trio of ukulele players played music of high drama, a highwire performer climbed one of the towers and attached a safety harness. With the normal flourishes and exaggerations, she started to soar overhead in ever higher orbits. A spotlight followed her. The ukulele players strummed a minor chord to maintain the thing of it. The feather headpiece she wore flew like a brave flame as she moved. She passed approximately and then almost exactly over the foundling on her widening transits around the ring. He thought their eyes met briefly. He thought that the moment would never end. She knew it was already over; but she glimpsed a little boy looking up at her as she 'flew' over the audience. Maybe she saw something in his eyes. Maybe she would only remember that thing years later – long after the Circus Minimis had lost its performance licence for reasons of Health and Safety, and for certain political reasons.

To the foundling, now, she flew like a myth above him. He didn't know the rope callouses on her hands were bleeding. He knew nothing of the pain in her muscles and sinews, or the smell of her sweat. He couldn't imagine how much she feared falling, even after all these years. All he knew was that she was flying, and that he wanted to fly, too. All he knew was that she was the most beautiful woman he had ever seen.

He therefore stuffed his mouth with sweets until he drooled and laughed with Tally and mummy and always serious daddy. This was fun!

After the circus, they said little as Jericho drove them home. Tally's wheelchair seemed to clank slightly louder than usual in the boot as the car moved. The foundling glanced at his sister as she took his hand as she often did. He held it until she fell asleep. It was sleep from which Tally wished no awakening, but he could not know that yet. For him, there was only the bliss of a journey home from an evening out with a family that he wished would always be exactly like this.

Even though he wished, however, he already knew that change is the only thing that exists; and change indeed was already among them like a reaper in unready corn.

*

Seeming average was hard because everything was so easy for him – especially maths, which he loved. In primary school, they did basic adding and subtraction. At home, he immersed himself in fractals and homological conjectures in commutative algebra. Tally crowned him King of the Nerds. The Krull dimension enthused him so much he named himself King Krull. One evening after primary school, he went into Tally's room and stood before her as a mythical king – complete with cardboard sword and crown. 'I am

King Krull! Kneel, earth woman, kneel!' He drew his toy sword and stood dramatically. Tally barely reacted, however. As King Krull accepted the praise of his minions, Tally stared at the horizon somewhere beyond the window inside herself.

Primary school studies were easier than easy for him. 'I might as well just lie down and dream of buttons,' he said to Dashiell.

Because everything in class was easy, he did badly at everything to make himself seem average. Certain pupils thus mocked him. He also took great trouble to be bad at sport, and appear inept in physical education classes. Teachers thus rebuked him. Their scorn, though gentle, hurt him. He was already burdened by a sensitivity that had no limits, it seemed to him. Perhaps he just had no boundaries, he pondered. He was like a landscape without a horizon. He visualised this such that normal people lived on the outside of the sphere of the planet, but he lived on the inside; so there was no horizon. He liked this, and began to devour all the books he and Dashiell could find about geometry. He thus made 'mind-friends' with Euclid, and was already on 'first name terms' with Plato.

After primary school, he went to the state secondary school in the town nearby. There, as he had at primary school, when children scorned or shunned him for seeming different, faux-weak, or faux-stupid, he smiled or made them laugh. Dashiell had taught him that they, like he, couldn't help being what they had been made; so he couldn't logically persecute them for their intolerance.

Dashiell and Jericho had always celebrated his birthday on the anniversary of the day Dashiell found him. When younger, he had assumed that his birthday was just that: his birthday; but as time went by, assumptions fled from him like doves abrupt into the sky. Soon, Dashiell and Jericho would have to tell him that his birthday was not his birthday and that he was not their biological child; but they delayed this telling out of love, and fear of its consequences.

Just after his 13th 'birthday', a secondary schoolyard fracas got tongues wagging. They had wagged before, of course; but now the wagging became the tail of a told-you-so dog.

He grew angry with a boy called Eric Lipton in the schoolyard. Dashiell had long since made him understand how important it was that he never got angry. Anger was the enemy. 'Anger is fear,' she said with mock sagacity (as she always did when being 'wise') when he had, when a toddler, punched a hole in Jericho's car when frustrated at something long since forgotten.

At secondary school, by and large, teenagers treated him as younger children always had: with (now spotty) indifference, occasional curiosity, or tribally. Eric Lipton persecuted him daily, however. The foundling knew why, because he knew why people did things. He knew that Lipton's grudge wasn't against him. Lipton's grudge was against the experience of being Lipton.

Indeed, it would have been hard to dislike the Salter boy at that time for Lipton or anyone else. He was neither large nor small nor too attractive or unattractive; but he was polite, and clearly abnormally gifted, however hard he tried not to show it. 'Not showing it' now involved botching homework; botching classwork; misspelling words; and seeming like an all-round dunce.

Word got around. Was he pretending?

Dashiell told him he was trying too hard. She told him not to appear 'implausibly daft,' because someone might smell a rat '... and rats can ming, lemme tell you'. Trying not to appear 'implausibly daft,' he therefore stated in science one day that zero and infinity were identical because neither could be measured or reduced, and that in ways that mattered, the universe had no extent, so it could be as endless as it liked, but not in the human mind, which is where quantity lived.

This may or may not have been why Lipton pushed him too far the next day at eleven-forty-one a.m. on a Thursday: the day of Thor. When Lipton shoved him and sneered, Thor pushed Lipton backwards with much force. Despite being somewhat overweight, Lipton took off. Thor roared as he did it in the thunders of his mind. When he saw Lipton take off, however, Thor went away quickly, and the foundling returned in sudden regret. By the time Lipton landed, Lipton was on the other side of the playground. Lipton thus broke nineteen of his two hundred and seventy bones.

Since what had happened was impossible, other children reacted in impossible ways. The teacher on schoolyard duty, Mr Calisher, had not seen the impossible incident directly, so could shed no light on what had happened when later asked. All everyone knew was that the foundling could not have sent Lipton flying across the schoolyard as Lipton had flown.

That was a relief for everyone except Lipton.

Crushed by remorse and stressed, he was taken home early by Dashiell, who was still working at his old primary school. He apologised tearfully. He didn't need to, she told him. She was now frightened of the future as never before. Now, so was he. For the first time, he feared his abilities.

'How can I control it!?' he said. 'What if this happens again, and ...'

'You'll just have to control it,' said Dashiell as she drove him home. 'Always.'

'Always? How? What if I can't? And how am I never or ever going to tell anyone about me?' he said. 'I'm supposed to be less than I am, always – to hide? And what am I? How am I like this?!'

Dashiell took a moment to say it: 'I don't know.'

'Well was I normal to begin with?' he said immediately.

His new despair – that of the freak, the banished outsider – seared her.

'Well at the start, when you were little, it wasn't apparent, but ...'

'But?' Aware that she didn't wish to go further, he didn't push her.

He resolved to solve the mystery of himself. He already knew that he never would.

Sometimes, when despondent, he suspected Dashiell and Jericho and even Tally of knowing more about him than they were telling him; yet when he considered their eyes, he saw no deceit, and when he looked at people, he saw all that could be seen. Nothing was hidden from him. This was what sometimes made people like Lipton dislike him: There was nowhere to hide from his gaze.

Try as he did to seem normal from then on, his reputation as a freak was born in Friday's tribe. Gossip gave it beestings. Insecurity weaned it. Myopia fed it. Boredom bloated it. By Monday it was fully grown. Much as she inwardly loathed those who mocked him, Dashiell taught him to tolerate them. She taught him that tolerance was above everything but humility, awe, and laughter.

Of course Kenton got to hear all about the incident – though not from the foundling. Kenton obviously told Shanti, who was secretly intrigued, because the foundling fascinated her. Perhaps this fascination drove her fantasies about him. He seemed different. He seemed elemental. Kenton sensed that his sister was drawn to his friend. This troubled him, but he told no one of his trouble.

Kenton didn't go to the secondary school that the foundling went to. He went to a private school some miles away. This was apparently 'cos my dad's gazillions rich,' as Kenton put it. In fact Kenton's father Thomas Young wasn't rich; he was comfortably wealthy. He could afford new golf clubs not when he needed them, but when he wanted them. This, he felt, was the description of acceptable affluence. He told his wife Bella nothing of his wants. She had no wish to hear of them.

The boys were teenagers now, so tea at the Young's had become visits to the town to 'hang out' after school. The foundling saw Shanti around quite often. She had grown from a pickled egg into something else entirely. Her body was fed up with straight lines. It had been experimenting with curves, which made the foundling feel like he used to when he went high on the swing and left his stomach behind as he went down. Shanti ignored him completely, however. He thought that meant she didn't like him. In this, he was that thing he loved being more than anything else: wrong.

He thought he loved Shanti Young as much as he loved subtlety. He thought Shanti and subtlety were the same thing. Shanti didn't feel subtle, however. She felt like many teenage girls feel: bored and betrayed. The only person that Shanti didn't feel bored and betrayed by was her brother Kenton. The foundling was already fascinated by, and slightly jealous of, their relationship.

'I want to spend my whole life thinking about subtlety', he said to Shanti two weeks after the incident with Lipton. It was his young way of flirting with her. She laughed, but not cruelly. She wondered if she might one day love him. She was already drawn to the dark strangeness of him. Did he hide a secret? If so, perhaps she would keep her love a secret, too. She would wrap it in rose scent. She would store it away safely. When the time was right, she thought, she might give him this present. He would unwrap it. It would stand, naked, before him, and he would adore it; but not yet.

*

'If I can't lie, how will I become an adult, mum? Do you lie?'
　'I'm lying now.'
　To Dashiell, he already seemed like a young man. To her, he seemed increasingly burdened by his impossibility, and the self-knowledge denied him. How do people cope with the impossible? worried Dashiell. How do I cope? How will Jericho and Tally cope? We just breathe. This is how people cope. When the day is smashed down or built up too fast to climb, people just breathe.
　Dashiell kept breathing.

By the age of sixteen, he was already funny. Humour turned the world upside down, he said. 'That makes it easier to recognise.'

He developed a tendency to play with words. He listened to a radio programme about the Reverend Spooner on a Saturday and from that moment, became an ardent spoonerizer.

'Lunch is ready,' said Dashiell a week later.

'Wrench is luddy,' he responded. Spoonerizing made his parents laugh, too, and that made him happy. It made Tally guffaw. She encouraged him. She started spoonerising everything, too. They tried to outdo each other.

'Wheat my eel chair' meant 'eat my wheelchair' – something Tally often said (and often with her middle finger raised to flick the world the bird). He loved this one and took it further. 'Wheel my chair eat' 'Wheel my air, cheat!' 'Cheat my air-wheel,' and 'Wear my eel, cheat!'

He loved to call his mum and dad 'dumb and mad,' which prompted Tally to say, 'Which one's which?' Dashiell attempted to admonish him, but it was half-hearted. Tally thought her parents were harder on her than on him. She secretly hated this, and her hatred grew inside her until she could ignore it easily. Tally thought her dumb and mad treated him like he was made of gossamer. This was the ultimate irony, of course: as far as they knew he was physically invincible. His quintessence, however, was another matter: that was too sensitive to exist in the world. How he would survive, Dashiell did not know. If she did cosset him, who, Dashiell thought, could blame her?

When Tally said she was going to phone Dashiell's mother Molly by saying 'I'm going to phone up granny,' he said, 'I'm going to groan up fanny.' It was the hardest any of them had seen him laugh.

He laughed a lot. He adored humour. When he was sixteen and six weeks old, he decided to be a stand-up comedian. He rehearsed (something that to him and Tally was obviously two hearses in a row, which obviously meant the undertakers had to be in a boat that could be rowed) in front of the mirror in his room for weeks. He then rehearsed in front of Dashiell, Jericho, and Tally. Wiping the tears of laughter from her eyes, Tally hugged him after one such rehearsal. 'Love is a confused vole', she said. 'I love you too,' he responded, naked in his truth.

He advertised his first public stand-up performance at the village hall with enviable courage and professionalism, Jericho thought. 'Well pin for an eddy, pin or a found,' he said. Tally began to translate: 'In for a penny ...' She didn't need to finish. Jericho was getting used to the verbal mayhem, and becoming quite good at it, too.

His first stand-up comedy performance was on a Friday evening. The turnout was actually quite good. Thomas, Bella, and Kenton Young were there. Their presence made the foundling wonder why Shanti hadn't come. Was she really totally uninterested in him, or was she playing games?

Kenton read his mind. 'She's got a date,' he said, grinning and knowing the foundling wouldn't enjoy the knowledge. In fact Kenton was lying so as to mess with his friend. (The foundling knew this.) In fact Shanti was at home watching TV and chatting to a friend on the phone. Shanti knew that the foundling wanted her to be at the village hall. She chose instead to play games with him in a harmless way, as she felt it. She chose to make him miss her. To deny him the chance to impress her.

Now, in the village hall, he was glad, because he was sure he was about to make a fool of himself. His mouth became dry and his palms, sticky. He swallowed air.

Dashiell, Jericho, Tally sat three rows back (there were only four) as he requested.

'If you sit near the front you'll ffo em tup,' he had said that morning, masking his nerves rather badly. 'You put me off,' Tally had needlessly translated for Dashiell and Jericho.

Now, Tally was laughing already. It put the foundling off anyway. Tally tried to stop laughing, but the harder she tried, the harder she laughed. He screwed up his face at her and tried not to laugh too. He was clearly terrified. He took his place on the small stage in front of a small millpond of familiar faces, some of which harboured unspoken suspicions.

He cleared his clear throat thrice and dived in:

So thanks for coming. I'm talking to myself now.
I'm thanking myself for coming. That's called
good manners for onanists. It's a rare thing in a
world of increasingly rude self-service. (*He screams at
his penis*) Come on you little sod! What you waiting
for! You utter, utter twat! I could do this with my
eyes shut! With one eye shut! Stop bloody winking!
(*He stops screaming at his penis*) Well I suppose
the penis mightier than the s word. And self-service
is the way it's all going isn't it. Automated this,
automated that, automated the other. And
even the other is now best done on your tod.
Did you know Tod is death in German? I suppose death in
Germany is pretty much like death anywhere except
it's more efficient. If you think about it, you do
both things alone. Jerk off and die. No that's not an order!
And here I am jerking off and dying. But seriously.
I'm the only person here who needs to be here.
If you no-show, the show goes on anyway.
If I no show, there's no show. But the show must go on.
So on I go. I'm amazed I found the bottle to do this.
I mean. If anything I lean towards shy.
Actually, that's why I'm doing this now.
Except that I'm not. I can't.
Because I've given up leaning for Lent.
I saw a lovely girl last week. I asked her
What her name was. She said Denise. I asked
her what was wrong with her knees.
The conversation didn't go any further because
I chickened out and crossed the road.
Seriously: I lost it. My nerves overwhelmed me.
I got so nervous instead of speaking to

> Denise, I spoke to de shins.
> That didn't work, so I admitted defeat.
> Anyway, Uncle V came to visit at Christmas.
> He's so old he dyes his toupee. He said he
> he was born so ugly they had to tie a pork
> chop around his neck so the dog would
> play with him ...

He sank fast but battled on bravely. He spoke for over ten minutes of pin dropping silence punctuated only by the sound of Dashiell, Jericho and Tally laughing. It was the silence he heard, however. The silence told him that the beginning of his stand-up comedy career was also the end.

*

He began to pace the bars of his invulnerability.

He felt no physical pain and as yet, could not be physically damaged. In the garage, he turned Jericho's old blowtorch on himself to see if he could burn or hurt himself. He could do neither. He seemed to be physically invulnerable. His skin seemed harder than any diamond, found or forged. It was impervious to anything but ideas. Why, and what lay beneath, were mysteries. What philosophy could penetrate the ruse of his surface? What insight could deduce his substrate? Ontogeny would have to go hang. One day he would be happy to be the hangman.

Every day he pondered his making and substance. Every day and ever more, he wished to feel something – anything – with his skin. He could not. His physical numbness grew as he grew.

Because nothing could be known of his interior, origins or processes, Dashiell felt free to theorise about them. Her theories turned into clever fantasies. At first, she was unwilling to fantasise thus, but she couldn't help it. She felt silly doing it. Perhaps, Silly-Dashiell whispered, he was made of another form of matter entirely – something unknown to current science. Perhaps his structure was not based on carbon, even (as he said) his consciousness was not based on words, but on maths.

In time, Dashiell came to believe this fiction or that, and in lieu of knowledge, become certain of one or the other. In time, she came to call these certainties Truth. In time, she came to act on this Truth. Well-schooled and rational, however, she was privileged (she thought) to see her Truth for what it was: a dream as dislocated from the predictable world of experience as Alice down the hole. No. Truth would have to make do with a lower-case *t* from now on, italicised with scepticism.

Six months after he hurt Eric Lipton, he all saw them flying the planes into the towers on the news on the TV in the lounge. Later, when alone with Dashiell in the lounge, he saw the towers collapse. He said: 'Now their shadows will get longer and longer.' Tears fled the horror in his eyes. He was too old now for Dashiell to wipe them away as once she would have done.

'I don't know how to live.'

'I know.'

Dashiell hugged him, a teenager though he was, and outwardly too macho to accept her comfort. Just for a numb moment between them, he did not feel alone.

Sitting her wheelchair in the kitchen, Tally saw them embrace through a door slightly ajar. Deja-vu, she whispered to herself sardonically. She saw their hug end, and her mother walk away. The foundling suddenly met her eyes through the narrow space between the kitchen door and its frame. It was, to her, as if all of her was revealed to him, including her intention; but her intention was hidden from him. He would always regret this hiding.

Then the foundling smiled and went outside via the front door with a 'Back soon, boogaloo!'

The front door closing. Fast, fading footsteps outside. Then silence.

The silence told her what she must do. The need for varnish on the lounge door told her. The willingness of the always loose door handle to be turned told her. The jerk of the second hand of the kitchen clock told her. The trees interpreting the wind outside told her. Migrating clouds that did not need destinations told her. A fly that could not find a way out through glass told her. Her bitten fingernails told her. The click of the central heating pipes expanding when the boiler came on told her. The landscape of history told her (but kept it secret). The word avoirdupois told her. Alternatives told her. Her marble legs told her. Troy told her. Evolution told her. Things growing told her. Heat–death told her. Inanity told her. The old quarry waited to tell her. Holding her breath like this told her. Knowing too much told her. Not knowing told her. Pointless craving told her. Indecision told her.

Tally knew anyway.

*

The body is the mind.

His sensitivity to the suffering of others was already unbearable to him. Naturally, it would grow until it consumed him. When he pondered the worst cruelties people had inflicted in each other, he couldn't breathe. He couldn't speak for weeks.

When he finally spoke of these things and others like them at breakfast on a Saturday morning, he also said, 'I'm going to help everyone.' Jericho assumed Dashiell would respond, but she just lowered her head slightly as she pecked at her food, which now irritated Jericho.

'It's a lovely idea, but no one can help everyone,' said Jericho. He smiled dryly and winked at the foundling, aware of the look Tally gave him. Tally's glance was a mixture of 'oh-you-are-horrible-dad', and 'please-spare-the-boy-from-more-of-your-doom-and-gloom'. In response, Jericho pulled a face at Tally that actually, deep down, meant 'we-would-give-anything-for-things-to-be-different-for-you-and-us'.

The foundling saw it all without looking, as things are often best seen. 'And I'm going to become all I can become,' he said. 'What else would I do?'

'You don't have to prove yourself,' Jericho said to him. 'You know that don't you?'

'Course I do. Anyway – prove me to whom? Myself? The world?'

'Godzilla, silly,' Tally cut in. Her eyes remained on her breakfast cereal.

'Thanks, sis,' the foundling said. He reached out and squeezed Tally hand. She withdrew it and pretended to wipe 'the filth' of him off her like she always had. He mirrored her actions humorously.

Dashiell wondered if Tally had been crying. Jericho sensed and shared her concern.

'You're amazing. Just how amazing is ... amazing,' Jericho smiled at the foundling.

'It's amazing,' said Tally. Something in her voice. He heard it.

Tally's face suddenly emptied.

'You OK, Tal?' asked Jericho.

'Oh, you know,' said Tally. She seemed preoccupied. She often did, so her parents thought little of it. The foundling, however, felt a shadow pass over them. Then it was gone.

After breakfast, Tally went upstairs. He often helped her up the stairs. This had become their ritual. Their time. This time, though, she rejected his help and faced the North Face of the stairs alone. She did this by dragging herself, step by step. Today, her progress seemed agonising to him, as it did to her parents; but they were numb in that way adults think they are, and busy with chores.

'It's OK, dog-brain. I need the exercise,' she said when he came to help her.

'OK, Tal. If you're sure. But shout if you need me,' he said.

She pretended to shout comically and silently, and then she ignored him. He felt stung by this ignorance, though feigned as he was sure it must be.

Wasn't it?

He couldn't watch her struggle. Suddenly he needed fresh air. He went outside and walked. He vowed to heal Tally one day if he could. He knew he was kidding himself. Yes, he was stronger and faster and smarter than anyone else – but healing? That was wishful thinking. That was la-la land.

Self-doubt began to follow him as he walked in the woods and fields that were his familiar friends. Doubt inhaled him. Doubt breathed him out. Doubt laughed though nothing was funny. Doubt made everything funny. Doubt devoured shoelaces and bread pudding and rain on hedgerows. As he walked, he doubted the seasons that inlaid the land. He doubted the voices of the trees that fell into his passions, yet he adored their beauty. How would he ever bear so much beauty if he were strong enough to lift mountains? It was impossible.

As he walked pari-passu with his thoughts, Jericho and Dashiell went to the big shop near town to do the big weekly shopping. Dashiell drove. She knew Jericho wanted to speak. She knew what he wanted to say. She refused to hear it.

'We have to tell him,' he said at last.

'Why?'

'You know why.'

They talked in silence for a while. Then: 'He already feels like an outsider. He feels lost and alone. Soon he'll be shunned,' said Dashiell. 'How will telling him we're not his real parents help any of that ... Who are his real parents anyway ..?'

'He's always going to feel like an outsider!' Jericho interrupted. 'There's nothing we can do about it. What is he anyway? Do you know? Does anyone? The whole thing is – I don't know. He's ...'

'He's a freak and we're mad as bags of frogs. Well thank goodness.' Dashiell finished his sentence, as she often did. Today, he found this even more annoying than usual.

'We have to tell him,' Jericho said flatly after several things called moments.

She suddenly knew he was right. She had to swerve to avoid an oncoming car.

'Watch out!'

'I'm bloody watching – OK?'

Silence. This road had never seemed so banal.

'Is Tally OK?' Jericho said.

'Am I supposed to answer that?'

'No. I mean today – now more than usual. At breakfast. Did you see her face?'

Dashiell could find nothing useful to say.

'I'm so sorry,' Jericho said eventually.

'What the hell for? I bloody found him!' said Dashiell.

'When are we going to wake up?' said Jericho. He looked at her as he had looked at her almost twenty-five years earlier; but she was too preoccupied and upset to notice.

She pulled the car into the supermarket car park. As Dashiell she did so, at home, Tally decided to use reality. This reality was sharp, naturally; so it would cut deep. As her parents decided on the right brands of this and that in the supermarket, Tally filled the cold empty bath with revolution. She looked outside, where to her, the trees bled time.

As Tally shock began to comfort Tally, the foundling arrived home after his dubious walk. He wanted to make sure she had got up the stairs OK. He felt that something was wrong as soon as he entered the house. His parents were waiting at the supermarket checkout as he called out Tally's name at the bottom of the stairs. Silence replied. This was not the silence of contentment. It was laden. It was incorrect. It was heavy. It made his pupils dilate. He felt his pulse thunder.

'Tally? You there?'

No reply. Was he mistaken? Perhaps she was out. No. A sound upstairs. Something metallic dropped. A sterile clatter. Then perhaps a human sound, and then stillness.

He vaulted the stairs in one leap.

Dashiell and Jericho were one customer closer to the till when the foundling said Tally's name again on the upstairs landing outside the bathroom door. There was no inflection in the word this time. It wasn't a question. It was a statement. It was the patina on the bathroom door. All he could think was how much the door needed painting. He had meant to do it last year but hadn't. Why hadn't he? What had he been doing? Why couldn't he just paint, paint, paint?

In the supermarket, Jericho cracked a supermarket joke as Tally's strange mumble in the bathroom made him force open the locked door with less than a touch. What he saw took him over shock's edge and into its charming rictus. He was beside her in the bath in a millisecond. Her wheelchair waited patiently at an angle beside the bath.

'I'm sorry bro,' she managed.

'Tally. What you doing?' was all he could find in his shiny new devastation.

He saw without seeing the cold blade lying in the blood in the white bath. He knew without knowing that he was too late.

'Sorry bro. Look. You have to know. I'm not your sister. You have to know. Mum and dad ... They aren't your real ... Should have told you ...'

'I know. It doesn't matter.' His voice was a strangled croak.

'Mum said she found you ... Took you in ...'

He fought his tears with all his strength. He lost. His strength was suddenly the perfect curse. His hands hung like cruel evolution by his sides. Tally was pale as new soap in the bath. Blood oozed out of the mouths she had cut in her wrists and throat with the razor. Her blood against the friendly whiteness of the bath was enamelled violence. It was the violence of a home furnishings showroom. It was the violence of normality. He was astounded by the redness of her blood. He had not imagined anything could be this red. He was staggered at the quantity of it. Redness filled the universe.

A sob turned his throat into a despot balloon. Fear, confusion, and fear clogged his mind's flesh, his breath, his infinite zero. Time became viscous. Everything became red dreams.

Pretend-dad Jericho and pretend-mum Dashiell were packing their shopping bags as he plucked her out of the bath with sabre-toothed gentleness. He carried her downstairs just slowly enough not to snap her spine. He kicked the back door off its hinges in his panic.

Outside, his tumult drove him several metres up into the raging air. His grief was too great to be sure this was actually happening. He didn't care if it was real or not. He didn't care about anything - least of all their friendly nosy neighbour Mr Bourncleave rushing out of his house and peering upwards at him with suspicious incredulity.

Mr Bourncleave saw that strange Salter boy (if that's what he was) in the air holding Tally in his arms. He saw that Tally seemed grotesquely limp. There was a dark fluid on her. Mr Bourncleave knew immediately that this was a bizarre charade. Of course it was. The Salter children were performing a tacky vaudeville from some absurd melodrama they had concocted. The boy had left school and they were bored. They had devised some arrangement by which they could be suspended aloft like this. Wires and pulleys. Perhaps they were filming it. They were probably filming him. What a ridiculous stunt. How irresponsible. Did their parents know? Did they care? Had they ever?

Mr Bourncleave then heard the unearthly shriek the strange boy above the Salter house next door emitted. Suddenly he knew this was no stunt - no drama. The sound cut him to his quick. It was impossibly loud; but it was the quality of the sound that made it so devastating. It seemed to cleave the world in two. Mr Bourncleave had no idea if he or the world could ever heal from such a cleft.

This was no enactment. This was real. His instincts told him. His instincts were scared.

Tally was one and a half minutes dead when Mr Bourncleave called for his wife inside to 'Flippin call someone quick and fetch the camera!'

No longer under pressure from love, Tally's dead blood was now lazy in its effort to leave her body. Some blood still fell from her wrists, however. Yes, it was the colour of October. Yes, this was the time for new rain. It was the novelty of the rain that made it so welcome, so crushing.

It was the novelty of rain.

*

The shockwave passed outwards into their lives. It drew them together and flung them apart.

He didn't move for a week. He didn't speak for a month. He retreated into the silences of his mind, where grief and guilt become fanged metaphors. For him, Tally's death was a supernova. She had collapsed in on herself in the bath with such force that her core exploded inside him with energy sufficient to forge elements heavier even than those that crowned the Periodic Table. He could not name them. Why would he? Names were for blunt normalcy. He knew only that these new elements would seed the universe within him with boundless potential for new structures. One day the valences of chance and time would enable compounds of unimaginable possibility and power.

There was the inevitable police investigation. Official people and people in uniforms came and went like easy dreams. They were people with questions in their hands. There were procedures. Guilt and forgiveness went to war.

A week after Tally's death – they never used the word suicide – the house was forensically examined. They were interviewed individually. Where had they been at the time of the incident? (Grocery shopping.) Why did they buy? (Groceries.) Had Tally seemed different in the days before the grocery buying? (No she hadn't, though perhaps ...) Why did he go straight up to the bathroom? (He needed to pee.)

Why did he break the bathroom door down – this was his sister after all; did he usually enter the bathroom when his sister was in the bath? (He sensed something was wrong.) How did he break the bathroom door off without 'utilities'? (Fear, love, passion, rage, horror, love, love, guilt, love, youth, adrenaline, love, qualia, intent, things.) How did the back door become so badly damaged? (Trauma and rage – he was so upset that he had little memory of wrecking it.) Why did Mr Bourncleave state that he saw him hovering in the air holding Tally's dead or dying body? (Mr Bourncleave drank. Mrs Bourncleave admitted it.) Did he use drugs? (No thanks.)

All of it was slowly devastating.

Mr Bourncleave told everyone about having seen him hovering in the air holding Tally's bleeding corpse. Mr Bourncleave became a laughing stock. Dashiell was secretly glad of this laughter because their secret – the unknowable truth of him – could hide behind it.

The investigation went on for almost a year. Eventually it found the cause of death to be suicide. Still, they did not use the word. The word ceased to exist. No dictionary could possibly contain it. The attention of the police eventually waned. Dashiell had a nervous breakdown. She took a short holiday with a girlfriend but when she came back, she was little improved. Jericho felt powerless to help her. He was flawlessly heartbroken by Tally's death.

The rest of that year fell into an abyss of strange silences and stone faces. Dashiell and Jericho clung to each other in the tempest, but he could see that they were coming apart. They both reached out to him and reassured him, but he was beyond their grasp. He always had been, but now, he journeyed ever faster outwards into the void within him.

To him, for a while, life became a boneyard. Winter etiolated the trees and froze them into the grabs of witches. Winter laced the pond. It mimed the sky. It became still as a mother's hands at rest. It followed the last few birds south. It drowsed in everything like brittle mercy.

That Christmas was still as iron. New Year was hollow as an abandoned well. The next year rose and clung to the branches. The sky bloomed in the trees. The foundling watched the seasons change as keenly as he ever had; but now, nature was alloyed with a strange new fiction. No colour was as it had been before; and when the wind breathed on the land he loved, it seemed as if this might be its final breath. Always nature inhaled anew, however. In this he took dear hope.

The word 'Shanti' gave him hope, too – though where Shanti ended and nature began, he couldn't imagine. The tragedy drew them together, as it drew the foundling and Kenton closer. Hanging out with Mac and other friends in the town in early spring, Kenton told him, foursquare: 'I'm here any time day or night, mate. You're never alone, so don't you sodding feel that way.'

Shanti said the same thing in her own way, and her words became embraces, which became intimacy. He needed her touch desperately. He needed to feel it even more. His skin was silent, however; but he felt the sad kindness in her huge green eyes, heavy with tears as they were at first.

Their love was planted in Tally's field. Grief watered it.

His new and growing closeness to Shanti niggled Kenton. Kenton didn't show or tell anyone; but both the foundling and Shanti sensed it. They never spoke of the matter to each other or to others. Thus, Kenton's niggle lived and grew in his fathoms undisturbed.

The suicide of children asks many childlike questions: why? What did we do wrong? Who is to blame? Could this have been prevented? In after-years, there is the search for cause. Time might slowly numb the hurt to a stump. The seething brain may fumble for justification and rationality. A little sensation may even return, but it is a sham; sensation has long since found itself useless and withered. Most toxic of all may be the nag that the death was evitable.

To herself, Tally had become a broken toy. A dilapidated thing. A laughable ruin, as she thought. Laughter itself, perhaps. Tally had laughed at herself as a way of coping with the foundling's perceived perfection. He now laughed at this, too, but with perfect bitterness.

For a year after Tally's suicide, he didn't care if he lived or died. He therefore realised that waiting to die feels like waiting to live; because a voice was calling him to life. It was the voice of the sky, and the sky waits for no one.

*

A year after he found Tally in the bath, he finally said it.

'I did it, mum.'

'Did what? No …'

'I killed her.'

'Don't say that!'

'It's true. You three were doing fine, and then … I might as well have killed her.'

'Never say that again. Never think it. You have to promise me.'

'You know I can't.'

She knew. Dashiell found his tears far more devastating than her own.

'She told you, didn't she? That your father and I … found you.'

He barely nodded.

'Come on,' she said when she could speak.

It was almost dark when she drove him to the place where she had found him as a baby. It was less than half an hour's drive away. It always shocked Dashiell now how close it was. Unaware of the location or its significance, it now shocked him far more.

They stood together beside the verge on the bend in the broken lane.

'It was here, I think. Yes, here.' Dashiell stood near to and pointed at the place.

'And I was just lying there?'

'Just there, yes. Someone had swaddled you,' Dashiell had said.

'Who?' was all he said. He knew she could not answer.

He looked around him at this landscape of the mind. He had not begun here, so where then? Who had left him here? Why? He looked around as if searching for answers that he knew he might never find. He saw only long grass, hedge, air, darkness, being, movement, now, and the new night roving the stars. He crouched down at the place she pointed to in the grass. Here he had once lain. Now he touched the grass, but it's shadowy dampness only told him of itself.

Dashiell experienced this place with a poignancy in her belly that (ironically, she felt) reminded her of the early stages of pregnancy. She had stayed away from here until now. Why? She could have come back whenever she wished. Was this place too sacred? Now, too ruinous?

To Dashiell, little had changed here; but in fact, much had. Some potholes had been filled, but the resurfacing the lane needed had never happened. In the gloaming, she could see things that had not been here when she found him. A retail park had been built just over a kilometre away a few years earlier. Now, its modernity haunted this once quiet place with regulated self-importance.

'Did you ever bring Tally here?'

His question hit her hard. The answer was in her face.

'Why not?'

Why not indeed.

'What about dad?'

She barely shook her head.

'It's OK though, mum.'

'No it isn't. Jericho never asked, which must mean something, but ... Tal asked me to show her this place many times, but I always found an excuse not to. Shame on me.'

'No, mum. No.'

He came and stood in front of her and put his hands on her upper arms. He held her eyes.

No.

The moment became awkward, so he stood away from her slightly and averted his gaze. She was almost glad. Then he crouched down at the place in the grass she had pointed to. Here.

Dashiell looked at her found-son crouched low in search of answers. A dark shape within the growing dark. The shape stood. It came and stood beside her. Her was several inches taller than her now. Standing beside her, he became perfectly motionless. He heard the last sparks of birdsong and watched the moon sail behind the clouds. Then motility returned. He hugged her. Here they were. Then, like all things end, the hug ended. He stood slightly apart from her. He looked at the rumour of the land around them. He saw the vague lights of cars on the main road, and the shapes of industry and retail on the outskirts of the town nearby. This was his beginning. This was his homeland, or as close as he had to such a thing. Distant clouds sutured earth and sky. His love of the earth overwhelmed him. What could be more natural, nature thought? He felt great calm.

Then, suddenly, he knew he would soon leave this place and become other things.

*

Another year bloomed and thrived. It was now seventeen years since she had found him. Dashiell and Jericho's marriage had fallen into the change that happens too fast to adapt to called ruin.

The foundling saw that their divorce enabled them to love each other better, and that it was the right thing to do. He lived thereafter mostly with Dashiell, as she wished. He was aware that she wanted to watch over him. To protect him. By now, he didn't want her protection, however, and she knew it. Soon, he would fly the nest. Soon, he would need to find work, too. He didn't want to depend on his adopted parents for financial support that they could barely afford to provide.

Dashiell was the only person he told about lifting himself and Tally's body into the air. What shocked Dashiell was how little the revelation shocked her; but by then, of course, nothing shocked her about him. When he told her, she felt pride. She also felt the monolith of grief inside her yield for a moment for the first time since Tally's death. Only for a moment. Then Sisyphus had to start again.

Dashiell told Jericho on the phone. She told him he had levitated while holding Tally as someone tells someone else that it rained yesterday, or that they've ordered a new sofa. There was a moment, and then he just said, 'So you waited almost two years to tell me this.' Another moment followed in which, she presumed, he was soaking up the revelation – as if anyone could.

'Please don't tell anyone, Jerry', she then said. She regretted saying it immediately.

'Why would I?' he snapped back at her. 'Obviously I'm not going to tell anyone that my son who isn't my son can fly. Bloody hell, Dash. I'm not a complete cretin you know!'

She knew Jericho was right. Who could they tell, without fear of mockery or the indifference afforded cranks and sensationalists? They would thus identify themselves and their adopted son as card-carrying, self-promoting fakes - or flakes. She knew the world would always 'know' her adopted son was a fraud. She knew that those who conjectured otherwise would be considered marginal or insane. She knew that one day the world would try to imprison or exterminate him. It could do neither of course, but this did little to lessen her anxieties. She knew that so much power in one would require a morality more perfect than could be survived. Dashiell had always done all she could to educate him ethically, but she knew he knew of her 'faults': her reactions to others – reactions not guided by ethics, but by insecurity, ancestry, and selfish genes.

She presumed that her faults and Jericho's had influenced him, and would always dictate actions over which he had no control. She wished he had free will. Perhaps, uniquely, he did. She wondered if, one day, his isolation would become beyond even his endurance. She felt sure that his humanity was absolute. Even as she marvelled at him, she feared for him, and he felt her fear.

'Sorry,' Jericho went on. 'I'm just knackered. Oh – he told me you took him to the place you found him. That's nice. How come you never took me there? A state secret? Did you ever take Tally?'

'You know the answer to that question …'

'He's your thing, isn't he?' Jericho interrupted, controlling his stress. 'I don't blame you. Funny that it was so close though. I had always thought it was miles away. You still there?'

She was still there. Her phone had become hot against her ear. She moved it away slightly.

'Where is he? Job hunting I hope.'

'He's been looking for work, you know that. I think he's off with the boys at the moment.'

He was indeed hanging out with Kenton and Mac as Dashiell and Jericho spoke. He and Mac weren't quite so close and he and Kenton, but the three amigos were often to be found together. They would listen to music, talk, tinker with Mac's moped, or play football. The foundling liked playing football. He liked playing any game and loved most sports. He hated having to hold back and make it look like he couldn't excel at them all though. This was difficult. Sometimes it was impossible.

Occasionally he simply thrilled in his abilities no matter what, as any young person might. As he did today (against Dashiell's advice never to show anyone), he outstripped those he played football with and against to such an extent that there was no rational way of explaining, or experiencing, what had happened. On this occasion,

Kenton and Mac just verbally abused him after he made them look ludicrous in that way people sometimes do when they are close: crudely.

'Wanker,' was never far from Mac's lips.

'Prick' was a Kenton stock-in-trade derogation of the foundling.

Both such and other obscenities made the foundling laugh and love them more.

Kenton and Mac had come to treat (consciously) his apparent uniqueness, whatever its cause, as banal. Mostly, they had stopped being fascinated by what he did. Mostly, they had stopped wondering how he did it. 'This is how people are with things,' he wrote in his notebooks, which he filled with his thoughts and his art most days. 'Few people can exist in the permanent state of astonishment that is fitting to the phenomenon of human experience. It's simply too exhausting.'

Mostly. Kenton inwardly wondered what was going on with the foundling, however. How and why he did what he did. His friend's abilities asked questions that Kenton couldn't answer. These abilities made him resentful in the fathoms of his being. This resentment grew. Shanti was aware of it in her brother. It darkened Kenton's eyes when they spoke of him, which they did rarely.

Shanti, too, was inwardly puzzled. She thought the foundling was either a mystery or a brilliant illusionist. He couldn't be the former, so he had to be the latter. How, though, and why? She found herself reluctant to ponder the issue and wasn't sure why. Mostly, she was too busy being a girl turning into a woman, and the daily thing of being alive. Two years after Tally died, she and Kenton did talk about the foundling briefly, however. The brevity of the conversation was significant. They pondered him strangely casually.

'He's just seen too many superhero films and he's found a way to pull the wool,' Kenton said in an offhand manner to Shanti one evening. They were preparing an evening meal when their parents were out at the golf club.

'Some wool,' said Shanti, preoccupied by the music on her earphones. Her heart was preoccupied by the foundling, however, and she knew it. She knew he was a mystery, too.

'What about Tally?' Kenton said; but Shanti didn't hear him or pretended not to because of her earphones.

As they cooked, the foundling pondered their acceptance of him and felt a new hunger growing in his heart. He knew he couldn't 'tell' Shanti, Kenton, or Mac of his mystery, largely because he knew nothing of it himself. He had nothing to tell them. That made him laugh.

If he had said he could bend steel as other people bend rubber bands, they would have laughed and 'felt sorry' for him. Of course they would. Flying? Ha! Surely, he was too old for such childish fantasies? They might have asked him to prove it, and then what? Show them? Appear to defy gravity's meniscus? Seem to disrupt mortal contracts? Then what? Knowing it was an illusion, they would have insisted he show them how he had done it, and he couldn't. Then what?

No. If he told Kenton that he could defy gravity, Kenton would reject him as a friend and brand him weird. If he told Shanti, she would reject him as whatever they were, if they were anything (he often wondered what she felt about him, if she did). No. Shanti, he felt, must be impressed at all costs. It was OK to be strong and clever, but not too strong and clever. His cool lay in his acceptability. He determined to seem cool to Shanti. Of course he did. Love, he felt, was folding them in its élan. Desire was telling them its fluid secrets, and their passion had become a shared omerta.

His love for Shanti indeed grew. He loved her rhyming eyes and ready smile. He allowed himself to put her on a pedestal. He rebuked himself for doing so. He chose not to listen when voices in his head asked him if she really belonged on the altar of his esteem (AKA lust). He told the voices that of course she did: she was a living wonder. She was a person. People are masterpieces.

Shanti was aware of his adulation. She saw it as sweet, and welcome because it was praise – not that she was any vainer that most teenagers. How could she be sure of his love, however, or of her own? How could she be sure of anything about him? He was an enigma – most would say weird; yet his mystery was what made him attractive to her. One day she would know him properly, she thought, and then he would seem normal. She dreaded such a day, not realising yet that the less people know about each other the more willing they are to see each other as ordinary.

Kenton knew that Shanti was increasingly beguiled by the foundling; so Kenton belittled his friend to his sister when they were alone. Aware of this sibling jealousy in Kenton, the foundling began to wonder where love ended, and ownership began. Perhaps love was actually need. Yes, that was it, he wrote in his journals. 'I love you means I need you.'

A terrible thought burnt his mind as he wrote this: if he could never tell of or show anyone his abilities, how would he ever fulfil his calling, which already whispered to him? Was he supposed to live a stunted life like many, camouflaging himself so as to blend in? That was unthinkable.

No.

The sky beckoned.

The sky said be all you can be. No one needs to know.

The day of Tally's death had been the first time he defied gravity. It had seemed like someone else's dream at the time because of trauma. Now it seemed like his dream. Nearly sixteen months after Tally's death – months spent locked in and paralysed by the hell of the memory of that day – he therefore tried to dream again.

He knew that if he was seen, he risked further ostracism in the village. The gossip machine was already churning out rumours about him. Whispers hung like spiders' webs in chinwag air. No matter. The sky was his country. He would try to raise himself up again at night. At night, surely no one would see him – even Mr Bourncleave, who had taken to spying on the house with binoculars. Mr Bourncleave thought no one knew he was doing it. Mr Bourncleave was wrong about this. Mrs Bourncleave thought her husband was wrong about most things.

He tried again just after eleven o'clock on a Sunday evening. It was early in the year, so it had been dark for some time. It was also quite cloudy; he could therefore be sure of much concealment. He had thought there would be nothing to it. In fact, there was everything to it. Everything told him he couldn't do it. He bent every fibre of his being to the task. Nothing happened. Tally laughed love at him. That was better. Now something. A blocked gutter of a laugh. Untrammelled guffaw. Going to the woods just to hear birds' laughter. Fathead bro in the fire laughter. Darling laughter, suddenly gone into boundless guilt. Magma's rage. Up.

Then. A few metres at first, then several. Then, there he was in the dark, fifty-something red metres above the house. The thrill of it made him laugh. Then, sixty-something metres above the house, he felt something he could call contentment. For the first time since Tally's death, he felt something briefly that he might call freedom. To him, this new liberty seemed fair in shape, though pale. It felt benign. He loved it.

He wanted to go higher; but something made him return to the ground. That something was the need to pee. No matter. He would go in and pee and go higher tomorrow night, and higher still the night after. Tally would take him to the stars! He would pee first! Love is the divinity of the cells! He was sure that this was the beginning of something amazing. People would be amazed by him! He would make sure of it.

The next day, he told Dashiell what he had done. She didn't seem as surprised or amazed as he wanted her to be. Perhaps she was just tired. She had seemed more tired since …

'How did you do it?' she said as brightly as she could.

'I don't know. But I went up to about – I don't know, mum. Up there somewhere! It was like a dream!'

She could see the exhilaration shining in his dark eyes. It no longer shone in hers. That was, he was sure, his fault. The fault of life finding him. The fault of chances.

'But you dream when you're awake – you said it yourself.' She smiled as she said it, but he felt snubbed. She alone was his believer and confidante. Did she doubt him now? Even as he asked himself, he realised what he already knew: that Tally's suicide had changed everything. Of course it had. Dashiell had found him. Cause is cause. Chaos is. Who, also, can believe in what cannot be?

Anyone.

No matter what, however, he had to be all he could be; so he began to go up at night regularly. Up there, his guilt and Dashiell's regret felt like joy when experienced in a wider context. Up there, his pain became laughter, and his laughter became unbridled bliss.

At night he ascended. It became an addiction. Dashiell always heard him go out. How could she not listen? How could she not worry? Why didn't she stop him? How could she stop him?

One evening she looked out of her window so that she could see him do it. There! Was that him? That dark ascending in the darkness! Did the owls love him? Did bats manage to avoid him by listening to him? Who else might see? What would the world make of him? What would he do to the world? Didn't Tally know she couldn't just have left him there beside the road? Why was the road still in such a bad condition? Did his ears pop? If they didn't, how could he hear so perfectly? Did he suffer from a fear of heights? Would he ever die? Who was he? What was she? Would he ever be happy? Who cared that wisdom was so much more important than happiness? How would the world reject him? How would the world ignore him? Why didn't Jericho come back? Why didn't Jericho blame her more? Why couldn't she orgasm anymore? Would he ever have children? What would they be like? How could he ever make love? Why didn't Tally say goodbye? Were there any limits to human suffering? Why so many ways to be sad and only one way to be happy? Was there a logical alternative to joy? How would he navigate if he went far away in the sky? Should she buy him one of those satnav things? When was the sextant invented? Did invention cause consciousness? Why couldn't she spell astrolabe? What is why? Were there any limits to intelligence? Did he know there was no such thing as him? Did he know there was no such thing as her? Could she ever tell him how much she loved him? Why the hell couldn't someone else have found him? Would he ever do this on a clear night? What if his strength ran out when he was up there? Would the fall hurt him? What were questions? Had Mother Nature finally given birth to herself? Was he wearing enough up there? Should she have made him put a jumper on? Did he know she knew about his fruitless masturbation? How would she pay the mortgage next month? What was sleep? What was it like up there? Would she live happily ever after? Ever after what? Were Platonists right? Should she tell him she saw him do it? Was Jericho seeing someone now? Why don't I care? What is the square root of sorry? Can you hear me? Can the idea of a void be a void? What other kind of void is there? Should she try to make him eat even though he was almost never hungry? When would he hurt her? Would losing him destroy her or give birth to her? Why had her father been so bloody stupidly full of love? Was that him, there? Was he inside her? Was she inside him? Why are green things good for you? How can Shanti be worthy of his love? What is tallness? Why do I think I have a right to be happy? What about aeroplanes? Have I locked the back door? Do badgers know anything? What is knowing? Would he die for her? Could he be killed? When would he go mad? Why Mandelbrot? Which side to lie on? Why are puns funny? Is fun puny? What is fun? Would a PET scan be the thing? Is up down in a pickle? Is he showing off? Does this make him happy? Does his potential scare him? When will he who cannot be killed, kill? Will he have to? Will he survive? Can I sleep forever? Can I wake up? Who can I tell how happy he makes me? Do dreams have surfaces? Why can't he just come down and be pointless? Will he take me up there with him one day? One night? Would he hold me tightly? If I fell? How many tears was I born with? Where is the surface of the centre? Why am I laughing? Am I?

*

Children never know their parents.

Though still only thirty-nine, Jericho had gone from early middle age to late as quickly as April changes its mind. He now lived in a rental on the other side of the canal by the disused quarry. The foundling visited him there occasionally because he missed his faux-father, as Jericho missed him.

It was necessary and awkward and wonderful and unremarkable being with him there.

The foundling thought (or maybe wished, he admitted to himself) that Dashiell and Jericho still loved each other. They just wouldn't allow themselves to feel it or act on it. This made him sad.

He tried to describe love. He couldn't, even if he thought about Shanti with his whole body.

'Is love an honest lie or is it, like sentience, a fantasy about reality?' he wrote in his journal.

He wanted to look good. In this, he was like most people. Looking good now meant shaving. He couldn't shave or have his hair cut because razors and scissors buckled like feathers when matched against his beard and hair, however. He therefore looked ever more 'like a hippie,' as Mrs Courtrai from the post office said to anyone who would listen.

His nails resisted all attempts to cut them by conventional means, too. Keratin they were not. He therefore cut his nails by biting them. Dashiell therefore found herself saying 'don't bite your nails' to him rather often.

Dashiell ruined the kitchen scissors (both pairs), then her garden shears (both pairs) by trying to cut his hair with them. By the time they had reached the secateurs stage, they were in hysterics.

'Mum. I'm not a bush.'

'No. But you look like Moses. I supposes.'

'I do not supposes my toeses are roses. That would be erroneous.'

'Bring me the head of John the Baptist.'

'If you insist.'

Of course the secateurs failed too. Pruning his head was just not an option.

He came to crave a smart and stylish haircut and shave so that he could look like most others. He now realised that looking or being like most others was not his lot in life, however. He would never fit in, and though he would one day relish being and looking different, he couldn't yet do so.

There was, he felt, no possible rehearsal for the role of outsider.

*

At about this time, he discovered that he could see outside the spectrum visible to normal people. Like bees and butterflies, he could see ultraviolet, and like snakes, he could sense infrared. He could choose when and when not to use this ability. Sometimes he chose to, so he could marvel at the strange beauty of EM radiation. At times it was as brilliant and savage as a dance that lacks a dancer; at others, it was as ghostly and serene as grief's echo. It depended on the wavelength.

At about this time, Dashiell got her first Wi-Fi broadband router. They set it up and turned it on. It immediately filled the house with electromagnetic radiation. Curious, he allowed himself to see this radiation. Combined with the artificial and natural radiation already filling the space inside the house and beyond, it was terrifying in its ethereal excess. It was indigo and seething and coiling and blue and jagged and stubby and languid. He couldn't imagine that anyone was supposed to endure this electromagnetic super-storm. It was a heavenly vision of hell.

He switched the router off immediately. Dashiell complained.

'I need it. The internet - you know!'

She was a little tired, a little too alive, and so less patient than usual. She turned the router back on. Again, he was alarmed at what he saw. He worried for Dashiell's health.

'Mum. If you could see what I see …'

'Well I can't, OK? And I never will! So …' her words fell into exhaustion. He knew turning the router off again would be fruitless - she would just get angry with him and turn it on again. What should he do? He couldn't imagine how anyone could think exposure to this much radiation every day was OK. He found that he couldn't understand what people were thinking much of the time, however - he was far too perceptive.

Now, he knew he would have to let Dashiell and everyone else expose themselves to amounts and types of radiation beyond anything evolution had prepared them for and blame the consequences on someone else. He closed his eyes to this madness (as he saw it), as he would learn to close his eyes to many other kinds of insanity and inanity.

As he grew, he enjoyed keeping his eyes closed more and more. In this way his eyes couldn't blind him, and he enjoyed the view.

Julie Sacthrow lived in the new development near the retail park. They had gone to the same school until recently. She was slightly older than him, and (as he thought) attractive.

Jericho warned him that Julie would hurt him if he got involved with her. The foundling could hear a wasp wince a mile away if he chose to, but he didn't listen to Jericho's advice. Instead, he fell into a chemical frenzy. He knew he was using Julie to try to get Shanti's full attention, which had waned in the last year. He was sharing her. With whom, however, was not yet obvious.

He didn't care. Julie was hot. The year was young. So was he.

As intended, Shanti saw him out with Julie. Thereafter (and for several weeks) Shanti ignored him entirely. Naturally, his ruse hadn't worked; so he wooed and wowed Julie in a fit of pique. He thus learnt that he was as much the main performer in the charade of his life as anyone else.

Dashiell, too, warned him that Julie would upset him, though she knew such hurts are part of breathing and being. She realised that her concerns about his romantic ardour were in part selfishness: she wanted him all to herself and she knew it; but knowing didn't help. Her fear was also rooted in the likelihood that he would try to reveal his truth to Julie because of his innate honesty. Dashiell knew that Julie would only react to his 'revelation' in one way, and it would hurt him.

He knew, too; yet must he always avoid intimacy in case his truth was revealed? How could he live without acceptance and its perfect tense, love; for without love there is only horror.

He told her of his abilities.

His delusion made Julie angry. That he was at the least absurdly big-headed, hopelessly immature, or worse, insane, made her angry at herself for having fallen for him.

Thus doubted, he recited pi to ninety-eight places in three-point-four-one seconds and lifted a car up at the same time to prove himself.

'However you're doing that, I don't want to know how you're doing it,' she said, walking away quickly. 'Freakoid!' she said loudly enough for the people sitting on a park bench nearby to hear. It was the Montclewes - a family hell-bent on being as normal as possible that had no idea what normal was.

He put the car down carefully.

'But Julie ...' he began, but she was gone. 'But I love you,' he said to the wind. He would one day realise that he hadn't really loved Julie Sacthrow. On another day he would learn that his true relationship was with himself in nature, which is to say the nature of himself. He would also learn that such a relationship may seem like an ashen road.

Now, his sadness at Julie's rejection and mockery turned to sudden fury, which he supressed by habit because the Montclewes were watching. They had their sandwiches and their suspicions.

'You must never get angry,' Dashiell had told him many times when he was little. This anger, however, was increasingly hard to push back down into 'the bad water at the bottom' of himself as he thought of the places that he now rarely visited within him.

Now he visited them.

He went to the old quarry and found a 952 kg stone slab. He threw it upwards with such force it burnt up in the atmosphere before it reached space. As he did so, rage escaped him as sound. The sound and the mini fireball were later reported in gossip a hundred miles away and in a newspaper the next day as 'a mystery' attributed to military activity.

Dashiell found him strewn with tears in his room that evening.

'What am I?' he blurted. His eyes were pools of frantic light.

She had no idea what he was, and they both knew it. All Dashiell could do was cradle him as she had done a thousand times and hope. Hope, however, became heavier always, as an essential curse often does. One day, even he would find it too heavy.

The next day he went out drinking in the afternoon with Kenton and Mal. He was vulnerable to alcohol. He had one pint of bitter as usual, and as usual, was stumbling drunk and as funny as life is to a truly serious person.

'The lightweight gets lighter,' said Kenton, grinning.

'Let there be light,' echoed all two metres of self-improving Mal.

They laughed until there was only laughter. Then the foundling fell over into a Julie Sacthrow shaped phantasm of welcome sleep.

*

'What the most clichéd thing a freak can do, mum?'
    'You're not a freak.'
    'No. I'm mad.'
    'You're sausage and mash.'
    'I'll tell you. Freaks run away to join a circus.'

*

Joining a circus isn't easy. There aren't many circuses left in the UK. The few circuses that still exist are mostly quite well staffed, thank you much. Also: though as well-meaning (and not) as people anywhere, people who own and work in some circuses can be slightly more reluctant to accept strangers than, say, Hamley's door staff at Christmas.
    After much phoning around, he nevertheless managed to talk to the owner of the 'Big K Circus' – one Goran Kleberhaus – into seeing what he could do. Kleberhaus insisted on being called Kleberhaus. Not Goran. Not Mr Kleberhaus ...
    'Just Kleberhaus. Anyways. What matters with you?' Kleberhaus asked the foundling when they spoke on the phone.
    'How long have you got?'
    Kleberhaus laughed. 'Funny. Funny is good. I ken use a clogs clever round here.'
    'I can do things that no one else can do,' said the foundling.
    'Well not any once can else do amazing shits, sun of beam. Don't be later.'
    An hour more than a day more than a week later, the foundling travelled without the aid of technology to meet Goran Kleberhaus. The Big K Circus was pitched just outside

Marlborough in Wiltshire. Kleberhaus lived in a rigorously outdated caravan. His girlfriend was a bearded lady with recreational scarring, whom Kleberhaus lovingly called Millipede. Millipede welcomed the foundling warmly and offered him Lapsang Souchong tea with honey and snap fresh Rich Tea biscuits.

'I take it you have a police record,' Millipede said with a tombstone smile as she poured.

'How did you guess?'

'Well look at you.'

The tea was delicious but interrupted by an inconsolably happy, tattooed dwarf called Laski. Laski led the foundling out of the caravan to a small tent beside the big top itself. It was raining so hard it rained upwards. The rain fell in love with the foundling's long, jet hair and beard. It thus jewelled his hair with pearls that vexed as he walked.

The small tent smelt of borscht and damp kvetching. Inside, tetchy Kleberhaus was sorting through various props, costumes, and regrets. Among them was an array of rusty old kettle weights.

'You later. Strong men he other vamoose. Die in car crush least months. Otherwise, this is why I ask you. But look at you. Mere boys. You are John Baptist? This you no do, no?'

Kleberhaus laughed and winked at the dwarf, who winked with both eyes back.

'I'll try, sir. Thank you.'

'Well go do, John boy,' Kleberhaus laughed again. Tetchy Kleberhaus laughed a lot. This is what can happen.

The foundling arranged the heaviest kettle weights so he could work with them. There was a damaged blackboard behind him, on which was scrawled what were presumably circus routine plans. He waited until Kleberhaus was sitting on a retired chair near the door. Instead of performing acts of strength with the 50kg kettle weights, he juggled all six of them with his left hand with his eyes closed. He wrote an original impromptu proof of the Goldbach conjecture with his right hand on the blackboard as he did so. He juggled the kettle weights in high swirling loops of juggle that juggled this way and that in vast strange orbits around and about his body. He recited Paradise Lost as he did it, so:

> "Nine times the Space that measures Day and Night
> To mortal men, he with his horrid crew
> Lay vanquisht, rowling in the fiery Gulfe
> Confounded though immortal: But his doom ...

High swirling loops.

> "Reserv'd him to more wrath; for now the thought
> Both of lost happiness and lasting pain
> Torments him; round he throws his baleful eyes
> That witness'd huge affliction and dismay
> Mixt with obdurate pride and stedfast hate:

Vast strange orbits.

> "At once as far as Angels kenn he views
> The dismal Situation waste and wilde,
> A Dungeon horrible, on all sides round,
> As one great Furnace flam'd, yet from those flames
> No light, but rather darkness visible
> Serv'd onely to discover sights of woe..."

As he did this, Kleberhaus' jaw dropped in astonishment at the same time as Kleberhaus stood up. Kleberhaus was short, so in effect, his chin didn't move at all. Chin down; man up: high orbits. It was as good a day as days get if they try hard.

The foundling stopped juggling and reciting and writing. He looked at the equation he had written on the blackboard. He grunted in appreciation of its truth, and then rubbed it out.

Kleberhaus' jaw suddenly snapped shut. He suddenly felt silly as one deceived might, so he said, 'I not vant diss bullshit, boy-boy. I vent real things. Here we do reals. Tanks anyway, Baptist John.'

Kleberhaus examined the obviously (but not previously) fake kettle weights briefly and pensively as he exited the room. He may or may not have mumbled something about the old days as he went.

The foundling did not run away to join the circus.

*

Genius is madness with its sleeves rolled up.

He loved making things. He was forever inventing. His inventions lay around the house and garden like the residue of natural curiosity. He was also an expert at mending things. He loved mending as he loved healing. When things broke or wore out around the house he mended them. Mending things gave him rare contentment.

He was a matchless juggler, dancer, cheese maker, impersonator, debater, stuntman, window cleaner, driver, computer scientist, bricklayer, wit, cook, train driver, carpet layer, psychologist, car mechanic, cobbler, physicist, thatcher, biologist, surgeon, masseur, potter, architect, leader, surveyor, plumber, mime, pilot, mathematician, tailor, fence builder, interpreter, moralist, accountant, carpenter, painter, topiarist, spot welder, writer, cleaner, engraver, polemicist, road sweeper, magician, physiotherapist, actor, farmer, cartoonist, digger, teacher, surveyor, glassblower, macerator, pilot, art restorer, masseur, watch mender, architect, scrimshander, barber, therapist, hod-carrier, cleaner, chiropractor, roofer, nurse, dancer, criminologist, acrobat, engraver, notary, pacifier, film director, beekeeper, Cary Grant impersonator, diver, enamel worker, furnace operator, grip, civil drafter, steeplejack, tiller, botanist, cartoonist, ethical hacker, glazier, and weaver.

He was good at everything. He could do anything (apart from follow others) better than anyone else. Because he could do anything perfectly, he didn't know what to do.

Moreover, for him, doing things was a distraction: being was all, and being was thinking. Thinking was what he did better than anyone. Thinking made him sadly happy.

He knew he could be a professional sportsman if he chose to, but his sporting abilities outstripped anyone else to the extent that he would never be able to hide his abilities, or compete without being accused of cheating (even if no one knew how); and if he revealed himself through sport he would be at best mistrusted and at worst rejected. This would hurt him. No. He could only do sports for fun. He would have to waste the limitless potential of his sporting abilities. This made him sad because he loathed wasted potential. It made him glad because he knew that the acclaim that would come with success of any kind would be unendurable.

In time, he came to realise that he would have to squander almost all his abilities – sporting, intellectual, creative and of whatever nature. He was good at everything, so he couldn't do anything. This made him feel desperate to the point of physically sickness, and his sickness made Dashiell feel many things.

*

He found navigating while airborne much harder than being airborne. The former required experience and much learning; the latter, it seemed, came naturally. He took every opportunity to practise both.

He mostly went aloft at night to try to keep his secret. He had so far done it during the day only once: during a thunderstorm. Dashiell had tried to dissuade him, but he couldn't resist it. Experiencing a storm a thousand feet in the air was too tempting a prospect.

It was ecstatic. The enormity of the energies unleashed. The violence of the wind. The sheer absence of a strategy. The lack of purpose. The being of it. Above all: the lightning and the thunder. The epic nature of the experience made him laugh with joy. He couldn't hear himself, however: up here, the noise of the storm was so extreme that it made him half deaf for days. It hurt. He didn't care. He had never felt so free. He went back to earth unwillingly that day. He was always glad to be on the ground, however. Altitude made him look down on people, and he thought that was intolerable. Anything that threatened his humility was his enemy.

He had always found the colloquial names of winds fascinating. A few weeks after the storm, redness sent him up to find and experience differently named winds first-hand. This would test his navigation skills to – and beyond – his limits. It would also be his first journey to multiple destinations abroad without the use of technology.

He went to the east coast of Sardinia in search of the Bentu de Soli. Some three thousand metres up, he couldn't be sure he had found it. He didn't care. There was no sign of a Borasco anywhere near, and the weather in the Tyrrhenian Sea was clement at that time of the day and year.

He went west over Italy and then through what he chose to think was a gentle Maestro (rather than a Levantera – and he believed it too late in the year for an Etesian) in search of a Zephyrus. He convinced himself he found it (in fact he was amid various Contrastes). Might this have been an early Tramontana? He didn't know. He didn't care. He was too happy. Below him, the Aegean Sea jewelled with Helen's evening.

To the south-east, he danced with a Sirocco. Then he ventured further south over Africa. Haunted by a myth of dust, a sudden Haboob over Sudan challenged him. He rode the turbulence. It made him whoop with elan. Remembering a Sharki, he doubled back on himself but went north-west towards a ruined memory of Nineveh. He saw below him much that would bring him back one day for different reasons.

The word 'Williwaw' made him laugh. Tally would have loved it. Now, to the sudden west, an ocean went without hope in search of horizons. It was breath-taking in scope and reality. He wondered if he dared cross the vastness of the Atlantic to get to the southern tip of Chile. He felt unfamiliar fear, and knew it to be the leitmotif of the human aria.

His curiosity overruled his misgivings.

Redness took him higher than he had ever been. He crossed the glass Atlantic in a southerly direction. He was now in the southern hemisphere day – and winter. Loneliness chased him across what he suddenly realised were the Falkland Islands. He laughed. Fear's defiance threw him across the coast of Argentina. A Suestado caught him in its claws. He endured. The high cold savaged him. He realised the chances of finding a Williwaw were minute; so he went north along the east coast of South America. Should he go further north to seek out a Squamish playing amid the fjords of British Columbia? He resolved instead to find a Tehuantepecer, then go home. He went inland. He stayed above three thousand metres to try to avoid being seen. He saw the mark of mankind on the Amazon. He framed the cataclysm in a billion cubic light-years of space and a billion years of past and future, but still it devastated him.

Down, down, down, and across the Caribbean. Then inland and through the gap between the Mexican and Guatemalan mountains. He let himself believe he found his Tehuantepecer (but he called it a Papagayo).

A Matanuska Wind, a Knik Wind, a Fremantle Doctor, and a Brickfielder would have to keep. So would an Abroholos, a Brubu, and a Warm Braw. He loved them all by their names. He would go in search of his windy loves again one day. He would convince himself he had found them.

It was time to go home.

*

No heart is average.

By the age of eighteen, he knew it was time to move out. Living with Dashiell had become what living with a mother can become for a boy who aspires to manhood. Dashiell had dreaded this moment for years, but when it came, she found herself resigned to it. So when he moved out of Dashiell's house into a tiny flat above a bakery, she was curiously devoid of emotion. She knew, however, that her degage probably meant that what she felt was too extreme to feel.

His accommodation was provided by his new employer: soon before moving out of Dashiell's house, he found work as a trainee bread maker at the bakery in town. The bakery owner, Mr Gibbie, let him rent the flat above the bakery for 'a modest monthly fee'.

Within days, mentored by Mr Gibbie, he was kneading and plaiting dough with impossible dexterity and subtlety. The dough levitated at the interest of yeast. Thus risen, heat then created wonder.

The wonder was bread.

Word soon spread. Within months, the bakery became a destination for shoppers from near and far. Mr Gibbie soon became discreetly rich. On the up, Mr Gibbie already dreaded the day when his protégé would get fed up with working at the bakery; but Dashiell's son went on making impossibly beautiful bread. He kept going to the pub with Kenton and Mal and getting falling-over drunk after just one pint, too.

In private, he continued trying to ignore whispers and rumours about him that rose in the village in the same way that –

'With every burst of carbon dioxide that the yeast releases into an air bubble, protein and water molecules move about and have another chance to connect and form more gluten. In this way, a dough's rising is an almost molecule-by-molecule kneading.'

As he ignored glances and wove ordinary flour and water into wonders, the master bread maker tried not to romanticise and obsess about his heart's nonpareil: Shanti.

He failed. In truth, his red spirit soared whenever he thought about her. Like the searching wind, it wasn't rational.

That's why he loved it.

He kept making bread and playing games with Shanti and hiding his secret until his hair reached his lower back and his beard reached his chest. By then, becoming a celebrity bread maker had drawn much attention to him. His repute filled Dashiell with dread.

'Don't let them ever see what you really are, what you can do.'

He knew Dashiell was just trying to protect him from ridicule and isolation. It would be impossible for him to conceal his true nature and ignore his vocation always, however. To hell with the consequences.

He therefore continued to draw attention to himself and give grist to the local rumour mill. He did this by other means, too: he'd discovered a passion for sculpture when Jericho had taken him up to the capital when he was ten. He and Jericho had visited a museum. The foundling had been astonished by the skill expressed in some of the sculpture he saw that day. He knew then that he would one day explore that skill in himself. He now therefore started to go down to the old quarry at night.

To him, the rock there was as modelling clay is to a normal person – except that this rock split and fractured under pressure. To get around this problem, he forced air from his pursed mouth with such force that it sculpted the rock subtly. The first thing he sculpted in this way was a semi-abstract sculpture of an idealised woman. He returned on two more consecutive nights to create two more sculptures. Both were of human figures. One was certainly an adult male. The other was a young person trapped in an unnatural sitting position.

The foundling took Tally's memory to see the sculptures the day after he had finished them. He still had rock dust in his ears, under his fingernails, and in his hair and flourishing beard. He remembered Tally's tears of amazement at what he had done. Her tears were the keystone where beauty and sadness meet to hold up the want of wisdom. He hugged her while she wept. This moment would end forever.

'Guess who?' Tally said. Now she was laughing like water late for something important. She was pointing to the sculpture of the young person sitting unnaturally. He just shrugged and pulled a face.

She pulled the same face in loving mockery. 'Why are you such a nitwit?' she said, blowing her nose. Then her memory was gone; so he shrugged again and pulled a different face.

The next day he brought Dashiell to see the sculptures. They went when it was dark because new health and safety regulations meant no one was allowed in the disused quarry anymore. Dashiell found herself smiling immaturely as she skulked through a gap in the wire fence 'like special ops dudes'. She stopped smiling when she snagged her new cardigan on the fence. She swore. She was better at swearing than she wished to be. Now it was the foundling's turn to smile; but when he saw that Dashiell was genuinely upset by spoiling her new cardigan, he became serious again quickly.

'I'll mend it for you, mum. You'll never know.'

She loved his earnestness.

The special ops dudes approached the sculptures. As they did, the sculptures seemed to grow out of the gloom like avatars from a jet world. They took her breath away. She just stood there and looked up at them. He put her arm around her. They stood for a while like that. Dashiell then surprised him by saying, 'She isn't worthy of you.' He took his arm off her, but not unkindly.

He knew instantly what she meant and why she meant it. She thought he'd really done this to impress Shanti. This made Dashiell unexpectedly jealous of Shanti in those unlit places of the self where few venture, but where rich seams of cause wait to cripple and shine.

'I'm sorry,' Dashiell said, aware of his chagrin.

'No one should be sorry for being honest,' he said.

They went home into the night shortly afterwards. Special ops dudes went in. Mother and orphan went out, snagged by a quietude familiar to people who are interstitially bound.

He resisted the urge to take Shanti to see the sculptures. He doubted that she would be interested: art wasn't her thing, as she often told him. Not taking Shanti was also his way of trying to prove Dashiell wrong even though he knew she was right. He marvelled at the human manoeuvrings he found within him. He could find no anagram of ego.

The sculptures were found a few days later by a security patrol. They were reported in a local publication a week or so after that. Within a year, they had become a 'phenomenon of the art world'. How had they got there? Who was the artist? Art experts came from all over Europe to examine them. The consensus was that 'nothing as fine had been achieved since the Renaissance – quasi classical or not'. Wishing to be major, one minor art critic thought that this sculptor was 'clearly' influenced by the likes of Rodin, Giacometti, Lachaise, Anna Hyatt Huntington, Hepworth, and Moore, too. Such disparate influences! How subtly they had 'found confluence' in these @masterpiecesofthequarry!

How strange the change.

The consortium that owned the quarry and much land thereabouts started to charge people to see the sculptures. Consortium staff fenced them off and created a pay-on-entry carpark. Lights were installed so the sculptures could be rendered more dramatic and enjoyed at night, so that all might enjoy these 'Glories of the New Renaissance'.

He laughed.
Dashiell knew.
Jericho knew.
Dashiell laughed.
Jericho laughed.

One night after all the hoo-ha about the sculptures, he ventured below ground in the quarry. He forced his way down inside a fissure in the rock. He then descended by using something like a swimming motion. To him, the rock felt like water. As he went deeper, the blackness and silence grew until it became absolute. Its absolution enthralled him.

He got it in his mind to go as deep as he could into the crust before he had to surface for air. Down and down he swam, faster and faster. At a depth of 137 kilometres, he knew he had to resurface. As he turned to ascend, he felt something hard about the size of his fist. He grabbed it instinctively. He then impelled himself back to the surface. He only just made it. Hypoxia was all but upon him when he finally burst into the air almost a kilometre from the quarry. His gasp for survival caused a drop in local air pressure so extreme that a low vault of thunder spoke, and flora nearby bowed briefly before springing back to shapes. His vertical momentum carried him high into the air. He laughed at his folly. He laughed at the beauty of air. He laughed at his dirty, ruined clothes.

Aloft, he looked at the hard thing his instinct had grabbed. It looked like an ancient mango.

He took it home and washed it. He realised that it was a massive diamond. It was the same size as, and similar in shape to, a typical human heart. That made him smile a grim miner's grimy smile - though frankly, he found his metaphor a bit twee. No matter. He resolved to one day give the diamond to someone he thought he loved. He had someone in mind.

*

On his twentieth birthday he became a slave.

Now, his vocation became a tyrant. It could no longer be denied. He had often gone to the town nearby with Kenton and Mal looking for fun. Now, he went there alone looking for trouble so he could mitigate it and relieve as much suffering as he could. He told no one of such forays.

Word soon spread. Rumours became reports. Beggars were fed fresh bread by a 'bearded stranger'; a victim of a bar fight was protected; a burglary was thwarted; an arson was prevented.

People discussed these interventions online. The local police became aware. They warned about 'vigilantism'. The use of this word troubled him: he'd never thought of what he did when he helped people as being outside the law; he thought of it as a manifestation of profounder laws called morals. He had no intention of enforcing or breaking statutory laws. He only wanted to do what he felt was right. 'The right thing to do is a question of the degree of an individual's privation,' he wrote in his journal as he pondered the origins and substance of his morality, and its agenda. He nodded sagely and pushed imaginary glasses up his nose as he did so.

He already knew that his moral obligations would become a heavier burden as time passed. How long could he bear them? In any event he resolved to seek brief release from their heft in humour, the sky, mountains, his journals, water, beauty, and in creativity as long as he could.

His creativity flourished as he grew. By now, music was a passion for him. He played Jericho's old guitar as soon as he picked it up. He could sight-read music immediately, too. He explored most forms of music because he loved most music. His criterion for quality was originality: he had an exceptionally low tolerance of repetition. Most good music enthralled or enraptured him; but he found a joy in traditional jazz that he could find nowhere else. This joy provided him with temporary relief from his ethical obligations, and the endless hurricanes of his thought.

'Jazz is Nature's down time,' he thought. Jazz made him smile.

Bach showed him the infinite potential of humanity.

He could transcribe anything – even orchestral music – to the guitar as he played it. He loved to improvise. 'Jam's my favourite,' he would say. 'Keep your marmalade.' He took to supplementing his earnings at the bakery by performing at the village hall. Word spread. Soon, people came to hear the 'Salter oddball' perform. Clever Mr Gibbie began to charge for tickets to these performances. Mr Gibbie knew an opportunity when he saw it. Anyway, he rather liked 'his' funny smiling sad long-haired oddball musician prophet hippy perfect bread maker freak. Mr Gibbie never used the word 'freak' outwardly of course. Inwardly was another matter.

His guitar performances were never the same twice. He just started with a single note and ad-libbed. What he played was as original as it was inevitable. Those who came to listen seemed, to him, to be underwhelmed at his talent, however. Few soon became fewer; and then, one evening, he found himself performing to an empty hall. He pretended he didn't care, but it hurt.

He could taste the musical sounds he made and see them forming, convulsing, and fading. He could hear the light dance on his fretwork. It reminded him of birdsong. To him, it was silver and slim chains and tinsel and alloys and the rose in the rain and small steel and lost and echoes and alone and days bouncing and brittle and the happy exodus of dreams and Tally's bed left unmade.

The sheets of his days became the pages of sliceable bread he baked so subtly. He worked at the bakery and loved music and numbers and helped people and exercised his ethics and tried to ignore Shanti Young in his mind and loins. The impossible made anything possible.

*

He dreamt they walked and then ran in the quarry, and that they laughed as they ran and that she became breathless as she gripped him and kissed him and that she told him to lie down on rough ground and that he didn't mind and that she moved on top of him and that he saw nations in the air. He dreamt that he had never seen anything as human as her movement. He dreamt that the wind rose around them like a dark moment. He dreamt that he would one day be part of things, not struck out like a cold animal. He dreamt that their hands could dance to the music of silence. He dreamt at the centre of the galaxy, which moved around him just like things can move. He dreamt of his gluttony for enlightenment. He dreamt that there were such things as near and far and big and small and I and you and we and they. His dreams took him beneath things and above them and inside the inside of them. His dreams showed him Shanti's truth and the impossibility of his own. He dreamt that she understood what he understood and that he understood nothing. He dreamt that her unseen body was now seen and tense with something molten. He dreamt of inhaling her exhalation. He dreamt that her rapture fell about him and comforted him. He dreamt that he would arrive, too. He dreamt she wasn't frightened of him. He dreamt she said it didn't matter that he couldn't arrive with her and that one day he would. He dreamt she lay beside him, comfortable in the moment of this uncomfortable place. He dreamt that she looked at the sculptures he had done and wondered who the sculptor was but said nothing. He dreamt that love existed. He dreamt of happiness.

*

Hope is a free radical.
    By the time he was twenty-one, the suffering of others, regardless of species, had become so intolerable to him that it turned his days into nights and his nights into a living hell. It had become a weight that crushed he who could hold up the world.
    If doing what he had to do – relieving suffering – on a much larger scale meant global ridicule, then so be it. Inaction was morally illogical. It was abhorrent. It made him ill. Dashiell senses the rising illness in him. She talked about it with Jericho – not because the conversation would solve their adopted son's quandary, but so she could share her anxiety.

They sometimes met at the coffee place in town. They met now. It was as awkward and lovely and pointless and boring and vital and inevitable and frustrating and painful and evitable as usual.

'He can't right every left, Dash', said Jericho with half-hearted wit. He was reluctant to make eye contact with her.

'How can he do anything else?'

'What about *him*?'

'He doesn't think about that.'

'What about you?' Now he met her eyes. Now she avoided the embers of regret she saw in them.

If he'd found the baby beside the wounded road instead of her it would all have been the same. They both knew it.

'Where is he?'

'He's a grown man,' she shrugged.

'Is he?' Jericho meant 'is he human?'; but all questions about him had long since lost the weight of asking. Answers had become winter trees bowed by patience.

Certain that he was not inhuman, they had in the past wondered if he was not human (and if not, what?) or if he was the most human thing possible (whatever that was). They had never reached anything approaching an answer to these or similar question in the hushes of their minds or the wedlock of their conversations.

As they now sat in eloquent silence in the café, the foundling was elsewhere embroiled in a discussion with Mr Gibbie that was, as far as Mr Gibbie was concerned, an argument. Mr Gibbie had no wish to argue with him, however. Mr Gibbie knew this strange, likeable young man was too valuable to his livelihood to 'put on the wrong side.' Mr Gibbie also found the idea of getting on the wrong side of the foundling strangely terrifying. He wasn't sure why. Dashiell's son was indeed the most charming, kind, and usually cheerful young man. Some now feared him, however. Even Kenton now found himself occasionally treading with care when he was with his best friend. Mal was more reckless, but instinctively wary. The foundling sensed their fear. He hated it. The three musketeers were thick as thieves. Nothing would ever come between them, surely.

Some still remembered the day on which he had shoved the boy Eric Lipton several dozen metres across the primary schoolyard fourteen years earlier. Eyewitnesses – mostly other pupils, now young adults – said he had done it 'without visible effort.' How had he done it? How do conjurers ever do what they do? With clever tricks. Lipton's take-off had no doubt been a clever trick, but rumours persisted. Mr and Mrs Lipton had never forgiven him, and they had made their feeling clear to Dashiell and Jericho at the time. Dashiell had been relieved when they had moved away years later. Eric had remained, however, and the boy had the seeds of revenge born of humiliation in him.

What, also, about the incident with the car, several years later? The Montclewes had seen him lift the vehicle up to impress Julie Sacthrow. How had he done that? Another trick without doubt; but a clever one. Again, however, gossip mangled the event into something that-could-not-be-explained. This is what gossip can do.

Gossip also questioned (as did Eric Lipton, geologists, Mr Bourncleave, and certain art critics) how the metamorphic gneiss, schist, granulite, and occasional limestone strata at the old quarry had been smashed into such fine dust. Most agreed machines hadn't done it. Surely nothing living could have done it, and certainly nothing human. Had the unknown sculptor somehow done it? If so, how, and why – was this all part of a Banksy-type myth-making? Was there a connection with the Maker of Marvellous Bread?

Now, as Dashiell and Jericho sat in the coffee shop in love's echo, in the bakery kitchen the Maker of Marvellous Bread told Mr Gibbie (wary and glancing) that he wanted to give away all the bread they baked on Fridays. There were several poor families on the outskirts of the village. There were homeless to be fed everywhere, too.

'Don't be daft, lad. If I give all my bread away, I'll go broke, and you'll be out of a job!' Mr Gibbie said. 'Your generosity is admirable, but you take my point.'

'But there are people who have nothing. They're hungry,' the foundling said, using moral logic like yeast. 'You're frustrated because ...'

'I'm not frustrated, lad. And anyway ...' Mr Gibbie shot back, hiding his irritation. Did this young man *always* have to talk about reality and ethics? It wasn't good for business!

'You know I'm right. And if we lose our right to the rite to do what's right there'll be nothing left to write about, right? And wrongs will feel left out,' said the foundling at an angle. His smile was irresistible.

'You can't make a joke of everything,' said Mr Gibbie uncomfortably. 'You know we're on the same team, don't you?'

'Are we?' He held Mr Gibbie's gaze. Mr Gibbie quailed. The young man's gaze was impossible to hold, and yet utterly magnetic.

'"Are we?"' Mr Gibbie went on. 'Of course we are. Anyway. If you don't mind. I've always wanted to ask. My wife would love to know. How did you do the thing with the car? Remember? Jason Montclewe said ... Forget it. But actually ... if you don't mind: are you the artist? I only ask because of what you can do with, well, dough! My-my. Eat your heart out Michelangelo. Whatever happened to the rock? How? And really: why? You can tell me. Mum's the word, mind. I'm not Bella Young, you know. So when are you going to marry her daughter Shanti then?' winked Mr Gibbie.

'Shanti thinks I'm a freak.'

'Come on. I saw the way she ignored you last week. Dead give-away.' Mr Gibbie winked again as he laughed. It seemed like a nervous wink and a nervous laugh. 'FYI though, lad: don't get married,' Mr Gibbie went on. 'If you settle down, you only have to settle up'

Mr Gibbie laughed again to hide a fear he didn't understand.

'So the bread, Mr Gibbie. People are starving. And at this time of year songbirds are desperate for anything they can get. You know that.'

He held Mr Gibbie's gaze. Mr Gibbie felt feeble before its strange power, which was the strength of absolute humility.

'Tell you what, lad. If you're prepared to do a shift without wage on Thursday nights, we can give away half of all you bake on Thursday nights on Friday afternoons. But paying customers must be satisfied first. How's that?'

Therefore the following Thursday night, the foundling baked:

- Three hundred and seventy-two wish-fresh batch
- Two hundred and sixty-two reliable bloomers
- Exactly two hundred outwardly religious coburgs
- A hundred and twelve gentle-as-milk barrels
- Ninety-four dusty farmhouse-to-be-bitten
- Eighty-eight smooth-but-reliably crunchy cobs
- Seventy-six safe and asymmetric cottage
- Sixty-one of his speciality plaits
  - He plaited these as nimble as forgotten hair and as complex as things can be, as simple as they can seem, as lovely as anything can be, and as happy as if they were the contemplation of something good

Some said he must have outsourced mobile ovens and a team of good bakers sworn to omerta. His achievement was not possible with Mr Gibbie's resources alone, surely. Someone used the word 'miracle' with quite a Serious Expression. Someone else laughed at it.

In any event, the limited size of the customer base – celebrity Gibbie bakery or not – meant that less than twenty percent of this enviably crusted night-bake was sold on Friday. Somehow the rest had vanished by Saturday morning to the last crumb. Many local songbirds put on much weight. Numerous less advantaged people nearby and not so nearby ate a lot of toast. This was good for local and not so local butter, jam, and marmalade sales.

He said that the smell of new baked bread looked like safety.

*

Saturday morning brought Dashiell a loaf beyond loaves. The taste sounded like love.

*

He told himself of love. He heard of: love's cup-cheek; hands finding; its destination; the heart's alliteration; the quality of honey; a glance entwined; a secret yes; no one else's; absolute trust; the keep of a caress; joy's salvo; the self, second; an apple-bough; touches dancing; a zero dilated; dead suns laughing; the sanctity of a nape; sleeping awake; silly accepted; blood at pound; a game for two; actual divinity; the harbour of a name; clouds but who cares?; the sun raining; anticipation; gasp at yes; yes; a permanent now; bliss that needs no catching; a perfect fugitive; pure lust, pure lust; lust; a full stop; youth that charged age head-on; us v the dark; cold, warmed; sweet glad; the east in bloom; the sidereal human; spring understood; arrival; please spell the word 'tomorrow'; the portrait of Pangaea as an island; the word 'goodbye' now looking for work; the long hello; vulnerability; fear; fear's death; handwriting; the fatal west; who needs the west!?; a melody entranced; we.

*

When it gets a certain kind of cold, rain gets lazy. It falls as if it doesn't really care about falling. That's because it isn't quite snow yet and isn't quite rain any more. It's as if now, rain is unsure where to go or what it is.

In the cup of Tuesday's hands, he waited for Shanti near the Vere Oak, under which he sheltered from such rain. Dead outwardly but challenging final ruin, the ancient tree stood alone near the centre of a field used to keep sheep for slaughter. The field was part of the grounds of a pale mansion that moped nearby in history's mumble. He always thought the many windows of the mansion gazed out as if waiting for the return of someone who would never come back.

Some said the Vere Oak had been planted by Alfred the Great. Others said the tree could not be that old. Others, that it was older. When a child, Dashiell had told him that Vere Oak's roots reached to the centre of the earth, and that the roots were made of lightning. He had always wondered where the thunder was and when it would come. He thought he now knew. He often came here and always marvelled at the tree. From its dead bole, a sapling now sprouted against all odds.

While he waited in the oak's lee for Shanti, he helped a bee that had fallen to the ground nearby. The bee was on its back. It struggled exhaustedly to right itself. He gently put it the right way up. The bee then stood there in the way bees do as if traumatised or waiting. He helped it to a flower nearby. He put the bee on the lower part of a petal near the pistil. There, dew had gathered. As he placed the bee there, the style quavered slightly, bowing the stigma slightly. The anthers existed. The bee was still for a moment. It then moved so that it seemed to drink the dew. He watched it do what the aeons told it to do as a way to distract himself from the tumult in his body at Shanti's desired approach.

Shanti did not approach, however. She did not come. She was with another lover, etiolated by sunlight made hesitant by cold rain in a clandestine room. She was sure the foundling didn't know about his competition – at least by name. If he did, she was sure, he would withdraw from her, hurt and shocked. Might he be jealous – angrily so? She had sensed anger in him, though he was mild and gentle as anyone she had ever met or, she somehow knew, would meet. For her part, she owed him no fidelity. They had made love, yes, but that had forged no stated bond of faith. She expected him to have other interests, too; yet knew somehow that he did not. She found herself wishing that he did as she experimented now with her other lover. She realised she was thinking of the foundling while otherwise engaged. She stopped herself doing it, surprised by her preoccupation's connotation.

For his part, as he waited under the clench of the Vere Oak's ancient might, he expected no fidelity from Shanti. In his heart, she was free to do as she wished. He expected her to refuse to be owned, even as he refused to own or be owned. Good love might only flourish thus.

When waiting for Shanti proved futile, he walked away without pique or chagrin: this was the way things were that day, so he became the way things were, too – exactly as did the surviving bee.

That evening he helped an aged motorist with a flat tyre out near the silos. The old man was distraught. He no longer had the strength to change the wheel; he would have 'done it in a jiffy' years earlier, he said. The old man had no jack to lift the car; the foundling therefore lifted it with one hand while changing the wheel with the other. Beyond a small plosive, the old man disguised his marvel at this in a way that suggested his pride insisted on it. Perhaps his old hands and his voice shook more than normal. Perhaps not. It was hard to know. When the task was done, the foundling shook the old man's hand and saw him on his way.

That night, he went to the town because he knew could help more there. He could. He did. He stopped a gang of young men from beating up another man outside a pub. He let them waste their fists on him for a while. He knew that fear would do his work for him. It did. Seeing him unscathed by their aggression, the bullies soon made off along the pavements of disbelief and rejection. As they went, one glanced back at him in a way the foundling would never forget. He then helped their victim to go on his way: drunk, aghast, and grateful.

He saw a report online about a sea-container ship that had been in trouble for some hours in a storm on the borders between the old shipping areas (about which Jericho was passionate) of Lundy and Fastnet. To the west, Rockall, Shannon, Sole, and Fitzroy were already smashed by the storm, which was a limb of a Category 4, Atlantic hurricane. He found the ship with great difficulty. By the time he got there, it was listing and low in the water. A tug was attempting to approach the ship, but the conditions made it impossible to get a line onto it. He went to the bow of the ship. He pulled it. He had to use so much force that the steel at the tip of the bow distorted in his grip. The storm made visibility so bad that those in the bridge couldn't see him (forty metres away as he was at the bow). If they had, they would have seen him laughing wildly. The storm exhilarated him.

He towed the vast ship at around 10 knots to a jut of rock called Gilstone: the westernmost outcrop of the Scilly Isles. It took two hours. He grounded it – by now half-submerged – on a sandbank that adjoined the coast of the tiny island. The tug was by now nowhere to be seen. As he departed into the red, he looked back. He saw a sailor clinging to infrastructure looking up at him through the assailing wind.

He rescued a starved dog from torment at the hands of its owner: a man with a stoop and bad complexion. He had heard the dog's yelps as he passed the house. The dog's tormentor abused him verbally when he knocked at the door then asked if the dog was alright. The man set his other dog – a Pitbull – on him. The foundling was a gentle as he could be with the Pitbull. He then took the starved dog away from its tormentor. He took the dog to the local RSPCA. He was unaware that the dog's tormentor wept for his dead wife after the dog's departure.

He provided food for a refugee family which was living on the street in the town. He rescued a fireman from a burning house that had collapsed around him. He prevented a female police officer from being stabbed at a scene of domestic violence.

He yearned to close the abattoir near the bypass down. He knew that if he shut it down, however, he would have to shut all abattoirs down all over the world and find jobs for everyone who was then unemployed and who would then likely suffer, as would their families. Some of these people might turn to crime in order to survive. Would he be willing to bring them all to book? How – by force? By what right? How would he close the abattoirs down anyway – also by force? In so doing all of this he would have to reveal his abilities, too, and that would have consequences.

Everything had consequences.

He got lost in an ethical labyrinth that he would never find his way out of because nothing is either this or that, or is or isn't, or should or shouldn't: it is both and neither to some degree. Everything is the fruit of the tree of causality, too; and that fruit can fall far from the tree.

No matter, he resolved. He would do whatever he could do. Not to do so was not an option. There is no excuse for inaction.

Now, he therefore retrieved a boy's kite from the electric power cable it had become caught on. He asked the boy to tell everyone that he'd seen the foundling rise into the air to retrieve the kite. Naturally, the boy ran home in a state of vexation and told no one what he had seen because he would look like an idiot if he did, and no one would believe him anyway.

When storms threatened to flood homes prone to regular annual inundation in the West Country, he dug a two-metre-deep water channel. This took the floodwater out into the middle of coastal mudflats where light rested. Though some homes were still damaged, most were saved.

He stopped two men raping a girl in a graveyard.

Doing such things and others gave him a happiness that felt like wet cardboard.

Making a cup is harder than breaking a cup.

*

Saturday evening made him drunk on even less than his occasional pint.

The three musketeers were at their local pub. They were small-town bored. Bored, Kenton called the bored foundling a 'cheap date' in reference to his inability to handle alcohol. Bored Mal knew Kenton was referring to dating per se by saying this. By dating, Kenton meant the foundling's obvious romantic and erotic interest in his sister Shanti, who sat across the pub with her friends Zadie and Imogen. Shanti smiled at the foundling and held his gaze. He smiled back. The exchange was an unexpected statement of love in an unlikely place: the pub, busy at it was with parochial grandeur. It was love admitted. It was trust confirmed. It was a contract of hearts. It was their thing.

'You'll go blind, mate,' said Kenton, following his gaze to his sister.

'Well then I won't have to see your ugly mug, will I?,' he shot back. He regretted it instantly. It was the alcohol talking. He hated what alcohol did to him. He wondered why he drank it. He knew all too well: it was brief release from the burden of consciousness and the threat of a fatal future. In these burdens, he knew, he was as most people are. He shared a common need for periodic release from existence with everyone. He now wished he were sober, however. He wished he were in the sky, too: free and free and free. The sudden tension between him, Shanti and Kenton was unwelcome. Here and now came into sudden, sharp focus.

Mal was laughing. Kenton's eyes were dark.

Shanti met the foundling's gaze with her smile. To her, his eyes intimated a longing to be somewhere else – to be something else. His face always seemed to convey joy and sadness in a way that suggested they were the same thing. This, too, she had always found beguiling.

Then, aware Kenton was looking at her, she looked away and said something inconsequential to Zadie in order to defuse things. She failed.

'Bake her some bread. She likes a loafer,' laughed Kenton. Kenton made suggestive dough kneading motions that went on too long.

'Come on then boys,' said Mal, trying to calm them. Mal sensed something in the foundling. It made him uneasy, and not much made big Mal uneasy. On the other side of the room, Shanti sensed it too. So like most people do, she pretended to be interested in Facebook. Beside her, Imogen was Tweeting. Zadie took a pouty selfie and uploaded it to Instagram. Everyone everywhere was trying to be elsewhere: online. Kenton looked at Shanti in a certain way. Mal sunk his pint like an old schooner. Kenton's right hand closed like Davy Jones' deep fist. Mal saw him do it through the bottom of his pint glass as it emptied.

'Come on then Kent,' belched Mal, ever the peacemaker.

'Well it's all lies anyway. Found Tally like that then did you? Really?' said Kenton. He regretted it instantly. It was the alcohol talking.

The foundling was suddenly overwhelmed by a dream about a hydrogen bomb exploding. He dreamt that it seemed like the bright egg of physics. He dreamt of spacetime bowing to this expanding shockwave within him. He dreamt that this shockwave swatted Kenton across the pub like a shuttlecock. He dreamt that Kenton smashed against the wall and then crumpled like a ragdoll. He dreamt that he and Mal went to help him. He dreamt that Shanti hurried over and tried to help Kenton too. He dreamt that Kenton was unconscious. He dreamt that people were looking at them in a certain way. He dreamt of remorse that was bigger than size. He dreamt that Mal called an ambulance. He dreamt that there was nothing he could do to help Kenton, and that guilt cut him inside like a greedy-greedy shiv. He dreamt that aeons later an ambulance came, and that they wouldn't let him ride to the hospital in the back with Kenton. He dreamt that, strangely, Shanti didn't scold him, but asked to be left alone now and that they would see each other soon. He dreamt that this was OK, and that then, she went away into the zanies of the shocked night. He dreamt that he got to the hospital before the ambulance did. He dreamt that there was nothing he could do, and that they took Kenton into an unconscious ward where they did things. He dreamt that then he went to the quarry (because where else?), where he stood near the statues of silence. He dreamt that regret is a country that is too big to navigate. He dreamt that he would never recover from the grief and guilt that consumed him. He dreamt that he would never drink again, but instead suffer the barbs of his awareness like swindling hooks that would grind him and hoist him and let his blood like strawberry jam not yet set and thus ready to serve. He dreamt that if Kenton didn't recover he wouldn't recover either, and that his death would be living.

Then he dreamt that he woke up.

*

The next day, a policeman came to his flat above the bakery.

The policeman said, 'That young man almost died. He's conscious now, but how do you know he won't spend the rest of his days in a wheelchair?'

'A wheelchair,' was all he could find to say. He swallowed dry. Shock became a seething snake. Its scales were cheap swarf.

'You need to know that Kenton's mother, Mrs Bella Young – I believe you know the lady in question? – Mrs Young has stated that she will be pressing charges.

Grievous Bodily Harm is a serious offence, young man, for which you will likely pay the price under law. Don't think you and your ilk can do anything and just get away with it. Actions have consequences.'

He felt sick. What had he done? He couldn't speak. His consequential world was now regretting, burning, sinking, floundering, yearning, gasping, being, cutting, dying, forming, aching, roaring, hacking, invading, grieving, wishing, begging, piercing, staying, walled.

The policeman went on, 'You'll first be required to attend the station to give a formal statement. Try drinking a bit less next time, eh?'

He felt the snake shift. Metal scales hissed. Insidious hoarfrost!

After some 'standard questions', the policeman left him with his thoughts. This was not, and never would be, an easy thing to be left with. When the policeman left, the tears arrived. They soaked his beard, where they gathered like dew on a bosun's glance.

Later, Shanti phoned him.

'He's back in the land of the living anyway,' she said. He heard traffic noise in the background.

'He's conscious?'

'Yes. But they said something about an intracranial haematoma or something. And I think his ribs – a lot of broken ribs, and maybe his back. And a fractured pelvis.'

The truth flayed him alive. For a moment, he couldn't speak.

'It was just you boys being boys. Again,' Shanti said.

'How can you forgive me?'

'Frankly, I don't know!' Her eyes flashed dark but then she cooled, moved by the pain in him. She put the phone back to her ear. 'How did you bloody idiots do it?' She waited.

A moment on the line, then: 'I don't know.'

'How could you not know?'

'Look, Shanti ...'

'I'm looking.'

'I don't know. That's all I can say.'

'Now may not be the time to be enigmatic, you know.'

'I know.'

'You know or you don't know? This is ridiculous!'

'If I knew, I'd tell you. You of all people.'

'I'm flattered. And all because of me. How Trojan. How tragic,' she said.

Another moment, then: 'I'm sorry, Shanti. I'm going to tell you one day. I'm going to tell everyone. I'm going to show you.'

'Show me what?'

*

'Is this your way of showing the world what you can do!? Is it!? What were you thinking!? Were you thinking? He's your friend, and now ...! Real power is *never* destructive! You know that! You have to learn how to control it! Are you listening to me? Have you ever listened to me?!'

Dashiell was angry, and she was rarely angry. Her eyes were midnight detonations. Her hands shook. She breathed. He waited for her to calm. As he often did, he let his silence tell her what she already knew: That he was a young man exhilarated by himself. He had as yet found no limits to his power. How then might he ever bring it to heel?

'The world demands limitations, you know. It will only tolerate a certain amount of ability.'

'So what am I going to do?'

She had no answer. There was no answer. So she just embraced him.

Then the moment fled into the horizon of memory.

Kenton had two 'surgical interventions' over the course of three weeks. He was allowed to go home a week after that. The foundling went to the Young's house to see him. To apologise. To expiate – though he knew he never could. Bella Young rebuked him savagely and told him to go away the first time he went. The second time he went,

Thomas Young told him he wasn't allowed to let him in. Thomas was a broken 9-iron.

The foundling and Shanti saw each other occasionally during this time and thereafter. Strangely, as they both thought, they became lovers again. The few that suspected or knew this thought their intimacy 'a bit weird', given what the foundling had 'done' to Kenton.

Bella was incandescent.

'Him!? Of all people, him!? That freak!'

'He's not a freak, mum.'

'Then what is he?'

'He's just different. I want to help him.'

Bella didn't know how to react to that, so she didn't. She prepared Kenton's painkiller dose instead and took it upstairs to give to her son to swallow in his bed of new pain.

To the foundling it seemed that Shanti took pleasure in Bella's tormented disapproval of her daughter's sexual union with him. For his part, he wished to upset no one, nor did he wish to be hated by anyone. He wished to apologise to Kenton, too, however inadequate an apology would be. Of course he was seeking atonement. He knew he would never get it.

He called Kenton several times, but his friend did not or could not answer. He sent Kenton a text saying simply 'Sorry.' It felt painfully inadequate. He found out from Shanti that Kenton was wheelchair bound. She had no idea for how long. In that moment, his misery seemed perfect.

The case was heard by a magistrate a month later. He was required to sit through hours of preliminary iteration and reiteration, and formal procedure. The hearing only lasted some forty minutes. In the end, the magistrate was lenient even though Kenton remained in a wheelchair. In her opinion, this had been a case of youthful high jinks gone horribly wrong. It was Mal's testimony that swung the case in the foundling's favour. Mal testified that he and the foundling had set the whole thing up with 'mechanical stunt devices' they bought online to windup Kenton. Mal said he had since discarded the devices in a moment of 'regretful panic'.

The foundling never understood why Mal lied to help him except that Mal was his friend. When they spoke, Mal just said, 'Just the crack of it, mucker. But I gotta know. How'd you do it, really?' When the foundling told him he didn't know, Mal looked at him conspiratorially, shrugged, grinned, and resumed work on the car he was refurbishing for sale.

Though Kenton remained incapacitated, the doctors were hopeful of a full recovery in due course. Mal's testimony and this medical prognosis together meant that the foundling – a first offender, too – was merely fined and given a community order. This order stipulated that:

Supervision

He had regular sessions with an offender manager to help stop him reoffending.

Unpaid Work (Community Payback)

He worked in the community to pay back the harm he had caused; this almost entirely involved the cleaning and sweeping of public places. (He enjoyed to graft of simple work, but felt humiliated.)

Alcohol Rehabilitation

He was mandated to undertake an alcohol rehabilitation programme.

Activity

He was required to spend time with the victim of his crime. (He sat with Kenton in his room at the Young's house for half an hour a day. They spoke little, and about things of little consequence. Bella loathed having him there, but the law enforced it, so she had no choice.)

Exclusion

He was prevented from going to the pub where it had happened. (It was the last place on earth he wanted to go anyway.)

Attendance Centre (for under 25s)

He was required to remain at an attendance centre for set hours.

 He could easily have ignored the whole procedure. He could have gone into the red sky and disappeared without trace. He could have defied the law and ignored its enforcers. Instead, he took his punishment because he felt it was the right thing to do.
 He lost his job at the bakery. Mr Gibbie said that he had no choice, much as he wished otherwise. Mr Gibbie broke a tooth thinking about the whole ruddy mess.
 By the time he'd finished his community order, his misery felt as absolute as his contrition and regret. His sadness was only eased by occasional forays into Shanti's arms.
 He had to live with Dashiell again after he lost his room above the bakery. Moving back in with Dashiell felt like a step backwards, but he knew he'd go elsewhere again soon. Of course, his foster mother was secretly glad to have her boy back in her care but she, too, knew it was temporary.
 Kenton remained housebound – either through necessity or by choice, such as choice is. As soon as the foundling was no longer mandated to spend time with Kenton, Bella banned him from the house.
 Thereafter, Kenton went downhill fast. He rarely washed now. He didn't shave. He began to drink. Though

Bella 'forbade' it, Shanti smuggled bottles of anything she could get hold of into Kenton's room. Yes, she felt bad about being the partial cause of his injuries; but of course she wanted to assuage his pain. When Bella found out and admonished her, Shanti turned on her mother with a savagery that surprised them both. 'Drop dead, mum!' Shanti's words hurt Bella deeply.

Thereafter, Bella found her newly spoiled son an increasing burden. She looked after (tolerated) Kenton for almost four months. Then the storm broke. She visited Dashiell unannounced early one evening when Dashiell had just returned from work. There were no platitudes to smooth the way. Bella just stood on the doorstep and spoke words that smelted venom. 'My beautiful boy! What if he never walks again!? What then?' Bella screamed. Her dark eyes that had once been pretty were red from fatigue and, Dashiell assumed, crying. 'That so-called son of yours!'

'Mind your mouth!' Dashiell shot back, reeling from the attack.

'He was part of the family once!' Bella went on as if Dashiell hadn't spoken. 'And this is how he repays us? He should be in prison! It's a travesty! I don't want him anywhere near my son or my daughter again! You tell him! You tell him ...!'

Bella let the words hang like an aerial toxin. To Dashiell, she seemed half crazed. Then Bella stormed away into the crowded rain.

Now, the next day, the hurt and shock remained: Dashiell said little. When she did, she just said, 'Don't bite your nails.' She sat with the foundling in the kitchen of the cottage. Jericho had taken time off work to be there. Dashiell and Jericho made little eye contact. They sat at opposite ends of the table. To the foundling, the table seemed laden with the fickle fruit of guilt and the agony of true compassion.

'I have to tell them what really happened,' he now said to his foster parents. 'I have to tell them about myself.'

'You can't, and you know it. You'll just make a laughing stock of yourself,' said Dashiell.

'And you,' he said.

'That doesn't matter,' said Dashiell.

A moment followed in which words seemed unwelcome. Jericho's phone chirped a message alert. Then Jericho ventured, 'Your mother and I ...' Then everything between them and behind them and in front of them opened up like a sudden canyon; so Jericho went on quickly: 'The past is the past. It's not your fault. None of it ...'

'I did what I did, dad. All I know is I'm not like them. They know it too. To them, I'm weird.'

'They know what it suits them to know,' said Jericho. 'You said it yourself.'

Then he left them alone together to talk. He went for a walk. Night had collapsed. He went to the quarry. To him, the three statues seemed to sit in slightly different positions now. Their expressions seemed to have changed slightly. Without light, experience and imagination can become one. He marvelled at the effects of subjectivity. He also became resolved: it was time to tell people. If they mocked him, their mockery would be his punishment for what he had done to Kenton.

He organised an evening at the village hall, as he had nearly eight years earlier to showcase his talents as a stand-up comedian. He chose the Friday evening after his conversation with Dashiell and Jericho because there was a chutney convention on the Saturday evening that was organised by Miss J. Q. V. Dashawn; and on Sundays, and now most weekdays, the village hall was shut.

He told Mr Bourncleave about it because he knew Mr Bourncleave would spread the word like bindweed, which he did. The foundling also posted on the village's humble online network. He said that he was going to do a small 'performance – some comedy (again), and some 'revelation'. He felt that the word 'confession' would be apter.

He didn't tell Shanti about it and thus invite her for fear of making a fool of himself in front of her, and thereby losing her. He had been tempted to tell her on the phone five months earlier at the quarry when she had told him how badly Kenton was hurt. How long ago that seemed now. He had been tempted to tell her how different he really was, but he had realised even as the words clotted his throat that it was futile, and probably damaging. She would have had no choice but to reject him as someone with issues too deep to have 'normal' relationships. He had therefore edited his revelation to tell her instead of his ethical convictions and vocation, and his interest in magic.

'Show me what?' she had said on the phone then.

He had been glad they weren't face-to-face. The veer would have ghosted his eyes, and she would have sensed his obfuscation. She was unusually intuitive. There had been a moment on the phone, but moments happen, so she thoughts little of it, preoccupied as she was by Kenton's demise.

'Nothing. I just mean I have to be what I can be. I don't want to become another cog in the machine, you know? Show you I can do things.'

'What kind of things?'

'Things that other people find hard. I'm just lucky I guess. I'm going to do good with them, as far as I can. I don't care about myself in that way. For me it's not me, it's …'

He had laughed as if self-consciously, and let the conversation navigate back to Kenton, and how guilty he felt for hurting him, and how he could make amends.

Out of the blue she had said, 'Don't expect me to forgive you. For some reason I don't feel like I need to, and I don't know why. Anyway – maybe there'll be a better time for forgiveness.'

The phone conversation had ended shortly after that with expressions of endearment that he hadn't expected. Neither had she.

Now, when he thought about 'confessing' his abilities in front of Shanti in the village hall, he almost shuddered with aversion. No. If he were about to alienate himself in public and earn the rejection of his community, such as it was, he would do so in Shanti's absence. He therefore didn't invite her. If she came anyway, so be it. Shanti would be better off with someone more conventional – someone without a secret that was hidden in plain sight. He was ultimately alone anyway.

When it came, Friday greeted him with a cold stomach, wet palms, and a dry mouth, Shanti or no. Was he doing the right thing? Of course not, but, he reasoned, it's often essential to do the wrong thing. As he finally stepped out in front of the few assembled in the village hall, he was ready to regret the whole idea. It was too late.

'Ladies and gentlemen thank you for coming. You'll be pleased to hear I'm not about to deliver the next phase of my burgeoning stand-up comedy career. Actually, the Comedy Club called, but ...' Of the eighteen and a half faces that turned up, one laughed, three smiled, and the rest lacked manifest humour, genuine interest, or involvement. There was a pleasant degree of tolerance, however – or was it ghoulish fascination (or foolish gassy nation, as Tally would have called it)?

Unanswered questions littered the place like the lout of autumn.

Dashiell and Jericho sat near the back, which was near to the front. It was a small hall. The foundling was glad of their presence. He was beyond nervous. Dashiell sensed it. She bled for him. She knew this was a mistake.

He went to continue talking, but the door opened. Thomas and Bella Young entered. He had hoped they wouldn't come. It seemed perverse that they had, after what he had done to Kenton. Perhaps that was why they were here: to punish him in some way. Thomas was incapable of such behaviour, but there was something vindictive about Bella. He knew it was a product of some deficiency in her, as she saw it. Some bitterness. Some regret. It was in her altered essence.

Thomas and Bella Young sat down as near the front as they could sit, which was in the second row. From there, they could fix their gaze on the foundling. Bella's damp eyes were empty. Dutifully next to her, Thomas seemed embarrassed by everything. He always had.

As he prepared to speak again, and his throat was dry with nerves, Kenton entered, helped by Mal. Mal winked and grinned piratically at the foundling, who's nerves thus abated somewhat in the presence of big Mal's languid indifference to anything that mattered.

Kenton had a beard but seemed washed and presentable. That he walked – albeit with the aid of crutches, was beyond anything the foundling could have hoped for. Kenton limped directly to his old friend. He shook his hand. All was as all was. All that would be, would be. The universe waited for them. Then the moment ended. Kenton walked to a seat some way away from his parents, whom he ignored abundantly. Kenton sat next to Mal. They had supermarket beers. Kenton drank and toasted the foundling, who welcomed his friends' ribbing and returned it in spades.

'Where was I? Ah – in a foolish gassy nation.'

The meaning of the spoonerism apropos Tally registered in Dashiell and Jericho's faces. Otherwise there were some polite smiles and Tesco queue patience. Some stony faces. Some low expectations. Some wishing for something better to do. Some memories of better things done.

Bella seemed to wait for him to say or do something with manicured ferocity.

He swallowed air, then said, 'Anyway thank you for coming. I'm probably just about to make a huge mistake, but oh well.'

Dashiell seemed to cross her legs in a certain way.

He responded in kind to Mac's anticipation of his imminent pratfall. 'Crash and burn, mucker. Go for it!' said Mac. Kenton laughed and said something to Mac that made him laugh harder.

'I'll try, Mac,' said the foundling. 'Thanks for your support, mate! Anyway. So I know there have been rumours. Some of you think of me as, well, a bit odd.'

Someone sniggered and tried to disguise the snigger with a cough that advertised the snigger. It was Julie Sacthrow. The girl he had 'loved' in order to signal his truer love for Shanti to Shanti. Julie was surer than most that he was a weirdo – perhaps even 'wrong in the head'. Was she here now to watch him humiliate himself? Was this just blood sport?

Nerves got the better of him for a moment.

'Don't let us stop you, young man,' said Thomas Young. 'Carry on.'

'Here to apologise are you then?' said Bella.

'Take your time, mate,' said Kenton. His voice seemed to have aged. Speaking seemed difficult. Kenton winked at him. The foundling was thus inspired to continue.

'Because of everything,' he said regarding Kenton, but addressing all. 'I just think it's time you knew.' He saw Dashiell lower her head slightly. He heard Tally laugh in the lost lanes of his mind.

'The fact is that I'm not like ... I mean I'm not really ... I'm not really normal.'

'Course you are, luv,' a female voice said. It was Jenny Blairlow.

'Who is?' A sardonic male voice.

'You mean you're not like us.' A male voice liquid with censure.

'What's wrong with being normal then?' A voice with ramparts.

A mote of silence drifted up in ordinary air.

'So what are you – chopsticks?' A voice without a face.

'Come on, luv. Why we here then? You gonna sing and dance, are you?' It was Jenny Blairlow again. Jenny led a small flurry of laughter. Some of it was crueller, some kinder. Most of it was the laughter of people living lives they hadn't been led to believe they would live.

The foundling hammed it up a bit to play along. He pulled a 'weird' face. He smiled. He noticed that Dashiell seethed inscrutably, and that Jericho shifted in his seat.

He saw Mal's grin fade quickly as Kenton twisted in sudden pain. The pain made the foundling wince. He had no idea whose pain it was. He was aware that Bella checked her Gucci watch, and that Thomas Young's love for his son glazed his eyes. Thomas remained in his seat, however, to which he seemed (but wasn't) tethered by Bella's apparent (but false) indifference.

Everyone else, but for Dashiell and Jericho, was getting bored; so he got on with it.

'So anyway. What I mean is. The sculptures at the quarry,' he said, crucified by Kenton's pain.

Expressions went from 'told-you-so' to 'as-if' via glassy eyed indifference around the hall at his reference to the sculptures. For his part, Mr Dailty from Islington-in-the-day scoffed kindly. His classical ballet trained wife Tabatha was routinely weary of his self-opinion, which was that of professed art maven and literati. Mr Dailty had always tried to be a-little-bit-too-cultured for village life. Tabatha expressed her rote irritation with her husband's half-moon-specs-half-way-down-the-nose by shifting her recently gracile body.

'Michelangelo now are we then? And I suppose you had no help with them loaves, neither' opined Mr Thorpethwaite, who's bulimic wife was suddenly hungry with scepticism, too.

'Well no, actually. That's what I mean.' He took a sudden breath to calm his nerves. The inrush of air into his lungs was so powerful it stirred Abby Lulealv's recently bouffant hair in the second-to-front row. Otherwise, she didn't react. Why would she? The poor bloke was a freak. He was a charlatan. He had problems. So what? Who didn't?

He knew that they were all sure it was all a trick. He was a trickster. He was having a laugh. Nothing was real, after all, because everything was. There was no boundary between real and not real. Everyone was bored by everything. Only nothing could please them now.

'Look,' he began again; but then self-doubt stopped him.

The mote of silence rose higher still.

'Well I'm the wind,' he went on after seconds that felt like hours that felt like years. He suddenly regretted saying that as much as he regretted being here doing this as much as he regretted being what he was, which thrilled him like a good simile. He glanced at Dashiell. She was looking down at her hands, wishing this would all be over soon.

Someone left. There was that show on Netflix.

Jericho met his gaze. They were both the remains of a star.

He hesitated. Then he did it slightly. Dashiell shook her head no, but he raised himself off the floor anyway. Only a few inches. Up. Yes. He remained so elevated. Then he let himself descend.

No one reacted as the foundling wished. This frustrated him. What did he have to do to show these people what he was!?

Only Kenton seemed genuinely perplexed. Only Kenton had felt the force that had shattered his body, and how could such force exist in a person? Only he and the foundling and Mal knew there had been no mechanisms in place to make the 'stunt' work. How, therefore, had he done it? Now this levitation, too? How? Such questions had stifled Kenton's throat since it happened. They were starting to choke him; yet how could he ask without fear of ridicule, and who could he ask? What was the question? What answer, too, could he reasonably expect?

All that was why the foundling was doing this. To answer Kenton and others' questions. To set the rumours to rest. To prove himself. It was a proof, he knew even as he did this, that would never be accepted. Evidence is unacceptable if it disrupts protective assumptions.

In defiance, in frustration, in the village hall, the foundling elevated himself again anyway. This time higher and faster. This time a couple of feet off the floor. Again, only Kenton reacted with anything but polite indifference (or in Dashiell and Jericho's case: measured public smiles). There was YouTube, and what was the name of that magician who walked across the Grand Canyon last year without visible support? What was this, therefore, but tepid?

Someone yawned. Bella's gaze sharpened to a snake's lick.

'Go on, son,' yelled Mac, who didn't seem to care if it had been a stunt or if the Force was as real as cheese on toast. Kenton tried to speak but was convulsed by sudden coughing. The foundling waited until his friend could stop coughing. Everyone waited for Kenton to stop coughing. Every agonized cough seemed to justify Bella's hatred of the foundling and indict him for his macho idiocy.

'You OK mate?' the foundling said when Kenton had stopped.

Blank stares stared. Texts were sent.

His irritation grew.

'Right,' he said again, not knowing what else to say. He, who could thread an atom with the English language and use it to misunderstand the robin and the rose. Right.

'I'm so terribly sorry about what happened to you,' he blurted to Kenton, a couple of feet off the floor. Then he said to everyone: 'There were no wires, no levers, no tricks – were there, boys?' he said to Kenton and Mac. Slowly, slowly, Kenton shook his head 'no'. The room saw it; but the room was not impressed by silly young men and silly tricks. Or jiggery-pokery. Or foolhardy tomfoolery.

'I just did it', he went on. 'It was just me. This is me. I baked all the bread. I did it alone. I made the sculptures in the quarry. I worked the stone with my hands. I wanted to save my sister. Nothing can cut my hair except fire because, well that's why I look like Aaron who had a square 'un. I have to bite my nails because I can't cut them for the same reason ... I can ... And ...'

He wanted to tell them that gravity had no dominion over him, but by now there were glances. Legs were crossed. The legs and the glances felt sorry for Dashiell, yes, to be the mother of both him and a girl with such a terrible illness who some say killed herself and some say was killed by her brother (or is he, is he?) and to be the mother (is she?) of that boy, here, now, not nowhere else, who was clearly not just on drugs, yes, but also maybe now we think a bit special as in special like in the head, and standing here saying no wires or levers and the quarry, and the fact that she's come here tonight to support him so is she here out of shame or some cruel schtick that makes her want to open her hands wide to the whole village and say look, none of it's my fault because none of it is, and I just got the wrong throw of the die and that two is dice, and that nothing needs to be said and nothing can be done but here he is, my other one, so please just accept him for what he is, though heaven knows what that is, what with the hair and the beard and nearly killing Kenton who never did not much of harm to no one but was actually yes, a scamp, but that's no reason to get yourself smashed in a pub over some girl but wars are started over girls and anything with a penis can't be trusted though the penis mightier than the sword as you say without grinning now, finally, finally, and anyhow whatever game he's playing there's someone he can see though who knows why she hasn't sought help like that before now and maybe she had but she's ashamed to tell anyone and what about Jericho now and the Queen of Sheba she reckons she is all la-de-la-de, but someone who knows about whatever it's called, but all he needs is a dose of the big wide world not the www, which is where the youth of today is at, Liking this and not liking any amount of what they need though some say they have seen things at night they can't explain but he's a bit odd anyway, but if that's true then how can he do that up there, though of course that can't be true and what are we doing here anyway?

    Dashiell actually stood up as if to say to him 'stop, please stop; it's pointless. Can't you see? If you tell them the truth, they'll know you're lying. If you lie to them, they'll say they always knew.' Then she stood there and looked at him and didn't know what to do.

Two seating rows back, Julie Sacthrow smiled at Mal in a way that told the foundling things he always knew. Abby Lulealv adjusted her hair. A few people began to leave. Mr Thorpethwaite stood as if to leave, too, so his bulimic wife Trudy remained sitting. Mr Thorpethwaite therefore sat down again.

The foundling retrieved a Jerry Can of petrol from beside the stage. He started to douse himself with petrol. The few people stopped their egress, pronto. They either remained where they were and watched, or went back to their seats: clearly this show was just getting started.

The foundling poured the last of the petrol over him. He put the Jerry Can down.

'Don't do this.' Jericho stood up as he said it. Dashiell's hand went to her mouth.

'It's OK, dad. If anyone can, Jerry Can,' he said with a smile. 'Has anyone got a light?'

Mr flipping Bourncleave got a cigarette lighter out of his pocket quickly indeed. He gave the dripping foundling the cigarette lighter with similar élan. Mrs flipping Bourncleave gave-her-husband-a-look as he sat down again.

The foundling clicked the faulty cigarette lighter several times. Kenton watched with growing incredulity, as did Mal. Mal actually put his beer down.

At last, a flame.

'So this is how it is for me,' he said. He saw Dashiell close her eyes.

'You don't need to do this,' escaped Jericho's mouth like a rope of smoke lifting a chimney.

'Relax, dad. You know it's OK.'

Then the foundling met no one's eyes. In this way, he met all who gazed. He applied the cheap plastic flame to his petrol-soaked body. He turned himself into an inferno.

'Mate! No!' yelled Kenton. 'Don't do it!'

'What the fuck!' shouted Mal.

'It's OK boys. I'm OK. See?' the foundling said inside his cocoon of fire.

Reactions ranged from abattoir-eyed mortification through disbelief via hilarity to panic. Mouths gaped. Someone vomited. Shock shocked. Chaos spread.

Chaos rubbed its hands with glee and warmed them on the flames that had now burnt the foundling's clothes away, revealing a naked young man of unremarkable appearance.

Bella tried hard to seem disinterested, but she was fascinated. Thomas stood and pulled her to her feet. He pawed her towards the exit. His face was a mask of sceptical outrage and disgust. Their exit triggered a mass exodus. Everyone was either shocked, angry at a cheap trick, or confused except Dashiell, Jericho, and the foundling, who were actually more confused than anyone else.

'Call the fire brigade!' A stampeding voice.

'The police! The police too!' A wide-eyed, reflective voice.

As the assembled scrambled for the exit, Abby Lulealv looked around at Dashiell, whose soul was on fire. 'Passed it on then, did you?' Abby said as she made her way out. Abby just touched her temple with her fingertip to indicate madness.

'I couldn't have,' Dashiell heard herself say. Jericho heard her too.

Others who were still inside scrambled for their smartphones to photograph and video the nightmare/performance. YouTube wouldn't host this one, but someone would. There was no reality too sick to be rendered unreal by zeros and ones. There were no nerves that could not be enervated.

The scrambling for smartphones was as horrific to Mr Dailty as the horror of the boy on fire before them, and nothing was more horrific than that. Mr Dailty exited promptly.

What kind of drugs can do this to someone? some thought as they hurried out, giddy with gossip. Lingering to watch, Mr Bourncleave laughed hysterically. Then he, too, exited.

The naked foundling-inferno felt serene. He felt pure. He felt clean as if for the first time properly. Now the flamed had consumed his clothes, the flames turned on his beard and hair. As he had hoped, the unkept hairs of his beard and hair caught fire. As he had hoped, only the blade of fire was sharp enough to cut his hair. Why hadn't he thought of this before!?

Dashiell and Jericho remained until everyone else had left. As he stopped burning entirely, their adopted son closed his eyes and smiled at them. He then tensed himself in a certain way.

'No!' shouted Dashiell, but too late.

He took off vertically. His egress punched a hole in the village hall roof. They exited the hall via more conventional means: through the door, and asap.

They emerged at pace in time to see him hurtle upward into the clouds. Jericho burst into hysterical laughter. Then Dashiell did, too. They laughed so hard they cried.

Their laughter attracted the assumptions of those who saw it, and who saw the foundling disappear into the sky. Because what they saw in the sky made no sense, they assumed trickery, albeit inexplicable. Of course this had been another cheap stunt, and they had all been party to it. Of course. A stunt that followed other stunts and rumours and enigma and lots of bread. There was wryness and modern indifference; yet some looked up with the faces of gods in the making. They saw themselves vanish into the sky. They saw themselves as they wished to be: free and powerful, instead of fragile and trapped and enduring that fragility as best they could or denying it utterly.

Bella was already waiting in their BMW for Thomas to drive them away from this 'utter though unsurprising nonsense'. As they did so, Thomas saw his son Kenton looking up into the sky with an expression he couldn't fathom. Kenton seemed deadly serious. It could only be his trauma and pain, surely; but that didn't seem to be it. Thomas saw something he thought he would never see in his son: humility in the face of the inexplicable. How Thomas longed to find such a thing in the eyes of the woman he once loved; but Bella sat beside him in their car lost, as it seemed to him, in a maze of resentment and unfulfillment. He mourned the part he had played in her downfall and his own.

Mal helped Kenton to his pimped car. To Mal, Kenton seemed bedazzled by what he had just witnessed. He seemed dumbstruck. Banjaxed. Undone. Why, wondered Mal? A stunt is a stunt, however good; and this had been brilliant – even better than the stunt that had hurt Kenton so badly.

Mal looked at Dashiell and Jericho as they walked away. He saw them laughing. What did they understand that he, Mal, after all these years, didn't? Like Eric Lipton, who now pulled up in a police patrol car in police uniform and got out quickly, Mal wanted to know what they knew about their son. His apathy was punctured for the first time in his life. It felt strange.

For his part, Jericho was already wondering how much it would cost to fix the village hall and who would be liable. He went to take Dashiell's hand but stopped himself. That wasn't who they were anymore. At least for now.

Far above them, the foundling let himself drift among the clouds and the stars. Condensation jewelled his freshly seared (and thus trimmed) beard and hair.

It was the slightest of rain.

**

ha

Showing people his abilities had, and would always have, consequences. Those consequences now felt like ash in his throat. His attempt to demonstrate his uniqueness had backfired spectacularly. He had revealed himself (literally and literally) and paid the price. He felt stung and vulnerable after the incident in the village hall. It set a precedent for the future that, blinded by ego, he hadn't foreseen clearly: that showing people what he could do wouldn't show them what he could do; it would just 'reveal' him as a charlatan or freak – someone to be tolerated, or perhaps enjoyed as an entertainer.

He was acutely embarrassed by what he had done, too. This made staying in the village impossible. He had wanted to get away from the village for some while anyway. He was twenty-one years old. He had found his wings. He had spread them, albeit initially in the wrong place and in the wrong way. Now, it was time to use them. How he might do that, he couldn't yet imagine.

Instead of letting the sky take him to London then, he had caught the train as anybody else might for fear of further revealing his abilities. He was keeping his head down.

The train moved quickly on a long run between stations. Raindrops on the window outside were almost horizontal with speed. He watched them. He turned them into information. He saw Shanti in them. He chose not to turn her into information. He didn't want to. He chose not to reduce that which she was, and so quantify her. He allowed himself to glory in her gestalt.

Shanti had moved to London in the New Year. Their midnight parting had been hell. They had both cried, but she had mastered her emotions more quickly than he. What did that mean? he obsessed. Was his love greater? Was he cursed to love exceptionally, too? Wasn't everyone? He dreaded the beauty of the thought.

Her subsequent absence had burned him ever deeper. It had transformed the village into a prison. It had turned seconds into hours, and hours into years. Breaths became syllables of a merciless valediction. The air became futile.

It was hardly surprising then that here he was, three months after the village hall fiasco, following his heart to her. He had told her he was moving to the capital by text. Her reaction seemed neutral – certainly not joy at the prospect of his nearness. Had she been escaping him by moving to London, he obsessed, and so secretly dismayed by his relocation there? Perhaps.

Perhaps even she didn't know what she felt. Who does?

Fear of losing (and, strangely, seeing again) Shanti made the rain on the train windows cruel. He shut his eyes, briefly. He suddenly felt immature and neurotic. He pushed the thought of Shanti out of his mind with difficulty. He re-engaged with his surroundings.

There was a young man with elvish ears and an older woman with a leg brace sitting across from him. They didn't seem to pay attention to his astonishingly bad haircut and lunatic beard trim. (The self-immolation had done the trick; but as barbers go, fire is hardly the Michelangelo of the Follicles.) They were people alive in the world. They were on their smartphones. They were on the delayed 12.07 to Waterloo.

He was alone. Ultimately, he always would be.

Perhaps Shanti sensed this ultimate solitude. Perhaps she doubted her chances of breaking it down, and thus lost the desire to.

The sea. Plenty. In. Fish more.

His mind wondered back to what he had left behind. The council was taking legal action against Jericho and Dashiell for the damage he had done to the village hall. If someone goes mad and sets fire to him or herself indoors, someone else must be told, promptly. If the aforementioned self-immolation goes wrong and said infrastructure is damaged by (yet another) stunt, then more big words must be used in the report. Someone would have to be held accountable for everything.

Stories about the Salter boy ejecting himself like a rocket through the village hall roof varied in detail. Yes, maybe he did it – but how? Of course he didn't do it! No – not everyone present was entirely drunk. Drunk was a question of degree. When drunk? Who drunk? Who sober? What is? Who did what and how? Why? And people, and people.

The situation would rumble on for months, if not years.

So would the gossip, though gossip is notably mortal.

Dashiell hadn't said goodbye at the station earlier that rainy day. 'It's only forty-five minutes on the fast train. Or I can drive if it's a Sunday. Don't bite your nails. You're a man now anyway.'

'Am I, mum?'

After he had gone, Dashiell again drove down the broken lane on which she had found him. She knew she would never do this again, but not why. As she drove past the exact spot, she resisted the temptation to look at it. Instead, she was aware of it. She was also aware of herself as she had been when she first saw him swaddled in abandonment. She greeted her earlier self and supported that person's actions.

'What else could you have done?' she asked herself aloud. Then she did her silly roar, and that made her laugh. It seemed as if her roar was weaker now. She laughed at the pewter sky. She laughed at nervous rain. She laughed at Trappist ditches. She laughed at history waiting in cold earth. She laughed at adjectives. She laughed at the unreliable shape of her pending death. She laughed at the earlier than usual arrival of Siberian cranes. She laughed at here and there. She laughed at potassium. She laughed at needing to want. She laughed at shopping lists. She laughed at transparency. She laughed at Josiah Wedgewood. She laughed at the sap of evergreens cut with the blade of a first kiss. She laughed at what was real. She laughed at the west. She laughed at salt marshes. She laughed at treasure long lost in greedy sand. She laughed at the longest word in the dictionary. She laughed at his adaptation of the minimal surface equation to human swarm behaviour. She laughed at dents in kettles. She laughed at the lack of fuss in tractors. She laughed at the o in phlogiston. She laughed at cushions. She laughed at jelly made specially. She laughed at space being closer than Birmingham. She laughed at all the burps that had ever been burped. She laughed at the last time she had kissed Jericho properly. She laughed at the old age of new frost. She laughed at agony. She laughed at cogs. She laughed at the next ice age. She laughed at nonchalance. Her laughter ended.

As Dashiell stood at the place where she had found him lost in thought and memory, he was taking the London Underground from Waterloo to his digs. He discovered an immediate like of the Underground. He marvelled at the engineering feat. He marvelled at human ingenuity and courage. His marvelling was interrupted by the scream of the brakes as the Bakerloo line train pulled into his station. If the noise of the brakes was loud to others, to him, it was the banshee of a billion screams.

His digs were on Rockingham Street near Elephant and Castle. He shared a small, two bedroomed flat with Egor Hanneken. Egor was a thin, bespectacled student with a celestial nose and acne. Egor was keen on whisky, older women, and ice skating. Egor was studying ethical hacking at UCL. The foundling found his new lodgings difficult. It wasn't as clean as he would have liked it to be. Things that shouldn't smell smelt. He could hear Egor snoring and hacking and masturbating and Tweeting and being gradually alive, too. The foundling cursed his ears. He bought industrial ear defenders on his second day in London. That was better, but he looked daft wearing them, and he couldn't sleep while wearing them; but he barely slept anyway, so that was fine.

He had brought his guitar to London. On the evening of his third day in London, he busked on the Underground. Everything he played with impossible precision and emotional involvement was original. He played it once, and then it dissolved into isobars. The dirty air of the tube tunnels bore his perfect inventions for microseconds; then physics dismembered them. He could make five or ten pounds a busking session. Occasionally, someone would hesitate and stop to listen. Some who tarried tried to place the music by composer; others, by type, era, or genre. A few just allowed themselves to be consciously enthralled. All witnessed it with their unconscious minds as they hurried past. The music would thus dwell in their foundations for a while, and then bubble up into their awareness several days later. So it can be with culture of any sort, he thought. He thought that culture is the residue of curiosity.

Sleepless, he went out at night to exercise the horror that grew within him. It was the horror of the suffering of others. This horror had been growing inside him since he was a boy. It had grown alongside him. It had followed him wherever he went. It always found him.

There had been an indigent man in the village when he was aged five. The foundling had talked to him – against Jericho's advice. Sneering and brutish, the man had told him to 'get lost'. The man had disappeared shortly after the conversation. He must have moved on – or been moved on. His fate had worried the foundling ever since.

Now, in London, he was confronted with vagrancy on a huge scale. It made him sick with sadness.

After busking outside Leicester Square Underground Station, he walked down St Martin's Lane, then past St Martin-in-the-Fields church in Trafalgar Square. It was now almost 1 a.m. He saw was a young man sleeping rough beside the sculpture of the baby growing from the stone before the church's doors. He found the sculpture mesmeric and wonderfully troubling. The vagrant slumped beside it devastated him. He tried to walk past the vagrant because he knew there were so many homeless people, and if he did all he could for this homeless man, he should surely do that same for all vagrants everywhere. He couldn't. Even if he did, while he was doing it, more people would become homeless, so his task would be unending. It would fill all his hours to the exclusion of all else. That would not be ethically logical. It would also be impossible.

He therefore tried to walk past the homeless man. He couldn't. Hating himself for trying, he tried again; but his limbs became heavy and unruly. Then they stopped obeying him altogether. He found that he was physically incapable of walking past the homeless man. Hating himself even more, the foundling tried again by going down the steps outside the church and out of sight of him. This made no difference. He still couldn't walk past him. He spent several seconds pondering the situation. In those seconds, he thought more than a thoughtful normal person might think in a lifetime. The debate raged within him. All points of view were perfectly presented and expounded. They cancelled each other out. He therefore stopped debating and instead put all the money he had on him in the homeless man's begging cap. Hating himself even more, he walked away from the homeless man in the direction in which he had approached him. In this way he didn't walk past him.

This happened inside the y of a Tuesday. That Friday night, he found a homeless girl on the pavement near Elephant and Castle Underground station. She said her name was Libby. He made no attempt to walk past her. Libby had left home six months earlier when her alcoholic mother had stabbed her faithless husband. This was Libby's story. He didn't mind if it was true or not. He didn't look at her. He saw her. He saw her wretchedness and it stabbed him.

'Thanks, mate,' she said when he gave her two pounds fifty-five – all he had on him.

'Have you got anywhere to sleep tonight?'

'The hostel. But that's seventeen a night. So.'

'Well you don't need to do that,' he said. 'You can come and stay with us until you find somewhere. We're on Rockingham Street.'

'Fuck off will you. I ain't up for that.' Libby had heard it all before.

'No. Libby, look. It's somewhere you can rest. We'll have breakfast.'

'What, bacon and eggs and that?' Libby's eyes changed at the thought.

'Well maybe eggs. Whatever I can get.'

'You'll put it in me anyway. OK then.'

He was horrified that she thought he wanted her for sex. He was also infinitesimally aroused and entirely unsurprised at the arousal. He was what he was, and he would be as long as he was.

'I guarantee no one will lay a hand on you that you do not welcome or wish.'

'Course you do.'

Her DNA was scared of him. There was something in him. Something. But.

They went back to his digs together. The foundling gave Libby his bed, while he would lie awake on the settee in the living room. Egor Hanneken was not impressed.

'Mate. Serious. I thought she was your girl. You can't just bring homeless in here.'

'She's my girl.'

'I don't want to be rude, but she stinks,' Egor said when Libby was settled, fed, and showered, and in the foundling's bed.

'She showered. She can't.'

'Well then it's her clothes, mate. Chuck 'em – no? Whatever. Where does it stop? You can't bring them all in here. I thought you had a girl anyway. When am I going to meet her? You just can't. Shit happens, mate. Breaks my heart, too.' Egor scratched his balls as he spoke. He usually did. Perhaps the speaking made them itch; or perhaps the scratching made him speak. The foundling pondered this. Shit happens, he also pondered. It was shit in the making.

Plus sssh! Please be quiet, Tally! There's shit in the making! Shit's made of it happening! It's made it! Sssh! Finally! Yay! T! No pets step on palindromes. It was obvious.

Libby stayed for three days and three nights. She didn't go outside once. Egor learned to live with it and sleep on it. His balls just got itchier.

Libby stole nothing but glances. She ate what he gave her. She showered every few hours. She slept fifteen hours a day. She wore the new clothes he bought her and the Tibetan bracelet handmade by a woman who (he was told) had once had a shop near Seven Dials.

'Something different about you, mate. Do you find it all difficult?'

'How do you know?' he replied. His stomach tightened. A sense of being revealed.

'You're not the only one you know.'

'I wish you were right, Libby.'

She contemplated him for a moment that was like an island. Then she said, 'Look thanks, yeah? I won't forget.'

The next day, Libby left. She touched his face just once. She abandoned his eyes with hers. She didn't look back. Eternity reclaimed her.

In the weeks after she left, he missed her. Shanti sensed it when they met. It was the first time he'd seen her since moving to London. He had sent her a text telling her. Her reply had been a while coming; but it was she who suggested they meet. The suggestion made him happy.

Now, she greeted him affectionately and he responded in kind. He was glad because he was lonely. They talked. Naturally, he told her about Libby because it had happened.

'There are thousands of them,' he said. 'Millions of homeless all over the world. They suffer every second of every day. How can anyone bear this? Can you bear it, Shanti?'

'Oh, come on.' She resented the implication of indifference.

'Sorry. I didn't mean …'

'Did she pay her way?' Shanti smiled with sudden sweetness.

'I told you. She was homeless. I found her.'

'Do you just find girls?' Shanti met his eyes briefly and smiled because she was serious.

He disguised his irritation at this reaction from her, but she sensed it. She had always been an uncanny litmus of his moods. Her reaction seemed proprietary and petty to him. It also, he felt, misconstrued him. He was used to being misconstrued, but it never got any easier. He wanted Shanti to appreciate his good nature, too – she above all people.

'What should I have done?' he said.

'What most people do, I suppose.'

'Walk past? Turn a blind eye?'

'Of course not. But a blind eye can be a blessing in disguise, babe,' she winked slowly like an owl. 'Too witty to woo, hey? That's me. Look: let's not argue. OK? You just have to realise. You can't save everyone. Anyway. Here you are in the big bad city. Why did you come – you following me?'

'I couldn't stay in the village any longer,' he said. 'Not after ...'

'The village hall? Bloody hell. What did happen, anyway?'

He blushed and avoided her gaze.

'It doesn't matter. I'm just glad I wasn't there.'

'So am I,' he said.

She saw his embarrassment. She also saw his pain. She always had. She wanted to make it go away.

She touched his face. 'What is it? What is it really?'

He felt uncomfortable at being probed, as Libby had made him uneasy. He avoided Shanti's eyes. He smiled his usual smile. It was as intoxicating as ever. She wished it weren't.

'I don't know,' was all he could find to say.

'That's OK.' The world left her eyes, briefly. Love replaced it.

'How can you love me after what I did to Kent? How is he anyway? He doesn't reply to my messages and doesn't answer his phone.'

'He won't speak to me, either; so it's not just you. I think mum's got him. You know?'

He knew. Bella's care had become an act of imprisonment. Of course it had.

She suddenly fussed with his clothes. 'What you wearing anyway?' she ribbed him gently.

'I can't find a lie to fit.'

'Kenton's a moron. You're both morons, and Mac! A stunt like that! And the village hall!?'

Her eyes were like the sky after rain over blunt land. The way she looked at him said to him: What are you? I fear you, my love. I fear loving you. I love fearing you. I don't understand. Am I a fool? No. I am love's fool. I am a person, so I can believe or doubt anything.

'How did you do it?' she said flatly.

The flatness made him uneasy again. The prairie of it.

'Hurt Kenton? I don't know.' Unfeasible honesty.

'How can you not know?' Exasperation.

'Easily. Not knowing is easy. Knowing is harder still.' Fascination.

She wanted him to tell her everything, if there was anything to tell. Why play games?

Moments.

Unanswered questions vied within her. She wanted to ask him:

- Who did the sculptures in the quarry?
- How did you bake all that bread?
- How did you and Kenton arrange the stunt in the pub?
- What had happened to Mr Bourncleave to make him say those things?
- Is Dashiell Salter your real mother?
- Why can't you lie?

He wanted to reply:

- I did
- I can move quite quickly and do several things at once
- We didn't. I just pushed him. I can do that
- Mr Bourncleave saw my sadness
- Define real and define mother and define definitely (with a grin)
- This sentence is a lie (with a grin)

    Instead of this conversation, they talked about nothing much. This made him unhappy. As they talked, she thought that yes, she wanted to love someone who was different – unique, even; but him? A trickster? An outsider? A freak? And Tally? Really?
'Tell me what you are.'
'I am love's harmonic.' He meant it was over.
'I don't understand.' She meant she understood.
They went outside and flagged a cab down. The driver drove them south on Walworth Road then east on Peckham Road. Then the driver chose Consort Road in defiance of his satnav past Sternhall Lane and Nigel Road and Scylla Road 'though I do love thee, Charybdis,' with his gorgeous damn him addictive bloody smile and her loving the slow-motion fragility in his midnight milk eyes and Kinsale Road on the right going south and those eyes closing, closing, and closing. He rested his head on her shoulder. He seemed like a child to her at sudden peace.
    What was she doing? she thought. Why were they doing this? Because their love was over, despite or because of him following her to London, and this was to be their farewell? The thought hurt. Their make- believe childhood love. Had it come to this? A valedictorian intercourse? A final, sealed adieu? Did she still love him anyway? Because by habit? Because insecure? Because love is the kindest and cruellest of all use?

Then London opened its oxbow eyes, and it had night vision, and she was paying the driver, and then, minutes later, his reality of her in her flat in her bedroom in her bed in her just showered privacy.

Now he was the honoured lover, cursed to kiss and caress and enter the night. He was hard inside her. He was Anthracite and Amphibolite and Blueschist and Cataclasite and Eclogite and Gneiss and Gossan and Granulite and Greenschist and Greenstone and Hornfels and Marble and Migmatite and Mylonite and Metapelite and Phyllite and Metapsammite and Pseudotachylite and Quartzite and Schist and Serpentinite and Skarn and Slate and Suevite and Talc carbonate and Soapstone and Whiteschist inside her. And it hurt, oh yes. It hurt; but she was soft as an idea, so she was the most resilient of all things.

When he looked into her eyes as he moved with her, she saw what she had glimpsed in him that evening in the quarry. Then, too, he had been unable to reach orgasm. She had seen then what she saw now: that he was forever beyond her touch. Was it a disease of some sort? It made her weep for him. He knew her reason for her tears, but they didn't speak of it. Nothing spoke of them.

They rested together for a while. They left goodbyes for others. Then he was gone in a way that made her feel he had never been there, and her dream of him was replaced by the thing of life.

*

Six weeks after he moved to London, he went to Speakers' Corner in Hyde Park. He was determined to become well known for his speeches. He would provide insight. He would add his name to the list of renowned people who had spoken there that included Karl Marx, Vladimir Lenin, George Orwell, C. L. R. James, Walter Rodney, Ben Tillett, Marcus Garvey, Kwame Nkrumah, William Morris, Vincent McNabb, and Bonar Thompson. He agreed with a few of them. He admired them all.

He arrived at about 9 am on a Sunday. He was surprised to find himself nervous. He realised that the village hall incident had left him self-conscious, and fearful of exposing his true self in public. The audacious boy who had once fancied himself a stand-up comedian had gone. He had been replaced by a young man who was scared of making a fool of himself. He resolved to speak anyway.

'So why ...' he began, but his brand-new nerves got the better of him.

He suppressed his fear and went on: 'I mean why doesn't anyone question ... why is it OK for us to be bombarded by bad news all the time? How does that help any of us lead better lives? And ... yes and advertising. Buy this. Buy that. How is it OK for people to try to sell us things everywhere all the time? To manipulate us. They even come into our homes and do it.'

No one was listening. He was being completely ignored. It was galling. It was actually irritating. He felt that he had worthwhile things to say, so why was no one listening?

Irritation overcame his fear. Having no box to stand on like some other speakers, he raised himself by about 20 centimetres. This indeed attracted the attention of a couple of passers-by, but it was the wrong sort of attention: these people were wondering how he performed the illusion. He was in the wrong place; surely, he should be in Covent Garden or on the South Bank? He remained aloft anyway. He noticed a mature, cosmopolitan man look at him as he walked his dog nearby.

'It seems to me,' he continued 'that this creates a state of dissatisfaction ... the temptation ... to buy things that perhaps we don't need, and which are what – environmental disasters? Exploitation? And so those who can't really afford these things ... further into debt, and then it's another recession, and the poor suffer again.'

'That's your opinion, mate,' said a man in a modified boiler suit.

'Why would I have opinions?' asked the foundling, confused.

'Funny. You should do stand-up. Oh, you are,' said boiler suit.

The mature man with the dog stopped walking and listened.

'I mean: to describe is to know, but description degrades. Yet you tell me: the things in life that have been worth experiencing. They can't be described, can they?' he said.

The boiler suit rolled his eyes. He got a text. Other people drifted away. Those that remained seemed more interested in his ability to levitate. Someone photographed him on their smartphone. This worried him, but it was too late: he was pixels now, like everyone else was soon to become.

Unsure what to do, he remained slightly aloft and forged on: 'And people come into our homes ... they come into our lives to sell us things on television and online and on our phones every day, everywhere. They come into our homes. Homes are supposed to be sacred ... The difference between a home and house. Like a country and a state.'

He was aware of the mature man with the dog listening to him. He could also see boiler suit talking about him on his mobile phone and laughing. It made him feel stupid. It made him angry.

He realised this had been a mistake. He was here though, doing this, so he went on for a while longer: 'But if we let technology addle us anymore ... Though it is our gateway to the stars, our eventual home ... The bad news ... The news ... a thing that makes us think people are all bad, or the world is all going wrong and ... That doesn't help us do anything about it. We either become desensitised or suffer. Well I don't know about you, but I know what's worse. That we become desensitised ... or that we suffer with others. With anything that can suffer. I can't bear it. How can you? What I mean is ... And surely to bring children into lives of misery is child abuse. Or to limit their minds and confuse them before they can defend themselves. Call me young and idealistic ...'

He heard someone say, 'Please someone call him.' Someone laughed. Someone else yawned. A couple started to walk away, but turned back when their child approached him to try to work out what was keeping him elevated. He levitated then lowered himself rhythmically, which boggled the child and made people smile. The child made him feel slightly calmer. He felt a bit less foolish.

The mature man with the dog did not smile or laugh. His gaze was unwavering. The man was in front of the foundling now, who suddenly felt the need to lower himself. The man made him feel embarrassed. He therefore stood normally on the ground, much to the child's disappointment.

'And what about the jury system?' he went on uncertainly. 'Twelve non-specialists who are open to the persuasion of someone trained to persuade ... Then there's the quality of mercy, no? In the face of wrong, it seems to me that forgiveness is prior to a first reflex. And democracy. How can we be sure what we're voting for, and who? Well not to vote is unthinkable, but to vote is to buy a lie – and at what price? Ultimately which do you prefer: certainty or knowledge? I'm sorry ...'

His nerves got the better of him. He suddenly realised that this had been a mistake. Talking publicly made him feel like even more of a freak – an outsider, as he had always been in the village. By now, the mature man with the dog was the only person nearby anyway. The man approached the foundling as he began to walk away.

'Benen Clay.' Benen held out his hand. The foundling shook it. He tried to be gentle, but Benen still smarted from his grip strength.

'Sorry.'

'That's OK.' Benen introduced his dog: a black Labrador that was trying to wear the air out by panting. 'And this scallywag is Pepper.'

'Nice to meet you, Pepper,' he said, making a fuss of the dog.

'Your first time?' said Benen in reference to Speakers' Corner.

'I'm rubbish. It's so vain to think that what you say is worth listening to anyway.'

'Such humility. It's refreshing. But you just need practice. We all do.'

'I don't know what I was thinking.'

'With all respect: it was OK – better than I could do. I thought some of the stuff you said – some of those things need to be talked about and aren't. Well not enough, anyway.'

'My first and last time being preachy I think!'

'Don't be discouraged. If you don't mind me saying. Maybe just pick a subject and stick with it rather than jumping from one issue to another. I hope you won't think me rude,' said Benen.

'Not at all. Anyway …'

There was a moment. He suddenly felt uncomfortable. He smiled and walked on towards the Serpentine, and the commas of swans. Taking the hint, Benen encouraged Pepper to walk away with him discreetly; but Pepper followed the foundling, so Benen was obliged to follow him too.

'He seems to like you,' said Benen in reference to Pepper.

'Happiness has a tail.'

'I agree,' said Benen.

Benen felt unexpected kinship, then sadness, and then a most unexpected fear of this stranger. Why? It was disconcerting and fascinating. They walked for a while. The silence was fine at first, but then it became awkward again.

'Sorry. I'm intruding.' Benen slowed, then stopped walking.

'It's OK.'

Again, Pepper strained at his lead to stay with the foundling, who stopped walking too, and made a fuss of the dog again.

'Oh to be a dog, eh? Fed, loved and watered, and no idea you're going to die.'

'Oh to be a dog,' he replied as he played with Pepper.

'You're not alone,' said Benen suddenly.

'What do you want?' said the foundling sharply.

'Why do you assume I want anything?' said Benen.

'I don't. I shave with Ockham's razor.'

'I can see that.' Benen smiled apropos his unruly beard and hair. He then met the foundling's eyes and said, 'All that matters are silence and stillness. We both know that. Call me if you want a chat. No bull. No agendas. Just someone in the echo. Just some honest heckle.'

The poetry of his words gave the foundling pause. Benen gave him a business card.

'Tell me how you did it sometime, yes? The magic thing.'

'I can't.'

'Of course not. Well ... goodbye,' said Benen.

He shook Benen's hand again, and then headed off toward the Serpentine. Pepper tried to follow him, but Benen prevented him.

'Listen,' called out Benen. 'I'm having a bash at mine on the twelfth. It's my birthday. You're welcome to come – if you want to. Some people I'd like you to meet.'

It was suddenly obvious to the foundling that a party was exactly what he needed.

'Sure. Thanks. What's your address?'

'Message me and I'll ping it back to you. From seven onwards.'

'OK. Thanks again.'

Benen flashed him a smile. The smile felt welcome to the foundling. It made him realise how lonely he would feel if he let himself. It was lonely indeed. How could it be otherwise?

*

Dashiell phoned him in the a of a Saturday.
    'Dad's moving abroad.'
    'Who?'
    'He loves you. Come on.'
    'Without saying goodbye,' he said.
    There was a long pause. He could hear her breathing on the phone, and the sound filled him with love's shadow. Her breathing spoke to him. It spoke of regret, and of unspeakable grief. It dealt with reputations, and what it meant to work, and how food was bought, and how flat a ceiling seemed. Her breathing considered Tally's echo, and the village still murmuring. It dealt with keeping going, and searching for laughter, and finding it without warning, and regret, and tea cups stained with memory, and silence drying on those cups on the draining rack beside a patient sink, and late afternoon light as seasons change, and what hands are for, and a new hairstyle, and places once visited (that are still there), and car park permits, and the lust for distance, and tannin, and Boogie Street, and El Capitan, and the Wooden O, and the sound of gravel trodden, and how thunder is, and telling the clocks to Spring Forward and Fall Back, and telling the planets that Mum's Easy Map Just Shows U North, and the tendencies of neighbours, and a smile waking, and avoirdupois or troy, and a bull's come-get-me-girls dewlap, and May in Provence, and the place where knowledge runs out, and running after it, and the love of being somewhere, and the sharp desire to be elsewhere, and sleep at long last, and waking in gladness, and flying, and the weight of an albatross, a siege of bitterns, a scold of jays, tidings of magpies, carols of robins, a trimming of finches, a pitying of doves, a stare of owls, a fleet of mud hens, a plump of waterfowl, a mutation of thrushes, a lease of hawks, a bouquet of pheasants, a trembling of finches, a desert of lapwings, a kit of pigeons, a whiteness of swans, a coil of widgeon, a walk of snipe, a prattle of parrots, and the neutrality of oatmeal.

'I'm sure he'll call you to let you know himself, but I thought I'd tell you. I think in a month or so. He'll text you or call, I'm sure,' she said.

'I'll just come, mum. Hang on.'

'But ...' Dashiell began. Before she has put her phone away and put the kettle on and wiped the surface next to the cooker and dried her hands he was there in person. She couldn't hide her joy at seeing him. It had only been a couple of weeks, but now, here he was in front of her.

'Where's he going?'

'Do you want tea?' Dashiell put the kettle on anyway. 'I think he met someone. She's based somewhere. In Dubai maybe. So he's going back to live with her there I think. He didn't tell me much more than that.'

'Has he hurt you, mum?'

'Not in a way you should mind, as neither should I.'

The kettle began to whizz and flick as the water animated in its silly belly. He watched and listened to it intently.

'This is just the way of it, and as you know, and anyway ...' Dashiell let the words drift like things. She leant subtly against the edge of the kitchen surface beneath the kettle as the water went mad. 'Don't hold it against him. Don't do anything. I want dad to be happy.'

'Does he want *you* to be happy?' was all he could say.

'You know he does. And he loves you much.'

The water began to scream.

'What if he had found me, not you.'

She met his gaze. Doing so had always been difficult. It had grown harder as his youth became ever more laminated by adulthood, which is a thing that fills the cup of the present ever fuller with the liquid of the past. Now, it was almost impossible, even for her.

'Darling man. It would have been exactly as it was.' Her words seemed to find their expression in her body. It shifted and curved. Her jeans and T-shirt mapped her qualia with buckles and rifts and indifference Made in Wherever.

He ignored the kitchen table at which Tally had once roared with laughter at a new and cruder spoonerism or a fart. Dashiell had brought the table with her when she had moved. Now here it was. The wooden, made thing.

'Has Bella Young contacted you?' he said. His words seemed like the land as things change. Then there was the sky.

'No. But I saw her last week and she pretended to ignore me.'

'Well I destroyed her son,' he said as one who comes upon the end of such land. 'I'll call her again. But whenever I do its always voicemail. I'll go over there again now.'

'Again?'

'Yes. I went over there last week to see how Kenton is, but she slammed the door in my face again. I have to help him, mum. Look at me.'

She saw now for the first time that he felt cursed by his abilities. It shocked and saddened her. She had never thought he would feel that.

'Don't blame yourself. Things happen, darling ...'

'Do they?'

So she just hugged him. The kettle went mad now it got the idea. Mother and son and man and woman and time sad because of love bounded by once guaranteed kitchen surfaces. She could see and feel his torment with every cell. 'You couldn't help it,' was all she could say.

A million-banshee water howl nice safe kitchen sound.

'And there's no change in his condition?'

'As far as I know. Bella is keeping things private, but the usual tongues have wagged. You know how it is around here.'

'And I did that. Shame on me.'

'No you didn't. Things don't happen – remember?' She went to hug him again, but he didn't respond. 'Anyway, dad said he'd probably pop back quite soon. He's still got some stuff to pick up. Most went to charity or the recycling place. Oh. And the village hall? The council doesn't buy the accidental thing. There were a lot of witnesses, so the thing about the liability. I don't know.'

He let her words evaporate as the kettle came to orgasm.

'Come on.' She smiled up at him, face to face. Her face this close took him. Love was the dome of a magma chamber. He kissed her forehead and her cheeks deliberately and slowly. They were softer than he remembered them. Then he was embarrassed. The water in the kettle covered for him: it boiled until the kettle died. She made them tea.

'Don't say he isn't your dad. He wanted to be.'

'I know.' He meant I will protect and love you as long as I can.

She knew what he meant. So he smiled back at her. They wondered where water ended and tea began, and they chased happiness along the ways.

*

Moving to London had felt right and wrong immediately. He had been inspired by the city's creativity, maturity, eclecticism, potential, and unpredictability; but he was ruined by the proximity of so much privation and vulnerability. Within six months he knew it would be impossible for him to live there.

A party seemed like a good way to say goodbye.

Benen's house was on the south side of Moscow Road in Bayswater. As he arrived, Saint Sophia Church bell pronounced nine hours that seemed to him like iron eggs.

Someone who lisped that his name was Marven let him in and greeted him notionally. Then Marven nursed his drink and nibbles into a crowded, noisy reception room full of time.

There were music and voices and people and possibility everywhere. Fractions of the world adorned the house: peregrine things and the collected memes of a well-travelled person. The foundling stopped to look at each one and be amazed, as he was amazed by everything all the time.

Benen emerged from the reception room, which opened out onto a patio and small garden beyond. Benen was slightly influenced. He greeted him with a smile that had slipped its leash.

'My boy! Welcome, welcome and welcome and so glad ...' A middle aged and sexually beautiful woman Benen introduced as Missy walked past with another, younger woman whose hand she touched, and a young man who might have been Missy's son.

Benen gave him half a hug. It felt fashionable but genuine.

'It's good to see you. Where's Pepper?' the foundling asked.

'He's somewhere flirting as usual. He'll be pleased to see you. Look. There are people ... I wanted you to ... Listen. Meet Tymon. Have a drink!' Benen went on, but his attention was then taken by another guest who arrived right after the foundling.

As if on cue, Pepper bounded out of the living room and into the hallway. The dog headed straight for the foundling. They greeted each other like new old friends. Pepper remained with him for several minutes, then went away on instinct's caprice and found Benen.

The foundling tried to seem normal and mingle with other guests. He struck up the odd conversation, but phatic talk made no sense to him, so these conversations strayed little further than an initial greeting and a 'so what do you do?' This he dreaded. He didn't really do anything. This was because he could do anything.

Tymon said he was a reality TV producer. He was here with his ironically Oxfam dressed partner Lukas, who asked the foundling politely why he was only drinking water. He told Lukas that he and alcohol were about as useful a combination as stupidity and technology.

'You too, huh? On the wagon,' said Tymon through a mouthful of whatever it was. The conversation fizzled out.

Tymon and Lukas went off and experienced time. The foundling looked for Pepper. He found him being made a fuss of by other guests.

He had thought Benen had invited him so they could spend time together, but Benen showed little apparent interest in him. This was perhaps because Benen was drunk, but the foundling felt slightly miffed anyway. He observed his own immaturity with tolerant interest.

He browsed Benen's books. One wall of the living room was floor to ceiling books. A female voice behind him said, 'You can tell everything you need to know about someone by their bookshelf.' He turned. He saw an early middle aged redhead with a badly concealed scar running from her left ear to her mid neck. 'Alice,' she said, and met his eyes. Meeting his eyes made her frown, and her eye pupils dilate. Alice wore a large adornment clasped in silver filigree around her neck on a platinum chain.

Alice examined his hand as she shook it formally.

'A sculptor's hands,' Alice said. 'Drink?'

'I'm fine thanks.'

'So how do you know Benen?' Alice talked to him but scanned the room for better opportunities.

'I met him at Speakers' Corner.'

'Who? Oh – Ben. You were speaking.'

'I was rambling.'

'Rambling rose. Feeling thorny?' She looked at him dead as she said that. He was intrigued by her jaded flirtation. He became aroused.

'You look like someone who's seen the light. Are you blind yet? Anyway. You're not getting your hands on my baby doll.' She touched the jewel hanging around her neck as she said it. 'Remember the Hatton Garden heist?' She touched her nose as if imparting a secret.

Seeing someone she 'knew', Alice soon melted away from him. Her degage scarred and enthralled him. Then, bang on cue, Pepper found him. They were reunited for several more mutually delighted minutes. The foundling soon forgot about Alice.

An hour later, the party was waning. The music had been changed from generic bass to a form of reiterated Balinese Gamelan, which he liked. Leavers had left, leaving behind a coterie of Benen's apparently closer friends. They formed a small keen smiling scrum around Benen. To the foundling, they seemed easily cosmopolitan. He sought a quiet seat from which to watch them. He could hear everything in the house and in the neighbourhood beyond. It was difficult, but he had mastered the art of filtering sound. He had to, to safeguard himself. He now focussed on snippets of conversation. He joined in with some, but as he did so he felt the earth turn, expressing the diminishing rotational energy awarded to it when the planet formed. He felt he heard an ice chasm split open on Europa. He wished he could swim in the ocean beneath it. He thought he felt magma vomit with such force on Io that some broke free of gravity's idea. He loved Titan for its name.

Alice brought him back to the here and now. In conversation with a man dressed in a three-piece tweed suit, Alice kept glancing over at him. He smiled politely at her and the tweed man. The tweed man couldn't take his eyes off the jewel between her breasts. 'Through the Looking Glass,' the foundling thought. Then Alice looked away abruptly.

Benen found him moments later. A self-assured and drunk woman tangled with his arm. He noticed a tattoo on Benen's forearm he hadn't seen before.

'But you aren't having fun, my boy. This is Savannah. Be warned!' Savannah kissed his hirsute cheeks. She penetrated his eyes in a way the foundling had never experienced. Hers was an intellect he yearned to explore. Instead, he said, 'I am fun. Want to see some?'

'Ah, the thing.' Benen's speech was blurred by alcohol, but something in him remained sharp as a razor after the strop. By 'the thing', Benen meant the levitating at Speaker's Corner thing. 'This is a wise young man,' Benen said of him. Benen kissed Savannah as he said it. Was

Savannah Benen's daughter? He evicted the thought immediately.

'Well I'm not wise enough to stay stupid, alas; or stupid enough to stay wise.'

'See?' Benen pointed at him and enjoyed the room.

'Why did you invite me?' said the sudden foundling. His smile fled like the wind on a hill. He feared the word 'sideshow'.

'Why what?' Benen cupped a hand to his ear and shrugged about the music. 'So you could ... in case you might meet people ... someone. It's not what you know, you know. One day you'll thank me. When you're someone. Seriously: you know you've made it when someone is doing an impression of you on a stage and people are laughing. Until then!'

Benen laughed and toasted the foundling's success and got drunker.

Alice came downstairs with the tweed man, who was disguising a deep sense of rejection with pin sharp nonchalance. Alice ignored him and went to pour two drinks in a way meant to mean something. Alice approached the foundling with a glass of amber liquid in each hand.

'Drink,' she said, and passed him one of the glasses.

'I don't. I mean if I do ...'

'Drink,' Alice said. She downed her drink as if to show him how.

Yes. It would deaden the pain. Perhaps it would help him forget about Kenton. Yes. Perhaps it would stall the need to do something about suffering in the world and keep on doing something until he couldn't do it anymore. He downed his drink in one, too. It became magma in his midst.

'Et viva tequila,' Alice grinned with the opposite of humour. She seemed to him like someone who saw others as opportunities. He felt ready to be exploited by her.

She wiggled her adornment – the jewel hung around her neck – at him in a certain way. Then she was suddenly gone.

The magma became a summons. The tequila boomed within him like a liquid pulse. The room started to jazz. 'I should probably go,' he said. He stood, aware of the tequila's promising banjax.

'Not a bit of it, said Benen, suddenly beside him. 'Come on. Where's Dressler?' Benen looked around for someone he wanted the foundling to meet. The foundling was already moving, however. He thought he was needed. People were starving and being tortured and murdered and raped all over the world. He couldn't bear any of it. He couldn't imagine how anyone else could bear it either.

Suddenly, suddenly, suddenly he had to go. The world cavorted faster inside him outside him. The tequila owned him. 'Benen. Help me.' Hearing him say that turned Benen's eyes to jet. Sobriety threatened. This – this need – is what he had sensed at Speakers' Corner.

'What's going on?' asked Benen. Benen put a hand through the party and onto his confused shoulder. It lingered slightly. It seemed like the memory of fathers. It seemed like a question. It seemed like a self-made man lost in an au fait blizzard.

'Could you please ask everyone to go into the garden?'

Benen agreed with a bang-on meld of witty asides and worldly pantomime. He ushered everyone, chattering, bored, what-next!?, whyever not?, out into the ornamental garden. The garden was a kempt plot with a small fountain at its centre. It was a paean to second hand Zen.

Once outside, the foundling asked everyone – there were eighteen people left at the party now – to form a semi-circle around him. He then stood in front of the fountain with its silver whispers. Benen stood with Savannah near the centre of the semi-circle. Alice slewed with the tweed man to Benen's sudden left and to the foundling's right.

'Alice. If I might.' He pointed to the jewel around Alice's neck. She pulled a face. She overdid it. Others overdid it with her. Only Benen was serious, and Benen wasn't sure why.

'Well – just this once. And don't run off to sodding Bolivia or else!' Alice blurred.

He assured her that he wouldn't. She unclasped and passed the jewel adornment to him. 'I'm naked!' Alice hammed, deep in his eyes. Voices said things like 'there goes Lloyds,' and the like. The foundling assured Alice it wouldn't take long.

'Who is this matelot anyway?' Alice aimed at Benen.

Her laughter and smiles were tocsins. The foundling heeded them without care.

The jewel on his lower palm, he held his hands out in front of him, palms parallel. He then brought his palms together with so much power that the jewel shattered into fine dust instantly. The sound of his hands clapping was deafening, but not as deafening as the sonic boom that occurred as he took off, leaving exquisite vortices in the dust – all that was left of Alice's faux vanity.

Pepper started barking.

Alice froze. Others reacted as people for whom nothing is real react to things that seem to be real. Someone said something about 'getting the app' to Benen. Someone else made firework noises. The tweed man seemed genuinely impressed until he caught Alice's glance. A few people applauded in Benen's direction and laughed their thanks for a wonderful climax to the evening. Marven looked up into the night sky and said something about holograms to Missy, who was more interested in her young female companion. Savannah downed her bourbon with one magisterial glug.

Beside her, Benen's face turned to brief stone. He could only marvel at the beauty of what seemed like diamond dust that wove and roiled in air riven by the impossible. He looked up. The foundling was now the sky's memory. What seemed like diamond dust mingled with the stars until there was no difference. There was only beauty.

Pepper still barked, but his attention was now waning.

Nearby, Alice unfroze: 'What the fuck? That was my fucking grandmother's! Benen, you wanker. Stop messing around. I need that back ASA fucking P. Benen?! Where is it? This isn't funny!' Alice's outrage continued despite the tweed man's attempts to mollify her, which just annoyed her even more. Alice kept yelling at Benen, but Benen's eyes were dark as the eyes of someone who has just seen something they can't understand or explain.

Tymon approached him. 'That was fair enough, Ben. You old dog! Come on. How? But this is better than Livewire! How'd you do the boom thing? OK. I don't care. Can we get him on the show? Would he do it? I can get him an audition on Tuesday. Ben?'

Benen suddenly knew he had to try to protect this strange young man, whoever he was and however he had just done what he had done. In this, Benen already knew he would fail.

*

As he grew, something grew inside him. He came to call this thing The Thing. It became ever harder to bear as he matured. He could bear the world on his back, but The Thing crushed him as if he were a paper baby. The Thing was the suffering of all things that can suffer. It broke his heart.

The Thing told him that he was duty bound to relieve suffering and not to cause it. As he had grown, the Thing had seemed to changed colour. When he was a boy it had been a neutral hue. In his teens, it became a flavour of jagged and smooth auburn that he could hear. Eventually – now – it became unspeakably red, and the redness seethed.

Sometimes envious of them, he had wondered how others bore the Thing with such ease. Now he knew. They didn't. They just got on with their lives. Who could blame them? They couldn't live in constant awareness of suffering.

They had to survive. They had their own problems. It was different for him. Everyone's problems were his. His empathy was as complete as his compassion. His compassion extended to all things that could suffer. He knew this was absurd. Sometimes he laughed helplessly at this absurdity, and his helplessness. He laughed when he realised that only a god would be too compassionate to exist.

The Thing, however, saw people's indifference to the suffering of others as punishable cruelty. He told the Thing it was wrong. He told the Thing to forgive them. He couldn't make the Thing go away. He knew the Thing would destroy him. He knew that when he had been destroyed, he couldn't act upon his moral imperative. He therefore couldn't let the Thing destroy him. The only way to do that would be to do nothing. Nothing was the one thing he could never do, however.

The future was melting.

Wildfires now raged annually. Beggar tides had become frequent kings. Hurricanes had replaced breezes. There were tropical blizzards. The tree of life was being pruned by a myopic, genius primate drunk on ancient genes and new psychology.

He had to act. How though?

When younger, he had avoided the news because he couldn't bear it. He could no longer avoid it. The Thing now made him browse news websites so he could find situations that might benefit from his intervention. What he saw and read mutilated him. It eviscerated him. It crowned him with slothful fire. He now acted upon this coronation.

The Thing took him from Benen's party to the place from which a news report (he had seen online that day) had been broadcast by a now dead journalist. The place had been a small town in what had once been called the Cradle of Civilisation. The dead journalist's blood still darkened the abandoned concrete on which she had fallen. Her body had been removed. There was still sporadic gunfire coming from the surrounding buildings. These buildings were now devoid of habitation's flesh. They were now the bones of war's ego.

A school was being used by some people that other people had called 'terrorists' as cover. Cornered and desperate, they were using the schoolchildren as human shields. Local combatants and western Special Forces had surrounded the school but were reluctant to attack for obvious reasons. This was the situation the dead journalist had been reporting. Her family in London were now experts at grief.

At first, he tried to reason with the terrorists. He spoke their language as they did. His long beard and hair made them think he was one of them; but his eyes drew their suspicion, and thus fearful aggression.

He tried to dissuade them of their intent. He suggested to them that they had not been born thus. They scorned him. They drew the schoolchildren's fear closer to them. They wore it. They bathed in it. He told them to let the children go. They shot at him. Their bullets did nothing but birth his rage. Rage became a fist within him. He suppressed it immediately. That way lay disaster. No one can count on a fist.

He levitated in their presence because he hoped this might stay their hands. They were initially amazed, but soon identified his levitation as a trick. They felt patronised, and so started shooting at him again. Their bullets stopped like sentences before him. This initially amazed them. They soon realised that they were being fooled again, and so they attacked him again, sure of his opposing agenda. Their bullets still couldn't wound him, but their hatred cut him to the quick. He begged them not to hurt the children. They ignored his pleas with their borrowed certainties. He wept to see such cruelty and suffering. Some laughed at his tears. Some shared them, weary with certainty. Again rage unfurled within him. Again he furled it; but the rage was slow to return to its cage.

Determined to affect the western combatants and their allies, too, he left the terrorists. Aloft, he went to their enemies the other side of what had been a wall. The Western military personnel met him with protocols and suspicions. His appearance and attempts at placation focussed their guns on him. What was he doing? Why this showtime magic, here and now? This was a war zone. Their leader was a female Belgian army captain here under the direction of the United Nations. She warned him to 'evacuate the area with immediate effect'.

There were sudden voices. Shouts in languages at war. The terrorists were now threatening to begin the slaughter of innocence. Without warning, the slaughter was prepared.

He therefore went back to the terrorists instantly. He reduced their weapons to compounds. He tried to pacify them without hurting them, but it was impossible. He saved all the children but one: a boy was shot dead. The boy's death gave birth to something in him. Something new. Justice was tempted to become judgement and judgement, judgemental. He almost lost control. He fought with and barely managed to leash his rage. He merely scattered the boy's murderers like dust.

The terrorists tried to flee. He begged the Belgian army captain to spare them, but too late. They were all shot dead before he could disarm the Western forces and nullify their weapons, too.

He was vaguely aware of them providing their command chain with a sit rep as he stood over the dead child. Grief drove him to his knees. He wept the universe. He shattered buildings with his sadness, and the perfect beast roared like tomorrow for the death of yesterday.

He saw the bodies of the terrorists all about him. He thought of all they could have been, but for hungry dogma. Grief became love's dark rose within him. The rose bloomed into midnight. Its scent was fatal. Its thorns cut him. He would never heal.

He took the dead child in his arms. He would never put him down.

*

- Wow. Neighbour sure loves a good #party. Love ya Ben!
- Sonic what in Queensway midnight!? Pls #MOD speak Enlgish!
- WTF!? Windows broken last night by something! Another #alien invasion? Pleeeese
- There are fireworks and there are fireworks, #London! Someone own up now
- Reality is either #real or it isn't, so it's real. The #beard abides!
- #terrorism at large in little Moscow rd? Help? Are we laughing? Die anthr day pls

*

THIRD PERSON SINGULARITY (AKA: Why Beards Are Still Cool) [Reuters]

Eyewitness statements confirmed what social media have suggested – even if professional UK and allied soldiers are forbidden to tweet about their experiences in so called official theatres of combat. But surely this is war fatigue? Or is it propaganda? Smoke and mirrors? Fun? Who knows?

The 'facts': an unknown and unsolicited 'element' became involved in the As Sa'an school siege in which CNN mid-east chief correspondent Corolla Kahlo was killed in March. Eye witness and unnamed sources 'confirm what obviously war weary (or just flip) blogs and various hashtags claim: that an unauthorised male came between UN and partner combatants and so-called terrorists outside the school – or what was left of it.

Reports state that the so called 'bearded man' attempted first to engage both sides in flashpoint diplomacy. Failing to dissuade combatants from further engagement, he disarmed the terrorists and their enemies 'with comic speed' (sic) – whatever that means. It's alleged that the unauthorised element may have saved the lives of over a hundred school children that the terrorists were using as human shields. One (yet unnamed) child was killed in the exchange, however.

The unauthorised element was apparently able to render the ordnance of both Western combatants and their enemies otiose before 'buggering off' (more sic). How he buggered off remains a mystery. Sources claim he levitated himself without the obvious use of tech, and then just went 'aerial exfill' – military parlance for a sky evacuation from a combat zone.

Not to speculate, but in the hours that followed, various sources claim another (?) 'bearded man' became involved in a situation in Sierra Leone, in which a militia was engaged with government forces. Again, this 'bearded man' allegedly disarmed both sides involved in this theatre of engagement – though all parties involved deny such a theatre exists.

Other reports are coming in of similar events from around the world on the same date, and subsequently. Ivory poachers were found tied up and 'in a state of utter confusion' in Kenya just two days ago. In Indonesia, a man with ' long hair and beard' was seen helping survivors of the recent flash-flood there with quote unlikely mobility and force unquote.

A whaling ship was found in Reykjavík town square last Tuesday. Interviewed, the crew has been, shall we say, backward in coming forward with an explanation. Perhaps they are obliged not to rumble the prankster. Or maybe they are disinclined to seem insane. But watch them being interviewed and they seem strangely unsettled, as people do when they have encountered something they can't explain, and which contradicts the worldview that makes life possible.

So what's going on? The likely answer is: nothing. Fine.

But whoever or whatever is perpetrating this (and how and why), just what are we to make of all this popping of our subjective reality bubbles? What are we, the citizens of the virtual, to make of anything?

We must factor in the rise of the pixel. We must consider zeros and ones. Is this just a new level of wish projection in a world in which nothing is real – an always-on anywhere world increasingly polarised by tribalism those 'in charge' wish to frame in Manichaean terms in order to spoon feed voters? A world in which the real and the unreal have become so interchangeable that they have fused into a numb, materialist singularity?

Of course this is all likely a hoax. Or it may all just be yet another portrait of the media as propaganda. It could be a 'truther' offshoot. Or hot air in search of the right political balloon. Or an individual who has become so lost in the world of Marvel and DC comics that he or she has come to live the fantasy, and may soon die living it. Perhaps you lot are a figment of my imagination, too. So here's to solipsism. Yours, that is...

Seriously: is this all about the perennial necessity of individual and/or collective action – even if it is said hoax? Is this need a product of a world in which fanatics of any hue have shown themselves unworthy of power – even if it 'just' digital? Because our future, if we have one, cannot be fundamentalist in thought, action, or intention. The destination of the past is now, and as we all know, now is an illusion. And that illusion currently seems a rather frightening one.

Is this (if there is a 'this') a complaint against an over-regulated, safety-obsessed world that ever more restricts free thinking? Is it 'just' mad hatter, faux heroism, and online tribal rubbernecking? Whatever it is, and how, and why, and who, more than 100 children in the tragic human dust of what was once the cradle of civilisation and those who love them will always be perfectly grateful. As will, no doubt, a number of elephant calves, who still have tusker parents, thanks to whatever is going on.

Whatever is or isn't going on, some may find the distraction welcome. If so, thank you, bearded 3rd person peculiar – little brother is watching you.

@simonsays

*

During his time in London he:

- Used the money he made busking to buy food for homeless people.
- Spent so long in Harrods contemplating the ethics of stealing a wristwatch on sale for £120,000, selling it, and giving the money to the poor that he was asked to leave.
- Prevented an armed robber from robbing a small general store and restrained him until the police arrived.
- Helped a desolate man up from below the tracks on the Northern Line on the London Underground and got him back onto the platform (but then realised the man was trying to kill himself and so felt hugely conflicted about rescuing him).
- Got there too late to prevent dozens of people being killed by a man claiming to be the Messiah who drove his car into a crowd of people protesting about freedom of speech.

- Had to use force (and hurt people) to defend himself and his actions when rescuing several animals from vivisection, which he then delivered to the care of the RSPCA.
- Went back to Harrods and stole the watch then sold it for £50,000 cash, which he then gave to a 12-year-old refugee street-girl who had been the victim of sexual slavery and abuse (the girl later used the money to develop a Flakka habit that killed her).
- Broke up a brawl in a nightclub and was then asked if he wanted to 'cane it' in MMA or cage fighting by the nightclub owner (he gave it serious thought, but on balance…)
- Saved a disabled man and his wife from the inferno of their house in Hackney (but was rebuked by a fireman for his actions and threatened with legal action).
- Rescued four people from a boat that hit a stanchion of Southwark Bridge and sank.
- Confessed his theft from Harrods and awaited consequences that somehow got lost in a vortex of police bureaucracy, insufficient proof (faulty CCTV), and routine inertia.

He grew ever more frustrated by how little he could do, however, in London and around the world. The more he helped, the more he realised how little he could help. Without access to emergency service communications, finding misfortune was also difficult. Seeking trouble and tragedy out felt depressing and occasionally absurd, too. He was forced to accept that fulfilling his mandate would always be at best difficult, and at worst, impossible. He told himself he would never give up. He listened.

*

Shanti phoned him out of the blue. Seeing her name on his phone display made his stomach cold. He pressed the call accept button.

'Hi,' he said. 'How are you? It's wonderful to hear from you.'

There was a moment of silence. Then she said, 'It's Kenton.' The normal silk of her voice was brittle with emotion. 'They've taken him to hospital. He's lost consciousness.'

Her words numbed him.

'What happened?'

'A pulmonary embolism, apparently. Don't go – please? Mum doesn't want you anywhere near him. He's been drinking anyway. God knows. He looked like shit when I saw him last week.'

'Drinking? How would he get alcohol?' His words felt like ash in his mouth.

'Guilty as charged. Don't judge me, OK?'

'It's not judgement, it's ...'

'Well what else is it?' Brittle.

A moment.

'How are you anyway? I've missed you.'

'I've missed you too.'

'Fuck. Mum's saying something crazy about looking after him at home full time. Sounds like atonement to me.'

'Atonement for what?'

'Being a crappy mother and an all-round basket-case I guess.'

'She's just playing with the hand she's been dealt like the rest of us – no?'

'Why do you have to be so nice? It would make things easier if you were as judgemental and prejudiced as the rest of us, you know.'

'Where are you?'

'In town, but don't come. Not yet.'

Not yet.

They said nothing for another moment. The moment became the keystone of bridge built long ago by children's hands. Then, they had thought it could bear any weight. They had thought it could span any abyss. They had been wrong of course, as children are, and adults wish to be.

'I'll let you know if anything changes. OK?'

'Thank you.'

'Take care.'

'You, too. Bye.'

The line went dead. Guilt gripped him like a bora wind.

It was a wind without a name.

*

The Thing slowly split his atom. His cataclysm began to bloom.

The guilt he felt for what he had done to Kenton took its place at the centre of his hurricane; yet his awareness was global: the world was his parish. The torment he felt at Kenton's demise therefore took no precedence over the anguish of others everywhere.

No. He did not own his sorrow. Neither did misery, he felt, belong to anyone who felt it anywhere. It did not belong to a woman being raped by a militia gang in Mali, whom he saved from further violation and carried to the relative safety of her family. It didn't belong to the whale calves whose mothers he failed to save from 'scientific research' in the Southern Ocean. It didn't belong to those whose lives the tsunami in Papua New Guinea had destroyed, whom he helped as best he could by rescuing people from the impossible and returning them to possibility. It didn't belong to the bears tortured in cages in bile farms in Asia that his rage released, but who had become too frail to live. It didn't belong to a political prisoner in an ancient land, who he freed from the privations of solitary confinement: a punishment for the man's courage and originality. It didn't belong to the baby in Southern Sudan. The baby could find no milk in the famines of his mother's breasts. The baby was too dehydrated to cry. He brought ass's milk that saved both mother and baby. It didn't belong to the parents of the twin brothers shot dead by gangbangers in Los Angeles, whose grief he could not assuage with his own.

No. None of the pain he relieved or could not relieve belonged to anyone because, as it occurred to him, pain cannot be owned. Pain is as free as paradise is pointless.

Morality became a master of boundless cruelty. When he helped someone or some people somewhere, he then had to depart to help elsewhere. It was logical only to remain until their situations were resolved, if possible; yet their situations were contingent upon other situations, whose contingencies spread out in time and space like the unseen hands of trees at clay; so every time he helped someone or some people he had to do the unthinkable: leave them because someone else needed him somewhere else. Whether they needed him more was an absurd calculation.

The pain of those he helped devoured him. It accumulated. It filled him with hunger. Hunger became lust. Lust poisoned him with devotion. Eventually unable to bear such devotion, he sought escape. He saw himself flee into inflamed sky. There, he sought to cleanse himself of the hurts he tried to alleviate. He sought in vain but found quick solace.

Then gravity reclaimed its son. He plummeted from the brief sanctuary of altitude to the earth below. As he plummeted, air friction ignited him, so he seemed, briefly, to be a fireball to a few who saw him far below. The phenomenon was also witnessed by chance by two astronomers at that moment recalibrating the Keck A telescope at the W. M. Keck Observatory on Mauna Kea in Hawaii. The event was turned into digital data. The data were filed among other data for analysis.

As the fireball screamed to earth, he screamed within it, but with sheer and unexpected exhilaration. In this way, he knew joy, briefly.

In this way, he had a haircut.

*

The fireball went back to Dashiell only because he had nowhere else to go. Unable to pay his rent without a job, he had been obliged to move out. He was therefore homeless. He should therefore, he reasoned, be unable to walk past himself. He resolved to try one day soon.

He bathed in Dashiell's bath. Her water failed to wash atmospheric elements reconfigured by heat off him entirely. It failed to cleanse hair that had yielded slightly to 2051-degree re-entry heat. It wrapped him in safety for a moment, though. It laved him as much as one who is pure can be cleansed.

After the bath, he lay down in his old bed. He closed his impossible eyes so that he could see all that he had seen more clearly. Clearest of all was Kenton, lying unconscious on a bed. He tried to force the image out of his mind. It took the last of this moment's strength.

Soon, he slept for the first time for years. Because he dreamt when he was awake, his sleep was the purest absence of experience. He slept as stones and clouds and vortices and cacti and tides and height and kittens and ellipses sleep.

When he woke, he drank the tea that Dashiell had made him. It was beside his bed when he awoke, piping warm. How had she known he was awakening? It seemed to him that only a real mother could do this. Not necessarily a biological mother, but a real mother. Real maternity.

He hung onto the thought as he drank this liquid sanity.

Jericho stood when he entered the small lounge from the even smaller kitchen with his empty teacup in his hand. The foundling was surprised and pleased to see him. Jericho and Dashiell seemed comfortable in each other's presence; but it was instantly clear they weren't back together in any romantic sense or reconciled, as he yearned for them to be. He felt responsible for their separation. He felt responsible for everything. He craved freedom from this feeling.

Jericho hugged him. It felt good. Jericho appraised him with his characteristic wry glance. 'Get your haircut then?' Jericho said.

He then spent an hour or so with his adoptive parents. Not much was said, but Jericho told him that had taken the job offer in Dubai because he had little option because the company was relocating, and the new operation needed setting up in the new location. As Jericho spoke, a man was tortured to death in a disused garage near a police station in northern Qatif in Saudi Arabia. As Dashiell watched the foundling listen and wondered what he felt and what it was like to be him, a young woman was being gang raped in Sheffield. As Jericho accepted Dashiell's offer of some fig rolls – always his favourite – an orangutan died of stress having entirely lost its habitat to humans in the Aceh province of Sumatra. Jericho asked him what he was up to. A woman battered her baby son to death in Koshani in Macedonia. He told Jericho that he'd had to move out of his digs in London. A child soldier in the Central African Republic was shot dead by his cousin over an argument about arguing. He reassured Jericho that he hadn't told him about being homeless to ask for money or support. A suicide bomber blew up herself and in so doing killed twenty-six people in a restaurant in Beit Lechem Road in Jerusalem. Jericho told him he knew that, but did he need any money anyway? A nineteen-year-old girl thrilled to have graduated that morning was killed in crossfire during a firefight between police and a suspected terrorist in the Vaugirard arrondissement in Paris. In the time it took them to talk about the village hall and for Jericho to say silly him, he'd forgotten, but he had suggested to the council he share half the costs of the rebuild, nine hundred and twenty-two people had died of hunger around the world. In the time it took him to say he wanted to go to the Young house to see if he could do anything to help them with Kenton, just over nineteen thousand seven hundred and fifty-six dollars were spent on ineffective weight loss products in America.

As tocks ticked, the roaring in his head became a livid golem admirably bent on roaring. The roaring became waves and myths and subduction and the truth of the Earth's core. It became waves approaching beaches. It became their breaking. It became two tides a day. It became the war hand of thunder. It became the Tsar Bomb conceived in a human mind and made by human hands. It became Tally's reckless laughter at groan up fanny before she phoned up granny. It became the sun transforming 4.289×10^{12} grams of is into isn't per second. Of yes into no. Of can into can't. Of must into will. Of willingness. Of action.

He would follow the sun into the slaughter of the west and laugh at the flood of it. First though, he would drink more tea.

*

'Oh that. I'd almost forgotten. It was a fake. Like me. Like you.'

'I know. Reality is my only fantasy,' the foundling said with a smile. His smile tried and failed to hide his distress at Alice's assumption of his trickery.

Alice's diamond hadn't been real. He had known it as soon as he crushed it between his hands in Benen's garden. It had burst like a bubble between his palms. A real diamond would have felt to him more like a warm marshmallow feels when crushed by a strong person.

'Well I'm pretty real, babe,' replied Alice, fondling him gently. Of course he couldn't feel it. He almost convinced himself that he was used to the numbness of his impervious skin. Almost.

He did enjoy her tattoo, though. It was an Ouroboros inked with Gothic inflection. The tattoo was near the bottom of her spine. He watched the Ouroboros eat its tail. It felt like one big apology. He seethed with all pain and guilt for Kenton. He was already sick of it, but he knew it would never change. The snake seemed to laugh at him; so he tried to laugh, too. Alice thought he was laughing at her. She didn't seem to care; so he made numb love to Alice again. He did it with her for so long that eventually, exhausted, she asked him to stop. Then she begged.

'That's a first!' she gasped. With a token caress, she moved away from him. She was soaked in sweat. She lay there and caught her breath. He watched her body function. He was always awed.

She didn't seem to notice or care about his inability to orgasm. Shanti had always fretted about it. She had tried everything to bring his desire to conclusion. So far she had failed. Now, here he was in Alice's Shoreditch flat thinking about Shanti as information in action.

Later, they talked about nothing much but things. Then Alice asked him, 'So how did you do it? Benen's full of surprises. How much did he pay you? Come on. William Tell.'

'I don't know.'

'OK. Course not. The magic circle. OK.

'It's just something I can do. I can do things.'

'You certainly can,' Alice purred. 'Have to call you Tantric Timmy won't we.'

'It isn't that ...' he began, but faltered. He seemed like a little boy lost for a moment.

'What is it then? He's so sad. It's in his eyes. Poorest eyes. What we gonna do with him?' She pretended to caress him, then, 'You going to do the show then? Watch out for that Tymon. He still owes me money, the bastard.'

The show was a TV talent show. Benen had told him that Tymon produced the show, and that they were always looking for new talent and new acts. Would he do something? The extreme levitation thing would good, 'but it will be in a studio, so something else? Something similar?'

It made sense. He rarely ate, and he didn't really need a roof over his head or a place to sleep; so he needed little money anyway. Being homeless is devastating for anyone, however. He was fastidiously clean, too; so somewhere to wash regularly was vital to him. Busking only earnt him a few pounds a day. Doing the show might earn him some proper money. It might also help to distract The Thing for a while – though he could not disobey it.

'I might. What's the show for?' he asked.

'You telling me you don't watch it? OMG! It's like, the number one numero uno at the mo. Maybe you need to lighten up a bit, Timmy. Let your hair down. Oops – too late!' She smiled and tugged his hair as she said it. Re-entry six weeks earlier had burnt much of his hair away, so it now sat about his head like the last rights of scorched rats.

He didn't like her touching his hair like this.

'I'm really sorry about what I did,' he said. 'How about I give you a real diamond to make up for it?'

'I didn't know Timmy was a zillionaire. Is he?'

'I'm rich, but my wealth isn't financial,' he said.

She looked at him in such a way. Then she snarled some laughter.

'Of course you are, sweetheart,' she said through the snarl. Her cynicism betrayed her fear. He could see it in her because she hid it, as much that is hidden is only thus found.

He got off the bed and went to his jacket, which hung on the back of the door. He removed something from one of the jacket pockets. He went back to the bed and opened his hand. There it was. The diamond he had found in the ground deep below the quarry ten years earlier. It still looked like a dirty mango. She barely glanced at it.

'Fuck, chuck,' she mumbled into her glass future. 'Amazon Prime? No thanks. I just want my necklace back. It might have been a fake but was a gift, once.'

'I don't want you to be scared,' he said.

'Oh fuck off. Fuck off and get me the real thing then.'

'I don't need to do that.'

She tried to meet his gaze. She found it almost impossible. She saw a child within him that was almost free and never would be. A child with singular eyes, wide as beauty's edge. She saw the human singularity in his eyes but could not recognise it. What had they done to him?

They didn't touch each other for a moment. He was glad.

'I'm so sorry to ask but do you know of anyone with a spare room?' he said eventually. 'Just for a few weeks. Then I'll probably go back. I want to be here in London, to stay here, but it's everyone. So many in such a small, confined area. So many of me.'

The Ouroboros looked at him.

'Just give me my fakeroonies back. And then we'll see.'

'I told you. I'm the real thing,' he said.

'You're a strange one, aren't you, Timber? Do what you want. You are a poppet though.'

She shot him a sleepy glance that said we're all a bit odd deep down, aren't we? You're just a bit odder than the rest of us. Then her smartphone vibrated, and she got lost online or on messaging and he suddenly didn't exist. He put the dirty mango back in his jacket pocket.

Alice thus became more than £100,000,000 poorer. She could spot a fake, oh yes.

He knew it would be fine like this for a while, and then Alice would ignore him permanently, whatever he could do in bed for her. It didn't matter. He was just trying to forget Shanti.

He put the diamond back in his pocket, which sagged absurdly because of the jewel's weight. He dressed and left without saying anything to Alice. She was busy on her smartphone anyway, and he thought goodbyes redundant. She didn't react to his exit as he knew she wouldn't. More resilient than the huge diamond he carried, he was hurt grievously by her indifference, casual as their brief relationship had been. His blessing was his curse.

On the way out onto the street, he decided to go on Tymon's show.

'Don't do it, darling, please,' Dashiell said to him on the phone when he told her he was going to go on the show the next day as he walked towards the junction with Drury Lane on Long Acre in Covent Garden – a favourite haunt.

'Mum. I have to make something go. I have to make money so I can live somewhere. I'm homeless. To be without a home is to be in hell.'

'You can stay here until you find somewhere.'

'Don't say that. You know I can't. I'm a grown something now.'

'You're a man,' she said, laying that on him like a slab of fact.

His mouth formed the words 'Ecce homo' sardonically.

Their conversation flowed like water in search of levels as he walked on. Walking in London had become a passion for him. He was fascinated by the mark of history he saw in its structures and their names. Long Acre became Great Queen Street as he headed east. Why 'Long Acre', he mused? (Compulsively curious, he later and found out why, and found out, too, that imperial units replaced the Winchester Standards, which were in effect from 1588 to 1825. He then learnt that Winchester measure is a set of legal standards of volume instituted in 1495 by King Henry VII. By then, he was in love with Wikipedia, especially for its need for citations. What price, knowledge?).

He walked past the junction with Wild Street (why 'Wild'?, he wondered) and approached the Freemason's Hall on his right. As he did so, Dashiell said: 'I saw Bella Young yesterday. Sorry to mention. I think she just wanted to apportion blame. It wasn't, shall we say, pleasant.' New familiar coldness grew like a season inside him as he glanced at the Grand Connaught Rooms on his right.

Kenton.

'She said the doctors ... Ken may not wake up. The embolism thing. I'm so sorry, darling. Bella's going to look after him at home anyway, which sounds like a recipe for disaster to me, but I'm no expert.' She paused, then, 'You couldn't help it. You have to know that.'

They ended the call moments later. Dashiell said a worried goodbye and went off into time. The thought of

Kenton's predicament lodged in his throat and turned his limbs to jelly.

The junction with Kingsway approached. He thought of Shanti. What must she be feeling? Her brother was in oblivion thanks to his petty jealousy and macho reflex.

Of course he and Shanti were over. Tumult engulfed him.

He decided. He speed-dialled. His stomach turned to ice.

After several rings, the landline call (it seemed she had blocked his number on her mobile phone) was picked up on the other end. Bella Young's voice - the voice he had heard so often as a child when he had gone around to play with Kenton. Then, he hadn't been aware of the voice's unfulfilled edges, or of its resentful harmonics. Now, he was painfully aware of both. She answered with her usual declaration of her phone number - such an old-fashioned way to answer a telephone.

'Hello Mrs Young. It's me,' he began. 'I hope you are both well. Well I mean … Mum told me. I mean Kenton … Is he …?' His voice failed. A moment of polite, culpable silence, then: 'I just need you to know that I'm so deeply sorry. It was just an accident, and really …'

Smelling of tired lavender, Bella let him waver and dangle on the wavering. She let him swing pointlessly like a garden swing long in need of oiling. She had no oil. She didn't want any oil. She hated oil. She would make him hate oil too, and he knew it.

Knowing had long since become far too much of a thing.

*

Kenton was everywhere. The Thing was everywhere else.

Kenton's unconscious shadow had fused with the shadow of the dead child in his arms in the As Sa'an school. This shadow-chimera followed him everywhere. It quivered in late afternoon sun in quiet rooms. It grinned at him with a sickle mouth on bright mornings where trees moved. He thought he could hide from it in the dark because only in the dark is there no shadow. He couldn't. Now, it followed him as he waited to be told where to go and what to do in Tymon's talent show studio. He saw it in these bright studio lights. He saw it in the styled utility of the building he was in. He saw it in people's lives as they hurried about, utterly involved with their tasks. He thought he envied them for their involvement – for being so involved with the world, so inside it. He was, he thought, forever on the outside. Only there could he be at the centre of everything.

He closed his eyes. The dead child stared at him. He opened them. His eyes became the child's. Dead, the boy's dilated pupils no longer adjusted to light. They filled him with the infinity of the human zero. He opened his eyes and thus became blind as Benen approached.

Benen was here because he was Tymon's agent. The older man waved a greeting. Pepper was with him on a lead. Seeing Pepper shook the foundling out of his reverie, and made him glad. The dog tried to make a break for him. Benen let him off the lead so he could do so. He and Pepper made an almighty fuss of each other. Benen smiled and shook his hand, but he looked troubled.

'You're conflicted,' the foundling said in such a way.

Benen smiled unconvincingly. It felt strange to be caught off guard like this.

'You're reluctant to draw me into your world of talent whoring. You'd rather not see me as sullied as you feel you are. You look back at a time when you were pure, too, and you regret. You would rather I remain pure, but you're not sure why, especially as we've barely met. But you have uncanny instincts. You're a good man, but you're an agent. A businessman. So here we are.'

'Well,' Benen said, his smile wider now, and even less convincing. 'You've got it all covered.'

'It's OK,' the foundling said. 'If this works out, we both stand to gain. Thank you for the opportunity. I'm sure I'll crash and burn though, so hey.'

The men smiled at each other. Benen marvelled at something he couldn't name.

The foundling still made a fuss of Pepper. The dog went nuts with dog-joy. It made him happy.

'Well good luck, anyway,' said Benen. 'Come on then, Pepper.' Bene led the dog away. Pepper and the foundling parted company unwillingly.

He was soon ushered into a rehearsal/prep room with several other contestants. He tuned his guitar while he waited. Of the four hopefuls in the room, two were twins. They were extravagantly and fashionably dressed. They were a singing duo. They rehearsed their number now – a dynamic, popular piece with dazzling riffs that displayed their soulful range. When they were summoned to go onto the stage set, the foundling was left in the room with two girls, who signed that they also sang – though clearly deaf. He signed back that he wished them all that was best.

His eyes darkened. The Thing seethed in him like guilt's belly. He knew that the meniscus of excuses could only hold it back for so long. No matter. Here and now. On and on.

The talent show that he was competing in was called The Next, Next, Big, Big Thing. He won this heat of The Next, Next, Big, Big Thing by singing as none had ever heard singing in a dozen languages. He accompanied himself and played his guitar with impossible popular brilliance. He invented the music as he played it. Its mortality was absolute. Its brevity, eternal.

He elevated himself as he performed. After the village hall, he was reluctant and slightly embarrassed to do this, but the ecstatic reaction to his performance inspired him. His blood was up. At first just a few centimetres, and then a few metres in the air. He tried to put his fear of being revealed as a freak and an outsider out of his mind. He couldn't. He distracted himself by mimicking the judges to perfection. He did a comic routine as each of them. It brought the house down.

Drenched in applause, he loathed the adulation. It threatened his humility, which was everything. Praise was his enemy.

In the rehearsal/prep after the show, a faux-jubilant Tymon invited 'incredible him' to come back to compete in the finals the next week. He could make serious money! He could become famous! It could be the start of something! 'Thank you,' was all he could find to say.

'Thank *you*,' smiled Tymon, squeezing his hand in a contract of flesh soon to be engrossed in legalities. Then Tymon got a phone call. He gestured excuses, pretended to smile, and headed off.

Benen approached him moments later as the foundling made his way out of the rehearsal/prep and towards the exit.

'Well done!' said Benen. 'Amazing!'

'Thank you. Where's Pepper?'

'He's in the car.'

He smiled warmly and shook Benen's hand with slightly more pressure than was apt because he was still high from the performance. He had several hundred thousand tons of grip strength available. Benen flinched, as he had flinched when he had shaken his hand at Speaker's Corner.

'And you're back next week for the final! Wow!' enthused Benen.

'Apparently. Look. Thanks for the opportunity.' With level eyes.

'You're welcome!' said Benen, his eye pupils dilated by hand-pain.

'So are you my agent now?'

'Sure. Why not? What else can you do?'

'Anything.'

'Of course you can.'

There was a moment. He released Benen's pancaked hand.

'Oh. Alice says hi,' said the foundling.

'Alice is in Wonderland,' said Benen.

'I know.'

'And what else do you know? I'm curious.' With nervous laughter that exposed Benen by trying to camouflage him. With painful hand.

'I know how to bake bread.' With usual ready smile. Charming and with peerless enigma.

Again uncharacteristically flummoxed for a moment, Benen's nervous laughter peaked, then subducted. The tectonic human.

'Say goodnight to Pepper for me.' He started to walk away as he said it.

'Are you going to tell me? How you do this stuff,' said Benen.

'I don't know.'

He glanced back and shrugged as he walked away from Benen towards the future. Then he and his easy smile and the wars of his calm eyes were gone.

*

Kenton lay in a state of potential.

His brain remained his brain; but it was unable to become again the tick and the tock of mind. Kenton was six letters. His ego could not pronounce itself. The gestalt was broken.

Bella sat beside his bed in the quiet of his room. It was morning. She hadn't slept. Sunlight enquired of the curtains. She stood up and let it in. The light ravaged her dark adjusted eyes. She smeared at them with her hand as if trying to wipe away the plan that grew within her. She couldn't. The plan just smeared yesterday's mascara. Reality blurred her vision into a kaleidoscope of truth that turned her son's face into a decision.

This could not go on. This was pointless. This had to end.

Love was certain of it.

*

He competed in the finals of The Next, Next, Big, Big Thing a week later. He won with ease. He apologized to the other contestants. He asked them if they would like to be the winner instead. They looked at him askance or spoke strangely to him. He sensed aggression.

'I've been thinking. What happens if I don't do this?' he asked Benen in Benen's lived-in Wardour Street offices beneath a Thursday two weeks later.

'Nothing happens,' Benen replied. 'You go back to being whatever you were. What were you? No disrespect.'

'Is there any way I can do this without becoming well known?'

'Seriously,' Benen smiled and laughed luxuriously. 'You must be the only person in the world who doesn't want to be famous!'

'Of course I don't.'

'Well if you want to be successful ... Or do you? Am I guessing you don't want to get rich either? Wealth is moral bankruptcy, right? I'm sensing morality. Good for you. Well think of how many people you could help with your wealth.'

'What splendid chicanery.' With a grin.

'Guilty as charged,' said Benen, smiling his agent smile. The smile soon faded.

The foundling sensed abiding regret in the older man. They both knew that Benen had swept himself under a carpet that was once delightful and calm underfoot, but which was now threadbare.

'Well anyway. Now you've won the show you'll probably be asked to do some radio. Some TV. But you've really got to want this. Do you?'

'I just want it to stop.'

For less than a moment, Benen glimpsed something in his eyes that almost made him almost gasp. It was an inner conflict the like of which he had never seen before, and yet it was utterly serene. What might it be like to carry such a thing around within you? Benen wondered. It mesmerised him. Was this what had drawn him to this strange young man in Hyde Park?

The answer was suddenly obvious to Benen.

This man in front of him was his mirror, but it was a shabby fairground mirror that distorted what it reflected. Such is the human in time.

'Is there anyone you can see? I'm sorry. Not to be rude. But there are people who can help. I've been there. Trust me. You can talk to me, though I ...'

'You've been where? Where have you been?' he snapped like a sudden branch underfoot.

Silence coiled around them like a snake's plan. Then the foundling calmed.

'Sorry,' he said. 'It's only that I've hurt someone, and it hurts, and I feel bad about it, worse than bad, and I'm sure I could have prevented it happening if I'd tried harder.'

'It's OK.'

'Anyway ... I just wondered ...' The foundling opened his holdall. He produced several sketchbooks and a notebook from within it. He put them on Benen's desk for Benen to assess.

Benen looked at them, while emails amassed in his inbox and his smartphone vibrated message alerts. By the time he got to the second sketchbook, Benen was astonished.

'These are ... I mean ... You did these?'

'And these are some of my music compositions,' he said as he took several musical composition books out of his holdall and put them on Benen's desk, too. 'I've also written a couple of journals, but they're work in progress of course, as long as I draw breath I guess!'

'I don't really know what to say,' said Benen apropos the foundling's work. 'I can't read music but the art ... It's incredible. But this isn't how it works. It isn't about being talented. It's all about knowing the right people. It's about what's trending. Hashtags. It's about what's hot and who's not. Talent is dead. Now, everyone's a genius, so no one is. You're cursed by real talent, and in my world, success is just well managed mediocrity.'

'Oh no. I was wondering if you might like to buy it, or some of it.'

Email and message alerts tuned the air with urgency. Benen tried to focus.

'Only a fool would put a price on this stuff. I'm humbled. Look, sorry, but ...'

'I've been kicked out of my digs, and so I need to find somewhere, and that takes money.'

'You can make a fortune now you've won the show. It'll take a few months to filter through, but ...'

'I need somewhere to call home. Today even. I don't suppose you know anyone?'

'You'll find somewhere.' Benen went on. 'OK look: I may know someone. Actually I have place – a room. It's small, but you could stay there until you find somewhere.'

'But how would I pay you?'

'Let's just see how we go, shall we?' Benen looked uncomfortable.

He made eye contact with Benen. He saw that Benen had trouble holding his gaze. 'Benen, I value your interest in me. I really do. But Tymon and the show and things. It's not really for me.'

'Not for you? Well what are you going to do?' asked Benen.

'What I'm here to do.'

'And what's that?'

The foundling knew there was no point answering.

Politely angry, Benen suddenly found something to do on his Mac.

'I'm sorry to have intruded, Benen. You're a busy man. I might just take you up on the room offer. I'll let you know later today if that's OK. Anyway thank you.' He then indicated his notebooks and art. 'Do you mind if I leave them here for a while? I have to run some errands.'

'It's fine,' said Benen 'Sorry,' he carried on, then went back to his emails and messages.

The foundling stood. They shook hands. Silence showed him the way out. He descended the stairs down to street level in silence. He heard Benen's question in his mind, 'And what's that?'

It's everything, his mind answered.

His mind was suddenly clear. He existed to relieve suffering. No matter how hard. No matter the quandary, the dilemma. If The Thing were the only thing that could kill him, so be it. Kenton could not be his exclusive priority. Neither could he let what he felt for Shanti rule him. He set them aside in his heart. He resolved to go from here to wherever he could find need, and provide succour. Anything worth doing takes courage, and fear is never a reason not to act. All this was obvious.

He quickened his step on the stairs, energized by a sense of purpose.

He reached the building atrium and headed out onto Wardour Street. He got a text from Shanti. Her name on his phone made him churn, not least because he had just determined to focus on his vocation, not his passions. The text was: '*I miss you. x*'. His resolve blurred. Conflicted, he texted back: '*I miss you too. xx*'. He walked south towards Shaftesbury Avenue en route to Chinatown – a usual and preferred haunt. Shanti texted back: '*Be whatever you are x*' He replied: '*I will if you will xxx*' His resolve came back into focus. He walked faster, enjoying the rhythm and power of his gait, and Soho's pulse. Here, he could be himself (within reason) and no one would judge him. If he belonged anywhere, it was in this place and places like it; yet he couldn't stay here or anywhere.

Be whatever you are. At what cost?

*

The Next, Next, Big, Big Thing made him an extremely unwilling, minor celebrity. He found himself being photographed when he didn't wish to be. He saw the photographs online. He read the media reports about 'the bearded man' and his remedial activities around the world, and theories about the bearded man's identity. He feared that two and two would one day become four.

Three weeks after his meeting with Benen, a Yasen class Russian nuclear submarine that 'wasn't there' sank to the seabed off the coast of Newfoundland after 'a possible explosion inside the reactor housing'. He dived into the freezing abyss and, eventually finding the stricken vessel pinned to the seabed by unimaginable water pressure, hauled it back up to light and life. The Thing thanked him. The crew of the submarine and their loved ones didn't know who to thank; so many of them thanked their gods. The rest were forever puzzled, as were 'experts'.

He helped victims of tragedy, saved many from death, and fed the starving. Always and always, however, the climate further destabilized, and biodiversity was obliterated by human activity. He could do nothing about either. The Thing extolled him to greater efforts. He bucked under its tyranny as easily as he warped steel.

All the while, Dashiell read the pages of her days and tried not to miss her adopted son or her ex-husband. She failed and she failed. She visited Tally's grave rarely because of the grief that bloomed there among the daffodils in spring. The need to say sorry to Tally clotted her entirety. It clogged the places where it needed to come out in dreadful torrents. It accrued.

Jericho picked away at the flaking patina of his heart in the Middle East. The love he harboured made the edges of things uncertain, and their substance regretful and bitter. He lost himself in work to protect himself from his heart's famishing. He found himself in reflections.

Benen tried to ignore the foundling's notebooks and art in a corner of his office as he worked.

Kenton did not stir. Bella waited for an opportunity.

Two months passed. He played the role (badly and usually AWOL) of reluctant minor TV and social media star, and followed his vocation. The two agendas did not marry well. Benen grew frustrated with his unwillingness to publicize himself, and his frequent absences.

Renewed contact with Shanti in London didn't interfere with his vocation as he feared it might. He did what he had to do, and spent time with her frequently enough that they sated each other's emotional and sexual needs. He told her nothing of what he did or what he could do, of course. He wondered how long such a secret might be kept. Kept it must remain, however.

Shanti told him that Bella Young was indeed now looking after Kenton at home – against the advice of medical consultants. If it was atonement, atonement for what? He had his suspicions.

Despite having achieved clarity about his priorities, the urge to help Kenton started to overwhelm him. Bella insisted on banning him from their home, however. He had no choice but to respect her ban for a while longer and hope against hope that Kenton would recover.

Benen negotiated several appearances and performances on radio, TV, and podcasts for him. He didn't turn up for most of them because he was 'busy'. His better nature, as he saw it, balked at the attention and adulation he received, while part of him enjoyed it. He mostly suffered it so he could (when Tymon eventually coughed up) give the money he earned to the poor and pay the rent he owed Benen, who had leased him a room in one of his properties in Battersea.

In June, Benen got him a guest interview on a popular morning UK current affairs TV show as a monsoon raged. The show was hosted by a man called JJ Mulder and a woman called Evey Sunday.

EVEY: So what made you enter Next, Next?

THE FOUNDLING: Well I need to make money so that I can ...

JJ: Don't we all? Are the producers listening?

JJ grins at someone off set. Someone says something, off set.

EVEY: So it was about getting rich? You don't seem like that sort of person.

JJ: Evey likes to judge books. She's on the Booker panel!

THE FOUNDLING: I'll bear that in mind! Well for me ... I want to make money so I can help ... I just needed to put a roof over my head for a while. Not that I really need one.

EVEY: Really? How's that?

THE FOUNDLING: Well I don't have the same needs for food and shelter most people have.

JJ: Oh. How come?

THE FOUNDLING: I just don't have those physical vulnerabilities.

JJ: Oh. OK.

EVEY: We're all vulnerable though, aren't we?

THE FOUNDLING: Of course.

EVEY: So you entered the competition really just to give yourself an income for philanthropic reasons?

JJ: Phil an' who?

THE FOUNDLING: Pretty much. I mean what I do is less important to me than my vocation.

JJ: More of a vacation fella, me. But seriously ...

THE FOUNDLING: There's so much suffering in the world. I have to help. That's it, really.

EVEY: Well that's noble. And yes, we all need to do whatever we can to help, right? But it's not all, all, all suffering. Some of us are having a good time. Aren't we JJ?

JJ: Yes we are. But this is such a great point. So how will you help? Get bonkers rich and have a charity foundation like Billy Gates?

THE FOUNDLING: That's a good idea. But no. I'll just try to go wherever there are problems and try to sort them out. But it's difficult. And the thing is: suffering is quite hard to find – especially from the air.

JJ: You'll fly everywhere? That'll cost a fortune.

THE FOUNDLING: You'd think so, wouldn't you?

EVEY: With huge respect – and I think what you're saying is so cool – what bothers me is that this sounds so ...

THE FOUNDLING: Sanctimonious?

JJ: Well kinda.

EVEY: But it's what we should all be doing though – right?

JJ: Right.

EVEY: It's true though. We do need superheroes ...

THE FOUNDLING: I'm no superhero. But say I was. How could I be regulated? The idea of one entity ...

JJ: Entity?

THE FOUNDLING: The idea of one person being judge, jury, and punisher is worse than dangerous. He she or it would have to be perfectly wise, wouldn't they, and who is?

EVEY: Well this is far heavier than I had planned.

JJ: And she plans heavy, lemme tell you.

EVEY: It's true.

JJ: And so how do you see the future of reality?

THE FOUNDLING: No one believes in reality.

JJ: I meant reality broadcasting.

THE FOUNDLING: Oh. Well I have no idea.

EVERY: So come on. Your fans will want to know ...

THE FOUNDLING: My what?

JJ: Your fans. You're all over social now. How does that feel?

THE FOUNDLING: It's not for me.

EVEY: Why's that then?

THE FOUNDLING: Well who wants to be famous?

JJ: Everyone!

THE FOUNDLING: I guess, but ...

EVEY: So why don't you want to be famous?

THE FOUNDLING: It's just not for me, that's all I can say. But social networks. I think they may be a kind of disaster ... Well nothing is entirely good or bad, is it? Most things are somewhere in between. But we're being tribalized faster than we ever have been. Cognitive bias and confirmation bias are running amok, though of course they always have, but not like this, on this scale ...

EVEY: Well hashtag that!

JJ: Every Sunday!

Evey ignores JJ with habitual skill.

EVEY: So you said you don't have the same needs for food and what – shelter – like the rest of us? Why's that?

THE FOUNDLING: Again, I can only say that it's what I am.

JJ: I am what I am what I am. What?

EVEY (*of JJ*): Well he is anyway. (*to the foundling*) Go on.

THE FOUNDLING: About what? Social networks or my physical needs?

JJ: Whatever you like. I mean, what's your opinion about ...

THE FOUNDLING: I don't have opinions. Sorry to interrupt you!

EVEY: Oh. Why not?

THE FOUNDLING: It seems to me opinions are just reiterated conditioning. I think a more fluid approach is required, because of the subjective nature of reality in sentience – if we decide there is such a thing as reality, which of course there is because there either is or isn't such a thing.

EVEY: Wow.

JJ: Where did you study philosophy?

THE FOUNDLING: Oh, nowhere in reality. Everywhere, I guess!

JJ: Every Sunday.

EVEY: Well this *is* heavy.

JJ: Well he's my brother, innit. Go on. This is interesting. What about free will?

THE FOUNDLING: It's an illusion, obviously; just like you and me ...

EVEY: So what about your music? And that incredible voice!

JJ: You're saying I'm an illusion!

EVEY: I knew it!

THE FOUNDLING: My music is, well ... I think in mathematics; so, if anything, music is my meta-language ...

JJ: Meta-bloody meta-hell.

EVEY: But did you train?

THE FOUNDLING: To sing? Oh no.

JJ: How about a little number now? The world's your oyster! Give us a pearl necklace.

Voices, off. Evey and JJ laugh. Evey whacks JJ's shoulder.

EVEY (*into camera*): Sorry about that.

The foundling laughs with them for a while.

THE FOUNDLING: I've got tonsillitis.

The foundling deadpans them. They all laugh again.

EVEY: Well if you're not going to sing, tell us all more about you, oh mystery philosopher minstrel man. I know the viewers will be keen to get to know you.

THE FOUNDLING: I'm honoured.

EVEY: That's lovely. We don't get much humility around here. Do we, *JJ*!?

JJ: No we don't, *Evey*!? So anyway ... I think what people most want to know ... (*consults an iPad and reads a tweet*) 'How did he levitate? Wow!' (*to the foundling*) Is it a Magic Circle thing? Impressive. Can you teach me?

THE FOUNDLING: My milkshake brings all the girls to the yard ...

JJ (*performs it*): And they're like ...

EVEY (*performs it*): It's better than yours!

THE FOUNDLING (*performs it*): Damn right, it's better than yours ...

JJ (*performs it*): I can teach you, but I have to charge. (*as normal*) OK. It's a tragic circle thing. If you told us, you'd have to eat us ...

EVEY: With sauce ...

JJ: Except that you don't eat?

THE FOUNDLING: Well certainly not meat.

EVEY: Yay.

JJ scowls at the notion of not eating meat. Evey fist-bumps the foundling. He is gentle, but Evey reacts to the impact, which clearly hurt.

THE FOUNDLING: I'm so sorry. Are you OK?

JJ (*sings, of Evey*): Falling in love again. Never wanted to ...

EVEY (*singing, of JJ*): He can't help it ...

The foundling laughs politely. He is clearly worried about Evey's knuckles.

JJ: Anyway you love birds. (*he consults his iPad*) People are talking. Another tweet. From @Mistersister: (*he reads from his iPad*) 'His hair is all wrong, lol. Big beardy means zilch on top? Eye-eye Cap!' (*he makes like a one-eyed pirate*) Well, cap? I think the beard and the hair rock!

THE FOUNDLING: I can't cut them, unfortunately.

JJ: Seriously. Why's that? Oh. Your religion. I'm so sorry ...

THE FOUNDLING: Why would I be religious? No. It's just impossible to cut my hair with normal scissors and things because it's too tough.

JJ: Welcome to my world!

EVEY: We're not talking about underarm hair now, JJ. Blimey!

THE FOUNDLING: Well that, too! But the only thing that will cut my hair is fire, actually.

JJ: Oh. OK.

JJ glances off at someone off camera. He looks serious for the first time.

EVEY (*into camera*): Anyway time flies when you're having fun!

JJ (*into camera*): Too true, you!

EVEY (*into camera*): And there's more fun to come, so ...

JJ pulls a face at Evey. Off-set, the show producers prep for an ad break.

JJ (*into camera*): So stay with us. More juicy fruits in a mo!

EVEY (*into camera*): Watch that space!

The show cuts to an ad break. The foundling sees the break on TV monitors. JJ and Evey fall into discussion with a producer. A busy assistant approaches the foundling, thanks him politely, and guides him off-set. As he leaves the set, JJ and Evey shake his hand; but they seem preoccupied in a way that may or may not hide professional embarrassment.

*

The seasons changed from major to minor. He could not endure the beauty of it.

He couldn't stay away from Kenton any longer, despite his vocation and Bella's ban from their house. If it got nasty, so be it. He had to help his old friend. How, though? He had no idea.

He felt anxious as he approached the front door of the Young's large house. Hearing about Kenton was one thing. Seeing what he had done to him was something else. It was time to face the consequences of his actions though. The prospect of seeing Bella made him uneasy, too. He had no reason to fear her, but it wasn't about that. This was about being hated. That was hard.

His pulse quickened. Shanti, he knew, was here today. She had sent him a text: '*At the house from Monday. Pls come. I dreamt you made Kent better. And want to c you. To hell with mum. xx*'

He went up the three wide steps that led to the front door as he had done hundreds of times as a child. He remembered earlier visits long years past. 'Can Kenton play please Mrs Young?' – as eager as only the pure can be. 'Is Kenton in please, Mrs Young?' – a polite child, free in the flight of play: that most essential of all pointless activities. Then, more recently, his teenage glance as he entered the house in secret pursuit of Shanti as she bloomed on the thorn step of puberty.

Now, his thumb was poised over the bell push. He hesitated. This was what he had to do. This was the right thing to do, yes. Not to say sorry, but to show it. To apologise to Kenton and to his parents Bella and Thomas, whose lives he had shattered with a flick of the wrist. How could he ever make amends? By doing the impossible. Be helping Kenton. Shanti had faith. Therefore.

He pressed the bell push. He heard the bell respond from somewhere within. It was a sound so long familiar to him that it seemed part of him. Now, the doorbell seemed rotten with accusation. The sound seemed uncertain of itself. It seemed lost.

After a moment, Shanti opened the door. It looked like she had just washed her hair. Still wet with dark, it licked her neck. A subtle smile haunted her lips. It told him she was still on his side – but why? Love is forgiveness, he allowed himself, knowing there was more to it than that.

She opened the door, hushing him playfully. Beckoned, he stepped inside. He glimpsed her familiar skin beneath the bath towel she wore. Her body thrilled and cursed him with memory.

'Is he ...?' he glanced up at Kenton's bedroom. It was the door first on the left at the top of the stairs that he had once thought Scarlett might have fallen down into the truth of Rhett's apathy.

She barely responded. Her sadness was the beauty of truth.

'What about ...?'

'Mum's gone out,' she answered, licking the devil to heal him.

They went upstairs. She pulled him gently into her room. It was next to Kenton's. Heaven is the door next to hell. She guided him towards her bed. They kissed. To him, this was so unexpected and so contrary to his intention. He was here to fail to make Kenton better, not make love to his sister in the next room. Driven by love, passion overwhelmed him, however. She pulled him onto the bed. Her bath towel fell away.

They made love as they never had before. It was furtive and frantic and stolen and theirs. It was he was she was it was him Then, an epiphany: he felt her body as any normal person would.

At last! Sensation! The tactile! He wept with joy as he reached perihelion inside her for the first and the last time. For him, for a moment, there and then finally became here and now.

Afterwards, they lay together. She held him. He felt it. A divine rapture. To him, the universe wheeled and hurtled and began and ended and collided and faded and fused and divided around them and within them and with them until its trillions became unity.

Then footfall beyond the door dragged them back to the world of their senses. An internal door closed somewhere.

'It's just dad,' she said.

Shanti wrapped the towel around herself quickly and got off the bed. He dressed quickly and stood. They met each other's eyes. Time began again. Then Shanti was gone.

He heard her descend the stairs outside the room. He waited a moment, then he exited her bedroom. He stood on the landing in front of Kenton's bedroom door. He went to enter, but Thomas Young emerged from the bedroom he had once shared with Bella in lighter days. Thomas paused across the landing from the foundling. A man under siege.

'Sir,' greeted the foundling, soiled with new and established guilt.

Thomas acknowledged him with decency and without accusation. Then Shanti bounded up the stairs as if on cue. She smiled as if all was good and bright and blithe. Thomas and Shanti. Father and post-coital daughter. Thomas went downstairs. He had to walk past them both as he did so. Not quite embarrassed, Shanti went into her room. She met the foundling's gaze as she did so.

He hesitated again outside Kenton's room. His heart pounded.

'Just go in.' Shanti's voice from her bedroom's whisper.

He opened Kenton's bedroom door. He went in.

It was calm in here. It felt safe.

An oxygen concentrator was on the bedside table. A nasal tube was attached to it, which ran to Kenton's nose. There was a half full packet of nappies on the ground, and a small stack of wet wipes and cotton wipes beside that. Kenton lay on a relief mattress, which was slightly too big for the frame of his normal bed. He had a substantial beard. His hair looked unwashed. His eyes were not quite shut and not quite open. He chest barely moved up and down as he breathed.

Brute shock at seeing Kenton like this distorted him. He felt primordial denial. What was his friend doing? Was this some game? He almost laughed. He somehow expected Kenton to greet him. To smile. To flip him the bird. To 'Aha!' His friend didn't stir, however.

He saw himself approach the bed they had once played flying carpets on. He saw himself sit beside the bed. He saw Kenton's empty face. He heard a voice he recognised say, 'Kenton. I'm so sorry.' Heavy with normality, the curtains seemed to wait. Steel was steel and wood was wood, and cotton was. He knew it. He heard someone speak again - this time in a tight whisper: 'I don't know what I can do. If only you hadn't annoyed me. I love Shanti. We both do. It didn't have to be like this. But this isn't the end. You'll be up and about in no time. I'll find a way.' He lowered his voice to barely a whisper. 'I wish you could hear me. I wish you could help me. I'm so sorry, Ken. Forgive me.'

Kenton didn't stir.

He resolved to act. He didn't know how to do it. He had never done it. He didn't know how to start. He moved his hand so that it was over Kenton's head. He then almost laughed at his own cliché and melodrama. His sheer cinema.

He held Kenton's right hand in his. Still a bit dramatic, he thought, but slightly less Star Trek! Following instinct, he bent his instinct to curing Kenton. He willed healing into Kenton. He insisted on Kenton's wellbeing. He insisted on his survival. He insisted on his flourishing. He did these things for several minutes. He was unsure. The machines hummed. A floorboard creaked beyond the bedroom door. He insisted. A creak. He willed. Nothing happened. Light tasted craven. Stillness was brilliant. Nothing happened. Of course it didn't. He stopped suddenly. He breathed sharply. A plosive huff. His body lilted backward.

How had he hoped this would work? Had he? He felt stupid. He felt like a spare fool.

He stood a fool's stance. He wiped his foolish eyes and focussed. 'Forgive me,' said the fool.

A sound beyond the bedroom door, which seemed protective now. He heard the front door open and then close. A woman's voice. Bella. His stomach crawled. He went to the door and listened. After a moment he heard Bella coming upstairs. He put his hand on the door handle. Why hesitate? Why fear? Go out there and care nothing for her acidy. Go. No though. No go. Not though.

He heard Bella's footsteps reach the top of the stairs. The dread hand of guilt cold upon him. The writhing conscience. The burden of total integrity. Then he heard

Shanti's bedroom door open. Then Shanti, voice wall muffled, but obviously tight with emotion: 'Hi mum.' Then Bella: 'What have you been doing?' Then drama: 'What's going on?' Then what sounded like nervous laughter from Shanti. Footsteps. Then the door of Kenton's bedroom opened in front of him.

He was face to face with Bella.

'You!' It was a finger of a word. It jabbed him.

'Mrs Young ...' he began, knowing beginning was pointless. 'I'm so sorry.'

'So am I.'

Bella: a woman who had given him tea and kindness so many times. Her eyes were pinched by alcohol and reality and irony and responsibility now. She had a thin wound for a mouth that had once laughed readily. Words tore the wound around: 'Come to gloat, have you? See what you did?'

'Leave him alone, mum! He just wants to help.' Shanti was there beside her, insisting.

Bella turned on her daughter suddenly. The scent of sex. An abomination. 'He just wants to what? Don't make me laugh! You slut!'

Shanti went back into her room. She slammed her door with hatred's hands. She started drying her hair to drown Bella's next-door voice out. Her hair smelt like the Sunday papers on a Bank Holiday weekend, and a clifftop shelter, and seagull weekends, and safety.

Bella turned her gaze back to him. 'He'll be like this until hell freezes now. You sick freak,' she hissed. He could see the flecks in her irises were actually hazel, not blue, as he had always thought. This surprised him. They looked like the surface of life.

'All those years we fed you and treated you like another son. More fake parents, eh!? And what when we can't pay for the bloody machines anymore? What about his life!? You did this! You! Well get out!'

He understood the futility of the word 'sorry'. He felt like his blood was full of stinging nettles. All he wanted was to be out of there forever; so he squeezed past Bella without touching her. She shrank away from him like he was a delicious disease. A disease like desire. He descended the sensible stairs three by three. He fled the house as fast as truth flees conversation.

He was thus unaware of Thomas, prompted by the founding's recent presence alone in the room with Kenton, entering his son's bedroom just before Bella did. He didn't see Thomas and Bella's eyes meet, and Thomas welcome the safe shock of the impossible he saw encoded in Bella's gaze, which lodged in his gorge like a wild thing. He didn't see the unexpected serenity in Bella's face that Thomas saw, which for the first time in years became beautiful again. He didn't see Bella remove the oxygen tubes from Kenton's nose and then pinch shut that nose with one gloved, mother's hand and cover Kenton's mouth with the other hand. He didn't see Thomas stand there paralysed by horror. He was several miles away by the time Kenton's body became a numb fathom. He was a thousand miles away by the time Bella emerged from Kenton's bedroom and Thomas stumbled after her, preserved in the amber of self-loathing at his weakness.

'Shanti! What has he done!? Stop him! He's killed our boy!' Bella shrieked. Bella slumped against the hysterical landing wall in horror. Thomas stood near her in shock's detention.

In her room, Shanti continued drying her dry hair to hide the horror ciphered in her mother's razor voice. The horror could only mean one thing, and that was clearly absurd. The hairdryer moaned a dirge of cut-price banality. The sound made everything normal and safe.

*

Redness took him higher than he had ever been. His failure to heal Kenton trailed behind him like a wet umbilical. The birth of doubt in him was a haemorrhage against the darkening of the stratosphere. Doubt screamed as it was born. The scream found little volume in the thin air. The air cared nothing for his limitations.

He went faster than he had ever gone before, too. He became a streak of information that raged across the earth's blue curve. By fluke, he passed a high-altitude weather balloon at 128,210 feet. The balloon was near its maximum bloat – the helium within engrossed by low pressure without. He barely had time to see it because he passed it so quickly. What registered was a silver pregnancy. Time gravid with brilliant indifference. A tear, brief against the night.

Red took him higher than he had ever been, but not high enough. He looked up. Somewhere up there was the Kármán line – the notional boundary between the atmosphere and space. He longed now, as he had always longed, to reach it; but he couldn't. Doubt had weakened him. Now, reality forced him to descend in search of survival, too.

He was suddenly moved to seek out suffering and relieve it as never before. He descended quickly to an altitude of just a few kilometres. He searched. From the air, it wasn't easy to see the human tragedy in action – or the extreme altruism it could inspire. He headed therefore back to the place he knew he could almost certainly help. Redness took him back to the As Sa'an school in Syria.

When he got there, he found that things had gone from bad to worse.

*

When Shanti's got this dry the ends frayed. She kept on drying it, however. The smell of singeing got worse. Soon, it seemed universal. Surely everything smelt of burning hair now. Mercury, quotes, Saturn, distemper, the Crab Nebula, gerrymandering, macrame, devotion, a pas de deux, Charlemagne. Surely they all smelt of burning hair. How could they not? How could anything?

She sat in front of her mirror in her room. Her eyes were glass. No expression inhabited her face. The urge to vomit overwhelmed her. Had her mother just murdered her brother? Had she and her father done nothing to stop it happening? That was impossible, surely; yet there was a certain silence in the house: a silence she had never heard before. It splintered like glass annealed too fast.

She dreamt she could hear her mother shattering the glass by doing what she, Shanti, wanted to do: vomit properly. The noise of her father making a strange animal noise somewhere in the house sounded imaginary, too. It sounded so distant and close. Thomas might be downstairs. He might be in Kenton's room. He might be a memory. She couldn't tell. Reality had just been obliterated. That was why her mind rejected the truth of everything.

The echo of the rapture she had experienced with him lingered in strange counterpoint. Why had he left without saying goodbye? He had left part of him inside her. Should she leave things to chance? A douche? No. It would be OK. What if not? She was too young for parenthood, yet some instinct told her to do nothing. It would be fine, whatever fine was. Alright then.

Him though. Him. Her lover. How could he move that fast? Could he? Was she imagining it? Had he ruined the banister with his escaping grasp? How? Mr Sledgeforde the carpenter would have to look at that.

Normally such thoughts would have seemed ordered and familiar. Now, in deep shock, they stumbled like a drunk somewhere within her.

'Now look!' Bella's disembodied voice. Thomas' shocked, desperate reply. Then 'Murderer.' Shanti heard someone say it. Whisper it. She realised it was her. She herself. Her she. Her voice. Her voice now lived somewhere else. Not in the house of her body. Yes, she, Shanti. She would now have to live somewhere else too. Later this evening. Tonight. Now. She would have to finish drying her hair first. Go out like that and you'll catch a chill, an' that'll be the end of you my girl – mark my words.

'Mind your mouth young lady!' Bella's hiss. Suddenly in the room with her, or suddenly imagined. Somewhere a serpent close. Somewhere near, the lizard mouth and the snaky search–flick–stitch–thin–tongue. The split tongue end. The two-way tongue. Tasting the killed air. For escape. For food next. For danger.

Then Eden spewed Eve.

'Well this is how it will be.' The hiss. 'There will be a trial. You will testify. When it comes, because it will surely come ... That boy did this to his best friend ... And you will say, you will swear under God that he did it. And if you don't, young lady ...'

'Yes?' Shanti span around as she said it. Now she was the serpent tongue. She was the squama. The bifurcate. The dragon scale. The gleam. She was the snake tongue forked into left and right, into this and that, into is and isn't, into good and bad, into yes and no, into did and didn't. Now she was the mould–black harvest at the mother heart.

'Yes.'

Yes. The word was the arrow that vexed the apple. The word sought to destroy the mould. The devil at the head of the queue. Show and tell. Under oath, you will lie for me.

Then Bella wrenched her bloodshot gaze from Shanti's. Shanti saw murder leave her room. A feather in a hurricane, Shanti turned her hairdryer on again.

Bella emerged from Shanti's room exactly as Thomas emerged from Kenton's room next door. Thomas' eyes were broken. His hands pressed at his twisting mouth. He made a mewling sucking groaning thrumming noise that belonged in a vault best left sealed and legendary. He stumbled. He was the shuffle of a man who had worked in a room for decades and gone home to a woman who had become an unwilling virago. A man who made babies with that woman while love was still in bloom and the fragrance between them. A man who has only just embraced so savagely with love the already cooling corpse of his son killed by the poor, poor darling he married, who could see no future but the humming of machines and a broken vegetable.

Out of nowhere as it seemed to her, Thomas veered at her with his middle-class face with a golf club grimace. They collided in a clumsy gasp. His formal hands sought and found the stem of her withered neck. His 9-iron grip stemmed her sob-screams. His face pressed to hers in a roar-body against which she crammed for the first time in years. His whole body shook with the pathetic monster of it. It was that the weight of him crushed her down, and Shanti emerging from her room and watching, and his broken glass beseeching his daughter, and Shanti observing as one might observe a bus approaching on a rainy morning going who knows where and who cares.

'How could you!? My son! My God!' Thomas' broken words danced around Bella like damp twisted dolls torn from his mouth.

Then there was Bella crushing him to her underneath him on top of her like a wrecked baby and Thomas the dead doll fumbling and her sudden eyes grasping and gasping in the rich carpet and Shanti losing sudden interest and going back into her room to be dry.

'What else!? What!?' was Bella's sound. What else could she have done? This was perfect. The perfect scapegoat. The perfect escape. The perfect goat. So they both suddenly bleated like goats together and laughed as they hadn't since time. So the hair dryer was turned up to full power to drown the sound of it forever. The seared hair smell became emetic. Shanti retched. Her hairdryer finally broke. The motor finally died and went down to silence in suburbia, which is strange in its normality.

*

He went back to Dashiell closing the night with her eyes.

He was exhausted and traumatised. After his chance rendezvous with the weather balloon, he had become embroiled in a conflict between so-called terrorists and their Western enemies a few dozen kilometres from the As Sa'an school. Arriving there, he had pondered the ideology, the politics, and the philosophy behind the conflict when he should have acted. In his pondering now as always, he found it impossible to see things from one point of view – least of all his point of view; so he had no clear enemies as far as he was concerned.

Despite happening in the nanoseconds of his mind, such thoughts had caused him to hesitate long enough that a Western combatant had died, whom he could have saved. This amplified his inner dilemma, rendering him even less capable of acting decisively.

Once again assumed to be a terrorist by Western combatants because of his appearance, he had become their target in a ruined suburban area now home only to the memories of bones.

Their bullets echoed off him. Though it didn't hurt, this prompted him to action: he disarmed the Western combatants, but this made the soldiers vulnerable to attack by their enemies. He therefore rearmed them. Verbal exchanges again failed to convince either side the conflict was only a guarantor of further conflict. As he had at the As Sa'an school, he found himself lost in a vortex of a dilemma that he couldn't find his way out of. He could leave and help people elsewhere, but that meant abandoning these people. He found himself locked physically inside his quandary. He stood still. As he did so, he saw people on both sides of the conflict talking photographs of him on their smartphones. He saw the consequences of this.

A decision made itself. He went from there to thirty-four locations around the world where he sought out suffering and did his best to alleviate it. Wherever he went, however, he felt he should be somewhere else. Whenever he went somewhere else, he felt he should have remained, so that he could continue to help. He soon became so conflicted he had to stop; yet stopping was utterly unthinkable. In the end, he became unable to go on. He therefore went back to that person and place where he knew he could find brief refuge and rest.

He let himself in. Dashiell was in the living room. She was sitting in the middle of the second settee as she often did. She smiled at him bravely, but the bravery masked terrible anxiety.

Two uniformed police officers were in the room with her – one a constable and one a sergeant. He knew what had happened instantly when he saw them. The knowledge devastated him.

He recognised the police sergeant. It was Eric Lipton, the boy he had launched across the primary school playground more than twenty years earlier. Lipton's juvenile corpulence had become that kind of bulk that might be either muscle or fat. Lipton had, in any case, become immense, and he was clearly proud of his powerful appearance. That pride and an old score unsettled were obvious in the way he now reacted when the foundling entered the room. The memory of being launched across the playground like a shuttlecock rushed back to him. Here was his one-time playground adversary, and he looked like a vagrant.

He looked guilty.

To the foundling, Sergeant Lipton seemed eager to tell him in his curiously muddy yet high pitched voice that Thomas and Bella Young had made a formal accusation against him '... for the murder of their son Kenton Allan Young at four-thirty-seven this afternoon'.

His intuition confirmed, winter made a home in foundling's heart.

Suddenly, briefly, nothing mattered, least of all the slight sneer he saw in Lipton's face that seemed to say: here he is – same old Salter freak. Now he's a prophet, too, looks of it. Found in the rushes like Moses, were we? Lead the chosen few out of Milton Keynes, will we? Everyone knows the quarry sculptures were done by art students for a prank, you prat. No one cares how many loaves of bread you had sent from Tesco or who cares where to make it look amazing. To make yourself look special. How come you ain't been done for the village hall fiasco, weird boy?

'Kenton? What? No,' the foundling said, shock engraving his voice. 'I was there. He was alive when I left. He's dead?' He looked at Dashiell as if seeking clarity in her face. All he found was dread.

Sergeant Lipton said, 'I normally leave this kind of thing to the beat boys. But I thought I'd make a special effort for you. It gets a bit dull behind a desk.'

At Sergeant Lipton's nod, the female police constable – PC Shah – quoted the foundling his rights. He noted how melodic her voice sounded, and how it wanted to be gentle. He noted the length of her eyelashes and the depth of her falcate eyes. He noted the slenderness of her wrists and that she wore her uniform with a style that refused to kowtow to the officialdom she needed.

As he noted these nanosecond things, Sergeant Lipton took his right arm at the wrist to handcuff him. Guilt robbed him of all his strength. Anguish turned his limbs to rubber. He let Lipton do it.

'I don't understand,' the foundling said while Sergeant Lipton handcuffed him. 'I went there to try help him. He was alive when I left … ' His voice died in the ash of his throat.

'That right?' said rhetorical Sergeant Lipton, complete with lipids. 'Anything you say may be taken down, sunbeam – including your underpants. I'd watch your mouth if I were you.'

The foundling saw all that would now unfold. He saw the questioning and the detention and his dilemma: to allow them to prosecute him, or to break their bonds like contrived gossamer. If he let them imprison him, he would wither; but he could only be imprisoned by walls he couldn't see. He was thus already a prisoner: he was incarcerated by a grief for Kenton that knew no bounds. In this formless jail he would wither. In this way, by this natural incarceration, by this emotional violence, society would get what it wanted from him: his normality. It was a normality he suddenly craved. It would be just punishment for his role in Kenton's death.

He therefore didn't resist Lipton's arrest. Why would he? In these moments he didn't care or think about anything than the death of his childhood friend. He wanted to be sick. He closed his eyes. He never wanted to open them again.

Sergeant Lipton stood in front of him. An old score lived in his blunt eyes. A bloodshot grudge. He had hoped the Salter boy might resist arrest so that he had to enforce it. Here he was, however, putty in the law's hands. His pathos and weak normality were thus revealed.

Dashiell was glad of his surrender. She knew its cause. She considered no one to be above the law, and she had taught him to trust the same. She knew he was innocent of Kenton's death. He may have turned Kenton into a vegetable, but he hadn't killed him. She knew that the legal system might not reveal that, however, or Bella's guilt; so when the foundling allowed Sergeant Lipton to handcuff him so easily, she also wished he would fly away from the law's grip and be safe and happy somewhere always. It didn't matter if she never saw him again; all that mattered was that he suffered as little as possible. Such are parents and their children.

He opened his eyes when Lipton whispered in his ear, 'Could have been me, couldn't it? Me or Kenton. How'd you do it then?'

'I don't know.'

'Course you don't.'

Sergeant Lipton then adopted more official body language as PC Shah gave the foundling a 'procedural overview'. He would be taken to the police station in the town. He would be held there for thirty-six hours while Mrs Young's 'accusation was formalised and initially substantiated'.

Dashiell held his eyes until Sergeant Lipton and PC Shah escorted him outside to the police van, which was parked within neighbour ogling range. She walked outside with them.

'It will be OK. We'll sort this out. Let them do it,' she said.

'Do as mummy says now, freakozoid,' Lipton whispered in his ear.

Lipton's mockery provoked a shockwave in him that came from a place too deep to be known. It blew through him, causing him to flex and twist in rage. The power of it made the police officers reel physically. Their cognitions reacted more extremely than their bodies, however. The shockwave, his power, broke Shah's grip on reality, though she managed to keep hold of his arm, which momentarily turned to living steel in her hand. Lipton's reaction was tempered by his experience of the inexplicable. For him, it was a kind of confirmation; but of what, and how?

The tempest lasted less than a second. When it passed, shock lingered. Shah was visibly shaken. Lipton less so, but his monkey-mind was afraid. He restored his grip on the foundling as he met Shah's panic-dilated gaze as if to say, 'See? Told you!'

Then it was over. Dashiell breathed again.

Then he went along with the charade, shackled by steel assumptions.

Sergeant Lipton and PC Shah escorted him into the police van. They locked him in. The white surface of the door and the reinforced van walls reminded him of the sharp sword of inanity upon which he often fell. He heard Sergeant Lipton and PC Shah get into the van upfront. He heard the engine start. His pupils dilated. His breathing deepened. The universe panicked. He who could not be imprisoned by any but himself feared this above all. Imprisonment.

To escape would be so easy. Their steel was as rice paper to him - unless the weakness he had experienced when he let Lipton arrest him endured. He sought immediate reassurance of his strength: he put his thumb against the door of the van. He pushed gently. The steel buckled. A concavity. Then the whole door started to warp, and the hinges complained. The relief he felt was a novel sensation. It made him realise how much he needed to be as he was, whatever that was.

Escape tempted him. Dilemma followed.

Yes, he could still flick the door away as he had once flicked Kenton across the pub. He could wreck the van and escape; but what then? He knew his escape would be taken as an admission of guilt. He would become a fugitive. That wouldn't matter unless it made it harder for him to relieve the suffering of others, which he could not endure. His own suffering made him laugh. It was his best stand-up comic routine yet. He actually laughed.

In the front of the van, Sergeant Lipton thought he heard the Salter boy laugh in the compartment behind him. The sound was proof of the insanity he assumed. The sickness.

Lipton thought he had heard the steel buckling in the cage behind him, too. It must have been a mechanical fault. Perhaps it was just this bumpy road. He would have the garage look at it the next day. In any case. What did he care? His shift was nearly over. Bringing in the Salter boy was a good way to end it. Who cared who killed Kenton Young? Kenton didn't. Kenton's worries were over, and Sergeant Lipton was startled and sad to find himself slightly jealous.

*

Shanti wept.

*

Weeks of questioning and uncertainty followed his mandatory magistrate court attendance the next day. He felt soiled and incredulous and outraged and calm and indifferent and sad. It felt disgusting to be so misconstrued.

When had it been otherwise? When would it be any different?

Never and never and never.

He forwent the opportunity of bail, which was in any case, a department counsellor told him, unlikely. They put a travel ban on him and demanded his passport. He told them he didn't have a passport. They didn't believe him. He let them search his room in Benen's Battersea property for it without a warrant. He knew it was necessary and wanted to help them with their enquiries, but he felt violated. When he let them search Dashiell's house for it (and in her absence) – again with his encouragement and without a warrant – Dashiell felt violated, too. On her return, she was furious with him.

'For God sake!' she raged. 'They can't just go rifling through my drawers like that! What were you thinking!?'

'I just want to get this over with, mum.'

'So do I. But there are limits.'

He knew she was right. Contrition feasted on his quiddity.

Naturally, they didn't find his non-existent passport. An adult citizen without a passport raises questions. It prompted them to assess his persona on their systems. They found little or no data on him. There was no record of his birth. The data vacuum prompted suspicions and drew attention to him. More questions were asked. He had few answers. This further aroused their suspicions. He was marked by the system as 'WD', which meant Wanting Data, aka someone the system didn't know enough about to take its eye off. Unblinking eyes therefore watched him. They sent data back to a sleepless brain that marked his absence in places it expected him to be as mandated by his situation. This brain also registered best-match IDs of him in places he surely couldn't and certainly shouldn't be. This brain was rarely wrong; so it refocussed its lidless eyes, ordered by legislation that demanded best possible intelligence about citizens it either knew nothing about or who seemed, as he did, indifferent to the procedures that 'strove' to keep them safe.

He strove to keep them safe, too. He was on the same side as the system according to its founding principles; but the system couldn't know that. He didn't seem like he was part of the system, too, and that made him dangerous. The system therefore made assumptions about his agendas and appearance – assumptions that were hedges against risk.

The system had a long memory. It remembered the damage he had done to the village hall with his incendiary stunt. It remembered doubts expressed formally by investigators about the part he played in Tally's suicide, and his strange behaviour then as reported by others. It heard the rumours about superhero roleplay played out with more enduring enthusiasm than could be attributed to imagination, youthful humour, and zeal.

Short of tearing the system down and watching one exactly like it take root immediately afterwards, he could do nothing about any of this; so he kept the Thing content by acting on his vocation in defiance of the bans they placed on him as they did all those who are pending investigation for serious crime.

Numbness grew inside him. Numbness followed him around the world. It made its numb home in him. It went with him back to London in defiance of the travel restriction order placed on him. It followed his instincts there to be near to Shanti, who had gone back to London to escape the tempest of Kenton's murder and the part she felt she had played in it.

Shanti didn't return his texts or his calls, however. Of course she didn't, he pondered. She must be in hell. He wished to follow her there and rescue her. Orpheus played his tunes upon the foundling's heart, but now the strings seemed broken, and the melody distorted.

Desperate, feeling bitterly alone, and homeless as he was, he went to Benen's Wardour Street office. He sat there with him now.

'This is insane. If you bolt town when you're bound over like this, they'll crucify you. Does anyone know? Christ, I'm sorry. He was your best friend, wasn't he? Shit. Look. We keep it out of the media. Off social. Have you told anyone? If he finds out, Tymon and the show will have to disavow you immediately. You'll lose the deal. We'll just have to see which way it blows. When you're found innocent, we can let the whole thing hit. It will be a case of you wronged by police ineptitude of the real perp, and all the usual bias and baloney. How does that sound?'

'I can't do all that anymore,' he said. 'I'm sorry.'

'Can't do what? Oh. But I thought you were broke,' said Benen. There was an edge of anger in Benen's voice that was sympathy re-forged on the anvil of inexplicable love. Suddenly Benen couldn't help but wonder where this young man was on the autism spectrum.

'Tymon is being a shitwit about my invoices – again. Cashflow this and blah and blah. I'm sorry. So as soon as he pays, I can pay you. Just give me your bank details soon, OK?'

'I don't have a bank account.'

'You said you'd open one. Fuck. So how am I supposed to pay you as and when Tymon coughs up? Anyway look. We'll cross that bridge. For now ... After the trial ... Will it come to that?' Benen said. 'This whole Kenton thing could make you a kosha star. The wrongly accused proven innocent at last. The real culprit is found and punished. We milk it on social. Tymon will work it. And bingo. You could make good money. Then you'd be freer to follow your vocation, or whatever it is you want to do. Ever heard the expression making hay while the sun shines? It's shining. Who killed him anyway?'

'I did.'

'What?'

'I hurt him. I destroyed him. It was me. This would never have happened if ...'

'Yes, but you didn't actually kill him, did you!?'

'Of course not. I couldn't have.'

'Why? Anyway I'm sorry. I know it must be hell on earth. God knows ... But maybe this trail – the whole shebang – this could really make you,' said Benen.

'Make me what?'

Benen's frustration with him became an unnecessary exhalation. The foundling's art books and notebooks were stacked up beneath the window. Dust was beginning to gather on them.

'What about those?' the foundling said of them.

'I can't sell that. Sure, I'm an occasional art dealer. I dabble, yes. But unless you become famous or something. Perhaps this thing – the death of your friend – the whole thing. Or maybe you'll need to die or something.' Benen laughed as he said it because he was serious.

'I may die. If I do, it will be soon. Otherwise I don't know.'

Benen eyed him for a moment. He was swamped by unexpected sympathy. 'OK. I can try,' he said apropos selling the art.

'Or you could just buy it all from me? Sorry to ask, but I may need some money for a lawyer, unless I can find a pro bono. Or I could exchange it for rent for a while?'

'What would I be buying?' With unforeseen anger. 'Beauty? Insight?' Calmer. 'How can those things be bought? The whole art market ... selling talent ... it's all about bullshit. Like democracy. Like pretty much everything.' Bitter. 'But you're not part of all that, are you? So what are you?'

The question hung like Foucault's pendulum. The Earth shimmied.

'So you won't buy it?'

'Dah-da-da-da-dah,' said Benen, oddly singsong and suddenly smiling; yet his eyes did not smile. 'Shave and a haircut,' Benen explained, implying the foundling's wild hair and beard.

'I know. I look ridiculous. But I think I've finally found a barber who can do the job. Anyway. How much will you give me? For all of it?' He indicated his art books and notebooks again.

The stress of obligation mangled Benen's reasonable id.

'I'd be insulting you.'

'How much? Two hundred? A hundred?'

'Please. Work up a career. Become notorious. Then this stuff could be worth thousands – millions if your tag is hashed.'

The situation waited. Laniakea was.

'Shit,' Benen said eventually. He seemed tormented. He mashed his face with his hand. He had studied acting. Eventually, he fished his wallet out of his pocket. He thumbed through the banknotes inside.

'I've got one-twenty on me. Who uses cash anymore anyway, right!? Open a bloody bank account and I'll transfer a thousand ASAP. Two thousand. Even that's an insult. Just tell me how much you need for a lawyer – OK? Pay me back in paradise.'

'I'm extremely grateful.'

Benen took one hundred and twenty pounds in cash out of his wallet and handed it over.

'Thank you much. It's all yours,' the foundling said re his art and notebooks.

'I'll keep it safe for you. That's all. OK?'

'No. It's yours. Thank you.'

Suddenly uncomfortable and swamped by stress, Benen indicated that he needed to get on with his work. His Mac pinged email alerts. Another phone call made his smartphone vibrate. Benen squirmed in a way that they both knew was a well-meaning sham. This was an opportunity. Benen was a benign opportunist. If the rumours about 'the beard' that were echoing around the internet somehow originated in this strange young man sitting across his weary desk, this art, bought now for a song, might be worth a fortune this time next year. His habitual strategies made him feel grubby. This was what he was, however. This was what life had told him to become. Benen had obeyed.

The foundling knew all this. He didn't seem to care. He stood. He offered Benen his hand to shake. Benen shook it reluctantly.

He went to the door. He looked back at Benen. Then he was gone.

Benen exhaled. He felt things. Mostly, his now squashed hand. Then his smartphone dragged him back to the quotidian life he loathed for murdering innocence.

The first breath is the last.

*

Independence Day

So now we're all talking about it: what was it (if it was an 'it')?

As everyone not living under a rock (pun intended) now knows, at 12.54 MDT on Independence Day (and how long ago does that already feel!?), the Yellowstone caldera was, well, lanced. Like a boil. And in the nick of time it seems.

According to Jed Alphorns of the USVPP (US Volcano Perils Program): 'The data on the Yellowstone caldera all pointed to just another hydrothermal eruption – a rock hurling geyser eruption kind of event. Essentially of the non-Armageddon variety. In fact, in the past, most eruptions at Yellowstone were not hugely explosive – certainly not global killers. And then the data last Fall about the magma chamber doming, then it got out, and all the panic after that which we all know about – and that evac. So like most people, suddenly we were worried. We were also wrong. How wrong is beyond scary. The new data suggested the caldera was set to throw us the biggest curve in geothermal scientific history.

'In earthquake terms, this was the Big One. I'm talking global killer – or at least many millions dead and displaced in the US mainland, and a likely breakdown in the global economy.

'I wish I could sugar it and I wish I wasn't saying these words. But then the event on the 4th. Don't ask me what happened, or what – or who – it was. I'm as baffled as everyone else. But whatever was behind this so-called lancing was exceptionally well informed, unbelievably timely – and a gambler: lancing a caldera is, frankly, absolutely certain to fail. It's like trying to set an atom bomb off slowly. But somehow, in this case, and don't ask me how, whoever is behind this got it right. Yes, Yellowstone Park will never be quite the same again; but that's better than what might have happened if, well, nothing had happened. I don't even want to think about the consequences of that. We likely wouldn't be having this conversation – and I'm a family man.'

Thanks Jed. Phew, then. So what was it? Theories abound. Of course they do. @everyone has an #opinion. Aliens. The good Lord. The Pentagon. The Rock. The ghost of Peewee Herman.

Brek Warmbier is a Yellowstone Park Ranger of some 27 years' service. Mr Warmbier was there when it happened. He had this to say: 'Well it came in too fast to see, I mean goddamn fast, then hit the ground like a meteor. In fact I thought that's what it was, except it wasn't on fire. It could have been ordnance of some kind, but none like I've ever seen or used in service. It hit like a thunderclap or bomb. But some serious detonation or impact sound anyway. Then maybe ten, fifteen seconds later, it – something, or something like it – resurfaced maybe two, three hundred metres away almost as fast. Then this whole in-out thing happened maybe three, four times. It hit, went under, then came out pretty much in the exact same spot multiple times. Then, I have no idea. It disappeared upwards. So this was no meteor. I'm baffled. What in heck does that? A miracle is what. But thanks-be is all I say. Like about a billion other people I guess,' said Brek this Friday gone.

Mr Warmbier is the only eyewitness we have because most others were happy celebrating the 4th. But frankly, *though we thank him warmly for his input, this sheds little light.*

Conspiracy theorists will no doubt tell us what happened in due course – if they ever leave 9/11, JFK, 'Q', or the moon landings alone. The rest of us may have to wait a while to find out what went down – a long way down, and into a vision of hell, and survived – and perhaps just saved all too many of us from a cataclysm.

Until then, all we can do is count our stars. Maybe it's time to start believing in those miracles again. I'm going with the tech-none-of-us-yet-know-about theory. Whoever or whatever was behind this enigma, however, from all of us: our heartfelt thanks.

Jyoti McRaven – Omicron SP @omicronsp

*

Parents never know their children.

He was talking to Jericho on Dashiell's iPad in her house three weeks after Kenton's death. His face was still a requiem.

'I'm so sorry,' Jericho said in reference to Kenton's death and the subsequent brouhaha. Jericho's image on the screen pixelated, then sharpened again as the stream picked up. Jericho's Dubai suntan was by now well established. He looked good despite this new anxiety.

'So am I,' said the foundling. 'I'm sorry for everything, dad. Sorry mum found me. Sorry for what I did to your life – to Tally ...'

'Stop it,' Jericho said sharply. 'I'm the one who should be apologizing. I couldn't cope, so I ran away. Anyway you said it yourself: no one is to blame ...'

'But I'm accountable,' the foundling cut in bitterly. 'Grievously so, as it seems to me at the moment.'

'We can work this out,' Jericho replied. 'Of course we will. Let me know if you need a lawyer. If you can't find a pro bono I mean. Actually scratch that. You'll need the full fat version. I'll help if you need me to. Or are you rich from the show and all the other stuff?'

'No. Some problems with invoices or something.'

'Jesus. Bloody sharks. Look. If this goes to trial ... Will you go along with it? Because you could just ignore it all ...'

'I'll go along with it. I did what I did.'

'Yes but you didn't kill him did you.' It wasn't a question. 'I don't know the first thing about you. But I know you didn't kill Kenton. Of that I'm certain. All the rest of it ... Everything else ... You've made everything uncertain, and that's the ultimate privilege, son,' said Jericho.

It was the first time Jericho had ever called him 'son'. It felt good. It felt essential.

A new silence hung between them for a moment, then, keen to normalise the conversation, Jericho went on: 'What have you been up to, anyway? I saw you on the show. Brilliant! All this stuff online, too. Is that you? All these rumours. Of course it is, right? Look. We'll find a way through this, you know. Truth will prevail. It always does.'

'You know that's not true. Everything is a lie out there, dad. It's making me ill, the lying. It's killing me.'

'I'm sorry,' was all his adoptive father could say.

Their Skype conversation didn't last much longer. He was still too conflicted by Kenton's death, his guilt, and his personal war with the Thing to say much to anyone – even Jericho.

Dashiell came back into the room. 'Don't bite your nails,' she said, and kissed his fire-bearded cheek. She then indicated that she wanted to speak to Jericho. He moved so that she could sit and speak to Jericho on the iPad alone. Then he went into the room next door.

There, he could hear Dashiell's voice in the adjacent room. It was a pleasantly familiar sound that provoked his emotions. He heard his adoptive parents talking about the village hall and the agreement they had reached with the council with regards its roof reconstruction as brokered (and partly paid for) by Dashiell and Jericho. He heard Jericho tell Dashiell that the new business in Dubai was so-

so despite the slump and all the 'other stuff'. Then it seemed as if their dialogue tailed off into the kind of talk that avoids what really needs to be said – like most conversation.

As they talked, the Thing warred within him. The Thing was becoming ever more intolerant of his guilt and grief for Kenton, both of which had become obsessive. There were millions of Kentons. What was he doing here? People needed him all over the world.

He started moving.

He went outside. He belonged out here. When he couldn't see the sky, he was anxious and diminished. He was about to follow his vocation up into the sky, but he remembered that he had another police interview later that day. He knew that the case would go to court, and that the odds were stacked against him; so he walked aimlessly instead of doing what he should do. The Thing followed, loathing him for his inaction.

The Thing, he mused, didn't have to read the derisory blogs, or see the National Enquirer quality photographs of a 'bearded man' doing things no human could do (and that any fraudster could do easily), however. The Thing didn't give a damn about all that, or him. It didn't care for or about the big fat ha–ha joke about a strange man who pretended to disarm aggression and help the helpless and oppose cruelty and rip hope out of blunt despair and wrestle with the idea of his strength and with dilemmas no other biology could understand or misunderstand so perfectly.

The Thing could go to hell. He could follow.

He heard a blackbird singing nearby in a field. The beauty of its song devastated him with its sad truth. The beauty led backward and forward to all causes and possibilities. He followed it happily into perfection. Heavy with grief, the beauty pierced him as nothing had ever done. It annihilated him. Annihilated, he was now free. An unexpected joy was born in him. Everything that bothered everyone would be gone sooner than the soonest imaginable thing, and like everybody's, his imagination was nature's imagination. His fear was nature's fear. His love was nature's love. His laughter was nature's laughter. He laughed now because he saw things as they were, are, and will be for a moment more fleeting than a shimmer on unquiet water.

Then he was gone into the air.

*

Love is a lie told by true tongues.

Later that day he got a text from Shanti: '*At the house with mum and dad. Joy! Where are you?*' The text made his cold stomach colder.

They met near the old quarry near the village. He got there early, nervous, eager to be with her and terrified of it. He reminded himself that there were Rules. In love's afterglow, ex-lovers must be Just-So with each other. There must be no sign of the intimacy and ecstasy they shared, no matter how absolute it was, no matter how intense. He knew he must obey these Rules. He must hide his love's brief permanence.

From here, the foundling could see that one of his quarry sculptures had graffiti on it. It was the sculpture of a young person in an unnatural sitting position as they might in a wheelchair. The graffito was quite near the base of the sculpture.

One word: '*Murderer.*'

The graffito made him feel sick. A defilement. A hooligan smear.

Who had done this? Bella. Who else? How sad that the branches should become so entangled in the roots that they shrivel.

Shanti turned up in her car. She got out. It was obvious to him that she had just been with her parents in the aftermath of the catastrophe of his making. Her eyes were empty. She avoided his gaze. He took this avoidance as her damnation.

They stood near each for a moment. It was slightly awkward.

'I can't begin to tell you ...' he began.

'You don't have to. It is what it is.' He found her forced nonchalance savage.

'I tried to help him. Funny that you dreamed that I ...'

'It was a dream,' she said coldly. She froze him to his core.

Following his pilgrim gaze, she saw the graffito on the sculpture.

'How did you do it?' Shanti said eventually.

'I didn't.'

'No, silly. The sculptures, not Kenton. Mum killed Kenton,' Shanti said. Her face emptied further, and then suddenly filled with something that he couldn't define. 'How?' she insisted.

'Oh you know. I was probably trying to impress you.'

Now Shanti met his eyes. She suddenly wanted to hug him. The impulse surprised her. She did not puzzle at the unknowable heart. She was content to be its puppet and to dance until music's end.

She held his gaze. It had become harder than ever. It had become impossible. She looked away. That troubled him. She had thought all was lost between them. To her, he seemed lost. He seemed like a child alone on a turncoat shore. It seemed to her that he looked at everything as if for the first time every time. It was irresistible but unsettling.

'I can't stay away from you, can I?' she said. 'What silly luck.'

'I'll go if you like,' he replied after a pulse. It was lame and he knew it, so he changed the subject: 'Doesn't waste time, does she?' he said in reference to the graffito on the sculpture.

"'She'?"

'Who then?'

'Baby. For someone so clever, and a bloody Michelangelo or someone, you can be deliciously dense. That daub's been there for a couple of years. It's that long since you were last here? Wow. Seems only yesterday they were the 'Glories of the New Renaissance' or something. Now, no one can even be bothered to clean graffiti off them. Go figure. Anyway, everyone says Mr Bourncleave did it – on another Glenmorangie bender, I guess. On the rocks.'

The foundling processed the revelation. Of course. Mr Bourncleave had witnessed him holding Tally's still bleeding body in the air the first time he had levitated. Mr Bourncleave had subsequently suspected him of Tally's murder and spread rumours accordingly.

How had he not seen that his onetime neighbour was the graffiti artist, when he could see forever? Because the answer was within touching distance, where he most often fumbled.

'Of course,' he said aloud, smiling wryly. As he said it, the memory of someone watching him perform the sculptures in the old quarry all those years ago flared and faded in his mind. A man, probably. A man who was not easy on his feet. A man who had stumbled slightly as he hurried away when he thought he had been seen by the sculptor. Mr Bourncleave.

Nearby, now, a tree vomited a crow. It hurled at the hooligan sky. All he wanted to do was hold her. He felt impossibly cold – or was it heat? High up, everything is one thing.

He looked at her. He dared not show his love. She saw it, nonetheless. She saw it in herself. They were the fractals of the heart.

'I'm so sorry,' was all he could find in the silo of his throat.

'So am I,' she said. Her eyes misted with tears.

He wanted to drown in her tears. He knew as he had never known before that love was all. It was the human moment, careless in the murder of the future and the resurrection of the past.

Then he laughed at himself – the king's royal fool: the overdressed emperor.

Mr Bourncleave. Of course.

His laughter and their sudden eye contact seemed to unlock their bodies. She moved close, then they hugged. Their hug was a perfect syllable. They existed as they had once existed without the need for anything else; but he knew that elsewhere, people needed him. The Thing bayed and roared like some fast beast awoken. It defied their rapture. It devoured everything. It ate whispers and words and hearts and earths and yes and maybe and caresses and purpose and now and reason and telephone lines and dustbins and hope and elbows and teacups and walking and counties and sacred and scared and polecats and countries and Pangaea and gifs and slums and palaces and suns and galaxies and clusters and super-clusters and light cones and everything, and still it was hungry. Its hunger could only be assuaged when it had eaten him. Only then would it be satisfied. Then it would sit back and with a contented belch, and fall into a dream-drenched sleep. Only then.

*

Tymon found out about Kenton's death and the foundling's prosecution.

Tymon dropped him like a wish down a well.

His contract with the company was annulled. The whole thing hit social media. He became a hashtag. He didn't like it, but he cared much less than most people would. 'Nothing lasts forever,' Benen said to him on the phone when he called him to tell him the deal was off. 'On the contrary,' the foundling replied. 'Nothing is the only thing that can last forever.' Benen was used to his habitual philosophising. He might have rolled his eyes at his client's unlikely and compulsive sagacity only a month earlier. Now, he felt a curious unease and sadness. 'I'll see you soon,' was all Benen could find to say, and 'Oh. Alice says hi'.

I'll see you soon.

*

Hope is a free radical.

His defence lawyer's name was Miss Eunice Swanland. Jericho had hired her online to defend him. Eunice had asked him to meet her at her office just off High Holborn to discuss his imminent trial for Kenton's murder. There was a considerable amount to go through. His position had to be made clear. He could either admit to it and take a lesser punishment without trial or deny the charge and take his chances in court.

As she now advised him, he looked at her sensible fingernails (as he bit his own). He thought of the Atlantic widening at about the same rate at which they grew. In his mind, he watched sulphur geysers erupting on Io as Jupiter's gravity caused tectonic tides, which generated friction heat inside the moon sufficient to melt its rocky core into convective magma. He heard the sonatas of whales as they voyaged the oceans. He was and loved and wished and felt and remembered many things.

He loved the fact that horses cannot breathe through their mouths. He wished a loofa weren't a vegetable. He remembered laughing to the point of pain with Tally when they found out that when male bees climax, their testicles explode, then they die. He remembered a female high-wire performer in a tiny circus flying as all little boys wish to fly. He regretted knowing that there are more fake flamingos in the world than real flamingos. He wondered if gravity was dimension transcendent. He felt mitochondrial DNA trickle down the distaff side. He saw the spear side wary beside legends of ice age fire. Woman and man. Bison daubed on cave walls by original hands. Sunrise.

She got his full attention when she said, 'You need to understand, Mr Salter – to realise that in the UK, euthanasia is murder. The punishment, your punishment, unless I can get you off the hook, unless we can win this, you could be looking at anything between five and twenty-five years. I'm sorry. But I'll do everything I can. But I need you to do your best, too. OK? Thank you.'

Shock stopped all the moons in their orbits. It gave the whales pause. It made daubed bison jolt and bees ejaculate. Accepting such punishment was unthinkable. Imprisonment would stop him doing what he had to do. It would also rob him of his uniqueness: any kind of constraint was catastrophic to him (yet he would never be free anyway).

If they found him guilty, he would have to resist their restraints, however much force they used to apply them; yet to do so would be to avoid punishment for a crime of which he felt profoundly guilty, and for which he expected punishment, even though punishment rarely works.

As Miss Swanland carried on briefing him, he felt his dilemma take on a new intensity. It bloomed like a mushroom cloud within him.

His nucleus was split. Only one thing could stop the chain reaction.

*

None are so punished as the innocent.

The moon went from tusk to blister five time. It had been five months filled with endless legalities and obligations. The magistrate's court had passed the case up to crown court as a matter of course. He had been electronically tagged. When he roamed the world to fulfil his vocation, he removed the tag so they would be unaware of his absence; but by doing this he broke it, and so fell further foul of the law. In the eyes of some whose job it was to bring him to justice, he thereby self-indicted.

Throughout this farce, the same question bickered with others in his mind: why did he tolerate his predicament when he could break free of it with such ease? He knew the answer of course. He felt he had to pay the price for what he had done. No matter that it hadn't been his finger on the trigger. He had loaded the gun. Justice had to be done. Justice is essential to civilisation. Civilisation is nature's finest sonata – a frail concord sung amid a near-barren cosmos.

He therefore sat now in the small dock in a London crown court. The dock constrained him notionally, but he was a truer prisoner of his conscience. Here and now, his conscience rankled, but then he realised he wouldn't have it any other way. He wouldn't choose to be anyone else. He was glad of what he was. He just had no clue what he was, though what he very much was at that moment was very much on display. He felt stupid sitting there like a performer in a side-show. It rankled. He felt misconstrued. It rankled. He was wasting time. It rankled. He should be out there doing The Thing's bidding. Here he sat though: lightning in a bottle. Thunderheads confined. Caprice on its knees. A tiger forced to smile.

Though he suppressed it, conflict raged in him as a storm at sea. Waves gnawed a monstrous sky. Wind drove rain to careless whips. All restraint was gone. Demons roamed the deep.

He forced himself back to land. He put the monster back in its cage. He focussed.

He glanced at Dashiell, who sat in the public gallery. Since his indictment for Kenton's murder, Dashiell's hair had become flecked with grey. He had told her that the greyness just added gravity to her innate grace (and that gravity, Tally, was just heavy gravy). Now, Dashiell didn't feel graceful, however. She felt like a hummingbird with a broken wing in a hurricane.

Having given evidence for the defence, Bella Young now sat in the public gallery. She was several seats away from Dashiell. Several continents away would have suited Dashiell much better.

Bella ignored her and the foundling in the dock with Old Bond Street distain. Bella knew he knew what she had done, and why. She knew her sick daughter had told him despite promising not to. How sad it is to have sick children for a mother of such quality. Beside her, Thomas' eyes were bankrupt. The foundling saw that Thomas hated himself for playing his part in a gruesome and expensive charade enacted in the name of revenge. He saw that to be near to Bella was now torture for Thomas, and that Thomas felt this torture was fit punishment for his weakness.

PC Lipton sat in the public gallery. Lipton was off duty and thus in civilian clothes. The foundling saw suspicion in Lipton's eyes, which seemed lost in his huge face like currants in porridge. He saw that Lipton didn't suspect him of killing Kenton, however. Lipton suspected him of disrupting normalcy. The overweight boy who had wet his bed most nights had felt a power that he couldn't explain in the schoolyard all those years ago. Fear of the unknown haunted PC Lipton's eyes now. This fear had a son called hatred.

When called to give evidence for the defence earlier, hatred spoke of the foundling's bizarre reputation and his violent proclivities. Hatred recounted in fine detail the incident in the schoolyard, and the affect it had on young Eric Lipton's life: the humiliation; the loss of confidence; the years of physical and emotional pain because of his injuries. Hate made everything clear. Hate left little room for doubt.

Mr Bourncleave sat behind PC Lipton and watched the trial like a boy with a new train set. He and various other village residents had already given evidence. A strange picture of the 'Salter boy' and his life in the village had been painted during the trial. There were more questions than answers. The Salter boy had hurt others. He had done strange things. Impossible bread had been baked and solid rock conjured into rumour. Alan and Daphne Montclewe had seen him do something with a car, too – but how? Had this been a moment of hypnosis? They had never taken drugs or done much to excess. They had eaten practical sandwiches and raised reasonable children who now studied at the right universities. No. Alan and Daphne Montclewe remained vexed to this day and all the well-behaved nights in between.

Questions remained as to Tally Salter's death, too. The police investigation had resulted in a finding of suicide, but some thought otherwise. Had her brother really found Tally bleeding to death in the bath? Was he really her brother? What, also, had Mr Bourncleave really seen that day anyway? Mr Bourncleave had sworn under oath that he had witnessed the aftermath of a murder. The fact that he drank like a fish in a sweat and said he'd seen the boy hovering 'several metres' in the air holding Tally Salter in his bloody arms rather undermined his veracity, however; but Mr Bourncleave was an ex-police detective with an impeccable record. Sober, he was considered as reliable a witness as could be found.

The foundling now watched the Young's relentlessly expensive lawyer Mr Julian Roshchard stand to say: 'I call Shanti Elizabeth Young to the stand, your Honour.' He saw the judge – the Right Hon Mr Justice Lu – nod in response. A clerk exited the courtroom briefly to call Shanti. He returned with her a moment later and led her to the witness box where she sat, and kept her gaze lowered.

The foundling noticed that Shanti had put on weight. He saw that her eyes were puffy. Her smooth complexion wasn't what it had been. Her face seemed drawn, yet rounder. She had dark circles under her eyes. All this made him love her even more. Her appearance could only be caused by immense stress, he was sure. Her mother had murdered her brother, and now this sickening travesty of which she was bound to be a part.

To the foundling, everything became like a dream of treacle. Shanti took her treacle oath, and Mr Roshchard started to ask her treacle questions. Shanti's treacle mouth assembled around responses as if packing them safely in treacle cardboard. Her treacle eyes fought the urge to look at him as she had many summers ago beneath apples in the sky's memory. The treacle eventually started to coalesce into meaning to which the Thing listened when Mr Roshchard asked Shanti: 'So who was the first to enter Kenton's bedroom immediately after the accused left the house?'

Shanti studied her hands for a moment. He saw her pulse in the tiny carotid drum beneath her jaw. Boom and boom. Her pulse had raced like this when they made love.

'My mother.'

'Mrs Bella Young here present,' said Mr Roshchard.

'Correct. My mother was the first person to enter the bedroom after he left it and went out of the house.'

'How long would you say she was in the bedroom?' asked Mr Roshchard.

Shanti's silence was a balloon abandoned at a child's party.

'Miss Young. In your own time. How long would you estimate your mother spent inside Kenton's bedroom alone?'

'She was in the room alone for maybe a minute. A bit more.'

'A minute or a bit more?' asked Mr Roshchard.

Boom went the drum.

'Maybe a bit more. But I've stated all this.'

'I know – and thank you. But for the jury. Thank you.'

'I'd say my mother was in Kenton's room alone for about a minute,' said Shanti.

'Thank you. I know this is extremely hard for you. You said she, your mother, Mrs Young made what you describe as a quote strange noise inside the room unquote. Can you describe the noise?'

'It was like nothing I've ever heard. But then imagine what she had seen.'

'Yes indeed. I honestly can't. And you didn't go into the room now with her, correct?'

'Correct.'

'And what about your father? Mr Thomas Young. Did he go into the bedroom while your mother was in there?'

Shanti could feel Bella's eyes drilling into her like wars into babies.

'No.'

'So your father entered Kenton's bedroom when?'

Thomas Young closed his eyes. Curtains against the night of lies.

'I don't know. Maybe a minute after my mother came out of the room. Maybe a bit less. A bit less.'

'I see. And when your mother emerged from Kenton's bedroom, where were you?'

'I was in my bedroom drying my hair.'

'You were using a hair drier?'

'Yes.'

'If you could please explain. If you were using a hair drier how could you have heard the noise your mother made?'

Boom and boom and boom.

'I felt something. Like something was wrong. So I turned it off.'

'It was then that you heard this sound your mother made. Then or before?'

'Before. Yes.'

'Before or then?'

'Then.'

'But you said 'before'.

Wars into babies.

'I turned the hairdryer off when I heard a strange noise. I could then identify it as my mother.' Shanti swallowed dry.

'I see. And why did she make this strange sound, do you think?' Mr Roshchard consulted a tablet, then continued: "like something being taken out of her by terrible force" as you put it'.

'Why do you think?'

'Please, Miss Young. Thank you.'

'Well she'd just found her son dead, hadn't she – or dying anyway.'

'Dead or dying?'

Eunice Swanland shot Mr Justice Lu a look of complaint, which was noted.

Stress etiolated Shanti. The foundling yearned to take her far away and learn how not to worship her as a theoretical goddess. Anger with Mr Roshchard began to gather like a posy in him.

Shanti found a small pebble deep within her. A tiny round thing, polished by time. It was her voice.

'Dead, I guess. I thought you had the medical report.'

'The jury needs to know everything. Thank you, Miss Young.'

The foundling saw Shanti waver. He craved eye contact with her. He wanted to reassure her. To tell her they couldn't hurt him or imprison him. That he would always be free inside the jail of his identity like everybody else. She wouldn't look at him, however.

His anger grew. It rebelled against the falsehood of this circus. Lies built out of greedy absurdity were being sharpened to sham points and hurled at innocence everywhere. Circus after circus was founded on deadly farce until a sick structure emerged that towered over its shadow like a swindler at noon.

In here, doing this, he was wasting time. Out there, cruelty thrived. The Thing mauled him for what he was doing. It was sick of his delaying tactics. He endured its talons. He knew that they would never stop lacerating him. He would bleed until there was no blood left.

Mr Roshchard's voice dragged him back to the here and now.

'Miss Young. As we have heard, and as you, your father and mother have testified for the defence, your father was downstairs when the crime was committed ...'

'I need to say something,' said Shanti. 'Can I say something?'

'Surely, Miss Young. As long as it is germane to the case,' said Mr Roshchard.

Something changed. Something caught in the foundling's throat. It choked Shanti. For a moment, a new silence existed around her like a child's seaside bubble. She had held the plastic hoop to her mouth and blown. The bubble solution had inflated and then pinched off into a petty universe complete with busy rainbows and seaside joy.

From Shanti's silence, a sound sprouted. Not the pebble, but a new thing. The new thing grew swiftly, fed by ancient winds. The sound heard the scars of birds fly south to seek warmth abroad. It took wing to follow them. The moon sailed behind a cloud. The sound was Shanti's voice.

'The accused. He did it. He killed my brother.'

Choked by her words, Shanti searched around, seeing nothing.

Bella's eyes shone with hollow triumph. Next to her, Thomas yielded his face to his hands.

Dashiell half stood and made as if to speak. She remained strangely at this crouch, as if ready for something that might be needed. Her gaze fled from Shanti to the foundling.

He had known this was coming, but when it arrived, it raped him. It wasn't that it stole his strength; it made being strong pointless. He suddenly didn't care about anything. Everything became nothing. Nothing became Shanti's face as she avoided his gaze and fought tears. He felt sick. His hands shook. He cursed himself for investing such love in Shanti, but forgave himself for doing it: like everyone, he was a slave of need.

Eunice Swanland looked at Mr Lu sharply in another complaint as soon as Shanti said it. Mr Lu responded as if needless of her fillip: 'Thank you Miss Swanland. Miss Young. Thank you, but what you have said is not admissible. We might consider it speculation, given that you were not present in your brother's bedroom at the time of his death, as you have stated. If you need a moment ...'

Shanti needed a moment. Her face was ashen. Her dark eyes glittered with stress and the threat of emotion. She avoided his gaze perfectly by closing her eyes. The foundling wanted nothing so much as to go to her and tell her it didn't matter, that forgiveness was a given, no matter the brutality of the crime. Her betrayal had frozen his limbs, however. He couldn't move.

This girl of moons. This love of days. This childhood verve. This adult treachery.

Mr Justice Lu gestured at the usher, who went to Shanti and said something quietly. She stood and allowed herself to be shown out of the courtroom, which buzzed with gossip in the public gallery in response to what had happened. All the while, Eric Lipton's eyes bored into the foundling.

As Shanti walked, the foundling was again struck by the changes in her – changes that could not be explained even by what she had just done. To him, her posture and gait had changed subtly. He pondered the condition but found no obvious explanation, unless …

Again, Mr Roshchard's expensive voice dragged him back to the world of his experience, which was riven by shock and jagged emotion, sharp enough now to cut flesh.

'I would like to question the accused, your honour.'

'As you wish, Mr Roshchard. We might as well abandon protocol entirely,' said Mr Lu.

Mr Roshchard approached the dock.

'Mr Salter,' he began. 'I'd like to wind the clock back some sixteen months. Exactly what were you hoping to achieve by orchestrating the so-called stunt in which Kenton Young was so grievously – and avoidably – injured on the evening of February the fourth last year?'

'I wasn't trying to achieve anything,' replied the founding, trying not panic. He wanted to escape by any means at his disposal, which was all means; but he was paralysed by hurt.

'So it was a prank. Young men having fun. And why not?' Mr Roshchard said to him. 'A way to get a laugh, perhaps. Were you trying to impress anyone?'

'I wanted to impress Shanti because I wanted to mate with her. So evolution made me love her. But romantic love is need dressed in the hem of possession, isn't it? So I felt jealousy.'

'I see. So you were in love with Shanti?'

The urge to weep almost overwhelmed him. Later, he told himself. Later, when they aren't watching you. Weep then as you have never wept before. Drown the oceans with your pain.

'I needed her. I need her now.'

'I see. So you say you felt jealousy. Of whom? Do you think Shanti was in love with anyone else at that time? Perhaps this put you on edge or made you aggressive,' said Mr Roshchard.

'Her brother,' said the foundling.

Seated now, Dashiell leant forward in her seat. Bella Young blinked once. Thomas existed.

'Please explain what you mean. And I remind you that you are under oath.'

'It's OK. I can't lie anyway. Kenton Young and his sister Shanti were ...'

He felt Bella's eyes flick to him as if daring, challenging, and fearing him absolutely. He sensed Thomas' body shift next to her. He felt everyone's eyes on him, waiting for more.

'Kenton and Shanti were what, Mr Salter?' said Mr Roshchard.

'They were close ... not *in* love but very close ... and how could I not envy them in that?' he said. His mouth felt dry. His heart pounded. He wished Shanti were still in the courtroom.

'Close?' said Mr Roshchard.

'Like siblings ... should be.'

Defending himself by instinct, he met Mr Roshchard's gaze full on. The barrister seemed to be trying to pull more out of him, to feast on some nugget of critical information that would change everything. The foundling therefore allowed his gaze to become unguarded for a moment. He allowed the furnace door behind his eyes to open briefly so Mr Roshchard could glimpse a perfect kindness and a fire so hot it could burn the world if it wanted; but it did not want: It wanted only to quell and cool and ease and heal; yet in this intent it burned hotter than a star's heart.

Mr Roshchard became afraid. Of what he knew not, but fear broke his gaze and threw it away.

Released from Mr Roshchard's attention thus, the foundling spoke again as a way to normalise the situation and appease the public seats. Hanging on his every word and wanting so much more, the public present were captivated by the prospect of gossip proven. Disappointment was unthinkable. Where was the meat in this tasty scandal-sandwich? Where were the garnishes and the French dressing? How might this be served? Surely it was lunchtime? Surely it always would be?

The foundling went on: 'So I think, being close to his sister, as a dear brother, Kenton was in some way jealous of my relationship with Shanti, as I must admit I was of him, of their closeness. In this way – in this capacity for jealousy and its havoc hands – I am like other people, and I regret it.'

'I see,' said Mr Roshchard. 'Well thank you for that. So ... if we can go back in time ... What part did Kenton Young play in the prank that led to this tragedy? What, I ask you, went wrong?'

'I just got angry. I was in love. I mean he just said something, and I ... I just pushed him. It's extremely easy for me you see because I'm not like you or anyone else. I did the sculptures with my hands. I can juggle cars and I can't be hurt. My skin. I'm not like any of you. I can fly. So doing this to Kenton was absurdly easy, which is a curse. My blessing is my curse. I can jump off cliffs and nothing happens. I don't know how. Fire is to me what water is to you. I don't know what I am ... I don't just mean that I'm an orphan ... I can't be known. I want someone to tell me ... Shall I fly now?'

Eunice Swanland's face clouded with remorse and professional humiliation. How had she not known of his condition? Had the system not diagnosed it? Why hadn't she been told? He had made a fool of her. This 'testimony' invalidated her entire defence – indeed the trial itself.

Fascination, pity, and ghoulish humour lived in different faces. To some, this publication of his insanity had been a long time coming. Now it was finally here, it was less interesting than anticipated. This reaction was best epitomised by Mr Bourncleave, who just looked sad and thirsty.

Dashiell closed her eyes as if she would never open them again.

The foundling's decision to end this charade came easily to him. It was time to stop this glove puppetry, whatever the outcome, for everybody's sake. Yes: Bella's tragic fabrication had to end. Yes: the truth had to be known. He could stand it no more. He stood up.

'Mr Salter. Please be seated,' said Mr Lu.

He remained standing. Mr Roshchard chose not to press the point.

'This is absurd. I didn't kill Kenton Young. His mother did,' said the foundling.

The public inhaled sharply. Lunchtime. The dessert menu beckoned.

Mr Lu began to respond to him as prompted by Eunice Swanland, but Bella was already screaming, 'Freak! My beautiful Kenton! All those years! Filthy bastard with your this and that! He's mad! Look at him! 'Shall I fly now!?' Yes, why not? You killed my son! Tally not enough was she?!' By now, Bella was lurching towards the exit door. False accusation and real grief intoxicated her mascara smeared eyes. As a man stands at a garden party, Thomas Young stood up beside her to follow her. He tried to calm her, but she was a quick sudden virago that smelt of seaside Bed and Breakfast soap.

Mr Lu began: 'Thank you. Mrs Young! Thank you!'

Bella ignored him and snarled at the foundling, 'Justice will be served. Rot in hell you freak!'

Bella stumbled out. Thomas Young followed her like a dutiful dog.

It was an award worthy performance.

Mr Lu pondered for a moment, while gavelling the hubbub in the court to silence. When there was, he said to the foundling, 'Proceed.'

'I played my part in his death, and for that I am more than willing to pay the price. But I couldn't have killed him.'

'Why not?,' asked Justice Lu.

'Because to kill is to die.'

**

kyū

Can I use mental health problems as a defence?

- If it can be proved that you were 'insane' at the time you committed the offence, the Crown Court may accept this as a defence (Criminal Procedure Act 1991). The Court still has the power, though to deal with you as it thinks fit, and this means it may impose an appropriate 'disposal'. The options are broadly the same as set out under the next question. This decision should be made after discussion with your solicitor.

- It might be possible that your mental health may prevent the "intent" required for the conviction of certain offences.

- If medical evidence shows you were suffering from an 'abnormality of mind', which meant your responsibility for the crime was diminished, then a finding of manslaughter will be substituted (section 2 of the Homicide Act 1957).

If I am found guilty of an offence, will I be sentenced to imprisonment?

- A psychiatric report must be obtained before sentencing if the defendant 'is, or appears to be, mentally disordered', unless a report is considered unnecessary. If the Court is considering imposing a prison sentence, it must consider the effect such a sentence would have on your mental condition and on any available treatment (section 82 of the Powers of Criminal Courts [Sentencing] Act 2000). This may lead the Court to consider whether another option is more appropriate.

*

A prison eventually becomes a sanctuary.

I don't know if I'm looking up or down. If I look down, I see them moving and speaking and doing things. They have been looking at me. If I look up I see them too. They seem the same. They seem to be saying the same things. It's further up than it is down. In either instance, they are a long way away. What's strange is that I get vertigo in both directions.

I think I can't, I must, I can't, I must go through with this charade. I must ride night's mare. I know I can't. I won't. I mustn't. I have to. The Thing is every tyrant. It beckons. It sounds like a cyclone forced through a small gap in jut rock. The constrained wind screams. Its throat is rock-tight. It is both rock and air. The air summons. The rock erodes. The Thing is all. All is absurdity.

Bella must be licking her lips at my demise with thin wet satisfaction. How she must loathe the taste of herself. How can she swallow such guilt? Perhaps she spits and spits and spits. Kenton will now be six months cold in sightless earth. They buried him long before the trial. A cheap and hurried affair. A pound shop valedictory. A matter hushed under humiliated dirt that will never fall silent.

The indignity is absolute. I am innocent of Kenton's death, but I feel more guilt than can be experienced. The pain of Kenton's death is almost matched (I cannot separate the two things) by the pain of being so misconstrued. My intentions were good, but they have been found to be bad. My hands are pure, but they have been sullied by false accusations and a legal system that could only treat me as normal.

I should never have gone through with it. Now here I am.

Truth feels dead, but in truth it just rests. Take note! Wake, most vital of things. Wake if only to attend your wake, then sleep again.

Lies bound me! And now. Lies curl like damp tongues around old meat at lavish tables where starvelings may not venture. The rest is the wobbly set of a stage play where every joke is a bit too obvious, and the Fool has wagged his last, jeered off at last to face the cold night without a mad king to love. Even this is a lie. All that endures is a brief gust that withers the skin of a lake on a summer evening. Then that, too, is gone.

Rise, fool, and quit your poetic self-pity!

If I ignore their constraints, what then? They come for me, but then? I will be a fugitive. I will be a fugue. Yes, but their grabs are the grabs of babies at the teat – or am I so weak now? Their doors and walls are rice paper conventions – or at least they were. Now though?

In doing this to me they think they are protecting people from me. They are protecting people from their sworn protector. This cannot be endured. I must break their walls, yet these walls will soon become sick darlings. Sanitary, secure, unbiased, sterile, functional, vertical dears.

They tell you that you are mad. Insanity cannot spread its wings. Not fly, no. Yoke it and they call it genius. They could use that, but madness they cannot. That's the difference. They don't understand.

The high winds summon. The blue says come back and be all you can be. Why should I be less? Why would anyone? Because the moon howls, fool. Because of the centrifugal fate and the centripetal. Because of escaping into the infinite or plunging in fire towards the zero planet.

Weak get weaker. Strong gets stronger. Rich, richer. Poor, poorer.

Still there are official echoes. I can't escape them. 'Your defence was recharacterized by your declaration of insanity under trial.' 'A state of diminished responsibility is reflected in the sentence handed down.' The echoes echo. Handed down? Why punish anyway? Punishment is revenge, and vengeance is inane.

Why had she testified against him falsely? He knew the answer. He had known at the time. Half mad with grief for Kenton, Shanti had panicked. Her anger at the foundling for the part he played in Kenton's death drove her to it, with a little help from her mother: Bella had enabled Shanti's violence against him. Bella pulled bitter strings and the marionette had flailed. Her wood limbs jerked. Bella the unable mother. Bella the child. Bella the murderer. Bella the compassionate?

Perhaps.

I cannot be here! Don't they understand? In this institution! There is a walled garden. How can the rose be prisoned? How can fire's petals be constrained? With wet ease. That's how, fool.

I fear the Thing. I fear failure. For me, there can never be success.

Mum and dad visited last week. It's the school holidays, so mum didn't need to take time off work at the school. Jericho's Dubai property business was 'in a period of transition', he said. This of course meant the business had gone to hell in a handcart. 'The business is due a boom,' Jericho said through a half-remembered smile. It was good to see him. He had flown back to the UK as soon as he heard about the court's finding and my sentence.

My only father. My pretend father. My pretend everything.

They let 'patients' sit with visitors in the secure room overlooking the oxbow. Jericho talked about things that actually meant he felt guilty about going abroad and not being at the trial. Mostly not being at the trial. I think he hated himself for that. While he talked, Dashiell looked out of the window. She watched the river carry history to the sea as it had done since history came into existence, born first of hearsay, then daubed and scratched on rock and clay in deep human time.

Dashiell's eyes were enamelled by distress that she sought to conceal. She had always been a stoic – at least outwardly. Jericho put his left hand on her right hand on the table. She didn't move her hand from under his immediately. Tally would have been glad. She would have pulled a face and rolled her eyes at her little brother, who would have giggled without knowing why.

'I'm sorry,' I said when Jericho moved his hand away from hers a few seconds later, then regretted it. I meant that I was sorry about everything that had happened. I was sorry about what I had done to their lives. I was sorry about the way people now saw Dashiell in the village. I was sorry about everything to do with Kenton. I was sorry the people who had played the role of my parents with utter sincerity now had to endure the pain of seeing me in a psychiatric ward.

Dashiell knew. She knew I didn't have to apologise, too. She told me with her silence. It was a silence that could dapple a familiar surface. It was the silence of slow afternoons. It could settle on things like old joy or clear new sadness. It could be daubed as if by curious hands, above which the steady shirts of heritage were buttoned back to free up expertise. It could wait as if forever on worn carpets, or the well-used handles of cupboards opened and shut ten thousand times as people become people, and then fade beyond memory and legacy. It could fill a favourite cup and be drunk by thirst that bursts into an excited kitchen with sticky fingers in a mortal summer.

So I listened. So did Jericho. Then the silence ended, as things do.

'I'm the one who should say sorry,' said Jericho. 'I'm sorry I couldn't make it to the trial. Sorrier than I can tell you …'

'Dad. It's OK. You know it is.'

'…But with things as they are – the restrictions are still in place. Anyway. We've begun the appeal. This is a complete and utter farce. You didn't kill Kenton,' said Jericho.

'Didn't I?'

'Don't be absurd.'

'How can you be sure of anything now, dad?'

'We just know,' said Jericho.

'No you don't. Two plus two aside …'

'Stop it!' said Dashiell. Sudden anger alloyed her sadness. She met my eyes as she often had when confronting me. She meant: 'This isn't the time, Plato: can it'. She was right. There was a time and a place. Sometimes I didn't recognise either. Now, I barely recognised myself.

'That witch,' Jericho whispered, of Bella.

Suddenly keen to change the subject, Dashiell then told me that the village hall was almost rebuilt. Her voice was tight with emotion and her eyes were heavy. She smiled falsely, which was unusual for her. She only smiled when she couldn't avoid it. She only laughed when truly amused. Jericho grinned and winked at me. It was his way of normalising things. Dashiell then told me a bit about work. Then conversation evaporated. We spent most of the rest of the visit in stillness. Before time was up, Dashiell stood abruptly to leave, as if unable to leave. 'Don't bite your nails.'

Then Jericho stood, too. He shook my hand, then hugged me. If only I could feel it. If only I ever had. Jericho then left, presumably so I could say goodbye to mum alone. This seemed melodramatic, but I appreciated it. Dashiell and I then hugged goodbye. It was fine. It would only be for a while. We would see each other soon, and anyway ...

That was last week.

I have heard nothing from Benen Clay since the trial, but perhaps they wouldn't tell me if he has called or emailed the clinic, if he can. Likely he wouldn't know where I am. They have taken my phone away from me, which seems criminal. I'm now glad I locked it with a PIN.

The screaming is louder now. The Thing is on fire. It rages at me to help and sustain those who wilt and flicker and congeal and squirm and endure and starve and parch and flee and fight and button their faces up with trauma. Yes: I will soon wash them again with my love; but not yet. Soon. Please? When I am strong again. Soon. The longer I delay, the more I betray myself and those I should be helping, and the more I am enfeebled by these walls, which grow ever more necessary.

Shanti looked different in court. Older. Not older. Different. Tired. Why? What must it be like to hate your mother so? What must it be like to love your brother so? What must it be like to know your mother has killed your brother? What must it be like to betray the love of your life? Unless she never loved me? Unless she fooled me? Unless she veiled her reality behind casual myth? I can see where hawks cannot; but was I blinded by chemistry? Of course I was. I know love is true, but is it truth? Whatever. Here and now love's cause seems irrelevant. I miss her so much. It hurts.

Knowing Shanti as I do (which of course is not at all) I know she must be ashamed of what she did to me. She must be. Did she do it because she hates me because I hurt Kenton? Did Bella force her, as I surmised? How? People are propelled in such fragmented and multifarious ways. Perhaps Bella's hold over her is stronger than I think, and much stronger than Shanti would admit. The influence of parents on children cannot be overstated, nor can it be purged.

The last I heard from my love was the day after the trial. A text. It was one word: 'sorry.' There was no x in it. No kiss. We first kissed by the brook near the windmill. That was almost twenty years ago. The kiss of children beguiled. I texted back: 'I am the one who should be sorry.' She didn't reply to that. Then they took my phone from me. I let them. Shame on me.

I am wasting time. I must act now. I am scared. If I do what I must do. If red takes me. But I am weak. If I avoid the black moon's gaze. But if I could. They will mock me. Be strong again. They will know me. They cannot know me. They wouldn't need to believe in me.

Does Shanti believe in me? Can she know how sorry I am? Of course not, dazzled fool. Is she what is she how is she where now how can she when will she how could she why did she who is she how can I when did I how could I when will we know how will we, we will be, we will, but what is how is who is what will how will it happen when will I see what love is how is love is need how are you today thank you kindly love and zero and you and me and the possible the stars have learnt to laugh at last there is no us only the me the I the natural mirror that is why which is why there is no who when will she will she come to me how will she I will ask these walls such questions I will carve them like thin air I will go to her but no she may not cannot see me hates me why is she the poor fountain Bella crying mother-acid over the clean the darling living land the pure the sacred memory of land unsullied and free and free of accusation and full of still red stillness mother oh sorry mother but I am here now I am I think I am glad as early meadows in the meme of here and now is there a then and when you are we are my darling oh my darling we are already history nearly the boiled sweet of an illusion in the mouth of minds hell bent on heaven in this crust of light-handed chemicals and carbon thuds sublimated and if you fight my rage for justice is this not right I know it is not right but if you fight your passion for Noh you will never be the empty space is the fullest you will never know but if you yield to this least forceful thing like me like you I will know you only as zip and nowt and zilch and nix and the irreducible nada knows no bounds.

 The time for excuses is over. Here I sit, however.
 I beg you not to forgive me.

*

Shanti tried water and detergent first. She rubbed with the soft side of a washing-up sponge for fear of marking the surface of the stone; but this had no effect, so she used the more abrasive side. That didn't work either, so she abandoned the effort that day and came back on Tuesday.

 Thomas had always said 'WD40 can sort anything except stupidity', so she came back with a can of that and another sponge. WD40 did indeed do better than the water and detergent, but the accusation persisted – albeit a ghost of its former self. She wanted to remove the word entirely.

For Shanti, now, nothing but entirety would do. She therefore came back later in the week – this time during the evening because she had been busy all day trying to find somewhere to live and visiting the doctor – and went at it with the WD40 again. She certainly didn't care if people saw her doing it. In fact she wished Mr Bourncleave would see her doing it (in fact he was watching her now through field glasses from under cover of what used to be the security shed near the entrance to the quarry. To him, she looked changed in shape and demeanour) so she could have it out with him.

Try as she did, the WD40 didn't do the trick. Not quite. The stone remained haunted by the word. Exhausted, she went back to the Bed & Breakfast she was staying in (living at her parents' house certainly wasn't an option any more, and she had no idea how they managed to do it).

She came back early the next morning with paint stripper and a few domestic brushes, and a new sponge bought for her by Thomas. Thomas was with her now. Father and daughter made the word go away. Where it had been, however, was the faintest discolouration: the rumour of the myth of the memory of the word. The word became a dream, as Thomas' memories of childhood had become. Were they memories or phantasms? He couldn't be sure, though he maintained a strong belief in his onetime innocence. Now, he and his daughter stood close and looked at their handiwork. To the casual glance, the graffito had gone; so they went, too, and Mr Bourncleave watched them go with a normal heart.

*

A sanctuary soon becomes a prison.

After three weeks in the psychiatric hospital, he started to feel like he was surrounded by busy or blunt ghosts. At night, they left him alone in the safe terror of his locked room. By day, they drifted and flitted around him. Perhaps some were patients. Perhaps some were staff. It didn't matter. Their voices were hollow plastic things. Their smiles echoed and veered. If they were lucky, the moon danced on their uniforms.

One day, the war within him combined with despair to converge on a moment in the bathroom after a breakfast he didn't eat. As he turned the hot tap on, it squeaked. It always did this. Squeak squeak squeak. Today, the squeak became the screams of those he'd abandoned.

He saw the reflection of his wildly bearded face distorted in the sink tap handle. He heard a shriek that roared. He saw a fist plunge through a tile, brick, and concrete wall. His cry was so loud it punctured the eardrums of the other two patients in the bathroom. It cracked the crack-proof bathroom mirrors. He tried to help the patients he had deafened. He tried to tell them there was no need to be afraid, but it was useless. He heard someone shout in the corridor outside the bathroom.

All of time and no time 'later', officials came running. Their voices were distant fluids. They entered the bathroom suddenly. Then they were near him. Then they were trying to calm and restrain him. He set them aside as gently as he could, but in doing so he sent one of them crashing into the sinks. He pushed the other backward with such unintentional force that the man might as well have been hit by a truck.

This most regrettable event gave him deadly hope: that his strength hadn't vanished entirely. It lay dormant. IT could be awoken.

The next day, he was confined to his room. This was his punishment while the bathroom event and its consequences were assessed. It had been raining. From the window, he could see doubt drip into stillicide from a blocked gutter above. He could see doubt sparkle in the newly damp grass of the small garden beyond the veranda. Doubt edged the veranda with moss. The wind doubted the clouds it chased through the carbon sky. He doubted the pebble of light that caught in the corner of the window. He doubted the solidity of the window, and the memory of sand within it. The doubted the vague sounds of staff and patients beyond the absurd door to his room. He doubted the door handle. The doubted the liberty he craved. He doubted his craving.

The damage he did to the bathroom wall, the injuries he caused, and the general fracas had inevitable consequences during the next few days. He was moved to a much higher security wing of the hospital. Letting them do this to him made him loathe himself even more; yet again, he felt powerless to resist. Awaken sleeper, awake! No. Sleep on. In sleep you will be safe. Rock a bye baby. Hush now. There.

They tried to inject him with what they described as a 'sedative'. Two well-built hospital warders were on hand. A doctor he hadn't seen before introduced himself as Doctor Chicago, with 'but you can call me Doctor Zhivago if you wish!' He didn't call him anything. He just looked at the ceiling as he lay on his back in the white-tiled room. He could smell the sterilising agent they scrubbed the pale floor with. The day echoed.

Doctor Chicago attempted to inject him with the sedative. Naturally, the doctor couldn't penetrate his skin with the needle. Doctor Chicago made some throwaway comment and unwrapped another needle – the first having snapped. He attempted to inject the foundling with the new needle. Naturally, he failed again.

'Déjà vu,' said the foundling. 'I'm sorry. I must pay for the needles. Anyway. I've decided. "Without stones, there is no arch" – Marco Polo.'

Doctor Chicago ignored him. He was slightly flustered. 'Well,' was all he said. Then he said it again. Doctor Chicago discarded the second bent needle and pondered the situation. The doctor then sought the pulse point on his wrist. He couldn't find it. 'That's odd,' he said through pursed lips as he continued to seek the pulse point.

'I'm wasting time,' said the foundling.

Doctor Chicago gave up on finding the pulse point. He was obviously flummoxed. He then adduced the needles, the hospital around them, and then seemingly the entire world in one eye roll and said: 'Quite honestly, you get what you pay for.' He then said, 'There are many forms of madness, young man. Some are sanctioned. Others are sanctified. You may have the misfortune to be curable. We'll see, won't we?'

Doctor Chicago put his equipment away in his bag. He was annoyed. He was annoyed because he was embarrassed. He was embarrassed because of what he thought to be his professional ineptitude, and/or faulty equipment provided by a cash-strapped department that was at the mercy of yet more austerity. He was determined to blame someone for this situation, so he did.

Doctor Chicago surveyed the foundling briefly before he left. Meeting his eyes gave the good doctor pause. A frown baffled his brow.

'Be well,' said Doctor Chicago. He then turned abruptly and headed for the door. The door ate him. Then he became a memory.

The next day, Shanti came to visit him.

'You were to have no further visitors for the foreseeable future after your little performance in the bathroom. Mr Carin is quite badly hurt you know. There are circumstances, however; and we are bound by law.' Mrs Essie Marr was the hospital manager. She had looked at him briefly as she spoke, then at her Mac screen.

'Circumstances?'

That was yesterday. Now, he sat in the visiting room at the allotted time. Two warders stood near the door – one large, one smaller. The foundling couldn't calm the butterflies in his stomach. His palms sweated. Shanti had come to apologize for her betrayal, perhaps. She had no need to. He understood. He didn't care why she was coming. She was coming. It felt like a complicated heaven.

He glanced at the large wall clock. Its vast hands jerked from second to second and from minute to minute in pursuit of the non-existent now. How silly. Time has no grain. How silly. It was.

He felt sick with heavenly anxiety when the secure door finally opened. Shanti entered. The reason for her changed appearance in court was immediately apparent; so was all that would now happen, to whom, why, and when. A tired smile haunted her eyes as she met his gaze. She walked from the door to the table he sat at and sat down. As she did so, all fear left him. As she did so, his strength began to return. He stood up. He sat down. His mouth opened. His mouth closed.

Shanti was pregnant with his child.

'You can't be in here,' she said eventually because she didn't know what else to say.

It was true. He couldn't be in here. Suddenly he felt he could be anywhere. He would soon be free. He smiled from east to west. Emotion roiled in him like dark oceans at bay. Shanti's eyes brimmed with tears as she held his gaze. The wind flogged the windows with safe rain.

As if overflowing with what he took to be contrition and regret she went to speak again, but she was suddenly conscious of the two warders and the other couple in the cramped room: a patient and her visiting husband; so she whispered, 'How are you, my love? I'm so sorry. I was so angry, and now I don't want to be angry any more. Is that possible?'

The answer was in his eyes. It always was.

His smile was perfectly gentle. It made her cry. He looked from her beloved face down to her eight months pregnant belly. His spark had taken. The fire of their genes had caught.

'It's OK. Everything's different now,' she said. 'Oh – big Mal says hi by the way.'

She took his hand. That made the slightly larger warder look over at them again. She held the warder's gaze until he looked away as if caught off guard. Then she winked at the foundling. The wink invented a tear. The tear escaped her right eye and spilled down across the cheek he had kissed a thousand times since he was eight years old.

'I'm so sorry, Shanti,' he began; but his voice stumbled and fell. It was the voice of a beggar who trod the streets of hope and faltered on its cobbles. When a coin was offered, the beggar doffed and winced strange thanks. Then his clubfoot voice was still.

'What for, you berk?' she smiled.

'For Kenton.' The beggar shuffled on.

'Well it's done, isn't it,' she said. 'I've told the internet what really happened anyway, whodunnit, so when she found out, Bella threw me out, so I'm dossing now. Look. I'm sorry I haven't … I couldn't bring myself to contact you. I was so angry with myself. I was too sad, you see…'

'It's OK.'

'No it isn't. What I did is unforgivable. How are you anyway? I've missed you like crap. What have they been doing to you?'

The beggar became the sudden king of itself – the only possible kingdom. 'Nothing. I'm fine,' he said. 'But you found me. I missed you, too. I thought … I'm sick of thinking. Sometimes …' the king said while he could. He looked at the dome of her inner fruit. His new world. Earth was his other world. Both needed him completely. His atom was split. The Thing awoke and regarded her condition. To it, all was instantly clear.

'What will it be?'

'I don't know. Does it matter? It's ours.'

He managed to shake his head. He managed to smile. Of course it didn't matter. She hushed him. She held his hand more tightly. If only he could feel her grip as he had felt her when they conceived this moment. Perhaps he would feel his child's touch one day. Perhaps he wouldn't. His child might never feel his touch, or anyone else's.

Help me help me help me help me help me help.

'It's lol hilarious though,' she said in her way. 'The whole thing's a lollipop. The deal was I testify you killed

Kenton and if I didn't, they disinherit me and accuse me of some filth they made up, well not dad but mum did. She's sick as fuck, right? And this is where it gets really funny ...'

'It's OK ...' he cut in gently.

'But they're flat broke now anyway,' she went on. Her eyes shone like being alive. 'Keeping Kent alive bankrupted them – well, poor dad anyway, as usual. That poor man. That's why Bella ...' she drew her thumb across her throat. 'One reason anyway. And you were the perfect scapegoat. And mum's not much for changing a grown man's nappies, or babies' nappies for that matter, so what better time to do it? It's OK, babe. Kenton loved me. You love me. We're all jealous, no? Why not finish the job, right mum? The goat escaped – ta-dah! – like you and Tally used to say, no?'

'Yes,' he said. For him, it was suddenly time to get out of this place. He shifted his position. The safe plastic and stainless-steel chair creaked beneath him. The smaller warder reacted.

'Where are you living now?' he asked, seeking again to normalise. He saw his desire to do this as a fault in his character. To seek normality; yet why would he ever do anything else?

'You remember Galway's B & B on Shallows Road?

'That sounds expensive,' he said. 'You could stay with Dashiell.'

'I couldn't put her out like that.'

'She isn't a cat, you know.'

She smiled her delicious tough-guy smile and said, 'Meow.' He was still cracking jokes – albeit awful ones. That was a good sign. Then they just looked at each other.

'When is it due?' he seemed to say at some point.

Shanti touched her pregnant belly.

'June the first, apparently. You and me, babe,' she said. She was laughing now. That made him laugh. 'The truth is,' she went on, 'Whatever you are, it's inside me now.'

'I have to be with you now.'

'I know! We will soon. And it's OK. We can appeal. You'll be out of here in a month or two and then ...'

He stood up. The warders reacted. She stood too in reaction.

'Babe? What's going on?' she said.

The warders were moving now. They sensed something.

'I was scared, Shanti.'

'Join the gang.' She laughed and cried at the same time. So did he.

'Come on,' he said. With suddenness and decision.

They walked to the reinforced steel door. The smaller of the two warders said, 'Excuse me. You can't ... Hey!' Both warders started to cross the room towards them. The other couple in the room – a female patient and a man who looked like her husband – stopped talking and watched. The patient's husband took out his smartphone and selected the camera/video function.

The foundling smiled politely and thanked the warders. He led Shanti to the door. She was still laughing and talking about something or something else, or something. It made him smile.

Then he stood in front of the reinforced door. He hesitated.

'What?' said Shanti, unsure of his intention.

The warders approached idly, as if they couldn't be bothered.

'Mate. Seriously,' the smaller one said.

The foundling lifted his hand and touched the door. He focussed. The universe swarmed in his head. His throat was dry. His palms sweated.

'Babe? What we doing?'

'You need to sit down again!' the smaller warder said officially. He slouched to make himself seem indifferent to his size. The bigger one put his hands on his official hips to big himself up bigger.

The foundling doubted his doubt. He took a breath that he started to believe in. He shoved the reinforced steel door. It resisted. How could it? Had he grown so weak? He shoved again. The door yielded slightly.

'Hey!' both warders choired as one TV dinner too many might, but they hesitated.

He shoved again – this time much harder. The door flew off its hinges and landed in the corridor beyond. The noise of it was so loud it made Shanti jump. She then recovered enough to swear expertly and say, 'Is your name Jose? What's the plan, Stan?'

He and Shanti walked through the now empty door frame.

'Hey!' shouted the larger of the warders on behalf of the smaller, who was struck dumb at what he had just witnessed. The larger warder fumbled for his portable radio as he followed the foundling and Shanti through the doorframe. He reached out to apprehend the escapee.

'Hey! Visiting is now officially ...'

The foundling brushed off the larger warder's large hand and walked on with Shanti down the corridor outside the visiting room. The warders replaced their fear of the impossible with irritation at poor maintenance, which they blamed on cutbacks. Their pursuit was somewhat casual, however, as dictated by self-preservation. They pretended to be busy on their smartphones.

He and Shanti walked on. She took his arm like a proper madam. At the end of the corridor, there was another door. It was less secure than the visiting room door, but reinforced and substantial, nonetheless. He shoved it politely. It resisted. He shoved it harder. The door suddenly flew off its hinges and its locks. Wrecked, it fell to the floor beyond noisily. He and Shanti walked through.

'I'm sorry,' he said to the dumbfounded warders behind them, profoundly anxious that he had caused damage.

'I'm curiouser and curiouser!' Shanti said, demonstrating her 'insanity' to the world. 'It's me! I knew it!' She laughed. It was nervous laughter, but there's no such thing as laughter anyway.

He and Shanti kept walking. The warders shouted after them and gabbled into their radios.

They were in another corridor now. They heard another commotion. More voices. An alarm sounded somewhere. He smiled at Shanti. Again, she was laughing and crying at the same time. 'I knew it was me, babe,' she said to him, and was suddenly sad.

He kissed her hand then held it with possible gentleness.

More warders and a manager emerged from the door behind them. More shouting. More commotion. The alarm.

He and Shanti hurried through another door – this one unlocked – and out into the foyer and reception area of the building. A receptionist looked up as they entered the foyer. She grabbed her phone immediately and started dialling.

'And ... action!' laughed Shanti through the thick thrill of it.

They left the running and the shouting and the procedures and the situations behind them. They walked outside. The rain had thinned to familiarity. A cool light said the clouds.

Shanti led him towards her car. It was parked in the visitors' car park nearby. The facility manager Essie Marr emerged from the door behind them in a controlled vex. She was flanked by the large and small warders (not exactly in her best books now) and others.

'Stop! You have to stop now – both of you,' Essie Marr shouted. She kept on walking toward them. Her scheduled cronies – people with hopes and histories and unknowable causes – followed. 'Stop,' Essie repeated as they continued to walk away. 'Now!' she bellowed.

They didn't stop then or ever. The warm air felt wonderful on his face as he walked. He hadn't been outside for several days. Pursued by Essie Marr and her sanitary cronies, they hurried to Shanti's car. On high, seagulls bewailed broken waves. His wonderment turned it all into a beautiful, strange, sluggish ballet that some call reality. He felt freer than he had ever felt. His strength continued to come home.

They got into Shanti's car. Shanti had trouble getting her pregnant belly behind the steering wheel. The struggle made her laugh like some glorious felon. He was already in the passenger seat by the time Essie Marr and the others got to the car. Shanti locked the car doors. Their pursuers remonstrated with them outside.

'I'm really sorry. I'll try to pay for the damage,' he said to Essie Marr outside. She just looked at him sadly like he was a thing found squashed in the corner of a room where time was resting.

Shanti started the car, banged the auto into Drive, and floored the accelerator. He put his hand protectively over Shanti's pregnant belly as a way of asking her to take it easy.

Shanti drove quickly and expertly out of the car park. She hit the button that opened the car roof. Summer sunlight thus caressed his wind-blown face. He shut his eyes for a moment and savoured the sensation. It was delicious. In the mirror, Shanti saw Ellie Marr and the others do an about-face and scatter towards vehicles and procedures.

Shanti put her foot down. The car responded. Sunlight strobed. He opened his eyes. Foreboding grew in the centre of his rapture. He forced himself to ignore it. He forced himself to exist entirely within this moment, even though all moments were now to him.

Shanti put her hand over his hand on her belly. She steered with the other hand. She hurried the car down the institution's leafy driveway. She turned onto the B-road at the end of the driveway. A road sign informed them the main road was four miles away.

'I've been such an idiot,' he said as they headed for the main road.

'Join the gang,' Shanti replied.

'This is madness.'

'You should be funny for a living,' she laughed.

'Shanti. Wait. We have to go back.'

'Again, Jose. No way. For why? I didn't tell you to break out of there. I have no idea how you did it, either. But hey. And what they going to do anyway? Admit they fitted cardboard doors and left them unlocked? I'm not taking you back there. They can't pin anything on me except visiting a wrongly punished man. The man I love. Anyway ...'

A siren started to wail somewhere. It drew near, then faded into Doppler sadness somewhere. The siren summoned him. The Thing awaited. It would tolerate little more delay.

'It's time to put the record straight,' Shanti said. 'The bitch is going down – if they can find her. I'm due to make an official statement to the police tomorrow. I'm going to reverse my testimony. I know I'm admitting perjury, but I don't care. The bitch is gone. I thought I'd come and see you first to tell you. And now look!' She was smiling. It was nerves. It was fear. It was exhilaration. It was the cosmos in a song.

'Whatever happens, you will be OK,' he said.

In that moment, she knew that she always would. She did not know how she knew.

'Your mother couldn't help it ...' he began.

'Well maybe I'll forgive her one day,' she interjected. 'Maybe I won't.' Shanti fought for control of her emotions for a moment, then carried on, 'She's done a runner anyway. The Costa del Broke, probably. Dad had to borrow in the end to look after Kenton anyway, so .... Maybe Bella was trying to help in her own FUBAR way. Oh shit. Seriously, babe. Who'd have a mother, right?'

She fought tears away.

'I'm so sorry,' was all he could find to say.

'So am I,' she said.

They went on in tender silence until they got to the main road. There was too much to say to speak; so they just let their situation – replete as it was with unknowns and uncertainties as all relationships are – speak for them. He saw her face became neutral in contemplation. A mask of sorts. Her mask revealed her to him. He wished he had a mask.

Foreboding hit him again. Her pregnancy was a new excuse not to follow his vocation. She would want him to be free, yes; but a present and involved father – however much they shared parenthood. His calling was to care for the whole world, however. However profound, parenthood can be written in the small print of schedules and routines, but such things were his enemies: he had to be free to be what he was. To be absent. To love all that lived. Only thus could he love life.

His new reality made him sick with its perfection. He kept his perfection to himself so as not to contaminate her with any more unease.

As they turned onto the main road, a police car – perhaps the origin of the earlier siren – appeared out of nowhere. It drove behind them for a while. There was no doubt that it was tailing them until it suddenly shot past them with its sirens and light on and vanished into the future.

'Where are we going?' he said.

'We need to find you some proper clothes, don't we? But they'll find us wherever we go. I hadn't planned on being a fugitive today.'

'Stop. Let's go back. I'll go back.' he said. 'They'll assume you played a role in my escape, that it was all planned, and they'll make you pay.'

'I don't care. It doesn't matter. As of tomorrow, they'll know who really killed Kenton.'

'A revised testimony will just start a review of the case – if they do. It will all take months, if not years. Until then ...'

'I don't care. Anything rather than you carrying the can like this. It breaks my heart. You're innocent. So am I. At least I was until you corrupted me.' Her eyes sparkled. 'How did you escape anyway? Back there? Is it some kind of test for ...'

'Patients?' he said, then leaned over and kissed her. 'Let's go to mum's.'

'Dashiell? No. After what I've done to you!? She must hate me. I'm filthy with it. How am I supposed to look her in the face?'

'Dashiell doesn't hate you. She's quite bad at hatred. Very bad, actually.'

'We'd be pulling her into this. You don't mind doing that?'

'It's what she'd want us to do.'

*

It was dark by the time they arrived at Dashiell's house just over an hour later. The journey had passed without incident. The furore that was to follow was inevitable, however.

Dashiell hadn't long finished work. She greeted them on the doorstep with astonishment. She hugged him without mercy. Her son's betrayer, Shanti waited for her rejection and hatred. Instead, she got a hug and an invitation inside and, 'You must be famished.' The forgiveness Shanti saw in Dashiell humbled her.

They went inside.

The hallway light was on, so Dashiell now saw Shanti's pregnant belly. She gasped. She hugged Shanti again. She wept. She hugged her son as she had first hugged him when he was swaddled. In those moments, life roared through them.

'You children. Oh my God. What have you done? What have any of us done? Come and sit down for goodness sake. I've got nothing to eat. I'll put the kettle on.'

That evening they ate the 'nothing' Dashiell had to eat (which was plenty) and talked.

'What will you do now?' Dashiell asked them both while fussing with her food.

'Start looking for another job I guess,' said Shanti.

'I'm so sorry. Once this blows over, you'll find something else. You'll see. Meanwhile ...'

'We'll leave in the morning, Dashiell. It's bad enough that we've made you part of this by coming here ...'

'To hell with them. You can stay here as long as need be,' Dashiell cut in kindly. 'When they come for you, they can speak to me.'

'Thanks, mum.' He managed to smile at her – as ever.

Out in the world, lights went on and off. People did things. Other things happened.

'What have they done to you, darling?' Dashiell asked rhetorically.

After dinner, they sat and talked in the small living room. He had put on his old T-shirt and jeans that Dashiell still kept there. The clothes felt like heaven, laundered. A documentary on the sun was on the television. He watched it in rapt silence. The room seemed vehement. Suddenly aware of Dashiell and Shanti watching him, he met their gaze as he met the sun's gaze. It was the gaze of recognition.

'We can't let them find you,' Dashiell said. 'You have more important things to do.'

Shanti didn't understand what she really meant.

'It's OK. I'm making a statement tomorrow ...' Shanti began.

'Wonderful, Shanti,' said Dashiell. 'I'm no lawyer, but even if they accept your revised statement ... It could all take months – even years. Not to mention the fact that you're guilty of perjury. Until then ...'

'I know,' said Shanti. She couldn't disguise her anxiety, which was amplified by the fatigue of pregnancy.

Dashiell smiled supportively at her and squeezed her hand.

'You two can sleep in the spare room. Lots of sleep.'

On TV, the documentary ended. The news came on. Dashiell took the remote control briskly from Shanti. She muted the sound to try to protect him from the horrors of a news report of an earthquake near Gölmarmara, in Turkey. As the newscaster talked, footage shot on a smartphone showed a scene of chaos. Dashiell turned the TV off, but she was too late: he had seen the report. She knew she was being a fool, but being a fool is part of a parent's job description. She shouldn't try to protect him anymore. She couldn't, anyway.

The foundling shot her a look that Shanti couldn't fathom.

'I don't want you to go,' said Dashiell haltingly.

'I have to go. I've been wasting time. I don't want to do that anymore.'

'Then go,' said Dashiell, avoiding his gaze to hide her feelings.

Shanti saw and felt it all.

'Go?' said Shanti. ' Right. If they come. Right. Definitely go. They'll turn up here soon and they'll try to take you back. My car reg and CCTV. It's just a matter of time.'

He suddenly stood up as if to leave. 'What was I thinking?' he said, his voice thick with stress.

'It's fine. I told you,' said Dashiell.

He went out of the room towards the back of the house. Shanti went with him. In the kitchen near the back door, he stopped while Shanti caught up with him. His eyes were haunted.

'Where will you go?' she asked.

'I'll be back soon,' he said.

'You'll be cleared. I'll make sure of it ...'

'No.' he said.

'No?' She took his hand. 'Do you think you drive everyone you meet mad, my love?'

'I try,' he said. He kissed her. 'I've been worse than a fool.'

They heard a vehicle slow and then stop outside the front of the house. They saw vehicle headlights.

Shanti said. 'We'll deal with them. They've got nothing on me anyway. Come back soon – OK?' She touched her belly lightly and kissed him. They heard a vehicle engine cut. Then a certain silence.

'I can't,' he said, conflicted.

'Come back soon, then it won't matter.' She smiled their troth and kissed him again. She started to usher him out of the back door.

'I can't leave you to them.'

Dashiell approached them quickly. 'Nonsense. Go. Hurry,' she said, propelling him outside more forcefully than Shanti. They seemed like dancers on the edge of music.

'Where will you go?' said Shanti again.

'I don't know. Maybe the quarry,' he said,, and the lie tainted his mouth.

Dashiell shepherded Shanti back inside and closed the door so Shanti wouldn't see.

Outside, he was convulsed by his conundrum, which Tally and he would once have hit with an imaginary stick to beat out a rhythm on while they conned it. Then he heard voices at the front of the house. His instinct was to scatter them to the winds. To protect Shanti from their assumptions and protocols. Others summoned him, however. He forced a decision from his tumult.

He heard a knock on the front door. He forced himself to do the impossible. To leave.

Hating himself, he let redness lift him up. He arose slightly – half a metre. He panicked. Perhaps he could no longer do this. Had they taken this away from him? What then? He forced himself. He rose higher. He reached the height of the house roof. He could see a car parked at the front of the house now. An unmarked police car perhaps. Ellie Marr's car, maybe. It didn't matter.

He willed it to happen. With all his might. Him against him. Yes against no. Then.

Suddenly he was gone into the sky.

Upstairs inside the house near a bedroom window, Shanti's heart followed him. Her subconscious wondered what the shadow was that had just crossed the curtains vertically. Something outside. Nothing that mattered. It was windy. Things were things.

She heard another knock on the door downstairs. She heard Dashiell answer the door. Then official voices. Her stomach churned. No. She must protect the baby. It won't like her stress. She forced herself to be calm. She searched for resentment for his departure. For leaving her to them. She found none. That made her smile. Then she let herself laugh and cry at the same time. On high, such things are the same, she knew.

Shanti felt sure their baby would one day know, too.

*

He arose slowly at first.

Doubt drugged his limbs. Guilt weighed him down. He was also out of practice. Incarcerated for over a month, he had become gravity's slave. The song of his nature had almost fallen silent. He had trusted his fear to protect him, but of course it had betrayed him.

He redoubled his efforts. He was rewarded. The higher he went, the stronger he became. He therefore went higher. The higher he went, the faster he climbed. Such is evolution.

After imprisonment, the sense of speed and the cold, fresh air on his face were bliss. As he went higher, the horizon of his awareness expanded. He speeded up. He soon outpaced sound. A sonic boom he couldn't hear because he was its source signalled his anomaly far and wide like vertical thunder. He no longer cared. He speeded up. The tiny, intestinal condensation trail below him would be noted, he knew. It didn't matter now. There was no turning back.

Seconds later, he reached his lifelong dream: the Kármán line – or thereabouts. Here, about 100 kilometres above Earth, the atmosphere was considered to surrender finally to the thought of space. Here, he glimpsed the place he thought he wanted to be: between the stars. His home.

Here, at last, he found brief bliss and the freedom of the unknown.

He slowed, then stopped his ascent. He could go little higher anyway: he had reached the limits of the earth's awareness. Above lay the unconscious vacuum. This was where he belonged.

The Earth rotated below. Day became night became day. At their boundary he saw infinite profundity. He saw that true beauty is fatal. He saw that violence cannot survive in space. The boundless desolation above made the value of life below overwhelmingly apparent. Hope bloomed in him because he was now free of it. Nowhere was revealed to be everywhere, just as no one was everyone. No one therefore let his tears freeze the stars into cold relief, more vital and less knowable than the zero of his infinity. He smiled in the face of his beginning's end.

He felt freer than he had ever felt. The freedom told him that love would be his darling jailer if he let it. It told him that love and courage are all anyone can hope for to face the inevitable night.

He looked down at the calling earth. Immediately beneath him, dayside receded and yielded to the terminator. Night was falling over Europe. On land, the mark of humanity became glitteringly obvious wherever night fell. Because of the earth's tilt, daylight persisted further south. North of Alexandria, the Mediterranean shone as it remembered the day. Still further south, a sinew of the Nile near Luxor gleamed silver for a moment, and then dimmed as the Earth turned on time's lathe.

To his left, Europe and Africa gave way to the quilt of the Atlantic. Here, the earth's pale radius seemed brave against the infinite beyond – but astonishingly exposed. All that had ever happened to people lay below him in extant or recorded form, or vanished beyond memory. All life that people were aware of called this chancy rock home. He looked out into space. His joy knelt before the possibilities of life out there.

Up here, Earth's nearest star was savagely luminous. He squinted. The sun's light seemed so bright it was almost a solid. It had a brutal, bluish quality to it that spoke of energies merciless to life. These energies were most obvious beyond the visible spectrum where he could see if he chose to. Now indeed, the ultraviolet and infrared wavelengths wove and played like fickle ghosts in his eyes. He looked down at the earth again quickly to save his eyes. He saw a certain part of south-east Britain – partly obscured as it was by cloud. Just there, Shanti would be breathing. The new life within her depended on it. Her life! His life! Their life! Breathe. Survive, my love! You will have a real father!

Nearby, everywhere, thousands of people like her and unlike her would be threading the fleet traceries of their lives. Actors on a glancing stage. Fail or prevail. Endure or succumb. Be. He looked over the Gulf. Back in Dubai already, Jericho would be busy playing the role of Jericho on a stage not of his making. Such is the human theatre.

He was suddenly deathly cold and panicking for air. He had tarried too long on the lip of the possible. He exhaled by reflex. He tried to control it, but he couldn't. He descended.

You will have a real father!

His ascent had been immensely quick by the standards of any machine. Suddenly desperate to live, his descent was far, far quicker. Air friction grew until the heat turned him into a fireball. The remainder of his old familiar clothes not burnt by friction on his ascent burnt away until he was naked. His long hair and beard yielded to fire's overlord.

As he plummeted, the urge to go back to Shanti was overwhelming; but he veered east across Europe and away from her. He couldn't feel the 1,000+ degree heat of his re-entry, but this choice of navigation seared his psyche. He felt like he had run out on Shanti. He knew that she and Dashiell were being questioned now. He reassured himself by knowing that they could handle whatever the authorities threw at them – probably better than he could. His presence would only escalate the situation. It would get ugly. He'd be back in a moment anyway. By and by, but not yet goodbye. It wasn't time for that yet.

He committed to his trajectory and intent. Descending at an ever-shallower angle, he passed over northern France, then Germany, then Austria, then Croatia. The airflow cooled his naked body and made the still burning ends of what was left of his hair and beard glow fiercely. He pictured himself. The image he saw in his mind made him laugh out loud. By the time he passed over Serbia, he had stopped laughing, and was at less than ten thousand feet. What telemetry had been recorded on what technology as he passed? He didn't care now. It was too late for caution.

He speeded up. The sirens of anguish summoned him. Seduced, he continued to descend as he passed over Serbia, and was lower than he intended as he passed over Bulgaria. He followed the River Vit approximately south-east. Just beyond Teteven, he saw a horse struggling in a mire. How could he leave it to struggle? How could he be distracted from the pain of the victims of the earthquake? Humans were experts at suffering. It was logical to continue. The dilemma burnt him. He was unable to continue, however. He tried but he failed. He found himself slowing and descending towards the horse. The decision crucified him. It toyed with him. The decision freed his will.

As he approached, the horse sensed him. It kicked and whinnied in response. This struggle further embedded it in the mire. By the time he reached it, only its neck and head were above the surface of the bog. He submerged himself up to his chest in the quag beside the panicking horse. Its eyes were wild and white with spook. He tried to reassure it. He managed to get one arm under the horse's twisting abdomen and another arm over it. The animal thrashed and kicked, then went suddenly calm.

'Good lad,' he said. He raised them both up. He could only just support the horse because it was so slippery with mud. He managed to get it to solid ground. The two swamp animals stood there for a moment and looked at each other. Only one of them smiled.

Then the horse was suddenly gone into the night.

He laughed at his appearance. The smouldering naked maniac in the sky was now the muddy naked maniac beside a river in the curious night. He walked towards a clear area of water in which to immerse himself and wash. As he did, he saw a local man standing as still as the i in bewilderment and looking at him. The two men looked at each other for a moment. Only one of them smiled.

'I'm going to be a father!' Then he was gone into the sky.

He followed the River Vit south-east again. He suddenly felt the acrophobia he had experienced years ago when he first learnt to do this. He didn't know why. He fought against it. He forced himself to look down. He saw his reflection in the river below. He saw a demented crow flying down a pewter vein. It looked up at him with invisible eyes. It battered its wings against the gooseflesh of the river's surface. It laughed at him seriously. It flew with ever more abandon until its wings splintered. Tatters blew away in sparks. He speeded up to try to escape it. It raced him. It outmatched him with joy. The faster he flew, the faster the crow's wings seemed to shred. Soon, it was no more than shards of night that flitted and dissolved in the black laughter of the water.

He awoke what must have been several hours later. He was lying beside Shanti in a bed in the spare room of Dashiell's house. She was asleep. For a moment, he struggled to remember what had happened. Then it came back to him. The River Vit had mocked him, so he had accelerated into near-vertical rage. The rage had taken him south-east into Turkey at several thousand feet. He had veered further south according to the map of his memory. He passed over the Sea of Marmara just north-west of

Gallipoli. From there, it took him several seconds to reach Gölmarmara.

South of the town, it seemed as if the bones of the earth had punctured its skin. The earthquake had all but obliterated the nearby town of Ozanca. He descended into an area that seemed the worst hit. He thought his descent was witnessed by the driver of a passing fire truck. Several of a group of displaced and traumatised people saw him, too. How could it possibly matter, now? There were a million things for him to do. There were a million ways he could help. Knowing where to begin was harder than doing any of them.

In bed now with Shanti, he screwed up his eyes against the strobes of memory. He remembered pushing collapsed buildings off survivors. He remembered trying to help and console them. He remembered preventing a church wall collapsing onto a group of firemen. One of them was the fire truck driver who saw him earlier. It didn't matter. He saved their lives, and then moved faster than speed to help others. He remembered that a teenage boy had stared at him as he pulled a car out of a newly opened fissure in a road. What had he been to them all? A figment of their trauma, surely? A dream of salvation. A muddy naked maniac who surely wasn't there at all.

After what may have been several hours assisting where he could, he told himself he had done all he could. He had bought his own lie, and let redness take him elsewhere. Everything had told him to go back to Shanti. He had therefore left the devastation of the earthquake behind and tried to go back to her. The Thing had other ideas, however.

From Gölmarmara, he therefore headed east over Turkey and then south into Syria. His destination was the ruined school in As Sa'an. The dead moon boy still summoning him with guilty tides. He never got there. New jihadists sworn to convert the world to their creed fought those sworn to stop them in a small town several kilometres south of Aleppo. The town had been ravaged by dogma years ago. It now stood as a dog day memorial to civilisation.

Descending there, he found even establishing who was fighting whom among the chaos in the dark almost impossible. Deciding who he should confront (and how) was even harder. For him (like most things) this situation was too subtle and complex to react to. Why had it felt easier before? Had it? Surely not. He would try again. He had no choice.

He appeared, naked and still ludicrously muddy (he heard laughter) in the theatre of battle. He was immediately shot at from either side of the war-ravaged moonscape that had once been a road he was standing on. Who was firing at him? It was impossible to know. To both sides, he probably looked like the enemy. To all present, he probably seemed like a madman. He resolved to do something about his appearance soon.

He moved among the shocks of war like a thought. He thought that individuals on both sides of the conflict had their own subjective, learnt versions of things that they called reality. These realities shaped their agendas. Who then should he oppose, and why? He froze inside the labyrinths of his pondering. He thus became an easy target.

A high-velocity bullet thwacked into him. The impact condensed these thoughts out into something that occupied time: a reaction. The bullet impact felt like a finger jab of accusation. It didn't hurt and he was unharmed, of course; but the impact of the bullet caused a subjective response in him that might be called aggression. He fought to quell the reaction and remain objective. He became a war within a war.

He went to the location of the muzzle flash. He found several men there in the remains of a row of houses. They were normal, afraid, unique, adult, defiant, thirsty children. They shouted abuse in him. As he approached, they shot at him – a western man, as they saw him. By the time he reached the jihadists, hundreds of rounds had hit him. By the time he reached them unscathed, they were in awe of his wellbeing.

He tried to remonstrate with the men. Some were so in awe of and/or confused by him they could do nothing. Others reloaded and/or re-aimed their weapons at him. Most shouted, so that none could be heard. He still tried to remonstrate with them. He talked about confusion and forgiveness and the pointlessness of their actions. His words fell like leaves from a revolution. His words drowned in their opinions and mandates. They started shooting at him again. He disarmed them and broke their weapons. They attacked him with knives. He took the knives from them and broke them. They attacked him with their beliefs. He could not break their beliefs. Seeing that they couldn't harm him, some fell to their knees before him. He begged them to stand. He helped them up. He was horrified by their worship. The more he begged them not to worship him, the more they did so. He felt poisoned by it. It was an attack on his humility that he could not defend. It was their worship, not their aggression, that made him back away into the dark and leave them.

He fled the buildings faster than imagination. He felt an overwhelming urge to return to Shanti and the future that grew within her. Defying The Thing, he departed the area quickly. He was aware of a combatant photographing his departure into the sky on his smartphone.

On the way back, he knew he must be moving above rapes and murders and famine and thieves and beggars and hoarders and suicides and poverty and illness. He could not ignore them. He had to ignore them. He had to go home. Just for now. He would come back.

Need and despair reached up and clawed at him as he passed aloft. He slipped through their pleading fingers like molten guilt.

Now, beside him, Shanti stirred. He glanced at the bedside clock. It was 6.34 am. The spare bedroom in Dashiell's small house they were in felt quiet and safe. Its banality was its beauty. Morning sunlight filtered through the budget curtains Dashiell had presumably hung herself. This light had struggled to the surface of the sun he had so recently been face to face with (as it had felt). Suddenly free, the light had then hurtled across the space between the earth and the sun in a little more than eight minutes. It now fell on his face like a simile.

'What's burning?' Shanti mumbled out of the dough of sleep beside him. Though he had showered before getting into bed with her, his skin and hair were still pungent with the sear of his re-entry and the acrid chaos of the earthquake, and the dreadful reek of the new Aleppo conflict.

He kissed her forehead tenderly. He got up and showered. He went downstairs and made her a cup of coffee. Dashiell was already up. She was sitting in the living room drinking her morning tea. He took Shanti's coffee up to her. She was still asleep. He put the coffee on the bedside table quietly. He went back downstairs to sit with Dashiell. They talked without words for a while. Eventually, Dashiell spoke quietly: 'You know you can both stay for as long as you need to, don't you?'

'Oh no, mum. I can't impose upon you. Especially with ...' He waved at the world beyond the window. Out there, the machine would be preparing to return him to 'a more secure facility'. 'I'll sort something else out. It's fine.'

'Well Shanti needs good food and somewhere safe to be at the moment. It's not like they can drag her away is it.'

'No. It isn't.'

She sensed the protective rage beneath his normal poise. It was the first time she had truly feared what he could do if he lost control.

'Thanks though, OK?' he went on. The blackness of anger left his impossible eyes. She was glad. 'Let's see what happens today,' he continued evenly. 'What happened last night? After I ran away and left you both with them like a sketchy coward,' he said.

'And if you'd stayed?'

He knew she was right. If he'd stayed, the inevitable conflict with the law would have happened then, rather than soon. He had done the right thing by leaving. So why did it feel so wrong to him? Why did it make him hate himself? It was obvious. Everything was obvious to him. That was his beautiful curse. He wasn't protected by the limits of perception. He was on high, scavenged by light. It was breath-taking and incurable. He wouldn't have it any other way.

'A young detective – he seemed familiar. I think you used to go to school with him – and someone from the clinic. A woman. They asked questions. Where were you? There are procedures. The clinic ... there was structural damage. You must turn yourself in immediately. If we shelter or protect you, we're obstructing justice. We're legally obliged to disclose your location forthwith. And did you plan your escape with Shanti, so her culpability et cetera. That kind of thing. I had few answers, but Shanti – bloody hell. She's strong. Strong and smart. I'm glad you have each other.'

He smiled agreement at her, but his ecliptic eyes said, 'I could have avoided all this. Long ago, a butterfly took flight. Now look.'

'I thought I'd never see her again.'

'Funny old life,' said Dashiell. Then silence put everything down and rested near them for a while.

'You've forgiven her for what she did,' said Dashiell eventually. 'I need you to know that I'm immensely proud of you.'

'Bella made her do it.'

'Poor witch,' said Dashiell. 'You mustn't hurt them. When they try to take you. Try to be gentle with them – OK?'

He met her gaze and turned his palms up slightly. He meant, 'I'll have to hurt them, but I can't possibly hurt them. What can I do? What should I do?'

The butterfly smiled.

He closed his eyes. She got up and came over to the chair he was sitting on. She held his head to her like she used to, but it felt awkward now; so she just stood there.

'You're wearing Jericho's old bathrobe. Are you aware?'

He nodded imperceptibly.

'I'll make some more tea.'

She hesitated. He waited.

He sensed something, and then knew what she had done before she said:

'I told her.'

He reeled from the enormity of it.

'You did *what*?'

He stood, incredulous and in tumult. His eyes bored into her. She couldn't meet them, such was their power, and the new turbulence within.

'What's better: that you tell her, and she thinks you're mad and rejects you, or that she rejects me?'

'Mum ...' he began, but was so incensed he couldn't speak more.

'Secrets are the enemy of love ...'

'Yes, but not ... How is she supposed to react? What's she supposed to think – that we're as weird as everybody thinks we are? I can't believe you've done this to me! What now ...'

Shanti appeared at the door, rubbing the sleep from her face.

'Hi babe. Oh crap. What happened to your hair?'

*

'I'm not running out on you again. We do this together. I don't care what happens.'

Shanti didn't react outwardly to his words as she drove them to the police station in the town. He sensed her demeanour flux as she assessed realities and decisions and outcomes, however.

He felt like his dirty secret had been revealed, and his status as deceiver had thus been made clear. He actually felt dirty, and it wasn't just the scent of last night's forays lingering on his skin.

'Where did you go last night?' she said just when he felt he couldn't bear the silence any longer.

'I went for a run. The longest I've ever ...'

'And what – there was a fire, right? You were out running, and you came across a house fire, and you stopped running to help the people trapped in the fire and saved them, because it's in your nature to do things like that, isn't it? You're what used to be called a hero, but you're too modest to enjoy the word, and to have told me of your heroism, now and in the past. Is that right?'

'Something like that.'

Moments lodged in his throat and made his core uncertain. When would he be forced to flat-out lie? Because he would have to lie to her every day of their lives together. Because obviously she would know that what Dashiell had told her was absurd. Pitiable, actually. Sad.

These moments suggested to Shanti that much as she loved him maybe she had made a mistake, and that he belonged in the sanatorium, but here they were. What now?

'I had weird dreams,' she said as if to silence her inner voices.

'You dream lots of things.'

'Are you saying I'm in some way responsible for Kenton's death because I dreamed you healed him, so you tried to, giving mum an opportunity to do kill him and blame it on you?

'No. I would have tried anyway.'

'You tried to heal Kent?'

'I was desperate.'

'Babe. That's nuts. No one can heal people like that.'

He just fussed with his singed hair and beard. She laughed unexpectedly. She laughed to clear the moment, and because she was stressed about making a statement to the police in which she would accuse her mother of murdering her brother, and thus admitting to perjury.

Suddenly she was laughing hysterically. She was driving too fast, too.

'Please slow down.'

'We're late.'

'It'll be OK.'

'How will it? I accuse my mother of murder and then? I've been a fool and I've caused you terrible pain. I don't understand. How can you forgive me?'

'I could say the same thing. There's nothing to forgive.'

Her laughter faded.

'If you come with me like this they'll try to re-arrest you,' she said eventually. 'They'll try to take you away from me again.'

'They'll fail.' Certain.

'How so?' Flat.

'I won't let it happen.' Determined.

'Wouldn't it be wonderful if we just didn't let things happen.' Rhetorical. Yearning. Bereaved.

He took her hand and squeezed it. She squeezed back. Relief washed his heart.

Then their hands parted.

'Seriously babe,' she said.

'What will be will be.'

'Want me to change my name to Sara?'

'No. I love Shanti just fine.'

'Just fine?'

'More than fine. Infinitely. Gratefully. Mysteriously.' He made a dramatic face that amused her. Something serious swam below the surface like a hunter though.

She checked her smartphone as she drove.

'Please don't do that.'

'Nag, nag, nag. Are you rehearsing for when we're married?' She laughed again. He pretended to laugh with her to disguise the enormity of his dilemma. She put her smartphone down dutifully and glanced across at him. This rag-tag, ancient child. It made her love him more, despite ...

'You of all people,' she said.

'Me of all people? I am all people.'

'If you say so. What happened last night? What really happened? You'll have to tell me one day, you know. You'll have to tell her, too.' She touched her belly to indicate their child.

'"Her?"'

She threw him a knowing look. He liked it.

'Your mum. Last night. She put the law in its place I can tell you. Wow'

'She spoke highly of you, too.'

'You're lucky to have a proper mother, you know.'

He knew.

'Shanti. For me it's everyone, not just me or us.'

'What does that mean?' When he didn't answer immediately she looked at him askance. The car consequently started to veer across the white line.

'Please.' He meant the road. He meant let's survive.

'What does it mean?'

'It means I love all that I can love as if I was loving my very blood. My own. For me, it's everyone. Everything that lives.'

'Should I be worried?' she said, correcting the position of the car on the road.

'No. That's the last thing you should be.'

'I never knew. I admire you.'

'Thank you. I admire you, too.'

'Why?'

Anxiety suddenly welled up in him. She felt it. To her, he seemed unexpectedly forlorn and conflicted, so she brightened her mood and became jolly to balance his disposition like she used to.

'I don't know what's what,' she said. 'I don't know why I don't care, and I don't know what's going on. Maybe it's me. Maybe I'm nuts. I don't care anymore. You know that thing when you're talking to someone in a bar, and you don't know if you're drunk, or they are? Anyway. And by the way. It's incredibly kind of your mum to offer, but I'm going to stay with Zadie until – I don't know. I need to find another job. The fallout from the trial and all that, and now ... HR says it's unfair dismissal, but now ...' Then her brightness faded in the stare of reality.

He felt her anxiety and distress immeasurably more intensely than she felt it. He touched her hand with perfect tenderness; but his touch was insufficient, and he knew it. 'I'm sorry. Look. Please don't do this. I'll take the blame ... Your mother ...' He stopped because her smartphone alert sounded yet another text or WhatsApp. The message alert stressed her even more.

She drove on in silence for a while.

'We stand at the grave of awe, and we don't mourn. I don't understand,' he said.

'What does that mean?'

'It means I'm hanging onto the tiger's tail like everyone else. It's just that my tiger is different. My tiger is on fire, Shanti. Steel is like gossamer to me, and I'm frightened. But the fear doesn't belong to me.'

'I don't know what you mean. What tiger? You can't love someone if they have secrets.' She looked dead ahead as she said it.

'I thought that if you love someone, surely you let them keep their secrets. It's part of who they are, who you love.'

'It depends on what we're talking about, right?' She smiled, but doubt edged the smile. 'In any case I'm having the worst time driving you back into the arms of the law, you know that?'

'I won't let you do this on your own. I won't leave you.'

'That sounds like you saying you have to leave me,' said Shanti.

'But I will always come back.'

'Will you?'

He realised that he might have just told his first proper lie. He was surprised to find it easier and less repugnant than he had anticipated.

They were passing a train station. Shanti pulled off the main road and brought the car to an abrupt halt near the station ticket office.

'Go. I won't take you back to them.'

'I can't.'

'Have you got money?'

'You know that I don't need trains.'

'*What?* Just don't. Please. You're out of that place now. We're going to be fine. You'll find work. We'll get a place together. You'll see.'

Her words buried him. He had foreseen this as soon as he knew she was pregnant with their child only yesterday. As a parent, he would have to work just as Shanti would work to make ends meet. He would be expected to work the week, prune Saturdays, and socialise with Sundays. To fit in. To become semi-detached. To conform sufficiently to become a cog in the contraption. To go from A to C by way of B, and to forget about Z altogether. To become what he could never become.

The world slurred and warped around him. A new, metallic sensation invaded his chest. He tried to hide his feelings from her as she met his gaze, felt vertigo, and then yielded.

'Fine,' she said, and drove them away from the train station and back onto the main road.

'Have you got a new phone yet?' she asked after a moment, checking the messages on her smartphone as she drove. She obviously saw a significant message. He saw her eye pupils dilate and her skin tone change. Their baby would be affected.

'Please don't do that while you're driving,' he said again, earnest as new bread.

'You're right,' she said, and then: 'This is ridiculous.' She put her smartphone away. She took a deep breath. Then they both laughed. Yes. Yes. Then their hands embraced.

'My milkshake brings all the boys to the yard.'
'And salt is just angry sugar,' he replied with a grin.
She turned left at a junction. They were getting close now.

She had to force herself to say it: 'Your mother ...'
'Please don't. I know.'
Kindness made her desist.
They were getting close now.
'If they take you back to that place,' she said, 'you'll break my heart and you'll miss the birth of our child.'
'They won't take me back. That I can promise you.'
She wondered at his promise. She wondered at everything. She felt sick with anxiety. For a moment, she felt more alone than she thought anyone could be. She had no idea she felt as alone as he had always felt apart from in the moment when they conceived the new life within her.
Then they were alone together.
How many times will you lie to me? she thought as she glanced in the rear-view mirror. For a moment, tired and stressed, she worried that she had said it aloud.
The mirror did not answer.

*

On arrival, they were asked to sit in the police station reception area.
'We're late. I told you. I don't bloody believe it', said Shanti.
He took her hand. It was shaking. He felt her pulse hammer. A demented blacksmith, crazed at the lip of ruin.
'I'm losing my mind, babe.'
'No you're not.'
Half an hour later they were shown into a small meeting room. Shanti entered the room first. The foundling followed. As soon as he did, he saw that the police officer who would receive Shanti's statement was Detective Lipton. He wore his recent promotion like a proud claim. Detective Lipton looked up from his tablet and saw him. He smiled.

The formal process immediately fractured into a strobe of action and reactions. Detective Lipton stood up. He fumbled for handcuffs. He barked an order out of the door. He went to restrain the foundling. The foundling let Detective Lipton put hands on him, but he resisted restraint. Again, Lipton was confronted with an enigma. In his mind, he was thrown across the playground at school again by a force that wasn't possible. This, now, wasn't possible either: Detective Lipton failed to bend the foundling's arm behind his back so he could handcuff him.

'No,' the foundling said. 'It's too late for that.'

'Leave him be,' Shanti said. 'He's innocent!'

'So you say!' said Detective Lipton.

'It wasn't him!' Shanti tried to get between them. Voices came running. Someone behind them. Other hands on him. Lipton's sweaty forehead. Damp corrugations.

'You are under arrest ...'

'No! I told you. It was my mother. That's why I'm here!'

Detective Lipton tried with all his might to bend the foundling's arms behind his back so that he could be handcuffed. Another police officer helped, then another. It soon became a knot of official human effort with the impossible at its centre and Shanti by his side. He pushed them away with all the gentleness he could muster, which was insufficient. They fell from him as trees bleed leaves in summer's India. They would not give up, however. He would have to use exactly the right amount of force. It was like trying to fine-tune a tornado.

Everyone (except the foundling) was talking or shouting at once.

'Your mother. So you say,' Detective Lipton shouted to Shanti. 'It could have been me!' The foundling could smell his breath. He saw evolution failing and fighting and succeeding and dying and breeding in Detective Lipton's eyes. It filled him with joy.

Shanti tried to wrench them off him.

'It's OK,' he said to her gently amid the scrum. She saw a calm in his face she couldn't understand. She didn't understand how he could resist their efforts. It confused her. The confusion made her feel queasy. Her mind played tricks. This couldn't be acting unless everyone was in on it except her. That must be it. So queasy became the deathly sickness of the confused outsider. It all slurred and buckled around her.

'Please listen to Miss Young,' the man she loved seemed to say to Detective Lipton. What might the policeman now say in this strange performance?

'Oh, we will, sunbeam. We will. Once you're safely back in the loony bin,' Detective Lipton said. He then hissed to a colleague: 'Taser.'

'No!' Shanti screamed. She wanted to be sick.

'This was a mistake. I'm sorry,' the foundling said to them all, but mostly to Shanti. He tried to reassure her with his gaze, but panic spread like fire in dry corn.

Someone pulled Shanti a safe distance away from him. She let them. They released the foundling for a moment while Detective Lipton fired up the Taser and touched him with it. Revenge licked him with physics' roots. Then they were on him again. He heard Detective Lipton shout 'again'. He saw the tongue of the Taser on him again. He felt nothing. Why didn't they understand? How much evidence is required to overcome certainty?

Then he saw their hands on him again. Detective Lipton and the other policemen continued to try to restrain, handcuff and arrest him. The foundling started laughing. He couldn't help it. He never could.

A WPC entered the fray. She danced with Shanti. It became a strange dance. To him, they all seemed like shadows that cast shadows called reality. The shadow that was Shanti tried and tried to stop Detective Lipton and the policemen try and try to arrest him. He laughed harder. He tried and tried not to hurt them. People said things. He suddenly became serious. He heard himself tell them that if Shanti was in any way harmed or treated with disrespect, everything would end. He saw fear and confusion and accusation and the thing of being human in their faces. He saw their births and their lives and the moment of their deaths as one thing. Everything was one thing. All moments were now. Everywhere was here. He was everyone. He was no one.

The WPC managed to usher Shanti out of the room. Her backward glance told him that she would do her best for Shanti. The foundling held her to her unspoken promise without words.

Fighting for breath and sweating devotedly, Detective Lipton met his eyes for a moment. 'Don't think I don't know all about you, mucker,' Lipton said, his face contorted by futile effort.

That gave the foundling pause. Then the moment was gone. He brushed them aside and exited the building. He shared a backward glance with Shanti, whose darling eyes were broken glass. His glance calmed her. His glance made her smile. His glance made her laugh. She had fallen in love with his laughter long ago. Now his laughter was everything.

Then he was gone.

*

I am laughing star stuff.

Of course she cannot know you, fool. Of course if you show her, you will lose her. If you don't show her, you will also lose her. How can you abandon her? What am I supposed to do? I can't hurt them if they catch me. I have to hurt them if they catch me. I want to be with her. So this is how it will be? I can't be with her. You'll leave her then? I can't. Watch me burn then. So you'll let the Thing die? The Thing will kill you first. It can't be killed. I can't. This new gall. This new back of the throat. How could I be so stupid? This pit of stomach. Of course she will expect me to carry the can. To accept my lot. The easiest lot to accept is a little. Of course she will expect me to get a job. Of course I will expect to wither with her. Boom–boom! Geddit? Everything is real, now. Of course you must abandon her. Of course you must abandon the millions. Of course you can't abandon her. To exist. Of course this is how it will be. They don't need you. Now, nothing is true. They are experts at suffering. They are overqualified. They need you. You need them to need you. To be what you are. I don't need them. I want above all to be free of them. Of myself. I want to be above them. I want to be free of their suffering. I can't be above them. I can never be free. I am no thing. In only one way. Of their scorn. I will be one day. Now, everything is. Scone or scone? Except me, that is. How though? Gone or bone? How will you escape? I will I will I will. How could you? I. And here's le devil d'evil, Tally laughed. There's the deep blue, see? I guffawed. Red sky at night. What else can I do? It's fine, fool! They won't believe, sir. They'll know it's all a trick. They'll know someone is just selling something to someone who doesn't know they want to buy it. Et voila, new world. Shepherd's delight. Sale on now! Why would Shanti understand?

    I find trouble online. There are websites. I feel like a pervert. Watching for trouble. Then I go there. Red sky in the morning. When I get there. I try to help. But much of the time I can do little or nothing. Shepherd's warning. And tell me, please: when and if I find those who break the law like happy wind, sic: How can I hold them entirely responsible? How can I be violent? How can I be anything else? What do I do to a rapist? A torturer? Do I go from here and knock on the door of the White House? Why not? The Kremlin? Zhōngnánhǎi? Goldman Sachs? Why not? And do what? Do I obliterate the Syncrude oil sands plant? And then? Livelihoods will be ruined is what then. And they will start again. And what about child slavery? And must I respond to female genital mutilation with rationality? How, said the How Bear to Goldilocks? How home the homeless? If I rip the bile farms apart, they will shoot the bears. If I sink the whaling ships in harbour, they will build more. If I release all the big game bred for hunting, what then? They will breed more is what then. And then? And so? And how, pray, may I unmelt a melting world? After you. No, I insist. No please. Après midi. Après ski. Après vous. Merci.

She will tell them, but they won't believe her. They'll see a pregnant woman protecting the father of her child – a man she testified against. A woman who had sex with her brother. The brother, she says, her mother killed! As if. It's gonna be hard to find you guilty of perjury, little chickadee. It's shepherd's pie. Oh, and why did you help him break out of the facility he had been placed in for the safety of others?

We think not, tiger.

My tiger sees time like a land ruled by a king who isn't interested in power. He uses his arms to tock away the ticks of time's horizon because he's an idiot. Everyone knows there's no horizon. To be conscious is to be there and then. Got the T-shirt. Everything I've ever experienced. I'm still experiencing it. Then seems to be now, too. So does the future. I feel what everyone feels. Can she imagine? I love her. I love them. No and no and no.

In the land of the blind.

On Chomolungma's peak, I'll rest a moment. Up here, the summoning silence. I have been called. Look – the slow seas of the peaks around me! A jagged song caught at beauty's edge? This is where wonder comes to weep. Not the poundshop version. Not the gameshow meaning. Not the hashtag. Real awe. Profundity on its knee. Peace beyond. If only she could see what I see. Below and far away, she will be pressed in an office with those who represent the law. I should be beside her. What then? What is growing inside me? No one can count on a fist.

The one-eyed man.

I must go back. I can't go back. Hurry, Harry! But if I go back to her, they will try to grab me back – at least until I'm acquitted (if I ever am, I am an iambic yam). Until then, they will lie in wait and then pounce.

My love has become bait.

Ctenizidae is a family of medium-sized mygalomorph spiders that construct burrows with a cork-like trapdoor made of soil, vegetation, and silk. They may be called trapdoor spiders. Some Conothele species do not build a burrow but construct a silken tube with a trapdoor in bark crevices.

Something moving, below. Of course! Even here. Five climbers. It is late May. The summit window is still open. I have come here to seek tranquillity in awe and a perfect solo; yet even here, people approach. I will come back in winter when there will be desolation to wear snug and safe. Laughing like that won't make it right. She was right. Up here, laughing and crying are self-same. Up here, the heart is fractal. What is the atomic number of irony? Laughing like that. Won't make it.

I look down at the climbers. I see them struggling. I know they are exhausted – probably dangerously. I know they are gasping at the oxygen they carry on their backs. Their pace is rasping slow. To them, this is the death zone. They shouldn't be here. I shouldn't be anywhere else.

They are what the world wants me to be. The only thing the world will tolerate. The struggling. The limited. The astounding. The only thing they refuse to worship when they should be building temples to themselves. I envy them their ability to become stronger.

The wind carries my laughter away into high canyons. Humour echoes. The sound makes the climbers look up, fearful of disaster. Long before they see me, I follow the wind away north and amazingly down. It hurls at me, vicious in its speed and cold power. I let it. I let it do with me as it will. I am glad to be out of control. I could let it smash me on crags. Would I be broken though? Would I thus be whole? No! My child will need me! I straighten. Shanti! I will never be free of my love! I resist. I regain control. I veer away down the North Col. I pass over a vast glacial pass towards Changtse in Tibet. Ahead and below lies the head of the fast-shrinking East Rongbuk Glacier. Soon it will be gone. I can do nothing.

I could go up. Beyond the troposphere, the azure stratosphere beckons. Beyond that, the dark violets of the mesosphere and higher still, the darkness of space. No! No more hiding at the lip of infinity. Up is away from my new reality. No. Down. Grasp the nettle. Down into the jaws of my truth. Faster and faster. Into the metaphor of experience. Yes!

What will I do though? Who shall I help first? Children amputated so they can beg for their families? How? Should I abandon Tibet to the fudge of history? I can't. I must. Go south anyway. Then back to her briefly. They will have done what they are doing by now. Soon. My love. I am with you. Not you're not: you're scudding in this direction when you should be going in that direction. You're betraying here when you could be betraying there. Who to make a priori? Priority? Hutu what? How help now help. Go! Flash there and do that then scream back to her to the nest of her breast and suck the hours out of her. Relish the kiss and the curse of love. You will be a father soon, and then? And then you must let the world burn, Baloo. Oh, Mr Magoo! South, then, into India! A jet, a jet! Did they see me? Fear not, thingumabob; it will all just be hokum in some corner of the internet where loons go. So up, up, and a day in the life of. But Africa. There must needs go I and go I because you read about the water. Help them drill the drought in South Sudan. Scream. They are drying out. Babies on mama teats flat as Shrove Tuesdays. Scream. OK so go there now then back to her to help her back to Zadie's to settle in. What will you tell her? She will see the dead babies in your eyes.

That cannot matter. It can only matter.

Africa, then – yes: South Sudan. Boom, said sound. But overlook the revolution in Yemen on the way? Yes, sir, I don't mean maybe. No, sir, she's my baby. Who's who at that zoo, Blue? What's new? Disarm the 'rebels' first? Nope. Bullets are the syllables of dogma, he sees. Ah, so those fighting for the ha-ha government? Right. Or those in

rebellion? But the flesh of the bureau is corrupt. So why them? So go with the rebels. Nope. OK so tell me the one about the stoning of the young pregnant woman on the peninsular. Boom–boom. Cracker. It's the way I yell 'em.
    Now what?
    Now but on to Uganda, prithee, where they sacrifice boys' body parts to bring businessmen luck. Roger that. That's the plan, Stan. Now you're barely less than bodacious. And after that, the new Somalia situation? Gotcha. Scream. And then the banjax in Nigeria you read about yesterday. Too right. That's for me. Yessiree Bob. Will that be next? Is the bear a catholic? I think therefore I yam. Or not. OK, so turn a blind eye and go back to her a king. Wink wink. Impressions are assumptions in their Sunday best. Ha! Dress up warm then and mind your p's while you queue, Hugh. You're hilarious. I'm hilly, Larry, and Bob's your uncle.
    OK, so stay away from your future and your future wife and family and the word 'love' spelt in genes and go around putting out fires forever. Be that fireman. Like you always wanted. Squirt. That's the ticket. Hysterical wisteria. Perhaps the cartels tomorrow after lunch? Can you squeeze it in? South of the border, they're still sending that white storm north and all together: breathe in! So, smash the cartels. Got it. How about writing a schedule? Something formal in Excel, perhaps, so you know where you are and when?
    Inaction is inexcusable and action impossible. I must act, then. I must play a role complete with breaths and entrances. Complete with sideshows and props and poppycock. Adept with queues. It entrances, so it does, and you are beguiled. Follow the echo or your rage around the world three times then fade away to molecules, too. It will send you star craving bonkers first. As a bag of frogs. Mad is as mad does, capiche? Mama always said. Tell me what to do. Do something blue. It's so you. Drink of her dew. Tell me what's new. No nose is good nos. Who knows? There snow business. It is bliss, this sweet unknowing. In the land

of the king. I wish even higher than I can go never to go high again, and for a puppeteer to jerk my principles. I wish above myself to be a marionette a'dance, jigged by a'one above whom I can rely on to spare me from up. Like show business. Benen old friend, if you could see me now. Make it all be dark I beg thee, and I bark, sirrah, and balance sugar.

    Make me into a dog.

*

'Where did he go? Where is he? If you don't reveal his location to us, you'll be charged with obstruction of justice, Miss Young. That's a serious offence. You've already admitted to perjury. That charge will stand until your revised statement is verified by material evidence or further witness corroboration. You've got to realise that to some, this might just look as if you're trying to protect the man whose child you say you carry. And whatever exists between your mother and you is your private business. You say you don't know where she is. Does your father? And with the bankruptcy as you say ... While your statement is processed, we'll need your passport, and place and proof of ongoing residence.'

    'I don't know where he is. If I did, I wouldn't tell you. He doesn't belong in your boxes. So you'll just have to put me in jail instead. I belong there with my mother.'

*

She held him. They would never be apart. They would always be apart.

    'I don't know how to be with you. I don't know how to be without you.'

    'What are you talking about?'

    'More than anything I need you to know me.'

    'I do. I mean I know it will all be fine. Somehow. Don't you?'

*

- #Loved the show! Wassup with #beardy again? I'm a believicator!
- Remember the boat rescue five years ago? The sub? And the Yello caldera? Seeing a pattrn? I heart #beards!
- He/she/it (pick a #pronoun) #shaved??? Check out last week's clip
- AC or #DC? Run, #Forest, run!
- Q: So where does #fake #news end and #reality TV begin? A: Somewhere behind the I? Well this pupil is dilating!!!
- Do it. Give it up for DC's best ever #summer #blockbuster #publicity campaign! Effing #Marvel-ous!
- Wise up, hash & tag weirdoes: its all the usual #pixels and bull
- @InHillarySteps is back at Katman base. Can report #hallucination on #Everest summit. Viva la #death #zone we guess! Or else?
- Its Big Foot redux. 'Authentic' footage of u know who being super at Ozanca quake last month. But #fakenews does not rock.
- Is it me or is our #guyinthesky the same bloke we are told broke out of an asylum here in the UK early last month? Huh?
- Be cool @InHillary'sSteps – it's all a #cosmic #hologram anyway!
- Do the math. It all adds up. Someone is selling. We're all #buying. But what the flock we #flying?
- Get real It all #SFX Manipulation nation. Ain't no thing but the thing itself

*

Shanti's morning sickness had long since abated. Nausea remained, however. It was amplified by insomnia. The stress of the trial and the part she had played in it haunted her waking hours, day and night. Being homeless and jobless also made sleep (and waking) difficult. No wonder she felt like hell.

His enforced (and, she felt, sometimes chosen) absence was the hardest thing to take. It was like a knife in her heart. She had been obliged to give them her current address – Zadie's address: the sweetheart had let her stay as long as she wanted; so this was where they expected him to visit her – here or at Dashiell's residence. This (or there) was where they hoped to entrap him and return him to the prisons of their sanity; so he stayed away. Where he went, she had no idea. She tried not to wonder, but often did so. She feared the worst.

Now, late in the evening, she hoped above all that there might be a footstep, a knock on the door: his smiling face – absurdly whiskered or ineptly shaven as it often was. She also feared such footsteps and intentions of ingress. When would that ever change?

She winced – but not because of such thoughts. She winced because of what she now saw online. Various blogs and articles – some even half creditable – discussed a presence and activities that she found impossible to associate with the man she loved. She saw words and phrases like 'cult', and 'second coming', and 'conspiracy', and elsewhere, 'crude media manipulation' and 'sad hoaxing', and 'gullible consumerism'.

She remembered what Dashiell had told her about him that night after his escape from the sanatorium – an event she couldn't explain and hadn't intended to cause. Dashiell had seemed to believe, and doubt, every word she said. She had seemed to hope Shanti would believe it, too; but no one believes in reality. He had often said that. Now, Shanti started to better understand what he meant by it. Poor Dashiell. She had always seemed to very essence of rationality, and now ...

Whichever way she looked, what she saw made her ever sadder and more anxious for him and for them both.

She remembered the rumours in the village where they had grown up. The trick he pulled in the village hall, and the subsequent commotion. The whispers about strange abilities and impossible strength. She had always denounced the gossip and fought to remain rooted in the only possible explanation for all of it: that his adoption (since admitted to her alone by Dashiell), Tally's suicide, and his presumed autism (which also caused him to feel shunned) had sculpted a unique human lost in his own world, the truth of which he sought to persuade the real world by way of trickery and illusion.

That explanation couldn't possibly account for the online and media phenomenon that now centred globally on the beardy hashtag, however. When she pondered that – which she often did – she drew a blank. She couldn't possibly link it with the father of her child. She didn't want to. Obviously #beardy was a fairly well-executed hoax, his hoax perhaps, with an agenda that required widespread collaboration. The alternative was obviously impossible. Myths were myths. The impossible was impossible. Those who thought the impossible, however, were the 'makers of tomorrows', as he once said. He had always said things. Some of them were strange, some of them were funny, and some were profound. He said far less now. In fact he had been deadly silent lately during the rare moments they could find to be alone together. His silences weighed on her.

Now, she let her exhausted online addiction control her for a while longer. She clicked through to ever new social media content around #beardy. She knew about the Facebook pages. She hated what she saw on them, but she felt compelled to look at them. Why do we do what we hate doing? she often asked herself. She had no answers. She felt she had no answers to anything – especially the question: why did he love her so completely, so constantly? He had mythologized her in childhood, she was sure. A unique orphan who sought to be accepted had fallen for her because she had accepted him and cherished him instinctively. Perhaps the ostracization that later grew up in the village around her rumoured relationship with Kenton had driven her empathy for him – a fellow outsider. Who knew? Who knew anything now?

She struggled to focus now on what she saw on the web. She had been online so long her eyes hurt. She had fallen into surfing these blogs and articles with the sullied habit of the junk content and porn addict. In digesting such content, she sought to disavow that which she feared: that there was any truth in the stupid 'truther' rumours, or that her true love was at the heart of some bizarre hoax. Such a hoax could only arise from things she either chose not to believe, or which proved the court right in its assumption of his insanity. Her thoughts went around in circles.

It was late. The curtained patience of her bedroom window held back and made obvious the wonderful, terrible, savage, rare, and infinitely subtle world beyond. Zadie had gone to bed more than an hour ago. The baby growing in her begged her to sleep. The baby inside her. Their child! What might such a child be like? They would soon know.

Exhaustion overwhelmed her. She turned off her tablet and lay down in the pale womb of bed. She turned the bedside light off. Where are you? I call to you. Can you hear me? When will this be over? When the truth is known and accepted? She saw hope swim towards her like a sensation of luminous safety. It got closer and closer. By the time it reached her, sleep had pulled her down into its darling folds.

Goodnight my love.

*

When he descended on them like a tempest and thus razed the opium poppy fields in Laos (because he could find no way of preventing the production off Whoonga, Krokodil, Scopolamine, Purple Drank, or any of the numerous drugs he couldn't research online), he was thinking of Shanti. Her stress would not be good for their baby.

When he met her in quiet concealed moments that they could engineer with Zadie's help or by their own guile, he was in the thrall of the Thing. The Thing said: go and relieve the siege of the Trinity Lutheran Church in Arapahoe. So, making his excuses to Shanti, he did. As he disarmed the mentally ill man who threatened to kill the congregation because theirs was the wrong hue of Christianity, he was painfully aware that Shanti hadn't eaten a proper dinner; so he went back to her immediately and made her a proper meal.

When he had made sure she was nourished and sleeping in his proximity, the Thing told him to assist at the train wreck north-east of Astana in Kazakhstan. So he tried to leave her without waking her like they do in films; but she woke, because this was life.

He couldn't tell her where he was going or where he had been then or at any time because he couldn't lie, and if he told her, she would know the court had been right in its assessment of him and that their love was doomed. He therefore said nothing, which as all lovers and spouses know, is the one thing that cannot be said with impunity. He often therefore left her confused and upset, which made him sick with anxiety because all he wanted to do was be happy with her.

This went on. When he was with the Thing, he was with her in his heart. When he was with her physically, he was called away by vocation. He was thus torn asunder perfectly. The atom was split. His conflicted moieties went about their quick ways, each busy with thoughts of each. Between them, Shanti tried to live normally and find her way back to something that made sense; but nothing did. They both knew this couldn't go on. Neither knew how it could possibly end until a loud knock on the door of Zadie's house disturbed them as they lay together one day on love's linen. It was clear immediately who had knocked at the door and what they wanted. They wanted him. He therefore fled so he didn't have to hurt them as they tried to apprehend him – a scenario that became ever more likely as his frustration grew and his dilemma overwhelmed him. Leaving her to deal with them again, no matter how capable she was, had become almost impossible. Soon he would never leave her again.

    Gone now, he went away to wrestle with the Thing. He knew he could never win, but he wrestled anyway. As they fought, hills rang with the gianthood of their battle. Oceans balked and the air buckled. The roots of lightning were dislodged. Eventually, thunder came. When it came, it escaped his throat like a million hurricanes. The tides of his heart were reversed. The mountains of his mind quivered. Chomolungma herself shuddered to her main. At first, the world was amazed; but after a pixelated moment it went on buying and doubting and being certain and blogging and begging and amputating and being lost and astonishing in other ways, and then history swallowed its amazement without trace.

*

He went back to Dashiell's house because Dashiell said Jericho had come back. He thought Dashiell meant that Jericho was visiting, briefly, and would then go back to Dubai. When he went in, however, Dashiell said nothing, but took Jericho's hand and stood by him in a way that told their adopted son that they had found each other again, and that they were glad. Joyous thus, too, he went to them and embraced them both together as he had when he was a child. Then he went out into the sky, where they knew they would never need to say goodbye to him again.

*

Benen sat in the study of his house on Moscow Road in Bayswater. Savannah had just left to go to her acting classes. He could still smell her perfume. Pepper lay on the floor near his chair.

Benen heard Saint Sophia say nine hours with her familiar iron voice outside. He heard Tymon talking on his Bluetooth in his ear, too. Tymon was excited. He wondered if Benen had planned this 'awesome publicity' that hashtag beardy was pulling with all this 'shit on the channels, now' – but how? 'Who cares?' said the digital voice in Benen's ear. 'And is it him anyway? But why make him shave? The beard was the shmeard, sunshine …'

As Tymon talked and the issue of unpaid invoices became ever less avoidable, Benen drained his glass of Eagle Rare bourbon. He glanced over at the foundling's many art and notebooks, which he had brought home from the office a month or so earlier. They were now stacked on the floor next to his desk. He stood, went over, and picked up a few. Pepper watched him. He sat down again and thumbed through a couple. Again, the art astonished him – as did the poetry and fiction and non-fiction writings. On other pages, he found entirely incomprehensible equations. Beneath one page of equations and what looked like technical drawings of big science machines he saw the handwritten words '*this is a tokamak workaround that will light the fusion fuse – ta-dah!*'

There was another notebook. He riffed the pages, which were dark with words. He glimpsed musings and aphorisms. Moments tattooed on time. The reflected human. Mortal genius.

He felt awe.

'You know what, Tymon? I'll call you back in the morning. I don't know where he is or what's going on. I don't know anything about him actually, and I don't think anyone else does either. Whatever's up, I'm fairly sure it has nothing to do with our yellow brick road.'

As Tymon began to say laughingly, 'Our what?', Benen killed the call. He took the Bluetooth off his ear and threw it on his desk with a degree of disgust. Pepper came to him. As usual, the dog was more aware of Benen's actual mood than Benen was.

'You miss him, don't you?' he said to Pepper. Pepper did nothing. Nothing made Benen smile.

Benen then looked again at the art and notebooks on his lap, and at the other art and notebooks standing dusty near his desk. He suddenly felt ashamed. It was all 'his'. He had bought it notionally, and for a song. Suddenly the whole idea of ownership seemed laughable. As he poured himself some more Eagle Rare, he was suddenly sure he would never see the author of these notebooks again. He wondered if (should the fictions and hokum about #beardy be attachable to these priceless works) he would ever attempt to attach a price to them and profit accordingly. He was ashamed to realise that he probably would, yet he took comfort in the erroneous sense of his own mediocrity he thereby gained.

*

'Your name, please – for the record?'

'Thomas Gideon Young.'

'In your own time, Mr Young. Would you like some water, sir?'

'No I'm fine, thank you much. That's good of you though. So here we are at last. Thank you. So yes. Well the truth is that my daughter – Shanti Young – Shanti lied, but then so did I, and that's why I'm here now really. I mean when Shanti gave her statement, and in court. We made her do it. Well, my wife Bella did … The truth is that my wife – Mrs Isabella Young – my wife murdered my son Kenton Darvish Young on the day in question. But the accused was visiting the house that day, so I think she saw it as the perfect opportunity … Bella saw her chance to rid us of what she saw as a terrible burden … To release our boy from his … From this awful prison that he was now in … So perhaps it was an act of love … She had so little love in her early life, you see … I tried, but …'

'Take your time. It's fine.'

'Thank you. Yes of course. So anyway, keeping my son alive – the private medical bills had eaten up all our money – our life savings ... I have no doubt that my wife also turned the machines off that day because we were facing an imminent financial disaster, too. But on that day – the afternoon – it was four-twenty-odd in the p.m. I forget that I had just found – there was no more Darjeeling, you see. Anyway I had gone into the room where Kenton was kept alive ...'

'You were already in Kenton's bedroom when your wife entered?'

'That's correct. Shortly after the accused left the room and then left the house. It was then that she did it. I saw her.'

'Mr Young you should know that revising your testimony, as now your daughter has done ... You will be guilty of perjury too.'

'I don't care. It's time for the truth. I didn't know what to do. Perhaps I never have, really. But now I do. I feel quite sure now actually. I don't care what happens, either. Shall I carry on? So yes: my wife and I were in Kenton's bedroom shortly after ... Just minutes ... A few moments after he left. Bella and I were alone in our boy's room. That's when she turned the machines off. That was all it took, as you know. We were looking after him ourselves by then ... We had the offer of a nurse but couldn't afford it. So this was her chance. To set him free, you see. I saw her do it. I will swear it. My crime is that I could have stopped her doing it, but I didn't. Is that a crime? I don't care. I wanted my boy to be free, too, perhaps. So finally, perhaps, a desire for justice. A rage if you will. I feel that I should tell you that certain things happened when the children were ... Perhaps she loved Kenton too much and didn't know how to show it so perhaps she loved him the wrong way, a way that isn't considered ... My wife did things. You might call it a sort of abuse ... She hurt them, you see, and I believe that drew them together, as siblings can – what: close ranks? And now she's gone. She ran away. I suppose I can't blame her. She's in Spain, I think. I have an address I can give you.'

*

Shanti's contractions began in the o of a Monday. He had been gone for some hours.

The first contraction prompted her to look in her bedside drawers for a reason. Instead she found a large, apparently dirty glass nugget on top of his journals, which he had given to her for safekeeping when he became, and she was reluctant to use the word, a fugitive. The journals were filled with vast profundity and extreme unlikelihood. She favoured the former and found no way to rationalise the latter.

She didn't know that the dirty glass nugget was an uncut 829-carat diamond. She wondered where it had come from. She would have it expertly assessed some time, perhaps. Seeing it, she felt the sort of vertigo she felt as a child when she went as high as a dare on a swing and then plunged down swiftly. It was a similar vertigo to that which she felt when she looked into his eyes. This seemed strange to her. She attributed the vertigo to her the contractions, but found herself smiling anyway. She shut the drawer and, for now, forgot about the journals and the glassy object.

The contractions soon became longer, stronger, and more frequent. There was no pain, however. None at all. Later, when instinct told them it was time, Zadie drove her to hospital through suddenly torrential rain that the bullwhip Jetstream had now made normal in summer. As the Jetstream flayed south like a maddened snake and Zadie pushed her car through drenching streets, he returned to Africa. Impulse had often brought him back to its burnt earths and ochre skies. He felt called here. It seemed to him that time came here to begin and end.

Reports of child slavery and abuse took him down the west coast and over the Gulf of Guinea, returning over land still further south.

There, south, searching, possible, hounded, driven, seething, bunching, instinctive, hot, the muscle of the air, the giant of the mantle, the pinwheel stars, an atomic hammer, all of the sea, convection's billion, the chamber, the magma, the bulk of math, unlikely, he found a monstrous hub of this activity. So far from her, all he could think of was Shanti. He could feel the life within her seeking exit. He had told her he would be there in time. Just this one thing first. Will you forgive me?

Zadie got Shanti to the maternity ward in time's nick. To Zadie's amazement, Shanti was serene and smiling, as she had been during their monsoon journey through blaring streets. Shanti now knew that this was to be a birth with no forcing, no pain, and no trauma. How could this be? The Thing knew how. She did not, nor did her absolute tranquillity care. As Shanti was rushed, crowning already, into a delivery room, the Thing took him to the shack village used by child traffickers. It was in a clearing in the forest there, where Africa's sun was born each day. As he descended among the shacks, he realised that the sky was a bloodbath.

As Shanti gave birth so far away, so happy, so easy, so near him, inside him, so calm, two men rose at him as if sensing his intent. He heard a child cry out. He saw children's eyes peering through gaps. His magma stirred. The caldera bulged upwards, domed by long captive rage. He heard another child-scream. The hammer of the sun raised up to strike within him. Rage wept as the two men attacked him. He merely hurt them. He tried. He tried. They fell off his agonies, but they lived. Their guns told him old jokes. His laughter ended. They ran away into the amazed trees. They took their shocked story to new places. They would soon plant the story in sceptical ground. It would grow.

Within him, now, his daughter was emerging from love's womb. So far away, he went to the source of the child-screams he heard. The shack door fell before him like beliefs. As their daughter's head emerged from Shanti's peace, he pulled the man off the child the man was raping. He dragged the man outside, where wild eyes lived. The caldera lost its battle with reality. Rage erupted. Incandescent, infinite, forgiven, zero, final: absolute. It took the form of sound. The sound went to live in the hills. The child wept. He wept for the child. He was the child. The child hit the man with such violation that the man almost disintegrated. His shattered body flew several kilometres away.

Somewhere, Shanti smiled the shape of bloodless motherhood. Everywhere, he knew what he had done. He told the broken child with simple tears that he would try to come back. The child believed him. He let go of the child's hand. He went outside. He found the man he had killed. Seeing him dead, he therefore fell dead beside him in the very moment that he became a parent.

*

After a dread night of free children, official people came. Searching, they found one dead body in the parched land. A Harmattan wind arose nearby. This caused some dry branches to stir in bone trees, and then they become silent, too.

***

290

Printed in Great Britain
by Amazon